Tales of Mystery and Suspense

From within the Library of Souls.

Tomas One

Contents

Part One

Monday

Location: Number 23 Waterloo Rd, Higher Glendale. Time: 8:15 a.m., Monday, the 9th of October

Nigel Benson, a forty-five-year-old probation officer, sat at his kitchen table eating a small bowl of muesli. As soon as he finished, he drank the rest of his black coffee before picking up his bowl and cup to place them in the empty dishwasher. On completing the small task, he picked up the dishcloth from the side of the sink to wipe the countertops down before putting the now-damp cloth back over the front of the sink to dry off. As soon as he had finished, he walked across the floor to grab his coat from the rack.

After putting it on, he fastened the buttons of the winter coat his wife had bought him in the previous year's Boxing Day sales. He recalled she had been quite pleased to save over thirty pounds off the original price. After picking up his satchel, he shouted up the stairs to his wife that he would see her later; he soon realised she must have fallen back to sleep.

Making his way to the front door, he opened it and walked out before closing it behind him. After locking it, he walked down the pathway towards the gate. On opening it and walking through, he closed it behind him before approaching his red and black mini clubman. Before getting in, he used his keys to unlock the driver's side door. Putting the key in the ignition, he turned it on before fastening his seatbelt. Once he had checked his mirrors to ensure the road was clear, he left his parking spot to make his regular trip to work.

Ten minutes later, he turned onto King Street and rechecked his mirrors to ensure it was clear before parking outside the probation offices. After he had turned the ignition off, he grabbed his satchel before exiting the vehicle and then locked the car door before returning the keys to his pocket so he could begin his usual journey past the police station. He headed towards the short-cobbled pathway that led to the probation office and walked the remaining few steps toward the double doors. Once he had reached his destination, he pushed at one of them to access the small reception area. After unbuttoning and removing his coat, he walked through the reception area's inner door and placed it on the simple coat rack. When he saw his colleague Sarah sitting at her desk while typing a document for the home office, he said, "Morning."

"Oh yes, good morning."

"So, whose company do we have the pleasure of helping today?"

The woman in her mid-thirties, wearing a bright-looking dress with a floral pattern, stood up to pass several files to her colleague. After taking them from her, he inspected them. The man sighed when the first name on the list seemed to be a regular visitor to their small establishment.

"Bloody hell, not again."

"Is there anything wrong?"

"Well, yes, it's Karl, Mario Andretti, Thornton. I thought we had gotten rid of him, but the stupid boy keeps re-offending."

"Nigel, you need to stop upsetting yourself like this. You must remember what your wife said about your blood pressure being too high already."

"I'm okay; it's just a little frustrating from all the earlier sessions we have had already. The lad lives and breathes in his imagination while thinking it is okay to race around the back streets of Glendale Heights as though he was driving a Formula One racing car in Monaco."

"If the information I received from a close friend is correct, he's one stop from prison if he doesn't change. Now that you have taken this little information on board, you will also see his two friends, the Weaver twins, who are also booked for repeat sessions. Also, the home office has sent us three temporary staff trainees, all of them in their final year of university, to help you out while George is on holiday with his wife, Suzy; one is an attractive-looking, busty young lady named Cathy Brookes. She is waiting for you in your office."

"How often do I have to tell them our small building isn't big enough for three juniors as well as you and me?"

"Do not worry; I have already spoken with the employment secretary to relay your concerns about the size of the building. The woman I spoke with told me she had already informed the other two women that one would be in tomorrow and the other on Wednesday."

"So, what's she like then?"

"Well, she seems okay, but I've only spoken to her for about five minutes before you came in this morning. She's here to add some on-site training to her Curriculum Vitae."

"If she needs some training, I will let her speak with Mr. Thornton to see if she can cope with him."

"You're not considering throwing the young woman in at the deep end on her first visit while expecting her to return to see us again?"

"Well, my dear, you said the three ladies need on-site training. The lads we must see again will be all these women will ever need to become qualified probation officers. So, let us see how the first of our trainees can cope with the arrogant, work-shy lad. If it's true and the woman has a large chest like my Jody, she'll keep his attention."

"When my friend Christy and I were chatting the other day, she informed me the system is so broken they are in talks to reinvent it, to stop the overcrowding in the already overstretched prison and probation service."

"Sarah darling, the home office is always coming up with these new schemes, but they never come to anything. Do you remember all the emails we have had about this scheme or this new idea in the past? They have all fallen at the first hurdle because they never want to put their money where their mouth is."

"Yes, but I've heard on the grapevine that actual change will happen soon. They're even considering employing a crime and rehabilitation minister to oversee the changes to the system, as the old system is clearly not working and needs a complete overhaul."

"Okay, all I can say about this new rumour is I'll see it when it happens."

"Just to inform you in advance, Mr. Thornton should arrive at ten a.m., but he's already telephoned in. The lad said he had missed the bus and would be at least fifteen minutes late. Then the twins are due in at ten thirty."

"Does the home office realise with George being away, I am supposed to take care of my appointments and his while he is on annual leave? Although I admit, I am jealous, as he has taken his wife on an all-inclusive safari."

"I believe it's their first holiday after the double cancer scares he had last year. Therefore, the home office is sending us the trainees to help you."

"Right, I'll talk to you later. I'll better introduce myself to this Miss Brookes to see what I make of her."

"Don't worry, she will fit in here while also being quite knowledgeable about the probation service for someone so young."

"How old did you say she was?"

"It says she's twenty-three years old."

"Thanks."

Nigel left his colleague to her typing and made his way towards his small office. As soon as he walked through the doorway, he noticed the pretty woman sitting down in front of his desk. "Good morning,"

As she stood up to greet him, the man could not help noticing her large bust being held behind a black see-through bustier covered by a white see-through, neatly ironed blouse. This was followed by a tight-looking black skirt with a small slit, giving him a quick glimpse of her seamed black stocking-covered legs.

"Yes, I'm here to learn from the best."

The man seemed to smile at the compliment. "So, as we have you for today, I'd like to ask what you've already learned about the probation service."

She informed the man about the training she had already received at university. As he listened to her, all he could think about was how the young lad would react when he saw the woman's heaving chest.

"Are you up for a challenge?"

The young woman with long black curly hair and bright blue eyes looked eager to begin work. Once he had informed her about the three clients they were to see later that morning, he pulled out his chair from his desk to sit on the comfortable swivel chair as soon as he was seated.

He passed her a few of their earlier preliminary reports, although each of them had been written to show the client's earlier visits to the probation service. He hoped that allowing her to read them would give her a brief insight into how they preferred to work at this small branch of the probation service. Every day, we have several people coming through our doors, and when it becomes time to complete a preliminary assessment for yourself, it should become second nature to both male and female clients.

After a few minutes, the woman returned the documents to the desk before looking up at him. "Do you want me to talk to all three men or just one of them today?"

The man seemed to smile as he knew how troublesome the three lads were. "With my colleague George being away, we're short-staffed, so if you feel ready to talk with Karl on your own, I will use the time to speak with our other guests, the Weaver Twins, in his office. After all your training, I hope you can manage him because he is an abrupt nineteen-year-old who will try everything to get under your skin. Now that you have read his reports, he is here again for twelve more sessions, including today. Once you have had your first session with the young man, you will soon see he is not that bright and seems to drift in and out of his fantasy world. This is where he believes he is a racing car driver. Therefore, I gave him the nickname Mario Andretti so you can get a clear understanding of his crude mentality. We have a few steps to go over.

Step One: Hunt down an expensive-looking car. The buzz comes from stealing it.

Step Two: Impress his friends with his fast-driving ability.

Sadly, we do not have a step three because they all desire to feel the wind in their hair. For some unknown reason, this excites all three of them."

"One day, their luck will run out, and their reckless behaviour will kill at least one of them. The problem here is they all like to guzzle down excess amounts of alcohol, plus whisky chaser top-ups, as soon as they are all drunk as skunks. This is when they decide to look for another fast car to steal. So, to analyse this more constructively:

1: Get Pissed.

2: Steal a fast car.

3: Race the fast vehicle around the back alleyways of Glendale Heights before looking for a police car to chase them.

Add all three to the mix, and you have an apparent disaster waiting to happen."

"Okay, I see where you're coming from with this lad, but may I ask you a question?"

"If you feel it will help you with your interview."

"I was just going to ask if you see this youth as the leader of this small gang."

"I wouldn't call them a gang, but all three are morons without a thought for the law or anyone's safety."

"You seem quite angry when you talk about Mr. Thornton."

"Angry, no, disappointed, yes, so you can understand this petty thug has no intention of getting a job. He lives off the taxpayer and only thinks about stealing high-end motors. In the last fifteen years, I have never met such a reckless, single-minded idiot as him."

"Although I've been trained to handle most cases, this will be my first proper case file. I must treat this as just another training exercise to become a qualified probation officer. I should then be able to handle whatever the lad chucks at me. Are the sessions recorded?"

"No!"

"Although my training has been extensive, will you be nearby if I need help?"

"If you can recall your journey from reception, you walked straight through the two swing doors before reaching the end of the pathway. From there, you turned right and walked along the small corridor to the office where you are just now. So, if you need me, Karl cannot concentrate on the task ahead, or he makes you feel uncomfortable; you will have to leave the office, walk back down the corridor, and knock on the door of George's office to get my attention."

"My training has been quite intense already, and my tutors all agree I can handle most situations."

"I'm sorry, but no amount of on-site training would give you an insight into how these three lads think."

"Don't worry. I have some talents that make men do anything I ask."

The man looked down at the young woman's heaving chest and could see she had a point, as her bust size was something to behold. Although he was married to a woman with a big bust, from what he could see, the woman's boobs were at least twice the size of his wife Jody's. Even though he didn't know her actual measurements from the size of her cleavage, it was clear her breasts were massive. Therefore, he had a little bother moving his eyes from her chest momentarily, making him wonder if she had ever suffered from a bad back.

"Just that look you've given me shows you understand where I'm coming from."

"If I were you, I'd cover those up, or the lad won't be able to think straight."

"That's just what I want; then he'll give me no trouble."

"Well, since I began working here, I don't think I've ever heard about someone using their breasts to get someone to do as they're told."

"Trust me, I know what I'm doing."

"Okay, I will leave it up to you. The lads are due in from ten this morning, although Sarah, our receptionist, has just informed me the young lad missed his bus, so he will be a little late. When he turns up, introduce yourself before beginning work on the new preliminary assessment form; while you are doing it, it will give you a brief insight into how he thinks. In my expressed opinion, the lad is even thicker than the Clampets from the popular comedy The Beverly Hillbillies. All I ask is that you support some form of professionalism with him."

At the end of the last meeting with Mr Thornton, we felt we had made some progress while trying to change him from being a total buffoon into someone who can return to society a changed man, only for the idiot to meet up with his friends at the pub within hours; they had made the same error in judgment and stole yet another car.

"From what you told me this morning about him, you're feeling he is getting beyond redemption. As this will be my first test with a client, not just another student, I will begin by using my talents on him. I've never had someone refuse what I offer them in exchange for their undying attention."

"From my experience, the first session lasts around two hours. Discussing what the earlier preliminary reports contained with the boy would take a while. Once this is done, we can use the information contained within the forms to analyse whether he is willing to change his ways and stop him from committing stupid, irresponsible, misdemeanour crimes against society. The problem with Karl is he can say one thing while promising you he will change and never commit another crime, only to get bored, and he'll go out and re-offend."

"Have you ever considered he does it because he loves the attention, even if it is negative?"

Last week, we had a lecture about all forms of control. It covered several topics, including Narcissism and Munchausen by Proxy, plus several other mental conditions which deal with intelligence and the use of it against other people, like ghosting someone, for example.

"I think I can see where this is heading if you are considering the Munchausen by Proxy illness; this is more about people who give minors unnecessary pills to satisfy their ego. A recent case to mention here was the Gypsy Rose Blanchard case.

The young girl suffered years of abuse at the hands of her mother, whom she killed with the help of a secret boyfriend. Also, he would need to have some form of intelligence if you are also considering the narcissistic angle, which includes ghosting as a form of control.

Having spoken with young Karl several times over the last few years. He is no Einstein, and his intelligence is well below par."

"With you saying he loves any form of attention, even if it's negative, it gives the lad a buzz."

"Having dealt with him frequently over the last three years. He tries to seem intelligent with someone new, but his temperament and immaturity show through, so I'll leave him with you and see how it goes."

The man looked down at his watch to check the correct time. When he saw it was about a minute or two off ten a.m., he informed the young woman her client would be with her shortly. As he turned towards the doorway to leave the office so he could make a brief journey along the corridor to his colleague's room to await his first two clients of the day.

As soon as she was alone, the young woman pulled out her mobile phone.

After calling a number from her contacts' speed dial numbers, she waited for an answer. "Hello, I'm in and waiting for the perfect person for the job to walk through the door.

"Just don't fuck it up."

"You're not the one who has to get her boobs out for the idiot."

"Darling, we went through this, and you agreed to let him do anything he wants to get him to carry out our plan."

"I should get a raise for allowing a man to touch me again."

"Amanda, think about it; you're getting paid more than enough, and you know I'll make it up to you once the job is done."

"I don't think we should say our real names on the phone just in case someone is listening." Stop getting so paranoid, darling. In a way, you are not lying to yourself. You are not using your full name; you have just shortened it for convenience from Amanda Catherine Parker Brookes down to plain Cathy Brookes. So, don't worry, your pretty little head about it; the plan is god damn near perfect."

Remember, the boss and I reviewed the plan thoroughly, so everything should go as planned. "When we talked it through, you waited till the last minute to tell me I'd have to let this idiot use and abuse me so he would comply with our wishes while knowing what happened to me when I was a child."

"I'm sorry, but you need to understand that without him, where are we going to find someone so stupid at such short notice?"

"You also need to understand my father, on the outside, was a loving parent. While I had no choice but to suffer years of sexual and physical abuse night after night behind closed doors, now, you want me to forget my miserable life before meeting you, so this perfect plan will work."

"Please, darling, how can I get you to stick with it? You must also remember you have already been promised fifty grand for your part in the job?"

"Yes, I know that, but you cannot pressure me into giving you an answer just like that as I need time to think things through in my head. How will I complete the first part of the job if I am unhappy? You also must understand if I cannot convince the lad to do our bidding because I am not down with all of this."

"Oh, my giddy aunt, I know what you are doing; it is not the money on the table; it's also not the fact I've asked you to have sex with a man again. Even though we are in a sexual relationship, you are playing up because you want my yellow Ferrari. Ever since I had it delivered, you have had your eyes on it. I want you to remember I received the vehicle as a reward for carrying out a tough assignment by killing someone and making it look like they committed suicide, and you want me to just hand over the keys to you?"

"You know I will take loving care of it."

"Damn it, Amanda, you're lucky I love you because it would be a straight no to anyone else."

"Okay, I understand, and I promise to take care of it for you."

"I don't think you really understand what this means. We are already going to lose the red convertible Porsche, so if I give you the Ferrari, the lad will carry out the task we need him to do. It only leaves us with the camper van; we go dogging in at the weekend left over." "Thanks, Lorna, for understanding."

"You better not crash my car because it goes from nought to sixty in about five seconds, so you better be extra careful. Right, I am going; let's speak later." As the phone went dead, the young woman put the phone away.

Monday Part Two

Just then, there was a knock on the door of the small but adequate office. "Hello, my name is Karl Thornton. I was told at reception I was having my first session with you."

"Well, good morning; why don't you take a seat, and we will begin? Nigel has instructed me to begin with a new preliminary assessment form. Once it is filled in, we will review your last three forms to see what went wrong. This may give us an insight into why you have re-offended."

"Wow, straight to the point, just like Nigel or boring George."

Preliminary Assessment

Name: Karl Thornton Age: 19

Address: 181 Palace View Terrace, Lower Glendale

Height: 6ft

Shoe Size: 12

Education: 1: Fallon Hall's School for young boys (5-13). 2: Kirk Levington Borstal Yarm Cleveland (13-16)

(16-19) Criminal Activity: Stealing and crashing high-end motors. Current sentence: fourth period of probation.

Notes: This young lad has continued to commit several misdemeanor crimes over the last three years.

He has been warned the next time he offends, he will receive a custodial sentence in a man's jail rather than a youth's detention centre handed down by the courts.

"I see, from the report, this will be your last chance to change your ways.

So, what can you say about this?"

"I am sorry, but I just cannot give you an answer to that until you tell me how big your tits are."

"Please, Karl, you need to concentrate on the question, not the size of my breasts."

"Do you have a fella?"

"Please stop this. We have so much to do but only a brief time to complete it today."

As the young man sat just a few feet from her, he lustfully tried to get her to respond to his crude requests.

"Although I may be new here, this line of questioning is not productive when we have only two hours to fill in this form. So let us begin again, shall we?"

"How do you expect me to concentrate on a stupid form when you haven't answered my question?"

The young woman knew she needed to respond to his request if the plan her girlfriend had set up was to work.

"Okay, if it will get your attention away from my chest so we can complete the paperwork. I have a pair of thirty-four double k breasts. I am five foot eight tall. Because of the size of my boobs, I need to buy my underwear from a lingerie specialist. Most women pay between ten and fifteen pounds for a bra, but I must pay eighty pounds plus because of the size of my chest. Although the bustier I have on today is a comfortable fit, it cost one hundred and twenty pounds."

"Okay, but do you have a man in your life?"

"Please, Karl, we need to get on with this form. Should I get Nigel to come in and sit with us?"

"Come on, darling, just answer the question, and I'll happily answer any of yours."

"Okay, I am single but love athletic men."

Although she knew this was a lie, she could not tell him she was now gay and detested men because of the number of times her father raped her when she was younger.

"Well, darling, I am athletic and quite strong; if you want, we could meet up later after you have finished work."

The thought of the lad with the bright blonde hair touching her was something she was not looking forward to, although the idea of the money was excellent. The best part of the plan was she would now get the use of one of the best and fastest cars in the world.

The only negative aspect was that she had no choice but to allow the stupid idiot access to her body for the plan to work.

"I have never seen such a beautiful, large-breasted beauty." He recalled all the stories his two friends would make up while in the pub when discussing the female form because of their inability to talk with a real woman. Moving his chair a little closer to her to get a better look at her treasures. He salivated at the thought of having a good grope of her massive chest. The young lad wore a bright red T-shirt with his favourite pub pool team logo on it. He was suited and booted in a stylish two-piece denim jacket and jeans, alongside a pair of black Dr Martins's steel-toe cap boots as he began to slip once more into his place of comfort between the realms of fantasy and reality about the sex kitten seated across from him. When he noticed the woman standing up before heading towards the open doorway, all he could think about was bending the wench over the desk so he could have his wicked way with her. He hoped she would not spoil his perfect fantasy, which filled his dirty mind. The young nineteen-year-old lad was shocked when the beautiful woman closed the door before locking it behind her. After pulling the blind down, she made her way over to him.

While slowly unbuttoning her neatly ironed white blouse. Although he was shocked by her actions, he got excited and found it impossible to keep his erection from growing in his pants as he continued watching her every move. When his dream date let her blouse drop onto the desk, his erection made him feel uncomfortable as it pressed against the zipper of his denim jeans. When the beautiful woman opened her black bra top, it took just a few seconds before her full, firm breasts were now on display. As she approached him, he noticed her areolas were at least two full inches in size, offset by her large button-like nipples in the center, as she messed around with the zipper of his jeans. He tried to follow her wishes. As soon as she pulled it down with her fingers, his penis sprang out of the now-undone gap in his jeans.

He had to admit he was happy with his ten-inch cock; although long, it was not thick; he hoped she would appreciate such a lovely member. As the woman of his dreams continued playing with the inexperienced penis before deciding to kneel. When she was ready, she took the lad's cock between the wet lips of her mouth to give him a blow job he would never forget. The troublesome teenager could not believe he was getting head from a beautiful woman at the probation office, of all places. It only took a few minutes before he could not stop his penis from spurting his thick semen all over the young woman's face. While realising what had just happened to him was much better than any of his fantasies. Watching the sexiest woman alive standing up as her large breasts wobbled against her chest made him want her even more. He had never been that lucky with a woman, so what had changed?

For the young boy, it had been a total surprise that someone so good-looking as her would entertain him as she had just done. As he continued watching the beauty wipe the remaining drops of his seed off her attractive face, it made his cock grow again. Minutes went by in complete silence as he watched her get dressed. Once she was seated, the young woman watched him struggle to get his semi-hard-on back in his jeans. Although she hated men, it made her smile because she knew her girlfriend's plan was taking shape. Once the teenager was seated again, he looked up at her curiously as if the act had not been just another fantasy, although he knew things like this didn't happen.

He tried to concentrate on her face to see if he could confirm the blowjob had taken place. He continued to look across the room at the beautiful woman he had just had some fun with, or had he?

Living your life in a fantasy world has several advantages and many disadvantages.

He thought about what had happened but could confirm nothing he had done since entering the small office, which made him realise he needed to change his ways.

The problem was that he had done nothing positive in his young life. All he had ever done was to live to impress others, like his two friends, Bob and Craig Weaver. He met them while in a young man's detention centre, and they became great friends. Both boys were on his wavelength, and they loved everything about fast cars. They also loved talking about alcohol; lots of it; the more robust, the better. After their release, they discovered they lived nearby, so they met up at the Bearded Tavern on Baker Street, Lower Glendale. While they consumed many drinks, their conversations had just a few topics.

The first was their love for fast cars. The second was women who were tall, short, fat, or thin; any female was on their radar. It is a pity they could not persuade a real girl into bed. So, the best alternative to that was talking about them. While reminiscing about his past events, he realised the beautiful woman was writing whatever he said, hoping she would understand his need to steal fast cars and crash them all continuously as the young lad finished talking. He soon understood why he could not get an actual girlfriend when the beautiful creature who sat only a few feet away discussed his crimes and his need to change.

He tried to concentrate on what she was saying, but even glancing across the room at her large bust for a second or two was a real problem as her tits were so big, wonderful, and marvellous. Stop it, Karl, he thought to himself. It would help if you tried to concentrate on something other than her chest. Looking down at his wristwatch, he realised his first session was about over. He wished the woman would be his lover. Not being sure about the blowjob taking place was just one of many obstacles he had. How could he face his two best mates and tell them the story was, this time, a reality, not pure fantasy if even he could not believe it happened? As the young lady looked over her notes, she thought about the plan again. She soon found out she had many unanswered questions. Looking at her watch, she also realised she needed more time to get the lad to follow her wishes.

"Right, Karl; before we end the session, we need to discuss the main reasons which make you re-offend. We must also talk about fast cars and your desire to steal them. For example, I am about to take possession of a fast, yellow-coloured Ferrari worth over eighty grand. Is this the type of car you like to steal?" The lad tried not to slip back into his preferred fantasy realm. Although he was six feet in height, his confidence was at an all-time low, so he preferred the fantasy world over reality anytime. In that scenario, he was a robust and handsome racing car driver with many women to choose from. He thought about the question before deciding to tell her the truth; yes, he loved that type of car, but he realised he loved the convertible Porsche sports car the best. Just the thought of driving something like that gave him an instant buzz; the problem he always faced was that Bob and Craig needed help to drive. He was the only one of the three who had passed his driving test. Bob's problem was that he had dyslexia, so he struggled with the theory test. Craig's' problem was that he had one leg shorter than the other due to a childhood accident and severe confidence issues. Therefore, Karl was the one who stole the cars, and they were his passengers. Night after night, all three of them would guzzle down pint after pint while talking about fast cars and fast women. Karl looked at his watch again to check the time before realising he still needed to answer the woman's question. As he looked across at her, he realised he needed to concentrate. He found it hard to think about his love for fast cars and women in the same sentence, as the beads of sweat formed on his hairline.

He realised it was his weakness to talk with sexy women like the beauty he had sitting across from him, which made him slip into his fantasy world in the first place.

"Come on, Karl, what is the problem? We need to delve into this a little more. As we are out of time here, why don't you come to my apartment this evening so we can talk about your problems with reality?"

The young lad was a little taken aback at the suggestion. As the attractive woman stood up, the split in her skirt flashed her stockings briefly, which the lad noticed. This made him think about the girls on display whenever he bought a sex mag from the newsagents across the road from his house.

Watching her walk across the room towards him, he could see her large breasts swaying from side to side within the confines of the black front fastening bustier she wore that morning her girlfriend Lorna had bought her.

He could not believe she was going to invite him to her flat. As the sexy girl handed him a small piece of paper with her address, she instructed him to be there just after seven that evening. The woman then walked towards the office door, opened it, and said she would see him later.

Monday Part Three

When the young lad left the room, the attractive beauty returned to her seat to look over her notes again. She needed to look for common factors to figure out how his young mind worked. Only then could she understand the reasons he needed to

re-offend repeatedly.

Although she was only twenty-three, her intelligence well outranked the teenage boys. Looking over the forms, she had not noticed that Nigel had entered the room to see how her first interview with the troublesome lad had gone. She looked up from her notes only when he coughed in her direction.

"How did it go with the young lad? I hope he was not too much of a handful for you. From all the reports you gave me to read earlier and reviewing my notes, I see minor differences in how you spoke with him and how I tried to get the lad to discuss his problems. Karl's issues are extensive. I am listing them to see if we can discover a way to break through this imaginary barrier he lives in.

1: Continues to live in a fantasy world

2: Drinks to excess

3: Breaks the law

We need to understand why he feels safe inside this fantasy world. From his earlier sessions, I see that it took him several one-hour slots to think freely. From the minute he entered the room until he left about five minutes ago, all I got from the lad was: "How big they were. Can I have a feel?"

"You wanted him to fill out the preliminary assessment form even though we only had a little time.

Although I told you, I would use my talents to see if the lad would communicate with me. I didn't want to rely on the size of my breasts. To get him to begin to talk about his problems. Just looking at the lad and the way he stared at my chest While wanting to have a grope of them made me think of how I could get him to talk with me like a woman, not as a sex object. I needed him to consider that talking about women so negatively was wrong and his actions were not very productive so I could get his full attention.

I moved my chair as close to him as possible without sitting on his knee and invading his space.

This action made me feel that I had his full attention, and I could see his face get a little red. I asked him how he felt about how close I was to him. Just this little action was just what I needed to see from him. I asked him if he would like to try a brief experiment As he could not turn his eyes away from my boobs. I wanted him to imagine that it was him instead of me who had the large breasts. At first, he laughed at the suggestion, telling me I was being silly. I asked him to stand up and unbutton his jacket. I then undid my blouse, allowing the lad to see my expensive see-through front-fastening bustier. Once I did this, I asked him to remove his t-shirt. Again, he felt the exercise was silly. I then removed it so he could see the size of my colossal bust. Almost at once, I noticed his penis begin to get erect in his pants. I explained I wanted him to massage my breasts so he could see how they felt and that they were a natural pair of tits. As soon as he did, he admitted he was pretty taken aback at how I was allowing him access to my boobs. After a few minutes, I asked him to pick up my bustier and his T-shirt from the table. This left him quite confused, which I put down to his immature mind. An awkward look came over his face when I told him to put it on. Luckily, the lad was not developed in the chest department, so my bra was quite a snug fit. However, he felt embarrassed at wearing an item designed to cover a woman's breasts. Only then did he begin to respond to me, which pleased me. Although I was still topless, I wanted the youth to continue with the test. When I asked him to push his t-shirt down the top of the bustier before trying to fasten it. Once, he had followed my wishes.

I told him he looked nice in my top, and I moved forward just a little more so I could grope at his fake bust. The look on his face was a picture. As I continued to feel at his chest, he tried to stand back a little. So, I moved forward. The young lad, by now, looked entirely flushed but tried once more to step back a little. I asked him what was wrong with him. The look on his face told me he had begun to understand the experiment. I also noticed he had lost his erection even though I was still topless at this point. So, I asked him again if there was a problem. Although he found it hard to answer me, I could tell that I had gotten him to realise how a woman felt when he continued to stare at them. At the end of the experiment, I stepped back and allowed him the time to think about how it felt to have someone wanting to grope their breasts. Allowing him the time to remove the bustier after pulling out the t-shirt from within the middle of it. He quickly passed me my bra and allowed me to put it back on while he put his t-shirt back on. Once I had put my blouse back on, I returned to my seat and allowed him to do the same.

After a few seconds, I asked him if he had enjoyed the experience. The blank look on his face while he tried to say something about how the experiment had made him feel made me think the test had been a genuine breakthrough. As the young lad was now beginning to talk with me. This leads me to a question: Should I continue testing him using my talents? In the hope that the lad will come out of his shell and begin to see how jumping in and out of his self-created fantasy world at a moment's notice was not a productive way to live."

"Although I cannot condone your actions, I can see that you have connected with the lad based on what you have told me. How about I get your tutors to agree to allow you to take over the lads' remaining time here? The principal goal is to get him to realise his actions are unproductive and that he needs to change to avoid a lengthy prison sentence. If, after four sessions of probation, we can use your talents to get the lad to change his ways, then it is all right with me. However, we cannot say that you allowed him access to your chest to give him the incentive to realise that he needed to alter his outlook on life and do something more productive instead. The lad loves fast cars, so we could use this a little by attempting to get him an apprenticeship in a garage or something appropriate to his mentality. I also feel a week in an alcohol dependency unit could help the lad stop drinking alcohol to excess. This could help him be more productive with his money. If this could be arranged, some relationship advice on how to talk with women may help here. George is back in three weeks; he could take the twins off my hands, lowering my stress levels, which will put me back in favour with my wife. If it is not her, it is Sarah; she is always there to help me stop getting stressed.

Jody keeps complaining to me because of getting too stressed out at work. This is affecting my sex life at home, and I am sorry to say this to such a young woman as you, but I love having sex with my beautiful wife. So, it would be beneficial to my work and to my home life, as something needs to change before I have a breakdown because of the build-up of stress caused by that silly idiot and his refusal to change his ways. So, all I need to do is convince your tutors to allow you to come here on a Monday."

"If you allow me to leave early, I will see them, and I can let you know the answer within an hour or two."

"Okay, while you do that, I will explain it to Sarah. Hopefully, she will understand my reasons for allowing you to take over Mr. Thornton's sessions while he is here."

As the man watched the young woman leave the room, the man felt slightly concerned about what he would ask his colleague to allow. As he returned to reception to see his friend, he hoped she would understand the reasoning behind his request. As the middle-aged man arrived, he noticed the concerned look on her face.

"What do you think you are doing by asking a student to take on that idiot for the rest of his sessions with us?"

"You know how you always ask me to watch my stress levels like my wife, Jody? Although this is a small branch of the probation service, quite a few clients pass through our doors. So, let me ask if you can tell me what days I get more stressed out."

"You get more stressed whenever Mr. Thornton and his two friends are in the building because of being stupid once again and have committed yet another crime."

"The young woman got through to the lad in her first session with him when it took me several stressful episodes to even get him to communicate with me without saying he was a racing car driver."

"Okay, the young woman is intelligent and has an excellent understanding of how the probation service works. Now, you have asked her to see if her tutors will allow her to take a break from her studies just to stop you from getting stressed out by those idiots. So, what happens when the next two women come in? Will you also farm off our other two problems to them?"

Just as Nigel was about to explain his reasoning, there was a telephone call to the branch. "Hello, can I speak with your office manager? I have an important matter I need to discuss with her."

"Yes, this is Sarah Goodwin speaking. Who, may I ask, is talking?"

"Oh, yes, my name is Tracy Webb. I am the assistant to the education secretary here at the home office. One of my colleagues contacted you earlier this morning to inform you that we were sending three students to cover one of your colleagues' annual leaves. The Probation officer is Mr. George Baker."

"I'm sorry, but I think you are mistaken. George's last name is Downing, not Baker."

"Oh, what is the location of your office?"

"We're based at King St Lower Glendale."

"I see this is where there has been a mix-up. As your offices are based around one of our more minor probation services, the students were allocated to attend the Topping Street Branch Higher Glendale. So, we can only send you one student to cover your staff member's annual holiday on a Monday only. How long is your colleague away for?"

"George is away for the next three weeks."

"Well, we can cover that, but once your colleague returns, the student must be transferred to the main branch. I am sorry for the mix-up. Goodbye. "

As the phone went dead, both staff members were shocked but relieved; they kept at least one student covering the Monday shift while George was away.

"So, you were saying before the phone call about trying to keep your stress levels in check. We are keeping Miss Brookes if your plan is to work. It is a pity we can only have her for the next three weeks."

"Yes, but the woman didn't mention any names. We do not want some other student coming here who doesn't know how to deal with idiots like the Weaver twins and Mr Thornton, so we need to confirm we're getting Miss Brookes."

"Okay, let me telephone them back to make sure who we are getting to give us the cover we need. Now, will you please take a seat and wait for confirmation?"

As Sarah returned the call, she was lucky to be reconnected with Mrs. Webb.

After a brief chat, the woman could release the name assigned to them, Miss Cathy Brookes. Sarah thanked the woman for the information before disconnecting the call.

Nigel began dancing a jig around the small office, making Sarah laugh. "It's a pity we cannot have her for the next eleven sessions, but at least we have the correct student to help me lower my stress levels for the next three weeks, at the very least."

Monday Part Four

As Cathy Brookes left the small probation office, she headed towards her blue Chevy Nova car, which she had had for the last seven years. On reaching it, she had no choice but to put her hand through the small gap in the window so she could open the driver's side door because the lock was broken from the outside.

Although her car had a few teething problems, she thought the seats were comfortable, and the stereo system was impressive. When she got inside the car and sat in the driver's seat, she put the key in the ignition and turned it on before closing the car door. After the third attempt, the car's engine fired up so she could return to her apartment in Higher Glendale. Once she had checked her mirrors, she pulled out of the parking spot she had used a few hours earlier.

As she reached the top of King Street, she turned left onto Fallon Street, which was the longest road in the city of Glendale, only to be shocked by the serious number of police vans and cars on the road in front of her. Wondering what was happening, she turned the radio on just in time to catch the last bit of the local news.

"A young woman's body had been found in a local park by a dog walker. However, the city itself had several notable crimes in its history. It was not unusual for someone to be found in a city as large as Glendale. The city included four districts: Lower Glendale, Higher Glendale, Glendale Heights, and the large shopping mall in Maiden Vale, which was on the other side of the Mallon Stone River." As she continued to drive home, she recalled a close friend telling her a tale she had overheard someone say while trying to give her a brief history lesson about the fine city of Glendale.

"I do not know if it is true, but a girl I knew told me that the actual location of the stone was where they used to drown the women accused of witchcraft in the sixteen hundreds. If you take the time to look, all the victims' names are carved into the stone written in old English. I understood back then that if a church member wanted another person's land. All they needed to do was accuse them of being a witch by using the now famous book written by Heinrich Kramer the Malleus Maleficarum circa 1486 (Hammer of Witches). Just an accusation would give rise to a severe amount of instability within the city's economy. Therefore, even now, Higher Glendale is the cheapest place to live. The church accused fourteen women and six men. Leaving the church elders to build a network of tunnels below the city's churches, connecting all four locations for easy access to all city areas. Most offices were in Glendale Heights, like the probation service and the local police and fire stations. This is also the location for the most significant appeal and rehabilitation building. It was named the House of Calamari, built in the fifties. It was run by a man named Frank Davies. While he was there, he had many notable cases to deal with. Some are okay, but some are sad on their own. He could never forget his first case, though he named it the Pools Win Tragedy. Mr Davies ran the House from the fifties until his premature death by suicide, even though his son Lorcan Davies could never accept that his father would have killed himself in that way. Lower Glendale had the most residents. You found them to be the yuppie-type office workers from the mid-eighties onwards."

She continued listening to the news while waiting for the road to clear. It took her at least half an hour more than usual because she had no choice but to wait at the junction.

As she made her way down the road, she discovered the perpetrator had hanged the woman upside down before cutting the victim's throat. However, there was a bit of other news concerning the city. The radio station kept repeating that a young woman had been found in a popular park filled with all the amenities any park should have. Several vehicles exited the busy road at the junction where the old hospital was found. This also led to the Priory Lane Mental facility for the criminally insane.

As the young, attractive woman reached her turnoff, this took several more minutes. Once she had reached the estate where she lived, she drove down the road towards the luxury block of flats until it was clear for her to park up. As she turned off the engine and opened the driver's side door, she thought about the made-up character she was playing. Cathy Brookes may have entered the car, but Amanda Catherine Parker Brookes left that afternoon.

As she walked down the pathway towards the stairwell, she stopped herself because she heard the familiar-sounding voice of someone she disliked. Which made her wonder what the bitch was doing leaving her apartment block with a seriously overweight man. She watched them both enter a chauffeur-driven Rolls Royce as they passed her. As she waited a few more minutes to make sure they were gone, she realised she also needed that time to calm herself down. Why would her girlfriend allow that woman into their apartment after what she had done?

As she made her way up the stairs towards her front door, she noticed her girlfriend standing on the front veranda smoking one of those French cigarettes the bitch must have given her. She only knew the fag being smoked was one of Gabriella's because the butt of the cigarette was coloured bright pink.

As she put her key in the lock, she turned it before walking through the now-open front door. Slamming the door behind her, she made her way to the living room and onto the veranda to speak with her girlfriend, as she needed an answer to a serious question. As the attractive woman chucked the remaining butt of the cigarette over the balcony before turning to kiss her on the cheek.

Amanda sidestepped her so the kiss didn't land on its designated target. "What the hell was she doing here?"

"Excuse me, who do you think you're talking to?"

"What was she doing here, and who was that fat bloke?"

"If you expect an answer, I want an apology for your evasive attitude towards me just now when I went to kiss you on the cheek."

"I'm not saying sorry until you explain yourself."

The woman stood there, a little shocked by her girlfriend's attitude. She pulled out another cigarette from her packet and turned to ignore her girlfriend of five years.

"Well, are you not going to answer me?"

"I will when you have apologised and not before."

"Damn it, Lorna. You know all too well I hate that bitch."

The attractive woman ignored her while puffing away on the French cigarette. Amanda felt a little let down but also wanted an answer to her question. "Okay, I am sorry. Will you now answer the question?"

"Only if you kiss me first."

The woman moved as the young, attractive woman leaned over to kiss her girlfriend, so the kiss landed on her lips instead.

"Now, what did you say?"

"I was asking you why that bitch was here and also who the hell was that fat bloke?"

"Gabrielle was here because Sir John wanted her here, and for your information, she has apologised to me about that incident at the prison."

"Okay, but she nearly killed you and didn't think how it would upset me if you died because of her giving you that cocktail of drugs down in the cellar."

"Look here, Amanda, I have forgiven her, so why can't you?"

"She may have apologised to you, but not to me. All she did was laugh it off as though it was nothing."

"Okay, next time we see her, I will ask her to apologise to you too."

"So, the fat bloke is the guy who's paying the wages then, or what?"

"Yes, that is the man who will shell out a lot of money for us to carry out several tasks for him."

"I thought we were only doing this one task."

"I am sorry, but you do not get fifty thousand pounds for jerking some guy off for the man, and that's it."

"Oh, I know that. I have to persuade the lad to nick our car and drive it into the target outside the House of Calamari as soon as he exits the building on a Friday Night."

"Yes, the lad only gets paid the full twenty thousand if he completes the task we need him to do."

"I know; I was there when you went over the plan."

"What the fuck, Amanda? Watch your fucking attitude."

"Bloody hell, calm down, Lorna. I am sorry now. Please carry on with what you were saying."

"Right, we better go on in, as it looks like it's going to rain."

As Amanda looked up, she saw some black clouds forming in the distance. Once they had retreated to the living room, Lorna continued to discuss the plan with her girlfriend again.

"Right, as soon as you have got the lad's rocks off, you tell him the plan and offer him the money. Are you clear about that so far?"

"I am not stupid, so why are you talking to me like I am thick."

"Say that again with that attitude, and I will give you a fat lip."

"Lorna, I am sorry to upset you, but I wouldn't do it if you would stop treating me like a thicko."

As the red-haired beauty sat down on the couch, she looked pretty pissed off with the attitude she was getting from her girlfriend.

"Ever since you have come in this afternoon, you have been at me to answer you, so I'm fucking answering you."

"You do not have to swear at me when all I am asking is to discuss the action plan, so I understand what happens next."

"Okay, I am sorry, but I don't like shouting at you, but sometimes you drive me up the wall with your jealous attitude."

"There is nothing wrong with my tone of voice. I was just a little taken aback by seeing Gabriella again."

"I have told you I will get her to apologise, so stop dragging up old events."

"Thanks; you were not the one having to watch your stomach get pumped while they got the potent drugs out of your system while she just sat there with a smug-like grin on her face."

"What do you want me to say? I have forgiven her, so why can't you?"

"You see, there you go again, blaming me when I love you, and all you say it, I forgave her as though it makes it all right."

"Right, I get it now. Let us change the fucking subject, as it is clear you will not move on to something else now because this is getting quite boring."

"Thanks, a fucking lot."

"Well, do you see my point?"

"I just want you to understand that the bitch nearly killed you and laughed it off as though it was nothing, so your attitude when it comes to that bitch pisses me off."

"This is getting boring, Amanda. Let us move on and talk about the lad, can we?"

"Bloody hell, give me one of those cigs?"

"Okay, tell me about tonight so I know what's happening."

"I have told the lad to be here for seven this evening. When he turns up, I am to seduce him, take him into the bedroom, and fuck him. Once I have done the deed, I will tell him about the action plan and offer him the money. You must understand the boy does not live in the real world like the rest of us. He lives in a fantasy world where he believes he is a winning and popular racing car driver and can get any woman he wants."

"Okay, how long will it take him to carry out the plan we need the idiot to do for us?"

"You know this is difficult for me. I hate men after what my father did to me. I am only doing this for you because I love you."

"Okay, the plan has a few pluses and minuses, but we need it done by this Friday. You have four days to get the lad to do as we need him."

"Why so quick?"

"That's what the boss wants, and he is paying the wages, so we do as he instructs, okay?"

"Yes, Kemosabe, your wish is my command."

"Look, I know I am asking you to do something you are not keen on, but I said I would make it up to you if you do the right thing by sticking as close to the plan of action as the boss needs to be done.

I fully understand your reasoning behind your reluctance to fuck the lad when you are no longer into men. When you are with him, you only need to think about something you want or need to forget what is happening in the room to you. For example, the Ferrari is much better than that old banger you drive around. I also understand the time restraints; we have no choice but to add to the mix. This is far too early when you need to cultivate and grow somebody as stupid as Karl Thornton and his two hangers-on; Pegleg and his dyslexic brother Bob, who cannot even pass a simple driving test."

"Lorna, darling, I struggled with the test, and I am not thick, so your analogy is relatively poor when you consider every year they try to add this and that to the test when you can safely travel the roads without crashing into someone."

"Okay, but you admit that all three of them are a little retarded in the brains department."

"There you go again; these days, you cannot say someone is retarded. It would help if you said they have a learning disability. It sounds better."

"Who lardy da, your majesty, for correcting my simple error."

"Lorna, darling, can I have the keys to the Ferrari tonight?"

"No is the simplest answer to that because I am using it to get around for now."

"That does not make sense to me if we are girlfriends."

"Yes, we are, so I need to see if you can handle a car like that before I give it to you."

"You never said I'd have to have a driving test to get your car before."

"I know I haven't mentioned it before because I've only just thought about it."

"Hang on a flipping minute. I must allow that lad to do whatever he wants, but my reward is a test to see if I can drive your super-fast car? I am a better driver than you are, and you damn well know it."

"Yes, I know, but I also said, if you recall, I told you I would make it up to you. What would make you happy to do, as we ask? I have decided that once you carry out your side of the plan to completion, I will give you a total pass when we go dogging at the weekend."

"You better explain that one, so I understand what you mean. As there is a pass and there is, I will not look if you are a good girl. I can easily recall you saying you would give me a pass the last time but then changed your mind when you saw who I wanted the pass with."

"Okay, if you do every part of the plan, darling, you can have whoever you desire."

"Nope, I want you to say it properly so it is clear."

"Damn it, Amanda, what more do you want me to say."

"You need to say very clearly that I can have a full pass, and I can fuck anyone I choose when we go dogging without you losing it and going crazy with pure jealousy."

"Okay, I will allow you a free pass to fuck who you like on Saturday, and I will not go off on one. Is that better?"

"Right, so we are very clear, as you are too chicken to say it. I can have a free pass and fuck whoever I like without you losing it, even if it's the sexy nun from the local convent."

"No, I didn't say that at all. I said you can fuck who you like, and I will not go off on one, but I didn't say you could fuck the nun, did I?"

"Why not? A full pass is a promise you will let me have some fun with another woman without trying to kill the woman in my book, so why can't I have her when it's clear she wants it?"

"Let's just forget it then. I just thought it would be a pleasurable surprise if I allowed you a pass, that's all."

"Now it comes pretty clear, so I must fuck a lad when I hate men after what my dad did. Although you will allow me a pass on Saturday night to fuck whoever I want if it is not the nun from the local convent because you want her too."

"Look, you need to give me time to wrap my head around everything."

"Oh, I must not allow my feelings to get in the way while allowing this bozo to do anything he wants in the next few hours, and my reward is what, exactly?"

"Okay, you need to understand that ever since the woman came on the scene, it has become clear to several members of the dogging circuit that she should not even think of giving her body to God when she needs a damn good shagging first."

"Ever since I saw her, I have wanted to her, but because of our loving relationship, I have just admired her from afar."

"It seems clear here that we need to agree on the terms of our dogging sessions. Alongside the rules we both need to follow when we're out looking for pussy without stepping on each other's toes."

"Yes, that is not how I would have put it, but you need to give me some release here to get over fucking a man again just for this plan of yours to go ahead in the next two hours."

"Okay, let's agree to disagree about that fine bit of skirt."

"Well, we both can't have her, can we?"

"What if we could both have some fun with the nun? Would that make you happy to fuck the boy later this evening?"

"Now, you are just being mean, when I was the one who saw her first."

"Yes, I understand you saw her watching our dogging session first. When I got to look, I was a little shocked to see the woman was a nun."

"I admit it was a bit weird seeing her there with that mutt she takes for a walk in the park so late at night. I wonder if she had not heard about the dogging community frequenting the park after dark on a Saturday night."

"What made my night was when she tied the dog to a tree so she could move near our van to watch what was happening inside."

"It was also a bit of a shock that once she could see what was going on, she didn't hightail it out of there and back to the safety of the convent to inform the mother superior about the other occupants of our dogging van."

"Right, when you pointed to her, I was a little busy getting some fine arse shoved in my face from the vicar's wife."

"Oh yes, when I think about it now, if the local parish only knew what their priest and his whore of a wife get up to late at night, it would shock the hell out of them."

"Yes, I agree, but Brigitte has a fine arse. You must agree on that one."

"It was funny watching you shag her while she gave her husband a blow job. That was when I heard the dog bark. So, I looked up, and there she was, a beauty standing there with her hand up her skirt, playing with herself as she watched what was happening."

"Yes, I recall you getting quite excited by it all."

"Well, it is not every day, I mean night, you see a beautiful woman, I mean nun, masturbate while looking in our van to see what was going on."

"Hang on a minute, let's go back a bit. How could we both have her without you getting upset with me for wanting to give her something the man upstairs cannot do in a month of Sundays?"

"Let me try explaining it so you are clear. As you must do something you do not want to do more than once if needed, I will allow you to go out on your own on Saturday evening to have fun with the nun without getting upset with you."

"Then, on a Sunday evening, you allow me to do the same with the sexy bitch without you getting upset."

"Ever since we began dogging, we have never done it alone; we have always been together."

"Yes, but I may be busy on Saturday, so you can go on your own, giving you a basic free pass."

"Why would you be busy when we always go dogging on most weekends?"

"None of your business now. Do you want the pass or what?"

"Yes, but why will you not tell me where you are going while I am fucking the nun with your full permission? I may not be able to concentrate if I do not know where you will be when I am getting some arse."

"Amanda darling, you can't have your cake and eat it. If I say I will be busy, I will be doing something important. Do you now understand?"

"Doing another job for the fat bloke."

"Look, we haven't got time to go into the fine details of it now when you need to be getting yourself ready to fuck the idiot this evening."

"Damn it, Lorna, you give me a reluctant free pass then will not tell me where you will be on Saturday evening. When I should be concentrating on seducing the nun, I will not be able to relax because I will not know where you are or what you are doing."

"Amanda, what do I do to earn money?"

"You're a contract killer for hire."

"That means I do not have the luxury of keeping my girlfriend informed about everything I do to earn money to clothe and feed us both and buy such fine cars."

"Which you are now donating to me."

As the redhead looked up from the couch, she noticed the clock on the wall. "Right, I better be going."

"What? Where are you going?"

"Amanda darling, you love showing off your intelligence and membership to Mensa. So, why are you being so thick?"

"I do not understand; that's all I meant."

"It's seven o'clock nearly. I do not want to be around while you fuck that idiot, do I?"

"Oh, I forgot the time we were having such an enjoyable conversation. We have not discussed how I will get hold of you once the deed has been completed."

"Amanda darling, stop being thick because the lad will be here any minute now."

"He could be late?"

"Stop this delaying tactic. Your job is to fuck the lad before getting him to agree to complete the job this coming Friday. Right, I am off. I will see you later this evening. Oh, one more thing before I forget: change the sheets on the bed once you have done the deed."

As they kissed each other goodbye, Amanda walked her girlfriend to the front door of the luxury apartment.

Monday Part Five

As soon as Lorna had left the apartment, Amanda headed straight for the shower to refresh herself. Ten minutes later, she stood naked, looking at her well-formed, shapely body in her bedroom mirror while admiring the giant maracas she had been blessed with.

Looking again at the bedroom clock, she walked across the room to her drawers to search for her sexiest bra and pantie set. After putting them on, she pulled out a sexy-looking pair of stockings with black borders and thick seams. Lorna liked her wearing them for her whenever they made love.

The stockings had been quite expensive, but they were worth every penny when she had orgasm after orgasm just because she wore those stockings for her lover of five years. She knew she didn't have the time to think about how they met, as she needed to get her mind around having to fuck the boy.

She just hoped the sexy underwear would do its job with a man like it did with her sexy, beautiful girlfriend. "Damn it, Amanda, you need to get your mind in the game."

Pulling a cigarette out of the packet, her sexy girlfriend had left her to calm her nerves as she left the bedroom to enter the living room to await the teen's imminent arrival. As the clock on the wall went past seven p.m., she fully expected the virgin boy to be banging down her door at once after the allotted time, but he was a no-show. Seven p.m. went by, then eight p.m. What was going on?

She had been wearing one of her most revealing outfits there, and he had not bothered to show up.

As the clock on the wall now said 9:30 p.m., she had gotten herself dressed and nervously awaited her lover's return. How could she tell her the lad had not bothered to turn up without angering her?

Just then, she heard a sound outside the front door, which made her leave the living room and head towards the front door to investigate. As she opened the front door of the apartment, instead of her angry girlfriend returning, there stood a very drunk teenager swaying around while trying to still stand upright. "Woman, your boyfriend has arrived. I am hungry for some love. Take me in your arms, and I will show you a fun time."

Amanda stood there in disbelief and tried her best not to see red. She moved to her left, allowing the intoxicated teenager a few minutes to step into the apartment, watching him with pure amazement as he struggled to lift one leg up over the threshold of the doorway while trying not to fall over

Once he was in, she slammed the door behind him while trying to stay calm. As the drunken teen tried his best to walk, she found she had no choice but to grab hold of his hands to guide him into the living room. Once he was in, he tried his best to kiss her but tripped and fell over, knocking himself out in the process as his head hit the fire surround with a bang.

Just looking down at the drunk as a skunk teenager reminded her of her beast of a father, who would always come home pissed. Even though she hated the man with all her heart, she recalled he could stand up after a few drinks. Having no choice but to keep her anger in check that evening, the attractive woman bent down to check if the guy was still alive after banging his head on the solid surround of the fireplace.

He began to snore loudly as she was about to check for a pulse, which made her smile a little. Just then, her girlfriend, Lorna, returned home. "What the fuck? I told you to shag him, not kill him, love."

After Amanda told her what had happened, she seemed just as amused but slightly concerned about what to do with the fool. "Lorna darling, you better put some strong coffee on while I try to get him to come round. Just think about it for a moment or two. The boss wants the lad to do that job this coming Friday, and you expect him to carry it out without fucking it up."

"I just knew it would be too soon, but the boss has a timetable he wants us to stick to, so we need to get him to stay sober long enough to be coerced into doing the job."

"I'm sorry, darling, he's well out of it."

"Give him a kick in the nuts. That usually works when you want them to wake up."

"I cannot do that when I've to talk him into stealing your Porsche this Friday night."

"I am not having him in our living room for the rest of the night when I have plans with you in the bedroom."

"Wow, sex, what a great idea, I could do with a good fuck to get over the night of frustration I have had this evening."

"Excuse me, what do you mean by saying that?"

"What are you on about now?"

"You just said you were feeling quite frustrated, which means you couldn't wait for the lad to come and give you one after I had left the flat."

"No way would I prefer a man over you."

"Calm down. I was only trying to lighten your mood."

"Well, stop it now because it is not that nice when I am now a confirmed convert to lesbian sex."

"Good. I have run the tap, so the water should be icy. All you need to do is pour it on the idiot to get him to come around. If that does not work, you can always revert to my first suggestion."

"I've already said I am not kicking him in the balls to get him to wake up."

"Look, Amanda darling, we cannot fuck this up because this idiot loves to have a drink; if I must step in and take over his training, I will get one of my sharpest knives out of the drawer and make sure he fully understands what he must do on Friday night. You also need to make sure he does not take a drop of alcohol on the night if he wants to get the full twenty grand, or I will cut his fucking throat. So, wake the fucker up and make sure he understands we are not pleased with what we have seen so far about his excessive drinking. Well, I am going for a shower, which should take me only ten minutes, so your goal is to get him back on his feet and out of the door, okay?"

"How am I going to achieve that in such a short time?"

"Okay, I will give you fifteen minutes to achieve your target if you want sex tonight."

"You know I will never refuse you sex, so I will try. That is all I can promise you."

"Fifteen minutes and counting, darling. That is all I am saying for now."

As the young, attractive woman poured the freezing water over the lad's head, she shouted at him to wake up because she was on a promise. In less than a minute, the lad woke up with a shocked look on his damp face. After she had passed him a towel to wipe his head on, the idiot had the cheek to ask. "Was I good enough for us to go at it again?"

"What the fuck are you on about? We didn't do a thing as you could not get it up because you were too pissed even to try. So, you can go home, but I want you here at dinnertime tomorrow, no later. Do you understand me? That means no drinking, Because I cannot sleep with a drunken fool, okay?"

"Damn it, I thought we had done the business, and I was great."

"We need to discuss why you live in your head, but we can do that tomorrow. Do you understand?"

"Okay, and one more thing, when I say dinner time, that does not mean teatime; okay, stay out of the fucking pub, and I will give you an afternoon you will never forget."

"Right, I better be off then if I'm to see you tomorrow."

As the young woman walked the lad to the front door, she gave him a peck on the cheek before making sure he would return at noon the next day.

Once he was gone, she stripped off her clothing to join her lover in the shower. "Wow, that was not even ten minutes. Well done, love."

"When I want sex, I want it, and I need an orgasm, so get yourself ready for a night of your life."

"I won't say no to that, my love."

Tuesday

When Amanda got out of bed that morning, she felt nervous. As she stripped herself down to shower, she had no choice but to begin clock-watching. She had done this as a child whenever she arrived home from school, knowing her father would come home for his tea.

Although he preferred a simple meal, such as beans on toast, it had to be served at precisely ninety degrees. Just one or two inches away from the target would send the man into a rage. Even though she feared the man, she learned from each beating her mother had received. Her age sometimes worked against her desire to know what to do and what not to do.

At first, she could not understand his mentality, but the man had not touched a hair on her head. This was the day she consciously decided to put pen to paper to record the beatings. Jeremy Parker had been such a nice man when he met her mother while studying at university. The problems began soon after he qualified as a probation officer. Each new case file brought its blend of excitement, which would positively affect him. Sadly, this thrill ride didn't last long.

Although he was intelligent, his inner demons began working their form of magic against him in dealing with the daily turmoil of being a probation officer; this led to him being a secret drinker.

He would hide the bottles of gin or whisky around the house. Instead of visiting a doctor to discuss his problems with stress, he took it out on his wife when the alcoholic drinks had not done their job and calmed the rage hidden in his very soul. The beatings began only when she discovered one of his hiding places for his favourite stress-busting alcoholic beverages. At first, her mother would make excuses for the bruises that appeared on her body.

Whenever a beating occurred, it was because she had thought she had done something wrong. Although the man worked ridiculously hard to hide the fact, he was a weak-minded fool whilst in the public realm. Behind closed doors, the man was the absolute ruler of his house. His father and grandfather had trained him to control their woman with an iron fist. Keep them from doing what they want. Beat them with a strap or cane so they learn to follow the rules. The man could become extremely angry for the very least of things.

The young girl was always sent to her room, and her beautiful mother asked her to wear headphones so she could not hear the television coming from the living room, and her noise-cancelling headset would cover up her mother's screams.

It was a Tuesday night when her mum left her. Her father told the young eight-year-old girl later her mum had slipped and fallen down the stairs while they were having a chat. All Amanda could remember of that night was coming out of her bedroom wearing her pink headphones. The blonde-haired woman in the tweed jacket and matching skirt walked her out of the house while the men dressed in black uniforms with badges talked with her father about the incident. She knew nothing about her father's job or her mother's so-called drinking problem as she was escorted to the waiting police car.

Taking notes with her brain, she saw the two men wearing white and carrying a stretcher from the house. Amanda could not understand what had happened, but later, the blonde-haired woman took her to the police station. Her father was interviewed by the police about her mother's addiction to sleeping pills and bottles of gin.

At eight, Amanda would believe anything Daddy would say. Once her mother's funeral was out of the way, this was when things changed, as she was now the only female in the house. One night at the dinner table, her father told her this meant a promotion. However, she didn't understand what he meant when he told her that now that her mother was gone, she needed to perform her wifely duties for him. He would visit her bedroom every night so she could complete her daily chores. At first, he showed her how to complete a blow job to the best of her ability. His nightly visits to her bedroom became more frequent once her girlish body went through puberty. As her body developed, this included her breasts, her father would beat her because of the cost of the lingerie she needed.

The larger her breasts grew, the cost of covering them up became increasingly expensive. Years of abuse followed, which included sexual, mental, and physical abuse. All this torment in her young life made her forget all about the night it had ended. All she could remember were the police cars and their flashing blue and red lights.

Her birthday. What should have been a joyous event turned sour when the bastard forgot her present but still wanted her to perform for him. With little thought or effort, she grabbed the knife from the table she had placed earlier to cut her birthday cake, and instead of cutting the chocolate cake, she stabbed the bastard repeatedly.

According to the coroner, she hit him so many times the original place of entry became concealed by so many knife wounds the man counted well over sixty separate points of entry before he lost count. What shocked the man the most who dealt with dead bodies for a living was when he found the man's penis resting inside the deceased man's throat.

When they asked her why she did it, she could only say the bastard had forgotten her birthday present.

At the court case, several months had gone by since her father's demise. When his nightly beatings on the girl were presented to the court by her barrister, who had no choice but to inform the packed courtroom of the young girl's journals detailing everything about the sex, the beatings and the mental torture she had suffered at the hands of that beast. Although it had been a harrowing read, the girl's written dictation was perfect. The diaries were dated year by year, detailing the days that were the worst and the least times she had been beaten in the name of love.

The jury at her trial soon came back with a manslaughter verdict with diminished responsibility because of the years of torture she had been subjected to at an early age. Judge Emery Christie gave a minimum sentence of just five years to be served at the Parkinson Hall prison for young women. Although she hated the place, it was where she met her life partner, Lorna Castle. From day one, the two women had an instant connection. Her only regret was that this was also where she was to meet the deputy assistant governor, Gabriella the Den Hen Unison.

The woman was pure evil and ran the prison with an iron fist. This was also the black guard's home, which included prisoners with special privileges, although any prisoner could join the black guard training program.

The seriously demented Den Hen had only one rule, which had to be followed: Do as I command, whatever that maybe on the pain of death if you do not follow this simple rule.

After stepping out of the shower, she returned her thoughts to the present. She dried herself before leaving the bathroom and headed to the bedroom the young woman shared with her lover.

She got herself dressed in some of her sexiest outfits. As soon as she was ready, she went to the living room to await the lad's arrival so he could begin his training. Dead at twelve, the young lad knocked on her door. As she entered the hallway, she made a brief journey towards the front door.

On opening, the eager young virgin looked quite different from the last time she had seen him. You could tell the lad had showered and put too much aftershave on. Just the smell alone would have knocked you for six, leaving her no choice but to spray the room with a perfume-flavoured scent to mask his dreadful odour.

Although she dreaded the next bit, she led the boy to the bedroom to begin day one of his training. After the first meeting was over, the young woman could not wait for the passionate young teenager to leave so she could wash the nasty smell of his awful aftershave from her body. She headed for the shower as she left him to get himself dressed.

Amanda ran the water to warm it up before she used the loo. It was not that long before she heard the apartment door slam shut. The young lad had been there for well over four hours, which was several hours too much. In that time, he had used and abused her body several times over, in more positions than she wanted him to. The lad may have been a virgin, but he had undoubtedly lost that within the first ten minutes. What he knew about sex was from what he had seen in the men's magazines he had bought from his local newsagents.

He didn't know much about sex to begin with; he knew enough to use her body to satisfy the lusty thoughts and dreams he had several times over. As she looked in the bathroom mirror, she noticed several bruises around her nipples as she recalled him biting her button-style nipples. She got into the shower to wash herself down while trying to get rid of that awful stench of his cheap aftershave from her body. There was no way Lorna, her girlfriend, would not say something about it if she still had just a hint of the smell left after her shower.

Usually, a shower took her ten minutes, but she washed herself at least three times to get rid of the odour he had filled her bedroom with. Once she had finished, she stepped out of the shower and headed for the bedroom. On entering the medium-sized room, she noticed the randy youth had left the quilt on the floor. As she looked across at the bed, she could see the now empty packet of condoms they had used that afternoon.

She had no choice but to pick up one of her girlfriend's expensive perfume bottles. She made her way towards the apartment's front door before turning around to return to the bedroom. There, she sprayed the familiar scented perfume to mask the dreadful scent of the teenager's aftershave. Although she would get a slap for using Lorna's perfume instead of her own, she felt it would be worth it. Once she had finished spraying it around the apartment, she felt a little guilty but would say nothing about it unless her beautiful girlfriend said something first. Looking at the empty bottle, she quickly poured some of her perfume into it, hoping that her girlfriend would not find out.

As soon as she completed the task, she knew she needed to change the sheets on the bed and dispose of the condoms and their empty packet. It had been several years since she had been with a man, but she knew she still needed to perform for the young lad, hoping it would motivate him to carry out her girlfriend's plan.

Although she didn't understand why Lorna's boss had targeted the man, she was not bothered. All she wanted was the Ferrari and the money—but most of all, she wanted to stop having sex with the lad as soon as possible.

While changing the sheet and putting a fresh duvet cover on the bed, her thoughts, for some unknown reason, returned to the young lad's cock. Although it had been many years since her father had used her for his pleasure, she remembered him having a small cock. The lad's ten inches had been just the right size for her to take.

What shocked her was that, despite his immaturity and her having to show him where to touch her, he had been a keen student. He had made her cum several times that afternoon, which surprised her as she now considered herself a confirmed lesbian.

She could not tell her girlfriend without risking a sulk. Whenever she had sex with Lorna, it felt completely different from sex with a man. She thought about it while leaving the bedroom with the dirty sheets and quilt cover, both covered in spunk, as the lad loved pulling off the condom to spray his semen all over her breasts or her arse.

When she entered the kitchen, she put the items in the washer, added soap powder, and set it to spin. Returning to the bedroom, she got herself dressed in a comfortable pair of leggings and a matching sweatshirt.

The young beauty slipped on a pair of sneakers before leaving the freshly made bed. Minutes later, she left the room and headed for the veranda to smoke. Just as she lit her cigarette, she heard her girlfriend's car coming down the road and into the square.

As she waited for Lorna to come up the stairs, she left the veranda to put her notebooks away, which she had tried to use with the lad that afternoon. Still, all he had been interested in was getting her kit off so he could finally lose his virginity.

As soon as Lorna entered the flat, Amanda hoped the perfume she had sprayed around the apartment would mask the lad's awful scent. As she walked across the room toward her girlfriend, she gave her a sloppy kiss on the lips while laying her hands on Lorna's shoulders.

"Okay, what have you done?"

"What do you mean? Can't I give the woman I love a kiss?"

"Yes, but you never move that quickly, and I usually make the first move. So, I'll ask again: what have you done?"

"Nothing, darling. Well, unless you mean carrying out one of my tasks toward our principal goal."

"No, you've done something. I'm not sure what yet, but give me time, and I'll discover your secret."

"Why are you being like this when I thought it would be nice to kiss you for once without you starting first? I want you to take me into the bedroom and make mad, passionate love to me right now."

"Amanda, darling, how long have we been together?"

"Five years this coming Sunday, I think."

"In that time, I've gotten used to your ways. Therefore, you've done something and are trying your best to hide it from me."

"So, you don't want to fuck me because you think I've done something wrong? Fine, I confess—I fucked the lad four times in several positions, and he made me cum loads of times. Are you satisfied now?"

Lorna pulled a cigarette packet from her pocket and offered it to her lover. As Amanda took the cigarette, Lorna took a lighter out of her pocket and lit Amanda's fag before lighting her own. She then went out onto the balcony to think things over. Amanda followed her, leaning against the veranda's balcony railing.

"So, the idiot made you cum several times. Why are you telling me this when your instructions were to fuck the lad and make it seem like you loved it?"

"I'm sorry, I just can't understand it. He had such a perfectly sized cock—at least twice the size of my father's. It was when he banged me from behind like you do that did it, I think."

"Amanda, darling, what am I to you now? Be honest."

"You're the love of my life, my sweet angel."

"When we fuck how many times do you cum?"

"Loads of times. Why?"

"More than that, idiot."

"Yes, sometimes you make me cum so much we need to change the sheets before we sleep."

"So, are you telling me you're being completely honest with me?"

"Now you've lost me. Are we still talking about sex or something else?"

"Forget the sex for now. I know you did something this afternoon and are trying to hide it from me for some unknown reason."

"There's nothing I can think of that I need to confess to you."

As Lorna threw the cigarette butt over the edge of the balcony, she left her partner there to think. A few seconds later, Amanda finished her cigarette and dropped it on the floor to stamp on it. After picking it up, she left the balcony to talk to Lorna and find out what she was going on about.

In the kitchen, she placed the butt in the bin and watched Lorna make them both hot chocolate—their favourite drink. After her lover passed her the cup, Lorna pushed past Amanda and walked into the living room. Once seated on the white leather couch, she looked directly at her girlfriend.

"I've just figured out what you've done. So, why couldn't you have told me before blurting out the fucking idiot made you cum?"

Amanda stood there, unsure of where the conversation was heading. They looked at each other silently as they drank their hot chocolate.

"What do I have to do to get you to confess your sins, my love?"

"If I knew what you were on about, I'd confess, but I have no clue."

"Amanda, who loves nothing more than telling me how intelligent she is?"

"Me. But I still don't know what you're getting at."

"Bloody hell, sometimes you can act so thick. Stop being stupid and confess your sins to me."

"What fucking sin? If I had sinned, then I would confess it instantly to you as I did about the lad making me cum with his gigantic cock."

"If you want sex, then I'm going into the bedroom, and I'm going to get on the bed, but you can only join me if you are prepared to confess your sins to me."

"Damn it, Lorna, please tell me what I have done so I can apologise to you."

"Sniff up. That should give you a clue, Miss Smarty-pants."

"Shit, I thought I could get away with that, but it has not worked, has it?"

"Now, you are back on my wavelength. You can tell me what you have done, take your punishment, and we can move on to making love if that is what you want this afternoon."

"Lorna, you know already I would never refuse to have sex with you. So, I confess the idiot wore too much aftershave and stunk the place out. So, I picked up a bottle of perfume and walked around the flat, spraying it to mask the lad's scent. There is my confession, and yes, I will take my punishment like a naughty girl should."

"Come here and strip for me."

"Yes, my love, I am sorry for trying to hide it from you. How can I make it up to you?"

"Get the strap from the drawer and get ready for your punishment, my love."

Wednesday Part One

"No! Please stop this right now. It was the time limit we were given. Please do not leave me, Lorna. I do not believe it is my fault the idiot would not listen to me. I told you I needed more time than just a few days. Please, darling, you need to understand me. It was not my fault, my love."

"Amanda, what the hell are you on about? Wake up. You are having a nightmare."

"I did what was asked of me, that is all. So, why are you being like this, my true love?"

Lorna sat up in bed, trying to get her girlfriend to wake up from the nightmare she was having. She shook her lover of five years again.

"Amanda, please wake up, my love. Clearly, we need to talk about this problem you are dreaming about."

The young woman seemed quite concerned, shaking her girlfriend once more while listening to what she was muttering.

"Darling, who is Tracy?" she asked a few minutes later.

Amanda stirred. "What are you doing? I was having a pleasurable dream about last night."

"No, you were not. You were screaming out my name, hoping I wouldn't leave you."

"Are you crazy? I know you would never decide parting ways with me would be better for you, my love."

"So, who is this Tracy, then? Is she your secret lover?"

"No! I do not know why I would call out another girl's name in my sleep."

"You also mentioned your mother's problem with drinking too much gin before blaming your father for beating you instead of your younger sister."

"I'm sorry, you must be mistaken there, my love. I have not got a younger sister. I have no clue how long I was jabbering on about this issue or that problem. All I can recall about my mum was that I was eight or nine when she died. If she had another child, I never knew about it. Also, it was around that time my evil fucking father abused me night after night. I think I can recall a woman with a tweed-looking suit of black and white, bright blonde hair, and perfume smelling of violets. She took me to the police station while the bobbies questioned my dad. I was supposed to sit in a room full of dolls and other toys while waiting for my dad to finish his interview. I may have spoken with a girl named Tracy there."

"How old was she?" Lorna asked.

"I was around eight or nine, so the young lass was about six or seven."

"Maybe those in charge thought the girl was your younger sister because her last name was also Parker."

"All I knew about the young lass was that she had also lost her loving mother the same night I lost mine."

"See, there you go. So, she may have been your sister. Do you know what happened to her or not?"

"I'm sorry. My memory wasn't that good. I was upset about losing my mother earlier that night. I wish I had paid more attention to the girl and asked questions. But what is strange is why I had a dream about her now when I haven't even thought about her since."

"Let me talk to the boss about this. If you had a sister, he could discover the truth one way or another. Right now, we are fully awake, and we need to discuss our boss's primary plan because it is clearly worrying you, my love. And we cannot have that, can we?"

"Okay. Do you fancy some hot chocolate with marshmallow topping to calm yourself down?"

The young woman with bright red hair got up from the bed and headed to the kitchen to make the drinks. Amanda remade the bed before joining her lover in the kitchen.

"I'm sorry I'm causing this minor issue. My subconscious mind must be trying to tell me something is wrong with the plan."

"There must be something we can do to help you get past this. I'll tell the boss you need a little more time to get the fool to comply with our wishes."

"Will he understand, though? I don't want to cause a problem two days before the event occurs."

"Drink your chocolate, my love. There must be a way to sort this problem out—one that keeps the boss happy and stops disturbing your sleep."

"If only I could get the lad to understand he needs to comply with our wishes and stop drinking until after the event."

"Well, there is a way, but I don't want to go overboard when we need him to do the job this Friday night."

"I'll do anything you suggest about the lad and his problem with following orders."

"You see that wall?" Lorna asked.

"Which one? There are several to choose from."

"I'm sorry, I should have explained my idea better. I was talking about the wall just to the left of our bedroom."

"Oh, okay. What's wrong with it?"

"Please, love, stop interrupting me and let me finish telling you my idea."

"Okay, I'm sorry. I was thinking about the lad. He will be here sometime this morning. I've asked him to come at ten a.m."

"Amanda, please let me finish before interrupting me again."

"I'm sorry, but carry on with your plan."

"There you go again. Please stay silent for just a few minutes, and then you will get the full picture of my idea, okay?"

As the red-haired beauty sat on the comfortable white leather couch, she explained her plan of action. Amanda sat next to her, finishing her chocolate drink and thinking about the changes to the original plan that were needed. This was because of the boy's problem with consuming severe amounts of alcohol to carry out even the simplest tasks.

Her interview with the lad on Monday at the probation service had answered the need to find an idiot for this simple task. Was the original plan perfect? No.

When Lorna received notification from Sir John that he needed her for a rewarding but straightforward task, not one of them thought about there being any form of complication. Now, they had only two days to get the incompetent idiot to complete the required task.

Amanda had allowed the lad access to her beautiful and curvy body, as instructed by her lover. Yes, she wanted people to understand.

She was now a confirmed lesbian.

After meeting her lover at the notorious women's prison at Parkinson Hall almost five years ago, after her three-day induction, she was escorted to the D wing of the large prison. Lorna was a trainee member of the black guard run by the Den Hen and her deputy Scarface Magee.

All that was in the past, and Amanda didn't want to discuss past events when they needed to sort this severe problem out so the plan would work. "The boss would be happy, Lorna would be satisfied, and I would get her car." After putting the now empty mug on the coffee table in front of her, she nodded her approval of the idea her lover had produced.

"So, I just wait for him to arrive, sit him down on the couch, and tell him about the serious amount of mullah he will waste if he cannot do this simple job on Friday night. I then stand him up and take him towards our bedroom so he thinks he will get his leg over again. I will then stop and make him stand against the wall near our bedroom. I then get his cock out and give him some head. While I do that, you will stand just inside our bedroom, watching what is going on through some hastily arranged mirrors in the suitable locations of the medium-sized living room. As soon as he gets lost in his world of pleasure, suddenly, with no warning, you pull out your sharpest flick knife and put it to his neck."

"You know he will do one of two things here."

"What two things?"

"He will either shoot his load directly down my throat because of the shock of feeling a sharpened blade touching his neck- Oh, I am sorry. I just thought about another issue regarding the first option."

"What problem are you thinking about now?"

"I was just thinking about whenever my father would insist I give him head, I would think about ways to stop him from abusing me so much. So, I thought when he spurted his load, I would simply bite his cock off."

"Oh, I had not thought about that minor issue. So, what was the second thing he may do?"

"He could shit himself with fright."

"Oh, and we do not want or need that, do we? We need to plan this correctly so it will work without him shooting his load so fast you have no choice but to bite down hard on his large member or crap himself in fear. Any suggestions? I am all ears, my sweet love."

"Why are you giving me so many compliments when we haven't devised a proper plan yet? I was just wondering if you would make another chocolate with double the number of marshmallows on it."

"Okay, but if you have the lad coming here this morning, shouldn't we return to bed to get some sleep?"

"Okay, but a lovely hot chocolate drink would help me sleep."

"Okay, one chocolate drink coming up with double the amount of marshmallow treats on top. You had better get back into bed, and I will join you in a minute. As soon as you have your drink, I will arrange the mirrors to give me a perfect viewing angle from my position in the bedroom so that I can strike when the time is right."

Wednesday Part Two

"Amanda darling, you better get up. Someone is knocking at the front door."

"What, what time is it?"

"Bloody hell, it's ten a.m."

"Shit, we haven't decided on the best plan of action concerning the idiot's drinking."

"I'm sorry, but he's already here. We will have to do what I said we should do."

"Do you mean the blowjob surprise we were discussing earlier?"

"Yes, that is the one, unless you can think of something else. There is another problem we must address now rather than later."

"Damn it, I hate being rushed into doing something without some form of rehearsal first."

"Yes, but this issue must be addressed right now."

"What the hell are you on about, darling? Let us go back to sleep. The lad can fuck off because I'm not ready to see him just yet."

"Amanda, my love, you need to check the sheets. Didn't you check the calendar for your time of the month schedule I put up in the kitchen?"

"No, damn it, it's far too early. I am not due on for another week. Well, it is not me, so either a rat just died or gone to heaven between your legs, or you have come on early because of the stress of this rushed action plan. Also, the lad's still banging on the door to be let in. So, you better get up and answer the door before sorting yourself out while I change the sheets."

"There's a second issue here you have not thought about or even considered."

"What's that, my love?"

"You, dummy, are the issue I was talking about."

"Me?

What is the problem with me?"

"The lad has not met you or knows about your existence. He thinks I am just a randy twenty-three-year-old bimbo, not a lesbian in love with my beautiful girlfriend."

"Bloody hell, just get up and answer the door while I wait here."

"How can I do that when I need to visit the bathroom first?"

"Amanda, the bathroom is next to the apartment's front door, so just let the lad in, show him into the front room, and then shower to wake yourself up."

"I hate having the periods once a month. It is so stressful. It's going to be more than a few days before I stop bleeding. This means I am going to be out of action this weekend, so I cannot take up your offer of a free pass with the sexy nun this weekend, so you better have your go with her until I finish with the period."

"Let us just forget about that for now. Put this towel around you, and I will hide in the bedroom until you have sorted the lad out."

"Okay, I just forgot, that is all, so you better check if I have not stained the mattress with my blood."

"I'll check it in a minute now. You better get going, and if the mattress is stained, I will have to punish you later for this minor indiscretion."

"That's sound just lovely. I cannot wait, my love."

As the young woman walked from the bedroom, she stopped briefly in the kitchen to check the chart they both planned their lives around. As she checked for her name, she could see her period was not due for at least another ten days. So, why had it come on so early?

As she left the kitchen, she approached the front door. When she reached it, she could feel the blood slowly dripping down her thighs. After opening the door, she could see the young lad moving around to keep himself warm because of the unseasonably harsh weather they had been having recently. As she invited him in, she asked him to make his way into the living room, as she needed to resolve a slight problem. The young lad offered to help her, but she thanked him for the offer but quickly denied his request.

As Amanda watched the disappointed young lad make his way to the living room, she entered the bathroom and closed the door behind her. After turning the shower to warm the water, she sat on the loo to sort herself out.

She used a few wet wipes to clear up the running bloodstains because inserting a tampon was not useful just yet, as she was about to shower. She stepped in to rewash her sins as soon as she was ready. Standing underneath the hot water, she usually took around ten minutes to shower, but when it was her time of the month, she loved nothing more than taking her time and having a twenty-minute shower. As soon as she finished her extended shower, she stepped out of the cubicle onto the mat before again grabbing hold of her lover's fluffy white towel. Once she had wrapped herself in the large bath sheet, she looked around the floor for the matching slippers to the towel.

After slipping them on, she sat down on the toilet while inserting a tampon in her fanny to give her a few hours of relief from the flow of blood she had no choice but to deal with monthly. After using a few more wet wipes, she ensured she was as clean as possible for the next few hours.

Once she felt ready, she wrapped her hair in one of the more miniature towels from the bathroom cupboard. She tightened the large bath sheet around her sexy body before leaving the bathroom to head to the living room once again. As the eager young lad sat on the white leather couch, she asked him to wait for her on the veranda, saying that she would be with him shortly as she needed to get dressed.

She needed the time to get dressed and confirm the action plan to have the lad stand in the correct location. As she entered the bedroom, Lorna sat at the dressing table chair, applying fresh nail varnish to her fingernails. Amanda made her way across the room to kiss her lover on the neck while trying to keep the volume down. After a brief discussion about the plan, the young woman dressed in relaxing clothing.

Once she was ready to leave the bedroom to meet the lad again, she saw Lorna had left her a few tampons and a packet of wet wipes on the bed so she could add those to her bag. "Darling, I have checked out the chart, and I was right. I came on well too soon; I was not due for more than a week or more."

Having finished applying her nail varnish, Lorna stood up, walked across to her lover, and kissed her while holding on to her waist.

"I will have a word with Sir John to see if there is any way we can delay the attack for a few days so you have more time to experiment with the young lad to make him more pliable to our desires."

"You know we will have to get a new chart either way or wait to see if I can stop and start again on my normal cycle."

"I do not think so; we will have to get a new chart and begin again. If your cycle has changed, all your dates must be altered."

"I have never had an issue like this before. I usually like clockwork every fifteenth day of the month until around the nineteenth, whereas yours begins on the seventeenth and ends on the twenty-first day of the month. This change will automatically fuck up our weekend plans until we can get used to my new dates. All I can hope for now is that your dates stay the same. Now, I'd better get this little plan of ours started. The sooner it begins, the sooner I will never have to ever sleep with a man again."

"Don't worry about it, my love. We will soon have the lad begging to stay in line and will carry out all our wishes. Once he has been warned and walked through the plan of action, he will have the choice to earn twenty grand or die because he cannot follow a simple set of rules."

Wednesday Part Three

The woman left the bedroom to go to the veranda to meet her waiting target. She knew she could not have a repeat of the Monday evening. When the young lad had turned up extremely late and was very drunk.

She never thought she would have to experience the stress of keeping this young teenager in line. Suddenly, with no form of warning, Nigel, the probation officer, popped into her mind, and she soon understood why he had a problem with stress when dealing with the childish idiot. She walked the young lad from the veranda to the wall next to her bedroom so her girlfriend could complete their plan.

Although they had not had the time to go through the plan step by step, all they could do was wish it would work because if this didn't work, nothing would. Once the young lad was standing in the right spot, the young woman knelt to pull out the young lad's penis from his trousers. Within a second or two, he was erect and happy to go with the flow. Meanwhile, Lorna looked around for her sharpest flick knife.

Once she found it, she retrieved it from under the bed, next to one of their strap-on dildos, which they used regularly on each other. As the young lad stood against the living room wall, Lorna moved to the correct position on the other side of the wall. Without warning, she got the knife in the correct location and slowly opened the bedroom door so she could place the sharpest of blades inches from the boy's neck.

As Amanda continued to suck at the guy's cock, he had been enjoying the pleasure of this with his eyes closed. This was until the teenager felt something sharp touching his neck. The shock of it was more than he could handle, as the pleasure was so intense. He at once cried out as his semen hit the back of the young woman's throat at a fierce speed. It was lucky that Amanda had been used to sucking on an enormous dildo before, so the speed of the spunk hitting Amanda's throat had not made her gag. As he had no choice but to open his eyes, he could see the red-haired beauty standing right next to him, holding the knife to his throat.

He had experienced nothing so intense as this, and even though it was a shock to the system, the thrill of the experience was more exhilarating than the fear any day of the week. This was not the reaction that both women had thought about earlier that morning.

As Amanda got to her feet, she still had hold of the young lad's cock in her hands. As they looked at each other, the weirdness of the situation enveloped them all. They never considered the lad submissive enough to accept his current dilemma. As she continued to grab at the young teenager's semi-erect penis, he felt intense pleasure in no time at all. His erection stood there like a springboard awaiting its first customer of the day. Leaving both women wondering how to continue with their plans.

Just the look the lad gave Lorna made her feel like a giant. As he turned to look straight at her, she had forgotten he thought her name was Cathy. As she continued to pull at his cock, it was not long before he could shoot his load once more into her waiting hand. Amanda, for some unknown reason, licked her palm clean while looking straight across at her lover. Lorna wished her lover of five years had not come on earlier that morning because all she could think about was bending her over and fucking her there and then with one of the many dildos they had in the bedroom.

Sadly, that would have to wait for another day, but their problem was keeping the plan going as the young lad had once again slipped back into his fantasy world where he could have any woman.

As soon as she had let go of his semi-hard-on, he wanted to have a threesome with both young women. Lorna had never considered herself bisexual; she had been a confirmed lesbian from birth, so there was no way she could have sex with a man, could she? Realising the situation was slightly more complicated than they had ever thought. Yes, they wanted each other, but the lad stood there with his enormous cock out and needed some attention from either Amanda or Lorna. They looked at each other with a look of pure passion in their eyes that morning.

Lorna even considered giving up her gold star crown and taking one for the team if it would persuade the young teenager to complete the deed. They needed him to complete it on Friday evening. Amanda was out of action because of her time of the month brought on by the stress. They needed to do something straight away before the intensity of the situation left them that morning. As Lorna led the lad into the bedroom, all Amanda could do was watch her girlfriend as she stripped the young lad of his clothes, leaving her partner in crime feeling like she just wanted to masturbate, but she had her periods, and so, was useless.

With Amanda standing close to the bed, Lorna pulled out her flick knife and waved it over the young, newly submissive teenage boy. As the young lad had no choice but to go with the flow of the situation, he had two sexy women standing there awaiting his loving attention, but he felt scared of what the woman with the red hair wanted to do with him.

Lorna pointed to Amanda to get the KY from the bedroom drawer and one of the smallest plugs they had to begin with. Karl could not believe it. Only the other week, he had dreamed of losing his cherry with a beautiful woman, and now he was standing in the lair of two of the sexiest women he had ever seen. They could do anything to him, and it would be a thrill to last him a lifetime.

He could not wait to tell his best mates that he had a threesome with two large-breasted women. First, he had Cathy, the trainee probation officer, and now he had this other beauty standing there wearing just a pair of tiny black panties and a bra set with stockings. Flicking a knife in his direction, just the intensity, was why he had a vast hard-on awaiting some female attention. Amanda had never seen Lorna this turned on before as she stripped herself.

Grabbing at the plug, her girlfriend had just passed her, which was something to behold. Placing the plug down on the bed, she forced the young lad to lay down on the bed before instructing him to raise his legs a little so they could squirt a generous amount of KY up his bum hole. Once she felt he was wet enough, she picked the butt plug and quickly inserted it into the young teenage arse hole. Just watching the young lad cry out in pure pleasure at the sensation the vibrating plug gave him. His cock sprang into action once again. Amanda bent down to grab at his giant cock and pulled at it, making him groan even more. The situation, which was quickly unfolding, was like the night they first went dogging—oh, what fun that was.

Once the lad had been used to the tiny butt plug, Lorna removed it before squirting some more of the lubrication oil inside the young lad's butt hole. Once she felt he was ready for some absolute pleasure, she grabbed at one of her collections strap-on dildos, wiping some of the KY around the tip before aiming it directly at the lad's anus. As she inserted it, a squeal of pure pleasure came from the boy.

Why had he only just discovered his submissive desire to be used and abused by a woman? As Lorna fucked the young boy, Amanda moved around so she could also have some fun with the boy's cock. She soon realised this new three way session they were involved in gave them both so much pleasure, which led to orgasm central on speed for both women. Yes, they had been dogging before, but they had always used each other's bodies for pleasure or fucked other women like the vicar's wife, Brigitte, who was up for anything to gain her orgasm. Minutes went by as the smell of orgasm juice was in the air that morning.

Then it happened: Lorna, the lesbian, was allowing the lad to fuck her with his enormous cock, while her girlfriend fucked the young lad's anus hole.

Never had Lorna ever imagined she would lose her gold star crown, but the situation had called for it. Having been used to Amanda fucking her with several of the enormous dildos up her pussy or anus. Allowing the lad to use her was more intense than she had ever imagined it would be, recalling her lovers earlier confession informing her the lad had made her cum several times that afternoon. Just the thought of a young boy using and abusing her beautiful lover of five years was not something she had ever been used to. Now she was the one feeling the absolute pleasure a giant cock can give you while the young lad had just one of the women's biggest dildos stuck up his anus.

As the young woman took it in turns to use the boy for their pleasure, they hoped he would now follow their instructions and follow the plan to the letter on the Friday without falling into the usual trip of drinking to excess when they needed him sober so he could carry out the task with no errors to fuck it up.

Thursday Part One

As the sun broke through the clouds that morning, all you could see in the medium-sized bedroom was a crumpled heap of flesh: two women and a teenage boy who had used each other to gain orgasm after orgasm.

Hour upon hour, throughout the day and into the evening. Suppose you wished to smell a room; this boudoir of sin smelt of stale semen and orgasm juice. In addition, the scent of strong liquor and the breeze of exotic cigarettes from Asia was present. The first woman dragged herself from the top of the young boy and out into the living room. The young woman felt quite rough but secure in her sexuality. Yes, she had considered all her options, which had been offered to her the previous evening as she indulged herself in the sexual orgy on offer between her lover and the young stud with the giant cock. If you asked her if she were ashamed of her actions, she would have to say no, but sex had always been a big part of her life, with the dogging sessions at the weekend to break up the loneliness of her state of mind. Since becoming a slave to her work, the freedom it gave her to stray from her increasing anger alongside her controversial relationship with her perfect soulmate.

They understood each other so well. Would you say they were criminally insane? It would be up to the receiver of their anger to pass judgment in that department. Years of being alone while hunting for the perfect person to carry on her choirs were initially a struggle, but since meeting her soulmate, they have gelled so well together. Sometimes, they worked together or alone, depending on the job.

Moving herself from the living room to the shower to refresh herself from the pleasure of the flesh.

As the warm water cascaded down upon her that morning, it was not long before her partner-in-crime joined her to wash away their sins of severe indulgence. As scented soap washed all over their young bodies, they could think of nothing but the sin of the previous night's indulgence with the young boy. Now, it was light; they had to bring the lad back from his wonderful world of sin and back to the reality of carrying out an essential task for their boss.

If they could teach the young stud all he needed to do that day, they could shower him with gifts of the flesh and plenty of cash. Their boss had promised them plenty of gold, which could be shared around now. All they needed was for the lad to understand what he needed to do. Once the refreshing shower had been completed, they returned to the bedroom to bring light to the room of sin, as they needed him to wake up and drag himself to the shower to cleanse himself so he could be ready to learn his actual role in a fresh state of mind. Lorna knew the lad needed to understand the rules. He also needed to be shown what to do and what was entirely expected of him so he could gain thousands of pounds and have generous sessions with both women.

Amanda sat on the couch with all her newly bought literature on how to help someone change their original personality to one of control, despite the strength of doing the right thing. Even though she had been doing this line of work for a while, it took her by surprise when she completed a simple test from one of her books, which experimented with the psyche.

The first few questions began by developing a simple scenario. The test was designed to see how far you could go within the confines of this imaginary framework. Questions one, two, and three were simple yes/no questions with no right or wrong way to answer each. However, questions four, five, and six formed an image in the mind, one that demanded closer examination. This time, there were correct and wrong answers to each question. Get it right to stay on the right path. Get it wrong, and through no fault of your own, you arrive at an alternative route to follow.

When Amanda carefully read each question, she found she had answered only one correctly. This made her question herself. In certain circumstances, those who answered all the questions either correctly—or completely wrongly—would then be transported to new structured pathways within the mind's eye. Questions eight, nine, and ten shocked her with their relevance to her current situation.

"How could a book written so many years ago correctly guess that its reader couldn't complete all ten questions?" she muttered to herself.

There were consequences attached to the framework of each question. Looking back at her answers, Amanda was surprised to find an answer to something she had often thought about: there was always a right way to do things and a wrong way to do them. According to the test, if you were normal-minded, you would correctly guess questions 1, 2, 3, 5, 9, and 10.

But Amanda had answered 1, 2, 3, 6, and 8. Its conclusion was a little disturbing.

"If this book is correct," she whispered, "I'm a disturbed individual with a keen sense of guilt… but only after I've attacked or killed someone. I mean… Daddy."

She sighed deeply. She had no choice but to admit what she saw when she attacked her father after he forgot her birthday cake.

"I saw a red mist form before me," she admitted softly, "and I attacked the man I should have loved as a father."

Her gaze returned to the book. The test suggested that, tragically, her guilt wouldn't last long. Once this job they were doing was over and she could spend time with her lover, she wanted to see how Lorna would answer the questions. She already suspected her lover had serious anger issues and knew how to keep herself in check in public.

Amanda briefly thought about her subordinate, Karl, and wondered how many questions he could answer correctly. She knew he needed to understand the reality of his limitations—not only in their work but in his life overall.

The foolish idiot had lived a life of excessive drinking, stealing cars, and surrounding himself with questionable friends. If he could stop living this way, Amanda thought, he might achieve a new sense of freedom. But she also saw his inner submissive nature—the part of him that had been exploited by two women indulging their own desires while using him to achieve their goals.

Would he be able to move beyond his self-created fantasy world? Could he leave behind the drinking, the stealing, and the trouble with the law?

Time had its own limitations, she thought. If he truly wanted to change, he would need to break free from the prison of his own mind. But Amanda wasn't sure he could.

"He's been working with that probation officer for years," she mused. "Still, no real change. But Cathy…" She smirked. "Cathy got to him. That large-breasted woman turned his world upside down."

Now, with not one but two women shaping his life, Amanda wondered, "Will this be the thing that finally makes him change? Only time will tell."

Thursday Part Two

With just one more day before the event, he needed to carry out the simple plan for his two large-breasted lovers. He couldn't quite understand how this had all happened to him after years of feeling trapped in his meagre existence.

Once he had completed the job, he would have plenty of cash to flash around, plus a lovely fast car to drive and impress the ladies of Glendale. Just stealing her car and knocking some guy over didn't seem worth the twenty grand he would receive, but the promise of freedom and excitement made it tempting.

"Yes, I can do this," he muttered to himself. "It's only one night without my favorite tipple."

He had been explicitly instructed not to drink, and while it was a tall order, the payout made it worth the sacrifice. He envisioned the red Porsche convertible he would drive around town—a flashy, fast car in his favorite colour, perfect for catching attention. Just the bragging rights alone would be worth their weight in gold.

Now, he was a "super stud," ready to have fun with genuine women instead of the imaginary ones that had filled his dull existence. The thought gave him a thrill he hadn't felt in years.

He smiled as he recalled the previous night, a sinful celebration he wouldn't soon forget. The redheaded beauty had taken control, using her rigid dildo to assert her power over him. The entire experience had left him in awe.

"That was the best thing I've ever done," he whispered, grinning at the memory. Their dominance and command over him had awakened something he hadn't known existed within him.

That morning, after leaving the two women behind, he was told to meet them again at three that afternoon outside the Bearded Tavern. They would walk him through the task to ensure he fully understood it. But first, he needed some well-deserved rest.

As he approached his home, a strange sense of freedom washed over him. For the first time, he felt alive. He no longer felt ashamed or burdened by the idea of being a submissive man.

"So, what's so wrong with it anyway?" he asked himself, almost defiantly. "Nothing. Absolutely nothing."

Tomorrow night, everything would change. Once the job was done, he could finally step out of his fantasy world and into a reality he had never dared to dream of before.

Thursday Part Three

"What time is it?"

"It's five minutes after three."

"We told him to meet us here at exactly three o'clock so we could go over the route he needs to travel tomorrow to complete the job he needs to do so he can get the twenty grand on offer."

"What time is it now?"

"Lorna darling, you have just asked me the time, and I told you. Now it is about seven minutes after three."

"That idiot better not be in the pub."

"After the pleasurable session, we gave him, I don't think he would be so stupid as to go against our wishes and go drinking when we want him to stay off the drink until he has finished the job."

"Will you check for me while I wait here?"

"Can't we give the lad the benefit of the doubt and wait another ten minutes? I'll check for you if he hasn't shown up by then," she said.

"Ten minutes no longer, and if he is in that pub, I will cut his balls off."

"Please remember, darling, that we only need to deal with him for another twenty-four hours. Once the job is done, we never have to see him again."

She sighed, "I am sorry for acting like this when we need him to follow the plan to the letter. So, we get paid, and you get the use of my car, and the boss will be happy once again until he needs us again."

"Will you replace the Porsche or just get another convertible?"

"I like my Ferrari, so I may get another one with a distinct colour this time."

"What colour are you thinking about?"

"I was thinking about a metallic red or even a black and burgundy one."

"I didn't realise they had so many colors."

"They do not, but you consider they can provide it in any colour you want if you pay over eighty grand."

"Okay, well, the lads had enough time. It's twenty-two-three, and the dragons have gone in for their tea.

"What are you on about dragons and tea for in the same sentence?"

"When I was a child, I remember reading a book about dragons in the library; if I recall correctly, they always went in for their tea at twenty to three in the afternoon," she said.

"Okay, well, check the pub for me because if I go in and find him there, I will lose it in front of all the customers."

"I do not think the lad would be that stupid, but we are talking about Karl here, who loves to live in a fantasy world of his creation, so I will check. Keep your hair on, and I'll see if he is in there."

"Don't bother. Look over there. Who is that swaying around near the back of the tavern while trying to light a fag and stand up straight at the same time?" Lorna asked.

"Shit, that can't be him when we gave it our all-last night."

"Wait here, and I'll make sure."

"No, Lorna, please stay calm. You wait here, and I will go and check because I can stay calm when needed when you want to strike out at whoever has done something wrong," she said.

"If it's him, he better have a good explanation for being late and pissed when we told him he cannot drink until after the job is done."

Thursday Part Four: The Warning

"What do you think you are doing, you blubbering idiot? We told you to stay off the liquor, didn't we?"

"I thought you said I must stay off the alcohol from tomorrow morning till the job's been done."

"Look over there. My girlfriend is not happy and is ready to cut your balls off, so you better have a damn good excuse for getting pissed."

"I am not drunk. I nearly fell over because of a powerful gust of wind coming from the north."

"Do not belittle the situation. You cannot even stand up straight."

"Okay, I had a few drinks to celebrate the twins coming twenty today."

"Well, you better come over and talk to my friend to ensure she will allow you to complete the job tomorrow. If you still want some fun with both of us, earn while also earning twenty grand."

"Nobody would refuse to have sex with you two beauties, so let me explain it to your beautiful friend, and it will be all right."

They went over to Lorna. "What excuse have you got, my boy? I have a damn good mind to take you back to our apartment and give you a damn good thrashing for not obeying the rules."

"I am sorry, my love. I was going home after leaving your flat when I bumped into Bob and Craig's. They told me it was their birthday, and I was invited to drink with them at the local pub. I could not refuse as my best mates were there."

"First thing, I am not your love; second, what are you going to say to them if you bump into them tomorrow when you must carry out the job with no fuck up's."

"I will not drink tomorrow, I promise you."

"Do you see that lovely red convertible Porsche over there?"

"Oh, yes, it's beautiful."

"Could you steal that car in your current state when you can't even stand up straight?"

"Darling, I am not drunk. I can steal any car. Just test me."

As the lad walked towards the red vehicle, Lorna put her foot out, and the young lad fell over, banging his head on a nearby kerb.

"Whoops, I slipped. It must have been a passing windblast, darling. I will get up and at once show you I can steal that car."

As the young lad tried to get up from the ground, Lorna approached him and, using her boot, she placed it slowly down on his neck.

"Now tell me you are not pissed. You didn't even see me coming, you fucking idiot."

As she removed her foot from his young neck, she placed her hand out in front of her to help him up from the ground while Amanda watched on.

"Darling, we better move. People are watching from the tavern windows."

Hearing that, she let the young drunk lad go, so he fell back once more, hitting his head once again on the curb.

"Get him up, and we better go back to the flat so I can sort this incompetent idiot out and give him a warning not to fuck up our plan of action."

As Amanda helped the young lad up before leading him to the red Porsche, she opened the driver's side door and pulled the seat forward, allowing him to enter the back seat. "Here, you better use this hankie to wipe up the bloodstain from your head so as not to stain the backseats."

Once Lorna was sitting in the vehicle's passenger side, she slammed the door shut while trying to hide her anger. Amanda then became the designated driver for the trip back to their apartment so Lorna could dish out the punishment they both felt the boy deserved. Just as they reached the busy highway, they found it full of police cars and other vehicles heading north.

As Lorna turned on the radio, they learned another young woman's body had been found in Northwood Park. Listening on, they heard the woman's body had been found just like the earlier victim, hanging upside down and tied to a cross-like structure. The radio presenter was already telling the listeners that the Sign of the Cross Killer killed both victims.

Lorna turned to look at the young lad before telling him. "I wonder what I could do to you if I had one of those crosses. Just imagine the pain I could inflict on a naughty boy who does not do as he is told."

The lad tried to smile, but his erection had already betrayed his feelings towards the subject about being punished by the two ladies.

As soon as they were allowed access to the estate, Amanda continued to drive them home. When she arrived, Lorna let the lad out of the vehicle's backseat. As soon as he was out, she looked down and could see the thick bulging in his trousers as soon as Amanda had locked the car door and joined them both on the pavement. Lorna pointed to the lad's growing erection.

"Well, at least the drink does not affect your cock now; get up the stairs so you can be properly punished for your indiscretions this afternoon."

"Yes, Mistress," the lad spoke out with a sullen-sounding voice while also looking immensely turned on about the forthcoming situation that was to come.

Thursday: Part Five: The Punishment

As soon as the lad had entered the apartment. He was told to strip by Amanda. Just the suggestion made the lads bulging hard on press firmly once more against his jeans. Lorna walked past the two of them into the bedroom to retrieve her cane and strap, which they used regularly on each other when having one of their usual sex sessions.

Sometimes, they even used it for their dogging partners who requested a little BDSM fun away from their usual dogging location. On her return to the living room, the young lad stood in the middle of the floor with a massive hard-on.

"Right, my darling, you strip because I feel you both may need a little punishment." Amanda looked slightly confused at first, but as she had loved her lover for five years, she did as she was told. As soon as she was naked, she looked straight at Lorna while awaiting her mistress's instructions.

"Right, my love, you need to show our young guests how we play our BDSM games."

"Oh, my god, yes, I love playing the enslaved person and mistress routine before we have sex. So, mistress, what do you wish I do for you this afternoon?"

"First, kneel and kiss my feet and ask my permission to play with my other slave."

"I'll do anything you command me to do."

As the young lad rubbed at his cock to keep it hard, he stood watching the beauty he knew as Cathy kneeling before bending down further to crawl towards Lorna's feet.

As she kissed them, she asked her permission to play with the young lad's gigantic cock. Although she had confessed her love for her lover and didn't want to fuck with a boy again. She had to admit she loved it when the childish idiot slammed his giant cock up her arse at speed; this was one sure way to make her cum bucket loads. The young woman had told herself she was a full-time lesbian even before she understood the word bisexual ever existed. But the pleasure the lad gave her with his enormous cock. On top of that, she had fun with her girlfriend when she was dogging over the weekend. The beautiful woman loved being tied to the bed and whipped with a strap.

As her thoughts returned to the present, she crawled across the floor again. Her target was the young lad. Upon reaching him, she slowly planted small, delicate kisses up the right leg of the naked youth.

Just the effect of those kisses allowed the young boy to stop using his hand to keep him hard. As a slight moan left the boy's mouth, he suddenly found that his young, naked bottom was getting slapped slowly with the thin cane Lorna was using. Just the hint of some slight pain alongside Amanda's tender kisses made him shoot his load over the hair of the young, big, busted lover of sorts.

As this happened, the black-haired beauty gripped the lad's ankles even more firmly now and moved even more quickly up his legs towards his massive hard-on, which was still leaking a little semen from the tip of his cock. After a few minutes, Lorna increased the pleasure he was feeling by making the cane move faster onto its waiting target of the young firm bare arse.

As Amanda reached her target, she opened her mouth and took the young lad's cock inside. As the young lad enjoyed getting a good blowjob while being strapped with a thin cane. He was in pure ecstasy. Nothing he had ever done before had ever been as good as this. He had given himself several wanks, even using one of those cock extenders from an early age.

This made his cock get hard fast and slowly, making him get bigger and bigger. He recalled the first time he had measured his cock. It was about seven and a half at thirteen. Not once had he thought he was still going through puberty and that his cock may grow naturally; he had used the erection motivator from the Texas Long Horn company for thirty- five pounds. He had used his dad's credit card to order the item, as he was too young to order something for himself. Once he had, he waited near the front door for the mail carrier to knock on it so he could receive it every day for two weeks.

On its arrival, he could not wait to get it to his room and give it a go. As his thoughts returned to his current situation where he was being caned at a medium pace whilst being given the best blowjob he had ever received. It felt incredible as he tried his best not to cum, but he knew he would explode his demon seed down her young throat any second now.

Just then, the speed of the cane hitting his tender bottom cheeks was now beginning to affect him. What shocked him about his current dilemma was that he had only just discovered he was submissive while losing his cherry with his trainee probation officer/student. He also discovered he was well into this thing called BDSM.

A weird thought entered his head about the two best friends, Bob and Craig Weaver, standing there watching him get some head while being caned by a contract killer, for god's sake.

Although he knew nothing about the two women, he was now having some BDSM fun with them. Now, the woman named Lorna was laying it on thick, and the pain was extreme. The young lad took it all, as he could not refuse when Amanda kept getting his cock so hard. As Lorna hit the boy another ten times, each time harder than the last, she demanded he ask for another one. She gave him some severe instructions on what they were to do to him if he fucked up the job the following afternoon.

"Right, Karl, tomorrow is only a few hours away, so keep from drinking and fucking up the plan; we are going to walk you through the plan entirely from stage one to the final stage. Then we will leave it up to you to do the job. We will leave the keys and ten grand in an envelope under the driver's side wheel arch. Do you understand these instructions so far?"

As the young lad could feel every stroke beating down on his butt, he could do nothing but shout out yes to his new mistress. Yes, he agreed he was now submissive, but he was getting to the limit he could take for now, so he asked her to stop, as the pain he was receiving was just a little too hard for his first lesson.

"Stop, you want me to stop?"

"Yes, please, mistress. I am a little weak, so I need some time to recover, but I will give to your will once I have time to rest."

"Would you like my lover to stop playing with your cock?"

"Yes, I need to recover from all this excitement my willing body is receiving for now."

"Do you want to stop Amanda, darling?"

"Yes, it is time the young boy used his talents on my fanny for a while."

Once Lorna had stopped using the whippy cane on the boy's bottom. She watched both her submissive students fuck like rabbits while she sat on the white leather couch smoking one of Gabrielle's fine French cigarettes. As soon as Amanda had reached the near state of orgasmic delight, Lorna wanted her turn with the young lad and his gigantic cock, which dripped with so much semen it was like a dripping fountain.

If at the time you were there, you would see the sure desire in both the young women's eyes for the boy's enormous cock. At the very least, one or two hours went by as they used the boy's talents to satisfy their every whim. Once they had used and spat him out, they began playing with each other while the young boy could only look on. Sleep enveloped the party of three because of the strenuous activities they had performed with each other that afternoon, which soon turned into night-time once again.

Friday: D Day Part One: The Tour

The day had finally arrived. Someone's life would end at their boss's instructions in just a few hours.

Amanda rose slowly from her position in the crumpled heap of flesh on the living room floor. Her hair was a complete mess, matted with layers of semen from their young stud and juices from her lover, Lorna. At only twenty-three, Amanda knew she had an insatiable love for sex.

As she glanced around the living room for her girlfriend, it took her a moment to spot Lorna smoking a cigarette on the apartment's veranda. She wanted to join her, but the pressure in her bladder from the alcohol and other "tasty liquids" consumed the night before demanded attention first.

Pushing herself to her feet, Amanda's eyes wandered, searching for the night's submissive companion. The most important man in their lives at the moment lay sprawled on the floor, still asleep, a large butt plug protruding from his reddened anus. His cheeks bore fresh cane marks, the visible welts forming a neat pattern. On closer inspection, faint streaks of blood seeped from the twelve strap marks etched into his skin.

Amanda smirked, recalling how, under normal circumstances, it would have been her body marked from their BDSM play. Both women had grown accustomed to a strange existence defined by a mix of violent thrills and death. Someone dying or being beaten beyond recognition had become routine for them. Then, of course, there were the weekend dogging sessions, always a fun escape for the pair.

Since the two lovers had met, it had been a whirlwind of chaos—this death, that car chase, gourmet meals, and unrestrained sex. Amanda shook her head, amused, as she padded toward the bathroom to relieve herself.

As she entered, Lorna followed, stepping in to warm up the shower for both of them. Amanda quickly checked herself for signs of blood, her memory jogging back to earlier in the week when she had been menstruating. Strangely, it had abruptly stopped.

"Hey," she called out to Lorna. "My period suddenly started this week and now it stopped again. Isn't that weird?"

Lorna turned her head, raising an eyebrow. "Yeah, that's odd. Could be stress—or something else," she mused. The two exchanged a glance, both noting the peculiarity.

Amanda's thoughts briefly flicked back to their young, submissive partner. His enormous size could have played a role in the bleeding earlier, though she hadn't given it much thought before now.

Shrugging off the concern, she rose from the toilet and joined her lover in the hot shower. The warm water helped ease the haze of the previous night's indulgences. They lathered each other with their favourite fragrant soap, the scent filling the small bathroom, and worked shampoo into each other's hair. The intimacy was routine yet grounding, a moment of calm before another chaotic day.

Once refreshed, the pair retreated to the bedroom to dress. Lorna glanced at Amanda with a mischievous smile.

"Go wake up our little stud," she instructed. "Kick him if you have to. He needs a shower. We've got a busy day ahead."

Amanda laughed, tossing her lover a knowing look before heading back to the living room. The day's events awaited, but for now, their strange, intertwined lives continued as they always had.

Friday D-day Part Two: Staying on the Right Path

Once they were all suited and booted, the two beautiful assassins were eager to get the job over with. In a few brief hours, the young lad would collect the car from the Bearded Tavern's car park after 4 p.m. and begin his descent into hell.

He had already been instructed not to drink; they needed him sober to carry out the job correctly and earn the next ten grand. What the ladies had not told him, however, was that he might get injured in the crash intended to kill their target. The man marked for death, simply because he was too good at his job, was a relentless figure in the House of Calamari—the city's leading appeals and redemption office located in the Glendale Heights district.

The Heights was home to the super-rich, like their boss, Sir John Stephenson, who owned a mansion worth more than twelve million pounds. For Karl Thornton and his two best friends, Glendale Heights was also the perfect hunting ground for top-end cars to steal and race through the district's backstreets.

The newly submissive teen walked gingerly that morning, a slight limp in his stride—a reminder of the previous night's indulgences. His young body bore the marks of his mistresses' attentions, and though he was embarrassed by the soreness, he couldn't deny the thrill of being used and abused.

Having never been caned before, let alone by such beautiful but dangerous women; the experience had left him dazed. Even so, he hoped to get the day over with quickly so he could rest. Submissiveness was new to him, but he was starting to embrace it. The pain, though intense, had given him repeated arousal, and the cane's stinging kiss had left its mark on more than just his skin.

Of the two women, the one he initially thought was named Cathy—the voluptuous probation officer—was his favourite. Still, Mistress Lorna wasn't innocent by any stretch. When she wasn't caning him, she had taken to pulling and stretching his cock. At first, it had been pleasurable, but after hours of torment, it had turned into a dull ache. Yet, how could he complain when Cathy had such massive, beautiful breasts and an inviting body?

Now, though, his bruised cock was all he could think about.

As they prepared for the job, the group piled into the car— a red convertible Porsche. Normally, Karl would have been crammed into the backseat with the others, but today, as "Mister Important," Amanda sat in the back instead. Lorna took the wheel, her fiery red hair catching the morning sun, and drove them toward the Bearded Tavern, their base for the day.

Upon arriving, they parked in the car park at the rear of the pub. Lorna locked the car and placed the keys under the arch of the driver's side wheel. She then slipped a large envelope, supposedly stuffed with cash, into the same spot. Glancing at her watch, she noted the time: 11:15 a.m. The lad had four hours and forty-five minutes before he could return to the car park and begin his deadly mission.

As the woman held his hands and began walking away from the car, Karl's curiosity got the better of him.

"Why leave the keys and money like that?" he asked.

Lorna smiled mysteriously but said nothing. Moments later, she led him back to the car. Leaning down, she retrieved the envelope from under the wheel arch and tossed it to him.

Karl caught it and opened it, his brow furrowing in confusion. Inside was only a single £10 note, backed by a wad of neatly cut paper.

"Wait… what?" he stammered. "I saw you put the cash there."

Amanda chuckled as Lorna revealed the real envelope, which had been hidden on her person the whole time. The trick was seamless, and Karl couldn't help but grin in admiration.

"Nice magic trick," he muttered.

Amanda's tone turned serious as she tucked the actual envelope back into her pocket. "You'll get the cash once you've completed the job to our satisfaction. Do you understand?"

The young man nodded immediately, his confidence returning as he realised the stakes.

With that, the woman once again took hold of his hands. As Amanda pocketed the money he had yet to earn, she leaned closer.

"Terry O'Neil is your target," she said, her voice cold.

"That man notices everything—he never misses a detail. He dots all the I's and crosses all the T's for the House of Calamari. He has to go."

Friday D-Day Part Three: The Road Less Travelled

When the trio was ready to begin the tour, they left the Bearded Tavern and walked up the road toward the summit of Glendale Hill. The journey typically took about thirty minutes, but it stretched much longer than expected. The lad, still sore from the previous night, slowed them down. His bruised arse cheeks ached, and his balls felt tender, but it was his cock that caused him the most discomfort after the intense sessions with both women.

The previous evening had been a blur of whip and cane strikes from the fiery-haired Lorna, followed by Amanda's relentless stretching of his cock. To maintain control, the women had instructed him to address them as "Mistress One" and "Mistress Two." It was a system designed to remind him of their dominance, but the teenager occasionally struggled to separate his reality from the self-created fantasy world he often escaped to.

As they continued up the hill, his mind wandered. He tried to recall whether one of the women had bitten his testicles the night before. Though his memory was hazy, the soreness in his scrotum left no doubt something intense had happened. He told himself he'd need a few days of rest before engaging in another marathon BDSM session. Still, he knew there was no room for defiance; disobeying their commands would likely bring consequences far worse than a sore body.

When they paused to rest, Lorna gestured toward a tall building in the distance. "That," she said, pointing, "is the House of Calamari."

From the summit, the full glory of Glendale stretched out before them. The view was breathtaking, and the lad couldn't help but admire the sprawling city below. After a brief cigarette break, the three of them resumed their walk, descending the hill toward their destination.

As they drew closer, the House of Calamari loomed larger. Its grandeur was undeniable, and it looked as though it had stood there for centuries. However, Lorna explained that it was a relatively modern construction, completed in 1953, shortly after the Queen's Coronation. The project had taken just five months to build, and the man behind its design was long dead.

"I should know," Lorna said casually. "I'm the one who killed him."

Amanda smirked, knowing the details of the lucrative job. Sir John had paid Lorna a cool million pounds and gifted her a yellow Ferrari in exchange for making the man's death look like a suicide. The payday had been life-changing, and the duo now lived comfortably, awaiting assignments that fetched six-figure sums or more.

When they reached the gates of the appeals service building, the lad got his first clear view of the site where he was expected to carry out the task. The heavy gates looked formidable, and he hesitated as the women released his hands. Turning to them, he asked, "If I'm supposed to crash this car at speed, won't I get injured by those gates?"

Both women exchanged a serene look, seemingly unfazed by his concern. Amanda was the first to respond, her voice calm and reassuring. "The gates will be open at that time, so it shouldn't be a problem."

The lad nodded, accepting her explanation at face value, though doubts lingered in his mind. Amanda's attention shifted to Lorna, her dark eyes catching the sunlight. At that moment, an unspoken understanding passed between them. If the lad were to die in the crash, they would save the extra ten grand—though they might miss his youthful enthusiasm and impressive cock. Still, they had other toys to satisfy their needs.

Their preparations were complete, and they returned to the Bearded Tavern. Amanda handed the lad an envelope stuffed with what appeared to be ten thousand pounds. She kissed him on the cheek and placed her hand gently on his shoulder.

"One last thing," she said. "Stay out of the pub this afternoon."

He nodded earnestly, promising to avoid alcohol and carry out the job to a professional standard. The sincerity in his voice was enough to appease them, though neither woman truly believed him. They kissed him one last time before leaving him alone with the car and returning to their apartment for some well-deserved rest.

As the women disappeared down the road, the lad glanced at his watch. **12:10 p.m.** He had just over four hours until the job, plenty of time for a nap—or so he told himself. But as he stood there, the pull of the pub grew stronger. With the envelope of money burning a hole in his pocket, he rationalised his next move.

"I'll just have a Coke," he muttered, heading toward the pub entrance. "Maybe one last drink with the Weaver Twins won't hurt." And with that, the young man stepped through the door, ignoring the stern warnings of his mistresses.

Friday D-Day Part Four: What the fuck happened

As the twins sat in the back of the fast-speeding convertible Porsche. They seemed excited but didn't realise they were soon racing towards their demise.

The young Mr Thornton would admit later that he was a brilliant driver when sober but having consumed six pints and seven whisky chasers at the request of his two best mates. He found it quite challenging to keep a clear head that afternoon.

The two ladies who had hired him to complete the job had made it clear that he should not consume any alcohol. Sadly, he entered the pub and walked straight to the bar to order a simple Coke. The attractive lady behind the bar was always serving him hard liquor, which she added to the Coke drink whenever he asked for it. So, she did what she had always done.

She added a powerful shot of his favourite whiskey to the drink. To understand Karl's mentality, he would have agreed to anything to get his hands on that wad of cash the two sexy women were giving him. When the drink touched his lips, he instantly forgot the instruction: Do Not Drink. He then ordered several strong pints of bitter with the added touch of the blended drinks of whisky. Once they were ready, the young woman placed them on the tray for her regular customer. He picked up and carried the tray full of drinks to the table to consume with his two friends that afternoon, sitting down in the snug where they always sat. He handed out the drinks to his friends. Once they had their beer glasses, he showed them the severe amount of money he had been given to carry out the task needed to receive a second lot of mullah.

Bob and Craig laughed as he chucked it in their direction. Three hours passed that afternoon, but did the boy's care? No, as they all were so rat-arsed by then. They found it challenging to pick up the money from the floor and hand it back to their mate. Twenty minutes later, some cash was stuck in his jeans pocket, some in his jacket pocket, and the rest still sitting on the table, soaked with beer or whisky droplets. Gillian, the bar girl, could see they were having difficulties, so she handed Bob a carry bag to pick up the rest of the money before giving it to the incompetent idiot. Four o'clock arrived and left, as they still had a few drinks.

When the bleeping sound on his watch bleeped softly and then much louder, Karl was brought back to his senses just enough to inform the boys they had a job to do. They all left the snug and went to the car park at the back of the Tavern. Craig, who walked with a limp, found it nearly impossible to walk in a straight line and could hardly walk by then. So, his brother helped him find the lovely, exciting red Porsche convertible their friend had pointed out. The only one of the three that afternoon who was sober was Bob.

He had a slight cold, so he only drank some of the whisky and some of the free drinks Karl had paid for with the loot he had been given. As the boys got in the car's back seats, they didn't put their seatbelts on because they knew their friend was a fantastic driver, and they were here for some fun that afternoon. The three of them left the tavern car park that afternoon.

Destiny awaited them all as the incompetent idiot reached the top of the hill where the young ladies had shown him early that day. His foot hit the accelerator pedal, forcing his two young passengers to think twice about not wearing their seat belts that afternoon. The House of Calamari was now in full view as the young lad put his foot to the floor.

Sadly, there was a slight problem with the lady's instructions. They had told him the metal gates would be open. So, he could easily hit his target as the man left the building that afternoon. The young lad soon discovered his error, and he wondered why the two women had told him not to drink when he hit the gates full-on. This forced his two friends to fly out of the top of the vehicle as the airbags on both sides of the fast sports car tried to complete their job and protect the driver from injury. All Karl saw was the white of the airbags as they enveloped themselves entirely around the young, highly intoxicated young lad on that early Friday evening.

Had he completed his task to the letter?

Had he hit the man exiting the building that afternoon?

The young lad's mind had stalled, so he didn't even see the guy he hit at full force that afternoon in the car park of the House of Calamari. Was the target dead?

Friday Evening D-Day Part Five: At Death's Door

It must have been around twenty minutes before the police arrived at the House of Calamari on that early Friday evening to check the damage to the gates.

When the ambulance arrived, the police could not let them enter the building's car park. Because of the damage the car had caused them, they needed to make sure the gates would stay open. All of them could see there had been fatalities at the scene, but it was the creaking gates that were their primary concern. The frustration was most clear in the ambulance staff to attend to their duties and try to save the lives of the remaining people affected by the crash that afternoon. As the local press arrived with their cameras to report to their viewers about the incident, other people arrived outside the gates of the building.

Not being able to gain access, they all could see what had occurred. It was the last night to rehearse for their extensive charity concert of the Calamari Choir. Made up of police officers, ambulance drivers and clerical staff from all the sixteen appeals service buildings around Glendale. It took the police one hour before they passed the gates, and it was safe for now once they had secured the rest of the metal fence attached to the brick wall surrounding the building. The fire brigade and ambulance staff were the first to enter the damaged entrance to the House of Calamari.

As the audience outside increased, a second ambulance and a removal truck were needed to take the damaged vehicle back to the police station for examination. Once the firefighters had ensured no flammable material was coming from the car.

They stepped back to allow the ambulance staff to remove the crumbled mess of what once were the Weaver Twins. Because of the speed, they had been ejected from the car as it hit the metal gates. Both lads' bodies had been squashed against the heavy gates; some of their flesh had even slipped between the railings of the gate that evening before dropping at a great distance and speed to the ground. Although the scene was a complete mess that evening, sadly, the ambulance men had not noticed the troublesome teenager Karl Thornton hidden between the car's airbags during the search and clean up because of the bad lighting on offer. This was also the main reason both men had failed to notice the middle-aged man stuck underneath the front of the once fast-moving vehicle.

Friday Part Six: A Hidden Surprise

As the car was about to be lifted onto the truck, the eagle-eyed police officer shouted out, "Stop!" The machine had the vehicle half on and half off the ground, swaying in the night wind. As the truck driver walked towards the policeman's location, he could see why the man had told him to stop.

He shouted to one of the waiting ambulance men to come over. Two men and one other police officer came over from keeping the watching crowd of people at bay; they could now see the hidden body of another man. He was lying directly under the vehicle. As one of the ambulance men bent down, he checked the man to see if he was also deceased. He felt a weak pulse spiking a little, and he could see from what he could see below him. The man wearing the pin-striped suit was seriously injured but alive. The man instructed the van man to move the vehicle, which was swaying in the wind, onto the waiting truck bed. To give them full access to the man so they could get him straight to the hospital for treatment.

The nearest hospital was Sir John's Rest and Rehabilitation Hospital in East Danby, a small district close to the Mallon Stone riverbank. It was only when the man with the truck was tying down the car to the bed of the truck that he saw what looked like a young lad lying in a crumpled heap inside the middle of the vehicle. They were shouting out to one of the ambulance men to fetch their colleague and a second stretcher so they could retrieve the young lad who must have been driving the fast car. As one of the men examined him, it was clear the youngster stunk of alcohol. Twenty minutes later, both men had been stretched off the seriously damaged vehicle and were on their way to the hospital that night.

Saturday Morning Part Seven: Hospital Part One, Patient One: Terry O'Neil

Doctor Karinea Krane introduced herself to the family before explaining their medical diagnosis of Mr. O'Neil's condition after the crash. The two women, Caroline O'Neil and her daughter Maggie, sat at the side of the bed. Listening to the attractive-looking blue-eyed redhead inform them both that they had lost what was once their loving father/husband because of the extensive head injuries that led to a fifteen-and-a-half-hour operation to try to put the man's brains back in his head.

The operation, although partly successful, had caused a minor bleed and brain wobble inside the head of the patient.

This was the reason they had no choice but to put him in an induced coma. In the hope this would rectify the problem with the brain seizure and many spasms which affected the patient during the lengthy operation. Doctor Krane explained that after several scans of the man's brain, the wobbling may or may not continue as the swelling in the brain will begin to settle down and subside.

As the patient's wife began to cry out in remembrance of what was a loving man, she had married twenty-seven years before.

Maggie asked the doctor several questions she thought applied to her father's diagnosis. "You say we have lost what was once a loving, healthy father, and so we are left with what?"

"I am sorry, but we have given your father several scans of his brain. It will take some time for the brain's swelling to go down after the car hit him at full force and crushed half of his body under the vehicle for quite a lengthy period. We cannot, therefore, give you a confirmed diagnosis of your fathers brain until the swelling comes down from what it is at present."

"So, it's just a waiting game for now?"

"Yes, but you must understand here your father's condition is very severe.

We recommend waiting for the next forty-eight hours. We should have him stable but in an induced coma to help the brain by giving it some time to heal itself. Once this time has passed, we may bring your father out of the coma, but it's touch and go at this precise moment in time. Sadly, I also must report that your father had several heart attacks on the way to the hospital. After being rushed into the theatre to begin the much-needed surgery to save your father's life, he needed to be renewed several times during the procedure. As a rehabilitation hospital, we try to help the patient as much as possible. Sadly, I do not recommend that you stay here as we will need the time to assess your father/husband's medical condition every day. The only positive thing I can tell you now is that the cost of all your father's/husband's treatment will be accessible due to him working at the House of Calamari. An extensive medical insurance policy covers all staff the government gives to such an establishment. I am sorry to say this, but it is my estimation, and several colleagues have agreed. Your father would have been better off dying of his injuries than living the life of a learning-disabled individual."

"I thank you for your acknowledgement, but if my father could live, we as a family would prefer that over losing such a wonderful father."

"As I said earlier, we here are a rest and rehabilitation hospital, so we will do all we can for your father."

"Thank you, Doctor; please keep us informed about any information you can give us, good or bad."

"As soon as we have been able to give the man some time to rest, we will scan him to see if there is any improvement in his condition."

As the two women were about to leave the room, Maggie asked one more question. "May I ask the condition of the driver of the car?"

"I am sorry, we cannot divulge that information to non-relatives but in this case, I feel it will be okay. The driver only received superficial injuries to his face. He also broke his right leg and left foot and a couple of ribs on his left side."

"Thank you, Doctor, for that."

Monday Afternoon, Hospital Part Two, Patient 2 Karl Thornton

As the young lad sat on his hospital bed, a junior nurse stitched a minor cut on his nose. Once it was completed, she left the patient alone so she could continue her other duties on the ward. A minute or two had gone by when the teenage drunk realised he needed to relieve himself. As another young-looking nurse walked by, the lad shouted in her direction.

"I need a slash. Can you get me something so I can relieve myself?"

Given the lad time to stew because of his crime of drinking and driving, the nurses had no sympathy for the teenager. So, I tried to ignore him and deal with the other patients on the ward first before handing him a bedpan.

"Nurse, I need some help. I cannot go on my own."

The young lad struggled to lift himself from the bed to position himself correctly so he could pee without causing him too much pain. He shouted at the passing nurse once more.

"Please help me. I need to pee, or I will wet the bed."

Several of the nurses tried their best to ignore the young lad until the sister came into the ward. As soon as this happened, three nurses rushed towards the lad's bed to help him in urinating. After they had helped him, they all walked away as fast as they had come to his aid once the sister had walked back out of the ward and into her office.

After he was settled back in his bed, he looked around the ward to see if he could see a doctor. He wanted to know how long he would have to stay in the hospital.

As a blonde-haired nurse passed his bed, he shouted in her direction when the doctors would return to the ward. The nurse stopped and looked at him. "Not until tomorrow."

Damn, the lad thought, because he wanted to visit his two friends, the Weaver twins. Asking another nurse with black hair if he could leave the ward to see if he could find the boys while enquiring what ward they were on. Just then, the sister came onto the ward.

As he noticed her, so did the other nurses, who all tried to look busy so she would not question them. When the young lad noticed her walking towards his bed, he shouted her over. "Excuse me, are you the woman in charge of this ward?"

"Yes, Mr. Thornton, I have come to see you to talk about your stay in our ward. You are not a popular person, which may be due to you being caught drunk driving. The clerical staff have made a grave error. This ward is usually appointed for those individuals who have been knocked down by the cars of drunk drivers. I have already spoken with them about you. They are now aware of their mistake and have been informed that you will be moved to a side ward this afternoon. The ward you are to be moved to is solely for those patients who caused accidents by being intoxicated. When you were brought in here three days ago, you were unconscious with a slight head injury and a broken right leg and left ankle, alongside a couple of broken ribs."

As the young lad listened to the attractive woman in her early forties, he could not help noticing her ample chest, but he wanted to know where his two friends were so he could visit them. "Excuse me, what ward are my two mates on."

"Mr Thornton, if you are talking about the other two lads in the accident, they are dead. They were killed at the scene. You also seriously injured a man who was well respected around here, as he did so much for charity. My friend Caroline may lose a good man because of your excessive drinking on Friday Night. It is Monday afternoon, just after two, so you missed today's doctor's rounds. Later this afternoon, a nurse will help pack your belongings to move you to the correct ward. The police have already contacted us to decide when they can see you to discuss the accident. On Friday evening, just after five pm. I hope you have long enough to understand the consequences of your actions. They say never drink or drive. This was something you ignored, didn't you, Mr Thornton? This is due to you needing to pay more attention to your speed. You hit those heavy gates, ejecting your two friends directly at those gates at great speed. However, the lads were fully clothed. The gates and attached bars were a perfect target for all that flesh. My husband, Tom, is a fireman and was on duty Friday night. So, he had no choice but to attend the scene of the accident you caused. When he came home on Saturday morning, he informed me about the accident because I was on duty, so I had yet to see the local news. Sadly for him, he had to tell me my best friend's husband was also involved in the accident because of no fault of his own. If only you had considered your actions before entering that public house to get drunk. Terry O'Neil worked at the House of

Calamari as an accountant/file manager and official auditor, which he had done for the last twenty seven years.

This is where he met and married my best friend, Caroline. Not only have you nearly killed her husband, but you have destroyed the chances of many children in the district and the help from the donations the charity attached to our choir would have received. On Friday Night, it was to be our last rehearsal for a concert we were holding to raise funds for charity. Now, this unfortunate incident has happened. This will now not occur; your decision to drink not only killed your friends. My husband had to inform me that one of the ambulance officers had no choice but to use one of the firemen's shovels to scrape what was left of their bodies up from the ground. So, the coroner could try to put the two brothers' bodies or what was left of them back together. So, I hope you are happy with your decision making to drink and drive. Well, I will inform you to get packed for your move to the correct ward, Mr Thornton."

If you could have seen the shocked look on the lad's face that afternoon, you might have pitied him. Karl Thornton could only wish for a time machine to undo the horrors of that tragic evening. The weight of knowing he had killed his two best friends haunted him—an unbearable guilt stemming from his failure to follow the explicit instructions the two women had given him.

His friends would still be alive if only he had listened.

As a junior nurse helped him pack his belongings, Karl's thoughts were far from the wad of cash he'd carried that fateful Friday night. Now, as he was escorted to a side ward where he would stay for the next few days, the reality of his actions began to sink in.

He remembered his sister's harsh words about the wasted money—money that could have helped so many children. The thought clawed at his conscience, and for the first time, Karl considered donating the remaining cash in honour of his two best friends. It was a small gesture, but it felt like the least he could do.

Once he was settled into his new bed, he asked the nurse to fetch the ward sister. "I need to speak to her urgently," he said, his voice heavy with regret.

Ten minutes later, the sister entered the room, her expression firm but neutral. "Mr. Thornton, I'm a busy woman," she said briskly. "What do you need this afternoon?"

Karl hesitated, then gestured for her to sit down. Gathering his courage, he began with an apology. "I… I want to say I'm sorry for what I've done. Drinking and driving—losing my friends—it was stupid."

He looked at her, trying to gauge her reaction, but her face remained unreadable. Undeterred, he pressed on. "There's something else. The money… If you can help me find it, I'd like to donate it to charity. Maybe in remembrance of my friends."

The sister's stern expression faltered slightly, replaced by a flicker of curiosity. "Well," she said, her tone cool, "I don't think many charities would want your bloody money, Mr. Thornton."

"It's a lot," Karl added quickly. "At least nine thousand pounds."

The amount gave her pause. After a moment of consideration, she asked, "Where is it?"

Karl pointed to his belongings. "It should be in my pants and jacket pockets," he explained. "Could you check?"

The sister rifled through his clothing, pulling out a significant wad of cash. After counting it meticulously, she announced, "Eight thousand six hundred and fifty pounds."

Karl frowned, his mind racing. "Could you… count it again?" he asked. She did so, confirming the same amount: eight thousand six hundred and fifty pounds.

Although it was a substantial sum, Karl couldn't help but feel frustrated. He realised that some of the money had likely been lost on the pub floor and in the car. Still, he resolved to make the donation. "Please, take all of it," he said, his voice firm. "Donate it to charity on behalf of the Weaver Twins."

The sister looked at him for a moment, then nodded. "Very well. I'll see that it's done," she said before leaving the room with the cash. Left alone, Karl stared at the ceiling, the regret crashing over him like a wave. If only he had listened to the women's warnings. If only he hadn't let the alcohol take control. His failure had cost him his friends, and no amount of money could bring them back.

Monday Evening, Hospital Part Three — Introducing Sister Death

The young lad tried to sleep in the side room he had been given. All he could think about was those two brothers who had befriended him in Borstal. As Sister De'ath passed by his room, all she could hear was him crying out in his sleep.

As she entered the small room to see if he was all right, he suddenly cried out again, but this time it was different, as the lad had started talking about the deal he had agreed to.

Twenty thousand pounds, but for what? She left the room till later. She turned once again to look at the lad struggling to sleep because of his broken ribs, which he had received in the accident on Friday night.

On her way down the hospital's main corridor, she noted the patient's room number for later. So, they could chat about this so-called deal he had made with the devil or devils in his case. If only he had known from the very start, the two women didn't care two frigs if he lived or died.

They were only interested in being paid. It seemed interesting, and she wanted to understand what drove the lad to accept the offer.

Was it purely for the cash or something else that had spurned the young lad to take on this financial arrangement?

Having worked for Sir John at his rest and rehabilitation hospital for well over ten years in their social services department, I know it was her responsibility to see to the needs of all patients who came through their doors.

She quickly recalled a simple mistake by an HR clerk when writing out her personal form the woman had removed the apostrophe from the wording off her name De'ath to Death which she found so cool so decided to leave it now she was simply know as Sister Death.

After leaving her office, it wasn't long before she noticed the boss was talking to the doctor who had seen Mr. Terry O'Neil to check his progress.

Doctor Karinea Krane was not one for intrusion when dealing with her patients. She felt uncomfortable discussing their progress with senior management, especially the hospital owner.

So, she told him she would need at least another twenty-four to forty-eight hours to see if the swelling in his brain had gone down before she could confirm or deny the man would or would not survive the procedure.

Although he was not happy with being fobbed off by the doctor, he didn't feel it necessary to involve her in his plans to get rid of the man in question as soon as possible. As the doctor left the room, he instructed the sister to return to the lad's room to see what he would say about his story to the police when they interviewed him about the crash on Friday evening directly outside the House of Calamari.

Just before she left the room, he instructed her to tell him at once if the boy would mention the two women and the deal involving twenty thousand pounds, as he wanted their names not to be mentioned. Having worked for a respected man, she told him she would follow his wishes when she returned to see him.

Monday Evening: Hospital Part Four — A discussion in Time

Eight p.m. is what it said to her when she asked her smartwatch for the exact time that night. She made her way back along the corridor towards the young lad's room to talk to him about the crash so she could inform her boss if there were any issues he should be concerned about. The sooner he knew of any issue, the more time he would have to seek the problem with the two employees he regularly hired to sort it out and make it all disappear.

So, his master plan was to eventually get the House of Calamari tariff-setting panel for himself so, he could change the way those idiots who ran the company for the rehabilitation of prisoners, not for profit, like he wanted to do. Sir John could see the untapped potential of selling the considerable building part by part instead of as a complete building.

This alone could make him even more millions than he already had in the bank. Whenever they met to arrange a new chairperson, he would try to swing the vote to his way of thinking. Sadly, Troy Castle, the current chair, and he didn't agree with each other. There were sixteen tariff-setting panels dotted around the city of Glendale.

Some minor departments were more clerical than the appeals service, but one person from each department made up the complete tariff-setting panel. The panel held meetings every two months to discuss the tariff prisoners received, among other prominent issues on the agenda. Sir John hated Troy Castle, the current chairperson, and the man hated him back after he had an affair with his needy wife. Although the woman said she loved her husband, he was never there whenever she wanted him. She needed attention and sex, plenty of it, as women had needs.

Her workaholic husband was always at that house instead of being with her. However, the affair ended abruptly because of an unexpected pregnancy. Sir John was not happy when she informed him she was pregnant and needed his support. His current model wife hated children and didn't feel right about raising someone else's kid or ruining her sexy body in the process of labour. Sir John offered the woman money to abort, but she was catholic and could never do that to an innocent child. When Troy Castle was informed about the pregnancy, he was not happy and would not let her return to the house carrying someone else offspring, which left her with a significant issue to sort out.

As she had a few months before, the baby would become a problem. She pleaded with both men for help from one who had used her to get back at the man he hated. To the other one, who felt betrayed even though he still loved her, his anger about who she had an affair with tipped the balance away from him to take her back to look after her other children. First, there was Joanna, aged twelve, who stood with her father on all family issues. Then there was Lorna, aged ten. Finally, there was also little Mary, aged five. She was far too young to have a problem with anything. Although Troy had explained to them why she was absent, only Lorna had an issue with it throughout her childhood.

As Sister Death reached the lad's room, she found him sitting up with both legs in a pot. The right leg had a pot up to his thigh, and the other pot ended just below the kneecap. He also had a large bandage around his belly. He was also fine, although he had been told in advance that the police would soon interview him. As she entered the room, he watched a comedy show on the television set provided, turning it off so they could chat about the incident on Friday that brought him here.

As they chatted, he informed her about the two exciting young women he had a deal with. He also mentioned the twenty grand, half of which he had donated to charity, hoping the world would give him some form of redemption for the accident he had been paid to cause. Not once had he thought about it as he told the woman if only he had not gotten drunk, if only he had not caused the severe crash that killed his two best mates. Money is not everything they say, but most people are gullible for some spy story they can be involved in, but not one that kills your friends. She could see the regret in the young lads' eyes. Moving the conversation away from the crash, she wanted to know more about this deal and these two women. After she had adjusted her chair, she asked him outright if he had seen the woman again. Would he recognise them both?

The lad nodded his response before talking about the amateur probation trainee with the massive bust. He informed the woman you could take advantage of the black-haired beauty. He then moved his attention to the other red-haired woman. Although he knew nothing about her, they had chosen him to carry out the task because he was great at stealing cars. Knowing that she would have to report what the young lad talked about to her boss, she hoped he would not discuss her friends Cathy and Lorna in such detail. They had a problem with him talking with the police. The less they knew about the pair, the better it was for Sir John.

He didn't fancy telling the girls they had a target on their backs because of an overactive underachiever like Karl Thornton. Over the next hour, she had him tell her everything he could remember about the two women, as though he was already talking it through with the police officers.

Although she knew her boss was a hard man, she hated staying in the same room with him for more than ten minutes because of those terrible-smelling cigars he loved to smoke. Yes, they were expensive, but the woman didn't smoke, so the smell was awful.

Once the young lad had gone through his statement with her, she asked him to repeat it so he could get used to telling the authorities. Because of his head being full of shite, in her opinion, she needed him to slip up and forget at least a few of the details, but the kid would not waiver and had an excellent memory to boot as well. Leaving the room, she felt sick at the thought of talking to her boss tonight and telephoned her friend Lorna, who she had met while serving out a minor sentence of just two weeks for parking offences at Parkinson Hall prison for women run by the deadly but friendly Gabriella, who the prisoners named the Den Hen.

As soon as she got back to her office, she picked up the telephone receiver and dialed the hot number of her friend Lorna, who had a fantastic job as a contract killer for hire. Instantly, the connection went through, and the young woman on the other end of the phone answered the call.

Monday Evening: Hospital Part Five — A Friendly Warning

Twenty minutes later, if you had heard the entire conversation between Lorna and Sister Death, you would have discovered a deal in the offer. Lorna asked her friend for a favour to end all favours.

She needed to silence the young man before he spoke with the police; so the sordid affair could be successfully concluded. Amy Death had not seen her friend Lorna for several years but would do anything for her and her girlfriend Amanda, her second cousin. Although it took a visit to a psychic tea lady on the front at Blackpool to find that one out, they had a weird aunt they would visit as a child who smelled of lavender. It was just that, and the dream they both heard about made them realise they were real second cousins.

Having the power to issue medicines to patients on any ward using a pen was just as powerful as someone using their voice to hurt a dear friend. After Amy's telephone call had ended, she made her way. To the young lad's room to check his medical notes. So, she could see if he had any allergies, the information she found there was just a question mark which didn't help her one bit to carry out the simple task her friend Lorna had asked her to do to stop the lad from talking to the police about the bosses plan.

As she arrived, she saw the lad had settled down for the night. This gave her the time to check his admittance notes. It would have his medical number on there, so she could check for anything she could use against the fool. Having not found something to help her out by there just being a simple ? under the known allergies part of the form. She had no choice but to look for another way of coming up with a solution to their immediate problem as she continued looking. After briefly leaving the room, she entered the medical bay each ward had at the end of the corridor, finding a glucose bag hung up close by.

She looked for some penicillin she could inject directly into the bag. Once she was ready, she brought it with her when she returned to the young lad's room. After setting it up, she held the lad's upper arm to attach it to him correctly. Once this was done, it would only take a minute or two for the youth's to receive the drug directly through the injection area. While waiting, she added glucose to one bag daily to the lad's notes. She then left the room to chat with her friend about what she had done to stop him from talking to the police. Arriving back at her office. If he were allergic to penicillin, it would not take that long to affect him. Ten minutes and nothing, Twenty minutes and still nothing.

Making the conscious decision to return to his bedside to check him and the machine to see what was wrong. As Amy walked down the medium-sized corridor, a porter stopped her and asked for directions to another patient's room. Although she was not nervous, she found the anticipation so exhilarating.

Once the porter had left her, she continued her journey back to the teenager's bedroom. On her arrival, she found the lad still fast asleep. Checking the connection between the patient and the machine itself, she found the injection needle on the floor with a puddle coming directly from the needle itself. Damn it, she thought, as she could not understand how it would have left the lad's arm like that. As she was about to reattach the needle, the lad turned over, grunted, farted, and went back to sleep. Having seen this for herself, she realised he had turned over in his sleep, loosening the lead between him and the machine.

As she cleaned the lead down with some surgical spirits, she changed the needle tip and reinserted it into his arm once again. Not even a minute or two had passed before the machine made an alarming noise. This showed the teenager was allergic to something, but she didn't believe it was penicillin, as it was just too quick for it to do that.

Using the sink to wet her hair a little, making it look like sweat, in case any other staff member ran in to see what was wrong with the patient. Leaving the room, she walked as fast as she could back towards her office with the knowledge they would need to contact her about any issues. Just as she arrived back at her office a nervous-sounding nurse began calling her on the phone, asking her to attend the boys room as all the alarms on the machine were going off.

Running down the corridor back towards the lad's room. On her arrival, she spotted the untrained nurse messing about with the machine, hoping the alarms would stop. "Stop messing with it. I will sort it out; move out of the way."As the nurse did as requested, Amy pressed all the correct buttons on the machine, and the alarm stopped almost immediately. She looked again at the young trainee nurse on her first night shift at the hospital. She could see a straightforward way of shifting the blame onto the young nurse. Checking over the machine, she could see a swelling around the young guy's arm where she had injected the penicillin and glucose drip early that evening.

"Who gave the lad a glucose drip?"

The panicking, untrained nurse was slightly taken aback by the accusation. She tried to stop the sister standing in front of her, blaming her for the problem with the purple-coloured rash now forming on the lad's right upper arm.

"Pass me his notes I need to see why the machines have gone off. Have you been trained yet on the use of all the equipment?"

"No, I've only just begun my training this month."

"Right, I see. From these notes, it seems someone made a mistake and added this drip to the lad's arm."

"What's your name?"

"I am trainee nurse Holden. Sarah Holden, if you want my full name."

"Well, Ms. Holden, looking through the notes; you can see the notes say allergic to surgical spirits in large red letters." Amy then recalled cleaning the lead attached to the needle to prevent infections from entering the room. Now, all she needed to do was blame the untrained nurse, but then she realised that if she were that new, she would not yet understand how to use the machine or sort out a cannula and connect it to the patient's arm.

"How long have you been in training, Sarah?"

"I have just started, and this is my first night shift. I am at nursing college four days a week and have one day of on-site training with a level four nurse to show me the ropes. So, where is the nurse in question? You better find her and bring her to me. Do you understand?"

"Yes, Sister Death."

Waiting for someone can become quite tedious, but the time Amy waited gave her time to examine the lad's swelling arm again. How did she know he was allergic to surgical spirits?

Just as she stepped back from the patient, it became serious as the young lad began to thrash around the bed in absolute agony. Amy had no choice but to press the alarm bell to alert the crash team, as the teenager looked seriously sick at this stage. If he died, it would help her, and her boss would be happy.

As she stood there waiting, a loud noise came down the corridor as the crash team arrived at the room to sort the young lad out. Amy looked on as she watched them work on the boy. As the patient continued moving about the bed in agony, the crash team tried to stop him so they could examine him in the hope they could discover what was wrong with their patient. After a few minutes of checking him over, they noticed the swelling on his right upper arm, where the cannula was. Seeing no alternative choice but to remove it so they could try to aid the young lad. As soon as the device was removed from his arm, he stopped thrashing around the bed. One of the junior doctors then scrutinised the area more and prescribed antibiotics to the boy to help in his recovery.

If you had seen the transformation that night from the young lad thrashing around the bed like the child in the Exorcist film to looking like a sleeping child, it would have been amazing. A few minutes later, the crash team left the room, after Amy and now returning trainee nurse alone with the patient "So, what do you think about what you have just been witness to? The lad looked like he was dying one minute and as quiet as a church mouse the next."

"Well, it shows I have a lot to learn when it comes to helping struggling patients."

"You better return to your assigned duties, trainee Holden."

"Yes, Sister Death."

Once the young lass had left the room, Amy looked once more at the young lad's medical notes to check if there was anything she could do to stop him from talking with the police about her two friends.

Finding nothing, she informed her boss, who at once rectified the situation to protect his key employees the sociopathic sisters of dread from being found. He had sent them both on another mission to prevent the police from tracking them down and asking questions about the deal between the lad and them and why the idiot had crashed into the gates of the House of Calamari at high speed while completely intoxicated.

Part Two

Name

Maggie O'Neil

Age

27

Address

15 Clinton Avenue (New Build)

Location

Lower Glendale

Employment Position

Interviewer

<u>Machinery</u>

New Video Monitoring peddle-based Audio system

Classification

V.M.P.A

Location of Equipment

Second Floor House of Calamari

Designation

Top Tariff & Appeals House

Owned By *Lorcan Davies*

Receptionist: *Alfred George Banks*

New Information

Miss O'Neil was brought on to the team after securing a first-class honours degree in Sociology & Preventive Counselling.

Awarded Blue Star Security Protocols Card

On completing a perfect score on her third test,

Reward

Instant Promotion

Sexual Orientation

Lesbian

Height

5ft 6.'

Body Mass Indicator

Slim

Measurements

34c-22-34

Foot size

4

Eye Colour

Blue

Hair Colour

Black

34c-22-34

Foot size

4

Hair Colour

Journal Entry One

Today is Friday.

This will be my last day living with my parents. My new life will begin next Monday. This gives me one weekend to hire a large van before loading it with all the latest items I have been able to buy for my new place. Due to the substantial number of boxes and bags, I already need a new bed, wardrobe, and dressing table with lamps and other furniture needed. I have side stands, plenty of rugs, and several new kitchen items I would need so I can set off toward the estate agents in Glendale Heights.

As soon as I have collected the keys alongside the official paperwork, I can make my way towards Lower Glendale and to my newly built two-bedroom house, which the large resettlement grant had helped me buy. My new home is only fifteen minutes from the new position I had been offered. Although the move seems rushed, I already feel excited and now I will feel better about it. As soon as I could unpack and sort out where I wanted to put things, I would have to spend a few hours assembling the flat-pack furniture I had just bought from the large department store in Brookfield Heights, which is an adjacent district close to the Mallon Stone area of Glendale.

Thinking about it made me recall what my mum had told me. My dad was the flat-pack king because he would spend all day trying to erect a simple piece of furniture. Due to not reading the instructions complaining, they were all in a foreign language. While having to reassemble whatever item he was trying to complete at least three times before giving up. As he had used too many screws, or a screw meant to fit in section Alpha in section Bravo. My mother, Sarah, would always remind him an inadequate worker would always blame his tools or someone else. Leaving it to her to put it together. Who would have taken the time to read the instructions?

Once it had been built, he would give her one of those sadly missed smiles. He had always intended to make a mistake so she would build the item for him. The one thing I hated about my mum's place was the overcrowding of her rooms with unnecessary furniture. Therefore, I went with the minimalistic Feng Shui method, which was designed to prevent filling a room full of unneeded furniture. Therefore, I chose two large futon-style couches, which will be turned into spare beds for future guests. I can have over to stay. At the shop, the display helped me realise. I would also require large potted plants and extra rugs to help my rooms look lived in.

My thoughts returned to all the training I now had under my belt. No more will I have to attend tedious lectures at the university. Last week, I was standing in what was once my least favourite lecture hall, listening to some boring lecturer. Yesterday, all this changed when my name was called out from the crowd of eager students to collect my first-class honours degree.

They were dressed in their finest robes made from pure silk with a matching hat, which was a cheap piece of cardboard shaped like a square covered in the same-coloured silk. Remembering when I saw the bill for it all, I would wear just the one to get a simple piece of paper wrapped in a little bow.

Those people should be ashamed of themselves for what they had charged for such a cheap garment. I must also remember I am one of many wearing the same costume. For just one day of hire, each outfit would cost a staggering. One-hundred and eighty-seven pounds plus V.A.T.

This was not the only expense we had to pay, for example. I had hired a photographer to take photos of me collecting my degree for two hundred and forty-seven pounds plus V.A.T. I only hired him because he had offered to take several photos of my special day, which would include framing and album costs so my relatives could remember this day for the rest of their lives.

Do not forget the dry-cleaning bill before handing it back to the shop you hired it from. So you can get your deposit fee returned. I now would have had a large student debt to pay back if it were not for the sizcable grant that helped me wipe the seventy-eight-grand debt out instantly.

Although the loan was quite large, you would need to consider that the course itself wasn't the most expensive you could get. Once qualified, I could earn several thousand pounds per week simply because of the volume of work needed to become a fully qualified interviewer. Yes, I have been quite lucky.

When I switched courses from being a simple counsellor to being an interviewer. It was an extra two full years of training and a one-year placement to assess if I had a certain quality.

They wanted someone to join their team at the House of Calamari which were the leading tariff-setting and appeals services sanctioned by the home office. My father's close friend Alfred took me under his wing and helped me achieve all my career goals. However, he had given up his spare time to help me as a favour to my mum.

I was surprised when he admitted he had always respected my dad and Terry's approachable attitude whenever they had worked together. My father had been the home office's official file manager/accountant/auditor. He was very competent, and nothing would get past his gaze whenever there were any discrepancies or a contract needed to be filed correctly. His office would be called in to check that all the Ts had been crossed and the I's had been dotted. Having come out to him, he hoped his colleague could understand his choice of sexuality. Alfred told me my father had just asked him one question. Would it affect his job?

When he said no. all my dad did was smile at him before pointing to his ring finger, showing his own choice of sexuality. From then on, they were great friends.

Even though my dad had said it was the way he spoke, with an effeminate-sounding voice, that had given the game away. If it were not for him, my mum and I would not have been able to hire a carer to look after my father. Twice a day, she would be there like clockwork. To help my dad out of bed and into the shower, helping him groom himself like he used to do before the accident robbed him of his independence.

I can recall my mum telling my dad he was silly, writing down the thoughts and tasks he had completed during his day. If she could return to those days now, she would not have been so short with him and allowed him this simple freedom of expression without being so objective about this task before retiring to bed. He would always stop what he was doing to look up at her while staring in her direction, and she felt guilty for interrupting him with this daily chore. He had done this since he was a little boy, just like his mother had done before him. Sadly, this task was now forgotten.

Like many of his other daily tasks, he would do before getting in between the sheets. Now, he looks out of the window, staring into oblivion.

I can recall his last words to us before the accident robbed us of his strong-sounding but friendly voice. Now, his days are like his eyes, so cold that he waits for his carer to come and get him up or put him to bed.

We were robbed of such a caring, wonderful father because of the mindless moron Karl Thornton.

If I must remember, a plain-clothed police officer asked me what I thought about the young man after I discovered he had tried to take his own life. All I could tell him was the truth from my position in the court, which was just to the right of the dock. When the young lad who was suited and booted was called to the witness stand, he began the short walk towards the small box, looking like he had no care in the world, with a simple luck of glee written on his face. This was until he saw the woman with deep black hair and bright blue eyes sitting in the audience. As my concentration turned towards the woman, only then did I see the attractive woman was wearing a nurse's outfit underneath her buttoned sheep's wool outfit.

Within an instant, his smile was gone to be replaced by a look of worry. As the man took the stand, he didn't look well. When the prosecuting barrister was ready to ask questions, he looked like death had warmed him up. When the judge could see, the lad was looking ill.

He allowed a thirty-minute break so the barrister could help his client. On his return to the court, there was no longer a sign of arrogance. A look of sheer concern had replaced this when the prosecutor stood up again. The worried-looking lad seemed to have lost all his willingness to lie his way out of any question. He concentrated on the woman with bright black hair and bright blue eyes. The woman stared at him while making a sign with one of her fingers. As though she was showing, one of the sharp ends of her fingernail was cutting at his throat.

The accused was the only person to notice this small suggestive signal apart from myself. Enquiry after enquiry, discussing what happened on that terrible night, my dad was nearly killed by this buffoon to discover what happened that night. Gone was the well-rehearsed youth trained well by the defence barrister so he could answer all prosecution questions quickly but with short replies. It was now replaced by what looked like a scared little boy.

His reply to all the relevant questions the prosecuting barrister asked him was being answered by a stuttering fool with the utmost fear in his eyes. When it was time for his counsel to talk to him about the horrific night the incident occurred, the suited gentleman tried everything to get him back on track so he would inform the court about the deal with the two beautiful but deadly women, but the young lad was having none of it.

The barrister asked for another break to talk with his client. Although the judge didn't want to give them a second break, he felt he had no choice but to grant them another ten minutes. Sadly, I cannot tell you what occurred down the stairs. Therefore, you would need to talk with the lad's barrister for the answers.

The police officer thanked me for my candid stance and reaction to the news of the lad's suicide attempt. He told me he had already checked the CCTV footage from the one in the court, along with the one close to the bottom of the stairwell and the final one in the accused waiting room.

"Normally, I would not reveal this, but as you are the victim's daughter, I will. All my colleagues and I were shocked when we discovered it was Terry O'Neil, who happened to be one of our Choir members. The group included several police officers alongside home office staff. Your father was one of our group's best voices. Therefore, I can inform you what the cameras revealed to me. As the pair left the courtroom to return to the prisoner waiting area, the barrister asked him what was happening. All those hours of rehearsal to get it right, why was he trying to change his story now? When the young lad asked for a glass of water. The smart-looking man in his late forties left the room to fetch his client a refreshing drink in the hope that it would clear his mind. When he returned to the eleven-by-ten cell with the full glass of water, he found his client on the floor. For some unknown reason, the lad had cut both his wrists. Having lost the grip of the glass, it fell to the floor.

He ran from the cell to look for someone to help save the nineteen-year-old. Less than a minute later, he ran straight into the young, attractive nurse he had noticed earlier in the courtroom. She was accompanied by an attractive redhead who looked like a solicitor or someone with a similar profession. He forgot his place and at once tried to find anyone to aid his client for a second or two. Once he had recovered his temperament, he remembered what he was there to do. He asked them both to aid him, to save the lad who, by self-infliction, had cut into both wrists with a penknife while trying to end his life. Returning to the witness room with the young nurse, Sister Death, and the attractive redhead. As the young nurse found out, she had no choice but to step over the lad's body to save him.

One of the women didn't want to get her expensive shoes dirty, so she left it up to the young nurse to do her duty and save the young, stupid boy. While trying to avoid the large pool of blood which formed around the small but sharp blood-soaked pen knife, she shouted at her shocked witness to fetch a first aid kit.

As the clerk of the court appeared, she shouted instructions to him to get an ambulance to help her in her attempt to save the boy's life. When the smart-looking barrister returned to the cell once again with the small but adequate kit, the nurse bandaged the man's wrists as best as she could with what little was in the small first-aid box.

Her precise white uniform was stained with several pints of the boy's blood. Once again, when the court clerk joined them, he had the ambulance staff with him. "I work at the police station, less than a minute from the court building. So, the young lad's treatment could continue at the nearest medical facility." Which was St John's Rest and Rehabilitation Hospital in East Danby. When the boy, accompanied by the woman with the blood-soaked uniform, had left the small but adequate room with the ambulance crew, the court clerk's duty was to inform the judge about the incident in the cell.

As soon as this was done, there was no point in having a hearing, so the case was adjourned for a possible later date. Leaving me time to ask the defence barrister several vital questions. "Right.

Can I first have your name?"

"Wilfred Credence Percival Snodgrass the third."

"Thank you. May I call you Wilfred?"

"Well, I cannot see a reason not to."

"Thank you once again. Can you explain why you feel the boy would do something so drastic? As to take his own life?"

"I cannot believe it. In the twenty-three years since, I achieved the title barrister after my name, just like my father did before me; I have never had someone do such a terrible thing. I had been training the lad on how to cope under the spotlight. The boy stood little chance of not being convicted for the offence. You must try with all your effort, and let me tell you, the boy was a two-tone plonker. He had this ridiculous notion that the two attractive women had paid him thousands of pounds to steal the red convertible Porsche from outside his local pub, the Bearded Tavern. This morning, we were to tell the packed court this far-fetched account of his actions. Although I thought it silly, he asked me to help him convince the court that the story he wanted to tell was an exact account of what had happened. So, I did as my client instructed me to do. The boy was fine just before he was taken to the dock. When my learned friend and colleague Anthony Fordham Pickles, for the prosecution, stood up, the boy was invited to take his place in the witness box. I watched him reach the box, which should take about two minutes. The lad smiled at the witnesses in the court. This included me, my clerk, Mr Pickles and his clerk, a couple of the local press, and a very few selected public members, which included a young, attractive black-haired nurse my learned colleague pointed out to me because of the size of her heaving chest."

"You do not mean the young, attractive lady looking lost while wandering around the tunnel which connects the police station and the court building?"

"Yes, she was the woman you saw attempting to save the boy's life only minutes ago. When I had looked for someone to help my client, I bumped into her and asked her to return with me to this room to see if she could save him. When the attractive nurse asked me to fetch a first aid kit, I did as she had asked. On my return with the kit, she used whatever she could find to help the boy while whispering in his ear to keep the lad conscious."

"Did you hear what she said to the boy?"

"Sadly not. The pervert in me was looking at her giant maracas, which were escaping from her top. She was kneeling over the lad and strapping his wrists up. I only came back to reality when she asked me to hold my client's hands up in the air to keep what was left of the blood remaining in his body."

"I see. So, the woman wasn't there to hurt the lad?"

"No, she did a decent job. The strange thing about this was how he reacted when he saw her earlier in the court. When he took one look at the woman, gone was his smile, replaced by a look of pure dread. When Judge Emery Christie saw the colour of the boy, he allowed my clerk and me to help the lad down the stairs to this room.

"I could not believe the change that had come over him in such a brief time. All he would keep muttering was that she was there in the courtroom. I could not understand what he was talking about. Sending my clerk to fetch a strong brandy from my flask in my locker, he said, 'I cannot do it. I need to make something up, or she will kill me.'

"Yet again, I tried to reason with the lad, but he was white as a sheet, with a look of pure dread written all over his face. Knowing we only had a short recess before we needed to be back upstairs, I tried to get him to stay with the story. All he would say was, 'No, I need you to help me, or she will kill me.'

"Telling the boy we had spent six weeks going through his testimony, I reminded him we cannot just make something up within fifteen minutes. All the lad would do was cry like a baby who had lost his dummy. When my clerk returned with my flask, the boy took several large gulps, to my utter dismay. I needed him to remain sober to give the court an account of his actions on the night he nearly killed Mr. O'Neil.

"After taking two more massive gulps and emptying my flask, he seemed to compose himself. Afterwards, I passed him a handkerchief to wipe his tears away. 'I'll just have to lie. That's it, that's what I'll do.'

"Even without telling me what he would say, he claimed he was ready to return to the witness box again. On his return to the court, the man didn't explain his reasons for changing his story. Mr Thornton admitted he had stolen the red-coloured convertible Porsche from the car park of his local pub. Once behind the wheel, consuming several pints of lager and even more whisky chasers, he began speeding down the road at ninety miles an hour.

"While trying to impress his two fellow passengers, Bob and Craig Weaver, the police officer had been the first man on the scene. He had earlier informed the court the lad had lost control at the bend, turning over the car several times and destroying the once-fast sports car. The look of shock on the jury's faces when the man for the prosecution informed them how intoxicated he had been—while showing them images of the now-wrecked car—was palpable. Alongside several photos of the two fatalities and the condition of the other tragic victim, the car had hit him at full force.

"He destroyed the man's life to have a drink. Yes, I drink sometimes to excess, but I would never get behind the wheel of one of those sports cars. When the copper finished telling me what the barrister had said alongside what I had told him, the man allowed me to leave the now-empty courtroom once he wished my father well. Sometimes, I wish the stupid idiot had taken my dad out as well. All we have been left with is the stranger sitting there."

Staring up at the clock, listening to its tick-tock sound, I thought, *At least I do not have to be there all the time now I have my new place.*

I could never think of having a place of my own before, but since I had secured this new position at the house, I could now look forward to a world of endless possibilities. I didn't have to look for long when I was searching for a place to take my placement year. I can remember Alfred being able to sort such a generous grant.

Looking back to the first time I put my card in the cash machine and saw the number of nines alongside the serious amount of fives, I smiled. That grant allowed me the freedom to buy my own home. Although I had enough money to buy the property outright, I took out a mortgage instead. This would free up more cash to do the place up.

He had discussed my talents at one of the panel meetings, telling them about my upcoming degree success. This may be why the grant had been so large. When I think about my new role, I am quite nervous, but I am also excited to be the first person to use the new video monitoring pedal-based system to interview patients needing a tariff.

During my training, I was told that the machine included a receiver terminal and a monitoring station. One machine would be based at the House of Calamari. The second was based at Priory Lane, a secure hospital for the criminally insane. My job would be to interview the patient using my terminal, which would be the receiver.

The one based at the hospital would be the monitoring machine. Both would work in unison, using a pedal-based answering system. Alfred explained that I would press a pedal with my feet to ask a question, which would be relayed over a satellite audio system. The patient would respond by pressing a pedal at their unit's base, which would turn the microphone on and record their response to any question.

Even though I was nervous about trying this new system out, using Mr. Banks as the person being interviewed became second nature straight away. Although it was amusing to see Alfred trying to make me laugh, he warned me that when it was time to interview a real patient, the machine would be critical to record all the patient's answers. I would review the recording and author a full report for the panel.

This report would allow them to discuss and evaluate the patient at their next meeting and award them the correct tariff based on my findings. According to Mr. Banks, I must understand and record my views about the patient. This document would go alongside my tariff-setting report to help the panel decide. I was informed the panel was run by a chairperson named Troy Castle.

Alongside his private secretary, Cully Wish, who would be there to record the meeting minutes, there would also be two people standing for all sixteen appeals service members. A representative from the home office would also be in attendance to collect the written report and evaluate the sentence. This report would be passed to the relevant departments, who would draft a final report once the patient had been given their tariff.

Once I have moved and settled in, Alfred has promised me a full tour of the House of Calamari. Even though I have completed my placement year there, I had only ever seen the lower floor of the immense building. All the training and studying to become an interviewer is giving me butterflies.

Mr Banks has also told me I should be given a tour of the Priory Lane site when the time is right so I can familiarise myself with the other machine and its response times to my questions. Alfred has mentioned that he chose me over all the other people he had interviewed for the position. I was honest with him about how nervous I was. He said he needed someone who would understand the importance of the position.

As he was my father's dear friend, he informed me that each case would be different. Some patients would be easy to evaluate, while others would be more difficult. He also mentioned that the panel had seen my test scores and was quite impressed with how I managed to get the patients to feel relaxed enough to tell me their stories. Although these were all outpatients, it felt strange saying the word *stories* instead of *conditions,* which might be a better term to use in my reports for the panel.

Alfred explained that the Priory Lane site held three distinct types of patients. There were low-risk patients and referrals with low-rate mental health issues. These individuals fell into two categories: outpatients and those sectioned for twenty-eight days. Patients attended one-on-one sessions with psychiatric counsellors on specific days. Due to budget restrictions, these counsellors were often fellow students studying for psychiatry degrees, while qualified psychiatrists handled the monthly patients.

Alternatively, patients could choose group sessions held once a month while receiving low-rate prescriptions to help them manage their conditions. These meetings were either held in the clinic or during monthly visits to the wards on the lower floor.

Floor two, however, housed patients with a history of mental illness who required constant monitoring by a team of psychiatric doctors. These included individuals with schizophrenic personality traits and those with multiple personality disorders; unlike the lower floors, which lacked locks, floors two and above required extra security. A double-lock entry system was installed at each floor entrance to accommodate medium- to high-risk patients, many awaiting evaluation by psychiatrists or a tariff for related crimes.

Floor two contained fifteen male and fifteen female cells, along with a security station and medical bay staffed by medical personnel. Most patients on this floor were sent there by the courts, as they were considered medium to high risk. The floor also included a shower block and a small dining area, which doubled as a space for daily group sessions to assess patients' moods and conditions.

Alfred was kind enough to send me a few videos of these sessions and grant me access to several patient reports. This allowed me to see the differences between the patients held on the second floor and those seen in the clinic. He also made me aware of one girl who had been imprisoned at the notorious Parkinson Hall for the last six years.

He said she would be an exceptional case to help me gain experience with both short-term sectioned patients and long-term cases. Alfred explained that the woman in question was serving a fifteen-year sentence for her crimes but was regularly transferred to the Priory for treatment of severe bipolar episodes. The young woman was only twenty-three years old and had suffered from severe mental illness since childhood after enduring sexual and physical abuse at the hands of several foster parents.

Alfred provided me with her complete case file to review and kindly walked me through her preliminary sentencing report. It showed that she had found solace from her abuse by playing with matches. Initially arrested for setting small fires in office doorways, her crimes quickly escalated to more serious acts within months. Because of her young age, the arresting officer had hoped to uncover the reasons behind her anger issues to prevent her from becoming a career criminal.

Unfortunately, social services lacked the time and resources to address her issues adequately due to a shortage of trained staff and repeated budget cuts. Then, one day, it was too late. Her anger and authority issues boiled over, and she committed an unthinkable act—she set fire to her family home.

Although her mental health had long been a concern for social services, she had been given multiple chances with various foster families. However, within days of being placed with a new family, her severe manic episodes always led to her return to the foster care system. During these times, she had been treated at the Priory on multiple occasions.

At just seventeen, her latest crime led to serious jail time. While she would have ordinarily been tried in juvenile court, the case was transferred to adult court for a full jury trial due to its severity. If she had been tried as a juvenile, her sentencing would have considered her age and the severe abuse she endured as a child. However, as an adult offender, her prior juvenile records and history were excluded from preliminary reports.

The jury, unaware of her social history or previous treatments at the Priory, reached a verdict based solely on the crime. This meant she faced a life sentence for the fire that killed her adoptive family—a standard family unit with two adults and two foster children. Tragically, all four perished in the fire.

It later came to light that the family had not been given full access to her case history. Lillie's regular social worker was on leave, and a temporary worker handling her file failed to provide the Watson family with complete information. Had they been fully informed, they might have chosen not to take her in and could still be alive today.

Alfred shared that this tragedy was the result of preventable systemic failures. While Miss Cole had committed the act, he didn't solely blame her. Instead, he placed the blame squarely on a broken system that failed to intervene effectively when it mattered most.

Journal Entry Two

Where do I begin?

A lot has been happening in my life since I could fill in my journal.

I have now moved into my new house, unpacked, and sorted the rooms as I wanted to. Alfred warned me that the position I have been hired for can be stressful.

I will draft the preliminary reports, which will also hold my views on the interview. When he came for tea, he told me to buy several pots of incense to promote the stress-free lifestyle I wish to adhere to.

So, I returned yesterday to the garden centre. My friend suggested buying more houseplants alongside the incense packs and holders.

In my last journal entry, I mentioned I would be given a full tour of the House of Calamari's upper floors. I also spoke about my upcoming visit to the Priory. So, I can see where the new machine is located.

Alfred told me once I had seen the system from their side, he would have his friend Gina give me a tour of all the floors, including the third floor. This is where the most dangerous of inmates are held.

If you can recall my first journal entry, the second floor of the Priory had a double lock entry system.

Where the third floor had a security department alongside a triple lock device. To prevent any of the patients assigned to the floor from escaping.

Alfred also informed me I would get to meet my new boss. At present, he is away at a gnome collector's conference. I had heard of many collector clubs. This was the first time I was hearing about people collecting garden gnomes.

From the interview stage throughout my one-year placement, I had only worked with Mr Banks. Therefore, I was surprised when he mentioned he was not my boss.

The man in charge was Lorcan Davies. His father had begun the House of Calamari in the early fifties.

Because of his first meetings with a representative of the criminal branch of the home offices. Justice and Rehabilitation department in Glendale Heights.

Alongside those meetings, Mr Davies senior also spoke with several psychiatric doctors. So, they could include their observations of the criminal mind.

The Tariff-Setting Justice and Rehabilitation Bill was formed in the latter months of nineteen fifty-six. Passing into law in March of the following year.

From just one office back then to the sixteen tariff-setting panels on offer, today was some going. Mr Banks asked me not to ask Lorcan about his father, which was a strange thing to say. Although he mentioned, I would understand why soon.

Journal Entry Three

What a busy week I have had. I have done so much in a brief time while learning more about the Home Office and the House of Calamari. I also met my new boss, Mr. Davies, who had just returned from Langley's fifth annual gnome collector's convention.

Let's discuss all I have discovered about the house so far. I feel it would be easier to discuss my tours in separate journal entries. To do this, I could fill out several pages in one go. I have, therefore, used a hands-free voice recorder. The device allows me to record several hours without taking up too much hard drive space. So, in this entry, I will talk about my tour of the house.

I must admit I have been working here for the last fortnight, but I also spent my placement year here. When Alfred informed me he would show me around the upper two floors, I was taken aback at the enormous size of this old building.

While on my mini-tour, there were a lot of areas needing improvement, as there were several rooms you could no longer enter because of the age of the building, which was built in the fifties. Alfred told me he had often discussed this with the Home Office representative. He felt his claims about the age of the building were falling on deaf ears.

In his opinion, the building needed a complete renovation so the upper floors could be used again. He also mentioned that when the building was first built, there was a need for a more extensive annexe. This was built in the seventies to hold office workers when their original offices were no longer available due to the asbestos-covered rooms, which were now classified as unsafe to use.

Alfred also mentioned that the Home Office moved the staff around the building as their numbers decreased every year. Now, only he and Lorcan were using the lower floors. He also mentioned the outdated equipment, which needed a serious upgrade.

When I was shown the whole third floor, the number of rooms that had red crosses on their doorways was staggering. Alfred pointed out that these rooms could not be used as they were toxic. This had closed thirteen out of the fifteen smaller offices, which had been transferred to the much larger annexe in the early seventies. Although they were all now empty of staff, all they held were empty desks, typewriters, and reams of paper. Back then, case files were all listed on paper, requiring much more clerical staff to write the data out.

It was when the records were transferred to a computer—using a DOS-based system on 5.25-inch floppy discs in the mid-eighties—that the clerical staff based at the house was reduced significantly. As computers became faster, data entry became easier. The staff who worked at the house were transferred to the other houses that needed computers to continue their jobs.

While moving around the now-abandoned third floor, I noticed at one end a large stairwell that went down to the second floor. Alfred asked me to look across at the double room just to the left of the stairs. Then, he mentioned that this was where Mr. Davies's father, Frank, had committed suicide ten years ago this September.

Thinking about this statement while looking at the room, I felt the need to ask several questions that came to mind. Alfred looked at me as though he could read my thoughts. He mentioned that Lorcan had never believed his late father had committed suicide. From where I stood, you could see the room, which still had the police tape around the doorway.

As we made our way toward the entrance to look around it, I noticed a large bath in the middle of the first half of the double room, stained with blood. Just to the left, there were several empty bottles of what looked like prescription medication, surrounded by several bottles of liquor, including whisky, gin, and brandy. I looked back at my colleague before returning to the scene. I could see something was wrong with it, but I could not say what it was.

Due to needing to know the complete history of the building, Alfred explained that the scene suggested Mr Davies Senior was a heavy drinker and a prescription pill addict. Although Alfred had his own opinion, he respected his colleague's view about the suspicious way his friend's father had died. He informed me it was unclear what had occurred on that fatal day. If Lorcan's theory was true, the evidence didn't fit the man.

This showed that the person who had done this didn't know the man. Frank Davies Senior had been a heavy drinker who could not control himself, although he had been a religious man. He was also a Jekyll-and-Hyde character. All it took was one drop of alcohol to change the man from a pleasant, god-fearing person to an absolute monster in the blink of an eye. Therefore, the scene in which Frank Davies, who had never touched a drop of alcohol, appeared to have died was problematic.

He was also very responsible with his prescriptions. If he had been prescribed anything, he would not take it until he checked the strength and potential side effects. Therefore, the scene presented could never be correct. Alfred informed me it was he who had found the body.

When he had informed the police about the death, they sent the most inept man they could find. He never asked questions, took no notes, and just continued nodding while looking at the number of bottles of powerful spirits left at the scene alongside the empty prescription bottles scattered across the floor. The man had not even noticed the suicide note.

When my colleague told the officer the handwriting looked nothing like his boss's, the inept police officer disregarded this information. On Lorcan's return from one of his annual conventions, I had the sad task of breaking the news to him. To this day, he still cannot understand why the authorities didn't investigate his father's death. They just logged it as a plain old suicide.

When I asked about the blood-soaked bath, wondering if the killer had cut his wrists as well, Alfred informed me Lorcan had complained to the authorities several times. His father's death needed a full investigation, but his complaints had fallen on deaf ears, with the suicide record still standing to this day.

As we left the room behind us, we went down to the second floor using the large stairwell. I was surprised at how spacious the floor was. This was when I noticed the large room to the right of the floor, which had two large doors and a sign above the door saying, *The Library of Souls*.

When I looked at my colleague for an explanation, he simply informed me the room was where all the completed case files were stored. As soon as he used his pass on the door's security panel, the double doors opened. There was an eerie atmosphere within seconds of stepping inside the large room. It emanated from the large shelves, which looked like library shelves. Instead of books, there were endless files stored there.

Alfred tried to crack a joke about wandering souls looking for redemption from their past sins trapped within the room. Looking around, I had no choice but to put my hand to my mouth due to the dust from the files, which made my chest hurt. When we reached the centre of the room, I saw what looked like a round table with a few burnt-out candles. On top were three dust-covered signs with names, but the files were missing.

When I looked at Alfred for an explanation, he remained silent. He may not have known what had happened to the files or could not tell me about them. I felt I deserved an answer as we left the room, but he remained silent. Making our way toward the storage area, he could see the puzzled look on my face. He explained that his friend, Troy Castle, had asked him to remove the files from the library to protect them.

Yes, it explained things, but it didn't make me happy. When we reached the large storage rooms, they were full of stationery and outdated computers and equipment that no longer worked.

Once we had left the storage room, my friend walked me through a small corridor. The corridor led to a much larger room with old desks and filing cabinets to the left. To the right were endless boxes full of typewriters, boxes of pens, and reams of unused paper.

On reaching the end, we stood in front of what looked like a set of metal doors. He unlocked the doors using the card on the panel. It led outside to a small garage and a second car park, where there were several old vehicles, including an old grey bus alongside several motorcars.

He told me, "They were last used between the late fifties and early eighties to transport the clerical staff around the many appeals services. Once they had broken down, they were abandoned here."

It was when his friend, Mr. Castle, had become the tariff-setting panel's chairperson. I had been given no choice but to demand extra money. The years of underfunding had left the building in tatters. Alfred informed me that things had changed, but there was still a meagre amount of funding, although quite a significant improvement. It still needed to cover the restoration of the house.

He added, "I've applied for more funding, but I've yet to see this ever being granted."

I asked him, "Has my grant been approved? And why hasn't the restoration grant been allowed?"

When he looked at me, I could see he had wanted to tell me something. It was one of those questions that would have to be left unanswered for now.

Seeing I looked frustrated, he said, "I'll answer all your questions once I've been given permission."

As we returned to the second-floor stairwell, Alfred took me into a side room just to the left of the stairs.

"This is where the old CCTV system is held," he explained. "It's operational for now, but if extra funding is ever granted, I'll move the security monitoring console to the third floor so that the new Aries security system can be installed."

He spent nearly twenty minutes telling me about the demonstration model he had seen being used while visiting one of their partner's houses across the pond in the USA. "The audio-based security system is second to none. Although the cost alone of one of these systems would blow through a sizeable part of any budget."

Looking at his face, you could see how eager he was to get this system. In the meantime, several cameras were positioned around the building. The monitors in front of me displayed the images the cameras were picking up. As I looked closer, I could see the room that held the video monitoring system.

Alfred apologised, informing me, "I'll have to cut your tour short. I'm due to attend another budgeting review at the Home Office."

I accepted his explanation but asked, "Could I continue looking around the place more?"

He shook his head. "I can't allow that until you've attended a security review. Even though you've finished your placement year, I had to bypass the system's security protocols for you to use one of the machines. To use one independently, you'll need a security protocols card. Since you haven't been granted clearance yet, you'll need to come with me to the budgeting meeting. I can take you across to the security office for your updated interview."

Alfred assured me, "Once you've been granted clearance, I'll continue the tour. There are areas of the building you can't see without proper security. And you can only tour the Priory through their security."

I was slightly taken aback by the need for not one but two security checks. This hadn't been mentioned when I was offered the job. My colleague's comment about restricted locations intrigued me. As we returned to the ground floor, I was eager to finish this review. Not only would I get access to the other areas of the building, but I'd also be able to do more than just the job I had been employed to do.

We were in Alfred's car on the way to the Home Office a few minutes later. As we travelled, he admitted, "I'm nervous about the upcoming review. I've asked for a significant increase in the house's budget. I'm also fed up with outdated computer models and programs when better systems and faster computers are available. The house has been treated as a second-class appeals service for far too long."

He explained that the budget responsibilities allocations manager would be at the meeting, along with his friend, Troy Castle, the chairperson of the tariff-setting panel.

Alfred added, "I'll take you to the security office after the meeting so you can get your official protocols card. The system is a ballache, but once you complete it, you'll have your card.

The security system isn't just there to protect the house's secrets but also its staff."

When we arrived at the Home Office's Crime Prevention Department, I felt nervous but understood the seriousness of the security services. We entered the building through a metal security gate and scanner.

He informed me, "Since the terror attacks in New York and the 2007 incidents in London, the old security system was overhauled. Now we have what you see today."

He pointed to the red security card around his neck. "Just this simple colour coding allows me access to the Home Office's more secure areas. Your card will be yellow when you get it. That'll allow you access to the machine you'll use, but certain areas will still be off-limits without a valid reason."

"It all sounds a bit like James Bond to me," I joked.

He smiled. "You're about to work at the country's top tariff and appeals service."

When we reached the security office, I wished him good luck, and he returned the sentiment before heading to his meeting.

Journal Entry Four

As I begin today's journal, I have to admit I'm disappointed with myself. Having gone through the security protocols test, I was informed I needed to get at least 23 out of 25 questions correct. I only managed 22, so my card couldn't be issued.

The attractive woman with bright red hair, wearing tinted spectacles, a white coat, an ironed grey blouse, and a black pleated skirt, reassured me, "Don't worry about this minor error. You'll be given up to four attempts to pass. The questions are quite random, so next time, you should be able to get your card."

On my way out, she handed me a form detailing my correct and failed questions. Looking at the sheet, I was shocked that the machine believed I was lying about some answers. I wanted to knock on her door again, but I saw Alfred approaching me.

He informed me, "The meeting went a lot better than expected. With Troy's help, I managed to get a total upgrade allowance worth four million pounds."

He seemed excited. "We can finally get the place overhauled. Installing the new A.R.I.E.S. security system will cost one million pounds."

When he saw the disappointed look on my face, he asked, "How many questions did you get wrong?"

I handed him the sheet. After scanning it, he mentioned, "I failed the test three times before I got my card."

His candidness shocked me. I pointed out the section where it claimed I lied about specific answers. He smiled. "Same thing happened to me. The tests aren't to check honesty—they're designed to see how you deal with different situations."

He added, "I got 17 on my first attempt, 19 on my second, and passed on my third. The machine isn't perfect. It flagged my responses because it wasn't designed for someone like me."

His admission gave me some relief. As we returned to Alfred's car to head back to the House of Calamari, I realised I also needed to be honest with myself.

Since I was a child, I've never been attracted to boys. Throughout my school years, I found girls attractive but was always scared to act on it. I've never experienced true love in my life.

I was now twenty-seven and had never had a sexual relationship. The machine had noticed my fear of rejection. I had never discussed my feelings with anyone. As we continued the journey home, my colleague saw I was deep in thought. He told me not to worry about the card too much or are you concerned about something else. I thought about his question but knew I needed to stop being afraid of admitting I was attracted to women.

So, I told him at once to gauge his reaction. He stayed quiet momentarily before telling me he had guessed as much but was waiting for me to confess my sins. The relief was written all over my face. I had told someone how I felt for once in my life. Without the fear of being told it was wrong to like another woman. Alfred had told me when he had come out to my dad.

He had been afraid of my father's reaction. As we arrived back at the House, he informed me my parents knew about my sexuality. They were waiting for me to tell them. His confession about my parents shocked me to the core. I had so many things I didn't know about being gay.

I didn't know where to begin. Once again, I confessed that I had several questions but no answers about whether he would come to dinner. I could ask him about the rules of being openly gay like he was.

Yes, he was homosexual, and I was a lesbian, but I needed to know how to approach someone of the same gender. At twenty-seven years old and still being a virgin, I felt it was time I lost my cherry.

My thoughts returned to the young, attractive, red-haired woman I had met earlier. Was she single, was she gay, and if she were, would she help me lose my virginity? I admitted to my colleague that I had fancied the security department woman.

Alfred smiled at me as though he knew I needed to know the answer. Was she gay or not?

He then put me out of my misery, telling me that the woman in my thoughts was gay, but he didn't know if she was single. He also mentioned the woman had a troubled past but didn't go into much detail about this issue. However, I had one answer I needed.

He told me to pluck up the courage to ask her when you are ready to take another test. I told him I had been afraid all my life of how people would react to me being gay. His answer was firm and direct. A loyal friend or colleague would understand and accept it. Like my father had done with him when he confessed, he was gay.

All I could think about was all those girls I had fancied when I was younger and afraid.

If only I had plucked up the courage to ask just one of those girls, I would not be a virgin at twenty-seven.

Journal Entry Five

Today is the day. Later this afternoon, I must travel back to Glendale to retake my security protocols examination. I remember Alfred telling me to be firm with the red-haired beauty. Tell her how you feel and how you want to go on a date with her. If she were seeing someone, you would find out there and then. If not, you could ask her out for dinner. He told me to tell her I was a gold star lesbian, but I said how could I lie to her when I had never slept with a woman, asking me to tell him how it went on my return.

He also informed me that he would be busy sorting out how to get rid of the clutter that had been in the house for far too long. I could not concentrate on my work one bit. All I could think about was the beautiful woman at the testing centre. Hoping she would accept my invitation to dinner.

I knew I would need to concentrate when reading the questions.

To get the required twenty-three questions correct to secure my card. Instead of testing myself on what questions I would be asked. When doing the test, I could only look at the rules of lesbian law. It surprised me how many rules of courtship there were when dating someone of the same sex. I didn't want to get it wrong because I wanted my first experience with another woman to be special. As I read up on the basic laws, I found several tests which would reveal the lesbian I was. I must admit, I had never even thought about there being more than one type of lesbian.

The lesbian community used several signs to inform another woman you were available for a sexual encounter. Some women trimmed an eyebrow. Others wore dungarees to show their preference for the fairer sex. Alfred would have been correct with his gold star lesbian statement if I had not been a virgin wannabe. As my car was in the garage for service, I took a taxi over to Glendale. I arrived almost an hour early as I tried to calm my nerves. I could not think about anything other than the woman of my dreams sweeping me off my feet. Just the thought of losing my virginity to such a beautiful woman made me feel quite embarrassed.

As the taxi reached the home office building, my first stop would need to be a visit to the ladies to sort myself out. Sitting on one of those cold seats while fantasising about the red-haired woman didn't take me long to finish myself off. I felt embarrassed when I used a tissue to clean myself up. I just hoped nobody had heard me masturbate.

My skin felt hot as I left the cubicle and walked over to the mirrored sinks to wash my hands. I had never in my life gotten myself off in a public toilet before. I only ever masturbated in bed at home using my fingers when I was a young girl, moving on to using various toys when I became a woman. My fantasies were always about dominant women tying me up and using me for their pleasure. I needed to concentrate while doing the test. But how could I complete it when all I could do was think about the red-haired beauty ripping off my clothes?

As I went to the room, I tried to think about anything I could to calm my nerves. The door opened, and the young woman invited me in. She told me I looked quite flushed, suggesting some water could help me relax. All it took was one stare, and I was gone.

My fantasies took over me once more.

Stop it, Maggie, I thought to myself. I needed to pass this test. Once, the woman returned with a cup of water for me. I was so nervous.

I needed to know if the woman was single and if she would go out with me. After sipping the water to calm my nerves, the woman guided me into the room. The test was about to begin.

One hour later, I left the room to await the results. After a few minutes, the young woman called me into her office. She asked me if I was coming down with some illness. To my eternal shame. The woman I had the hots for was revealed. I had yet to get one question correct.

I didn't know what to say as I sat there in silence.

When she took hold of my hands, she felt how hot they were. Asking me once more if I was feeling unwell. I thought about Alfred coming out to my dad. I felt the only answer I could give her was the truth. So, I plucked up the courage and came out to her to gauge her reaction.

When she went silent, I hoped I had not ruined it by rushing to confess my feelings for her. Looking into my eyes, she smiled at me before asking me out for dinner. I apologised for how badly I had done on the test. She said she understood why I had failed now.

Kate told me she had fancied me the first time she had set her eyes on me. We discussed having a meal at a local restaurant and I would telephone here later with the details. As I left her office, I was relieved my sexual frustration would soon be over, even if we didn't have a relationship, at the very least.

I would have lost my virginity to the red-haired beauty. She then arranged for me to retake the test at the end of the week. After leaving the room, I walked down the stairwell with a sigh of relief on my face. As I waited for my return taxi, all I could think about was her. The woman was so beautiful; I could not wait for our date when the vehicle arrived. I got in, sitting in the back seat of the fast-moving car. In no time at all, I was back at my house. Once I had paid the man, I walked into my home in a daze. Walking across to my laptop, sitting on one of the side tables, I began looking up local restaurants before booking a table for eight pm. After I telephoned her with the details and location, I made my way upstairs to take a bath while the tub was filled with water.

I looked for my sexiest underwear and the lovely dress I could wear for her. Once I had taken my perfumed bath, I made sure I changed the bed sheets. She would come back to my place for some late-night drinks. Having never been on a date before, I was keen for the night to go without a hitch. I just hoped she would like what I offered her.

Dropping my towel in front of the mirror, I briefly looked at my body. I thought my breasts were quite perky, and I regularly shaved my genitals. I just hoped she would strip me down and take me to heaven so she could release my pent-up desires and sexual energy.

As I looked at the clock, I had time for a brief nap before having to get ready for my date. After a few brief hours, I awoke full of sweat, having had another wet dream. It had been so intense that I believed I had experienced several multiple orgasms.

If this was just a simple dream about the woman, I was about to go on a date with. All I could hope for was that the woman was even better than the fantasy. Once I had showered, I dressed to impress in my sexiest outfit. I hoped she would strip me out of it in just a few hours. I wanted to arrive on time, so I called the cab and arranged for it to arrive fifteen minutes early. I could not understand why she had affected me so.

In the past, I had fantasised about several women, but this was not a dream; this was reality. When the taxi arrived to pick me up, all I could think about was making sure I didn't embarrass myself by being too overkeen.

Yes, I had the hots for her. I also wanted her to rip my clothes off and make mad, passionate love for me. I needed to relax, calm down, and not be a blubbering idiot and ruin the fantasy. I found she was already waiting for me when I arrived at the restaurant. When a member of staff escorted me to my table. I didn't want to make it obvious to the posh restaurant what I had wanted from this date. Kate stood up, leaning over to kiss me on the cheek, and then sat back down. I could see she was wearing a sexy little black dress that was easy to slip out of when needed.

Once the ordered meal had been served, we talked like we had known each other for years. When the meal was finished, we were served coffee and a small chocolate biscuit at the side of the cup.

Looking across the table at my date, I could see the look in her eyes. She wanted the pleasantries finished as soon as possible so she could escort me back to my place. I had to stop myself several times as the night war on. Once we had paid the bill, we were ready to leave, and I was ready for it.

As soon as we were in my house, we could not keep our hands off each other. Having never experienced genuine passion before, I wanted it all. I didn't want her to have sex with me. I wanted her to take me, to use me as her sex slave. Making our way up the stairs to my bedroom, the reality of the situation was better than any dream I had before. Minutes later, my clothes were on the floor alongside hers.

The intense pleasure I felt when she went down on me was like a breath of fresh air. All those fantasies were nothing compared to the real thing. All I could do was moan and groan with intense desire for this beautiful, exciting young woman. I was a willing participant and wanted my virginity gone.

When she moved on top of me, I was unsure what she was doing. Then she moved slowly, making her clit press against my own. At first, it was a slow movement that sent pure pleasure down my spine. Then she gyrated her bottom, so her clit rubbed me in all the right places.

Yes, yes, oh my god, yes was all I could say as she went faster and faster till my orgasm ripped through my bones. This woman knew how to turn me on. Several orgasms later, I needed to take a break from the intensity of the situation. I had experienced my first real-time pleasure with a woman.

Yes, I came several times, but was I still classed as a virgin? She asked me if I was ready to experience real heaven. As this was my first time, I was unsure of what to say to her. When she pulled out this large latex cock held by a strap from her bag, I was curious. As she allowed me to touch it, it felt quite soft. Once she had strapped herself inside, she made me kneel. She then instructed me to grab it and kiss the toy helmet.

I did as she instructed me to do, and my juices flowed once again. As she forced the large tool into my mouth, making me gag. I found the whole thing a turn-on. When she dominated me, I experienced genuine pleasure. Like I had never experienced before. When she positioned the gigantic cock in front of my moist fanny, I was ready to lose my virginity. As she rammed the large penis-shaped head into me, at force, I squealed with intense desire. No longer would I be a virgin fantasying on my bed.

I now had this huge latex cock moving in and out of me at speed. Then it happened: my orgasm hit me like a speeding bullet. Kate took me to heaven and back again, and I loved it.

When she removed the solid cock from my pussy, she turned me over, making my arse rise on the bed; she then entered me once more, thrusting the mighty tool into my anus. With no form of lubrication, she knew she didn't need any as I was so wet with desire for her. She could have ripped me in half, and I would have loved the intense experience. Orgasm after orgasm ripped through me as she took it in turns to take it from my bottom hole. She would then use it to ram it inside me faster and faster. This woman knew how to pleasure you. When she removed the huge latex cock from around her hips. It had completed its job.

My virginity was now assigned to history.

Returning to kissing my body all over once more. Those sweet kisses sent their signals to my already wet pussy. Making me dribble cum juice onto the already damp sheets. Not once had she asked me to please her. She just wanted me to lie there as a pillow princess would do. I had no choice but to push her off me and take control of the situation.

Yes, I was a willing student, but I didn't want to just lay there while she gave me pleasure. I wanted to give her just as much pleasure as she was giving me. If this was to be just a one-night stand, I would need to learn from her how to make love to other women even though I didn't want this to end. Throughout the night and into the morning, we made love, taking turns to pleasure each other till we could no more.

As we drifted into unconsciousness with our arms wrapped around each other, we must have slept for several hours. Only when my alarm clock sang its familiar tune did we wake. I always felt quite passionate in the morning light. Retrieving the enormous dildo from the bedroom floor to use once more on my new lover. Although she was a little tired, she loved me thrusting the thick dildo in and out of her damp pussy.

In and out at speed till the rhythm of the thrust made her squeal once more into an orgasm. As the plastic cock was once again assigned to the floor. I began planting kisses on her sweet-smelling, sexy body. I would begin at her large but firm breasts, taking her erect nipples in between my teeth before biting them.

This seemed to give her some intense pleasure. I moved down her body, planting kisses until I reached her clit. I once again took the little bud in between my teeth, gently biting it. This made her moan even more. It was only when I turned her over and rimmed around her anus hole she moaned and groaned with some intensity. As I got a rhythm going, using my tongue to dip in and out, she squirted love juice from her pussy onto my heaving chest.

When I spanked the cheeks of her firm bottom, beginning softly, I found she enjoyed it. As my smacks got harder, her moans seemed to get a lot louder. I can remember all my fantasies from my childhood years till this night. My dreams had always been about making love with other girls.

Not once had I dreamt I was going to dominate someone to give them pleasure, but it seemed I liked it.

Looking at each other, I asked her there and then to be my girlfriend. She stayed silent but kissed my forehead. We rose from the damp sheets and headed for the shower to wash away the night's sins. As the warm water washed over our bodies, we could only kiss each other. From the gentle kisses we planted on each other's lips. To me, kissing down her body till I once again began to bite at her clit, making her juices flow. Only then did she agree to become my girlfriend.

By Thursday evening, Kate had moved in, which made me happy. The next morning, I retook my security protocols test and passed with flying colours. Now, there was no pressure on me. I got full marks twenty-five out of twenty-five. When I informed Alfred about my score, he said he always knew I could do it. I also informed him about my new relationship with Kate in the same conversation. He said he was happy for me but had to cut the call short because he had the builders in. When I arrived at the house later, the place was heaving with men coming and going.

When I saw Lorcan, he congratulated me on getting my security card with a large bottle of whisky.

He surprised me again by taking me on a tour of the upper two floors of the building. Although several men were wearing loose-fitting jeans, baring their builders' bums at us. Lorcan took me to a room I didn't recognise when I had toured the floor with Alfred. When I looked at the label on the door, it had my name on it. This would be my new office once the work had been completed. And where I could prepare my reports for the tariff-setting panel. I thanked him for his confidence in me to do my job. He then handed me the security card my girlfriend had sent him earlier. Instead of the standard yellow colour, it was a bright blue; this informed me that this was the first time anyone had ever gotten twenty-five points in the security protocols test.

He felt I should be rewarded, so he immediately promoted me. Lorcan said I now have a blue security card, which means I would not need to go through extra security testing. I was confused. Because of my instant promotion, I need only scan my card at the security terminal to be granted access to any room. This gave me the entitlement to visit the Priory Lane site without having to go through a second security review, which would also cut out any formalities when I needed to enter a restricted house area. The card also granted me access to most sections of the Priory, apart from the third floor, which housed the more dangerous mental patients.

Most of the inmates there were classed as insane and should never be released back into society. Once we had left the small room, which would be my new office, my boss escorted me to the larger room next door. With the house now fully renovated, they had installed the V.M.P.A. machine next to my office for convenience. I only had to travel a little to use the machine daily.

I realised this room and the room next door were in the same location where his father had lost his life under mysterious circumstances. It must have been hard for him to allow the rooms to be included in the renovations. I remembered what Alfred had told me about not discussing it with Lorcan. Not wanting to upset the apple cart, I remained silent.

I wanted to see the annexe while on the third floor. So, I asked my boss to show it to me out of curiosity. As we passed by what would be the new CCTV room on the way to the end of the floor, Lorcan seemed pleased with himself. I asked him why he was in such a good mood. He then pulled out his mobile phone and showed me a picture of what looked like a simple garden gnome.

"This," he said, "is the cream of the collector's world."

He explained that he had just won it from a new collector in an eBay auction for two thousand pounds. His rival, Stan, would be envious if he discovered such an item in Lorcan's collection. Inspecting the photo, I recalled my dad picking one up for a fiver at a charity jumble sale. I wasn't sure if I should tell him or keep quiet about his blunder.

When Lorcan began showing me photos of his enormous collection, I had to bite my tongue. Did the man really think one needed to pay such an absurd amount for a set of cheap garden gnomes?

Just then, Alfred joined us to inform Lorcan that his wife was on the phone with something important to discuss. My boss took the phone and returned to his office. Now that Lorcan was no longer close by, I asked Alfred about the gnomes Lorcan collected.

Straight away, Alfred seemed pleased with himself for some unknown reason. I asked why he looked so happy. From his expression, he seemed like he was about to roll over with laughter. He showed me his phone, displaying another garden gnome. When I looked more closely, it was the same gnome my boss had bought from a woman named C. Davies.

Looking confused, Alfred showed me a second picture of the same gnome. This time, the picture showed that a broken rod had been replaced. Also, the chipped and broken bottom had been given a fresh coat of bright green paint. He then informed me that his friend had just bought it from the same woman on eBay. Apparently, the gnome had been sitting in Alfred's friend's garden only a few days before the auction began.

I was still waiting to see the funny side of the joke. Alfred informed me that last year, Lorcan had cancelled a skiing holiday his wife had booked for them. The trip was supposed to cost five thousand pounds, but Lorcan called the holiday company, claiming his wife was ill, and cancelled the trip. The company refunded the money, and Lorcan used it at the next gnome conference.

"Lorcan spent several thousand pounds on collectable gnomes from C. Davies," Alfred added.

I didn't want to seem thick, but I couldn't understand why Alfred found it so amusing. He asked me to look again at the first gnome. He showed me the photo once more and then pulled out a second mobile phone. Logging into an eBay account under the name C. Davies, he showed me a photo of a newspaper clipping.

Looking closer, I saw the clipping showed Lorcan holding the same gnome in his hands. It was supposed to be a rare find. Lorcan had bought it for three thousand pounds from a collector called C. Davies. Giving the phone back to Alfred, I still seemed confused.

Alfred, red in the face and on the verge of laughter, showed me yet another photo. It was of Lorcan's back garden, and once again, he was holding the same gnome. Then Alfred showed me the newspaper clipping again. This time, he pointed to something else: the initials C. Davies stood for Colleen Davies—Lorcan's wife.

"Oh my god," I exclaimed. "His wife has been selling his own gnomes under a pseudonym!"

Alfred informed me that she had done it out of revenge for Lorcan spending their savings on a garden gnome instead of their skiing holiday. When Lorcan returned, he informed us that his wife had just told him his precious gnome collection had disappeared. He then mentioned seeing the same garden gnome for sale on eBay.

"I don't have the heart to tell him the truth," I whispered to Alfred.

Lorcan announced that he would leave early to participate in the auction, believing he could outbid Stan with a five-thousand-pound offer. Once Lorcan left, I turned to Alfred.

"This joke has gone too far," I said. "You need to tell him the truth or get Colleen to end the auction."

Alfred agreed. Pulling out his phone, he stopped the bidding war and closed the auction, saving Lorcan from spending another fortune. Alfred then made another confession: all the missing gnomes were safe in the family attic. The gnomes Lorcan had been bidding on were bought from local jumble sales for mere pounds. Colleen had painted and advertised them as rare, knowing Lorcan's slight colour blindness would prevent him from noticing the difference.

Colleen, it turned out, was saving the money in a holiday fund and had always planned to confess her "crime." Alfred had only discovered the truth during dinner at their house when Lorcan kept leaving the table to watch the gnome auction. Colleen had revealed the joke to Alfred and asked for his help to recover the money her husband had spent.

When Alfred left to tell Lorcan the truth, I decided to explore the annexe. My boss had earlier assured me I could move around without compromising security. As I made my way there, I passed several modernised rooms. Eventually, I reached a stairwell leading to a large, empty room. Dust on the floor suggested it once held many desks.

At the end of the room, I saw a security scanner. Testing my new pass, the light turned green, and the door unlocked. Inside was a bigger room filled with shelves of files. Taking one, I noticed the title: *Ex-Detective Inspector John Smith.* Opening it, I found a detailed history of his crimes, including a preliminary report.

Preliminary Case File

45/01141999

Name *John Smith*

Age

45

Last known Address

Held at Fallon Wood Correctional Facility while on Remand, Moved to Maiden Vale Men's Prison.

Sentence Given

Twenty-five years to life

Appeal Date

24 January 2000

Appeal Decision

Denied Parole

Assessment Hearing Held

16 March 2000

Records Passed to Host

19 April 2000

New Case File Classification Number

45/01141999

Records Reviewed by Host

Parole Appeal Denied (Reason Given No New Evidence)

Determination Report Findings

Does not admit guilt

Final Report Decision

Without a guilty plea, the ex-detective inspector will fully serve his sentence.

Description *Brown Hair* ***Eye Colour*** *Brown* ***Height*** *6ft 5"* ***Shoe Size*** *12*

Distinguishing Marks & Tattoos

None

Preliminary Case File History

Ex-Detective Inspector John Smith was reportedly chasing a serial killer.

Several victims were discovered. Witnesses Identified Mr Smith as the killer. When detained for questioning, he could not give a reasonable explanation. Why did all witnesses point in his direction as the man they saw with the victim before they disappeared? He was arrested and charged with eighteen suspicious deaths.

Final Classification

Overwhelming evidence pointed toward Mr Smith, who would not admit his guilt.

My only thought was why the file had been moved from the dusty library to a room guarded by a security lock. When I returned the file on the shelf, I noticed another file from the table. This one said Brian Cross on opening his file; it listed his crimes also, so I also looked at Mr Cross's preliminary report.

Preliminary Case File

34/19061999

Name *Brian Cross*

Age

34

Last known Address

57 Jurby Avenue Manchester

Sentence Given

Sectioned under the Mental Health Act

Appeal Date

19 September 1999

Appeal Decision Denied Parole

Assessment Hearing Held

20 March 1999

Records Passed to Host

27 May 1999

New Case File Classification Number

34/19061999

Records Reviewed by Host

Parole Appeal Denied (Reason to be Sectioned under the Mental Health Act)

Determination Report Findings

Classed has Insane

Final Report Decision

Brian Cross was classed as criminally insane

Description *Ginger Hair* **Eye Colour** *Blue* **Height** *6ft 5"* **Shoe Size** *11*

Distinguishing Marks & Tattoos

None

Preliminary Case File History

Mr Cross believes his daughter told him to kill, kill and kill all his victims.

Final Classification

Mr Cross escaped custody on the way to Priory Lane.

Update

Mr Cross has never been found.

I could also see that an attachment folder had been inserted within the file. This seemed to have been added much later.

Second Update

Mr Cross's Son Harold was admitted to the Stephenson Rehabilitation Hospital after unsuccessful gender reassignment surgery.

Harold Cross = Born a Hermaphrodite. Released back to Mother's care six weeks later.

A second file about another operation was also included. It simply said that it was performed with the parent's full consent.

As I was about to pick up another file to examine, I could hear raised voices coming from downstairs. I could tell it was Alfred and Lorcan. This meant my colleague had confessed to his wife's scheme of getting her revenge on him for cancelling their holiday to buy a simple garden gnome. When it went silent after a door or two slammed, I returned my thoughts, looked through the various files on the shelves in front of me, and picked up what looked like the last file. This file was much heavier to hold and had several inserts. I took it to the couch near the back wall, and upon sitting down, I read the contents.

Several inserts were included, but nothing too specific about the young girls' criminal activity.

The name on the file is Jenny Louise Harper, and a preliminary report was attached.

Preliminary Case File

53/29031968

Name

Jenny Louise Harper

Age

25

Last known Address

Served three years at Parkinson Hall before being transferred to the Priory held at Priory Lane State Mental Hospital for the Criminally Insane in 2015

Preliminary Assessment

Not fit to stand trial because of Psychiatric Evaluation. Classed as criminally insane

Appeal Date

14 January 2015

Appeal Decision

Not fit to be released back into society, further determination is needed

Assessment hearing Held

23 May 2015

New Case File Classification Number

53/29031968

Records Passed on for Further Determination

5 June 2011

Determination sent to Host

Records passed to host records now held under strict home Office guidelines from 29 March 2015

Determination Report Findings

Classed as extremely dangerous, interviews are only conducted using a new video link monitoring system to protect the final interviewer.

Final Report 26th June 2015

To be held indefinitely to decide the earliest possible release date

Description *Shoulder-length Red Hair* **Eyes** *Blue/Green* **Measurements** *36EE-24-36*

Height *5ft 10 tall* **Size** *12* **Shoe Size** *Eight*

Distinguishing Marks & Tattoos

Scars on both knuckles, severe scarring above the right eye, and a heart-shaped tattoo on the right shoulder with the initials L.C. enclosed.

Preliminary Case File History

From an early age, the young lady has been shown to have aggressive behaviour, which seemed to have been inherited from her deceased father, Tony Harper. Further testing is needed because of the psychiatrist's view of a borderline sociopathic disorder.

Video Monitoring

Miss Harper was found to be a suitable candidate for the new Video Monitoring System. Held in the basement of the Priory Lane Mental Hospital. The system is also being offered to all leading tariff-setting panels for testing. Full installation funding granted is subject to home office guidelines and needs approval by a tariff-setting panel before grant allocation.

Final Classification

Extremely dangerous, visitors are only allowed if previously arranged with the Governor. No sharp instruments are allowed.

There was no history here like the other two files had held, but several psychiatric reports had made the inserts, which detailed the young woman's anger issues relating to her father. Some reports were from a school she had attended, detailing many fights she had been involved in, and one report included was something the other files had not held. The report was written by a man whose name was familiar. I could not place where I had heard the name before.

When the annexe door opened, Lorcan and Alfred came in together. My boss had forgiven his colleague. I asked them both about the familiar name.

Lorcan stated the man was a pompous arse far above his station in life. Alfred told me not to believe a word from the man's mouth. Having not met him, I could not make an honest opinion of the man. I wanted to ask my girlfriend later to see if she had heard of him. When I showed my boss the file I had on my knee, he said he was not familiar with the name. All he knew about was that the files were placed in the annexe, and they had been moved here by special request.

Alfred told me he didn't know why they had been moved, but the chairperson wanted them kept from the other files. When Lorcan picked a file up from the shelf, he informed me that with these files, there were hidden areas held within a sleeve. I needed to understand the relevance of what he was saying.

Alfred said if you turn to the back page of the file, you could place your security pass on the blue square, and it would reveal the full file, not the bits you may see at present. Turning to the last page of the file I held, I placed my security card on the blue square, which didn'thing. Lorcan looked at the file he had held, and when he tried to use his card, nothing happened either. So, Alfred picked up the other file I had looked at first and tried his card on the blue part of the file, but nothing happened again. He then said Troy Castle had asked him to keep these here.

There is some importance between all three files, but only he would know the significance of what it was. He looked concerned as he took the file from me to put back on the shelf. I asked him what was wrong, but he didn't answer me; he just looked once more at his security card.

When he left Lorcan and me standing in the annexe, I could tell he had something on his mind.

Maybe it was the card that had not worked on the blue square on the back page of the file. I asked my boss to try his card on all three files once again to see if they worked. As he tried his security card on the back page of the files, nothing happened once again. This made me wonder what information was hidden below the blue squares Troy Castle didn't want you to see.

As we left the annexe together, Lorcan and I made our way down to the reception area of the house. When we arrived, we could see Alfred on the phone. A few minutes later, my colleague put the phone down and told us we were meeting Troy at the tariff-setting headquarters In Glendale at 10 a.m. Turning to his friend Lorcan, he asked him to collect the files from the security bay. We would take the files with us, and at the meeting, we would be shown the contents of the back page. To do this, we would need our security protocols cards upgraded. Alfred also informed us that once we had had our cards upgraded to reveal a file's hidden contents, we could never reveal them to anyone.

We would need to sign the Official Secrets Act to upgrade our cards, which prevents us from revealing anything we have learned or else face imprisonment. When I heard this, I imagined my colleagues would have signed a document like this when they began working at the house.

Having no choice but to ask them, Lorcan said he had never had to sign the Official Secrets Act before. Alfred said something along the same lines. This surprised me somewhat, but my new girlfriend would have already signed this important document.

As I returned to what would have been my home, but now, it was simply Kate and I's love nest, I noticed several smells attacking my senses. My ears could hear a tune playing on the radio. My nose smelled of steaming vegetables in the slower cooker alongside what smelt like a beef joint cooking in the oven. As I entered the kitchen, I was greeted by my naked girlfriend using a rolling pin on some pastry-making homemade bread. When she noticed me, she smiled at me like my mum would do when I came home from school when I was a little girl.

Walking over to her, I stood behind her and put my arms around her waist before kissing the back of her neck. I asked her how long she thought we had before dinner was ready. She smiled as though she understood why I asked her for this basic information and said, at the very least, a full forty-five minutes or more.

I took her by the hand and led her upstairs to the bedroom. I wanted her; I needed her, and she was so beautiful. She made me feel happy. And all I could think about was how she made me want to fuck her, to release my pent-up desire for this incredible-looking woman.

She was something I had always wanted. When I was younger, I felt the need to be dominated in my fantasy world. Now, it was my need, my pleasure, to rock her boat and take her to heaven. She helped me out of my clothes to have fun on the bed before tea. I looked around for the strap-on once I had it strapped in place. I had her kneel before me so she could take the head into her mouth. As I forced the phallic-shaped head down her throat, she began to gag. Moving the latex cock in and out of her mouth in quick succession.

You could see the look of desire on her face. We were one; we were together. Grabbing hold of her, I pulled her up from the floor so I could use her for my pleasure. The pent-up sexual energy she had allowed to develop between us. It helped me to fulfil my need to dominate this beauty. Taking it in turns to thrust the large latex cock in her wet shaved pussy before removing it to force it into her open anus. I gave her several mini-orgasms, but this was only the beginning.

We had at least another thirty minutes left to take each other to the heights of pure pleasure. We intended to make every minute last to enjoy each other. However, our relationship had only just begun. We both wanted to fulfil each other's sexual desires. Once the dildo had begun its task, it was soon once again assigned to the bedroom floor. As we moved our sweat-soaked bodies together. The sexual tension grew and grew till our clits were exposed. Moving the tip of my clit against hers made us feel intense pleasure and desire for each other. Rocking back and forth on the hardwood bed together gave us pure pleasure. As we reached our simultaneous orgasmic joy with each other, we moved from the bedroom to enjoy ourselves in the shower so we could wash all our sins away. The desire for this young woman made me feel complete.

After the shower, we returned to the bedroom dressed in relaxing clothes. Once Kate was dressed, she returned to the kitchen to finish cooking our dinner. When I was dressed, I picked up all our clothes and put them in the laundry basket. I also picked our favourite strap on from the floor to wash it. On my return to the bedroom, I returned the latex dildo to its resting place alongside all the other toys we used to pleasure each other.

When I walked towards our small dining area, I took my seat to await my lover serving my dinner. As she brought the hot meal to the table, I helped her. After taking the heavy bowl full of steaming vegetables to lay on the table, we filled our plates with hot vegetables and mashed potatoes. Kate picked up a large piece of hot beef from its planter to put on my plate. Once she had seasoned the meal, we began to eat our tea.

While eating, we talked about our activities during the day. I asked her if she had signed the Official Secrets Act. When she asked why I needed to know, she tried to make out I was a spy for the federation. "If I must tell you, I must kill you," she said in a comical-sounding voice. This made us both laugh before she told me she had been ordered to sign the document due to the sensitive information she dealt with at the home office. I told her the reason for my question.

She once again tried to make her answer quite funny. Which made us both laugh once again. I asked her if she had ever met Sir John Stevenson. Her smile disappeared from her face in an instant. She told me to stay away from him as he was not a nice man to know. I didn't want to ruin our meal; the mention of the man's name made Kate feel quite upset. This was the third opinion of the man's name, which gained an unlikely response.

What was it about the man that made people hate him so much? I felt I would ask Mr Castle about the man. If his response were the same, I would need to know the reason he was so despised. For the rest of the evening, we sat watching TV together.

Although it was easy to see Kate loved me, I could not get over how her reaction had sullied the conversation. She said she felt a little sick when she retired to bed. I knew she was lying her arse off, so I needed to find the underlying cause of this issue that was putting my girlfriend in a mood with me, even while my boss and my colleague Alfred had told me the man was not somebody you would want to know.

When I slipped into bed beside her, I wanted to continue our earlier lovemaking. She moved away from me, saying she had a headache. This didn't make me happy one bit, so I told her to stop this stupid game she was playing. I needed to know her problem because I had mentioned a man's name at the dinner table. She turned her lamp on her side of the bed and sat up like a frigid damsel in distress.

She had not wanted to ruin our growing and intense relationship. I asked her if she loved me. She said I should not need to ask such a question when it was clear she did. I pleaded with her to explain how mentioning one man's name had destroyed what should have been a pleasant evening. As the tears began to roll down her face, you could see something had happened to her in her past. Just the mention of his name brought back the memory of an incident from her past, sending her into a weird mood.

Kate began to tell me about the man who had been her boss when she first started working at the home office. All I could do was listen to her explanation of why she hated the man. "One night, he had me stay back with the excuse he needed some extra filing completed on a new contract. He wanted to be put through the home office books. I told him I was not a file clerk, but he insisted I do what he had asked If I wanted to keep my job. Once again, I explained to him I was not a file clerk. He just looked at me for a few seconds before striking me with the back of his hand, knocking me off my feet. As I fell to the floor, he just laughed at me before kicking me in my stomach several times. He repeated his request for me to do something with the paperwork he needed to file away. All I could do was try to crawl away from him; I was also in a lot of pain from this unprovoked attack. As I tried to get to my feet, he put one of his heavy shoes on my back and pressed down hard, laughing as he did so. I could not believe he was doing this to me. As I lay there in silence, he again removed his foot from the small of my back. He instructed me to get up from the floor, but as I tried to get up, the pain in my stomach made me feel quite ill. He laughed again, complaining I was just a feeble woman. He would not have had to strike me if I had done what he had asked, he said. As I tried once more to get to my feet, he kicked me clear in the face with his right shoe, laughing as he did. I fell back down to the floor in considerable pain. A minute later, he said he was extremely disappointed in me. How could he complete his file if I continued lying on the floor? He then instructed me to get myself up so I could do what he wanted. As I tried to get up from the floor, it was clear he had me where he wanted me. My face was a bloody mess; all I remember was his evil laugh.

When he allowed me to get up, I had lost several teeth, my body was full of bruises, and my nose was broken. He told me that when I was at work, I needed to look presentable, so why was I dressed in such a manner? If it were not for my bra, my breasts would have been exposed due to my blouse being bloody and ripped. The evil man asked me again if I would do his filing for him. I was in so much pain I could not believe what he was asking me. I didn't want to be struck again, but I had no choice but to tell him once again that I was not a file clerk, and they were the only people who had access to the file store's access keys. I tried to explain this to the tall, heavy-stocked man standing in front of me as he began smoking a large cigar, but his face went red, and his eyes bulged with anger once more. He then grabbed me once again by what was left of my blouse, forcing me towards him.

"I do not give a flying fuck who has the access codes. I want you to file this away somewhere so I can get paid for this bloody contract. I have already lost the money once, so I want to be reimbursed for my loss," he said.

I was taken aback quite a bit by his fearsome attitude. Seconds went by before he forced me down to my knees. He then removed his cock from his pants. Instructing me to give him head for wasting his time. Having never been with a man, I didn't want to do as he instructed. This angered him, so he pushed me to the floor and stepped out of his expensive-looking trousers. He then forced himself on me by lifting my now-torn skirt. Tearing at my panties with his large bulky hands before viciously raping me."

The look on my face was one of disgust and anger. I could not believe what my girlfriend was telling me. I now understood why she had gone in a mood with me, destroying the pleasant atmosphere we had built between us. When I had made the mistake of asking her about the evil man, all I could feel was hurt and anger for my girlfriend. I needed to understand how this bastard of a man could get away with this unprovoked attack. I had no choice but to ask her to continue her story so I would know everything.

As she continued with her story, everything she told me shocked me. Not only had he attacked her, but he also belittled her before raping her. The reason was just not so clear. From her confession, the bastard wanted some contract filed away somewhere to be forgotten. He also wanted to be paid for it.

All my girlfriend had said so far showed me she had done the right thing. She had also said the right thing. This evil brute of a man just would not take a no for an answer. What right did he have to do this to my woman? I had no choice but to ask her if she had reported the attack to the police. Kate informed me he had torn her genital wall, as he was so rough with her. He may have been quite an overweight man, but his penis was at the very least ten to twelve inches. His girth must have been at least four to five inches in width, leaving her with extensive and severe internal and external bruising, which needed hospital treatment. He had broken her nose and her left eye with such heavy bruising. She had nearly lost sight in the eye as he had dislodged her cornea. This was why she would need to wear glasses whenever it was sunny.

The rape left her suffering nightmares for several months. Having no choice but to ask her to pass me the box of tissues I had on the small two-shelf bedstand, I wiped my eyes while listening to such a distressing episode from my girlfriend's past. I had to get her to stop so I could give her a loving hug. When I felt ready, I asked her to continue so I could hear every detail.

"After he had his pleasure with me, he stood up but before putting his underwear back on. He made the conscious decision to urinate all over my bruised and battered body. Once he was dressed, he took his mobile phone from his jacket pocket and made a call to some woman on the end of the line, saying he needed her to take care of some business for him. He said he needed some trash disposed of. I could not believe how such an evil man could exist. As the man waited for his guest, he stood near the window smoking what remained of the sweet-smelling cigar. Not once did he look at me. I was in pure agony, but I needed to get out of the room. As I tried with all my effort, I could not even move a foot or more. Minutes later, I tried again, but once again, I failed. I heard him laughing in my direction.

I could not turn around to see where he was because of the pain tearing through my body. All I could hear were heavy footsteps making their way towards me. As the laugh got louder, I heard him speak, "Where the hell do you think you are going?" I tried this time with all my effort to raise myself from the floor, but I heard the bastard laugh once again. I knew I needed to move yet again.

I heard the bearded man laugh loudly before pressing his heavy foot once more down onto the small of my back, saying, "Now try to move bitch." As he lifted his foot from my back, he slammed it down once more. The pain was so intense I must have passed out."

Moving towards her yet again, I had to hug her while wondering how she had coped with the bastard's attack on her; tears welled up in my eyes once again. As Kate passed me a second tissue, she returned to telling me her horrific tale of despair. "When I awoke, I lay on top of a bed in what seemed like a hospital. My left eye was covered with a surgical dressing, so I could only see from my bruised right eye, just enough to see several nurses moving about the room. When I tried to lift my head, I heard but could not see the person sitting just to the left of me. "I think she's awake."

The mysterious voice sounded like the voice of a woman. As a nurse came to check me over, the mystery guest moved her chair. "Can you see me now?"

Turning my head to see the attractive-looking woman sitting in front of me. "My boss has asked me to come and talk with you today."

Still not knowing who the woman was, I had no choice but to listen to her. "My employer wants you to understand. He wants you to get better. He also wants you to know he has found someone to file his lawsuit for him because of the unfortunate incident that happened last week. He has decided it would be best for you to take as long as you need to recover; he would also take care of all your medical expenses. I want you to understand me when I tell you not to tell anyone about the fun and games my employer and you indulged yourself in. He told me he had a lot of fun, and when you are better, if you want to do it again, he would love nothing more than to accept your request."

I nearly fell off the bed in disgust at what she was telling me. How could there be people like this in the world? They were not what you would call normal. I just could not understand how she had coped. She asked me if she should stop her story, and I wanted her to because it was so awful, but she needed to get it off her chest. So, she could put the memory to bed if it were even possible. I felt I needed a drink before she continued her terrible tale. I moved off the bed and made my way to the kitchen to retrieve what was left of the whisky Alfred had left the other week when he came for dinner.

As I returned to the bedroom with two glasses and the bottle. I poured us both a large glass of the spirit. As the drink hit the back of my throat, I could feel the strength of the blend. My father, Terry, had loved his whisky, whereas my mum preferred gin. Once we had consumed our drink, I sat next to her on the bed so I could hold her hand as she continued with her story. As she returned to the tale of despair, I continued holding her hand for support.

When she began, she reminded me she was lying on the hospital bed. The mysterious woman had just threatened her with a repeat performance. "This was to stop me from telling anyone about the serious attack he had inflicted on me. As the woman stood up, she moved the chair to one side of the bed. She made her way to the left side of my head, knowing full well I had my left eye in a bandage. So, I could not see her. "Just remember, tell nobody, or you'll have me to deal with." I didn't have a clue who she was. All I knew was she was not someone I wanted to upset. It took me several weeks to stay in the hospital to recover from the unprovoked attack. Several times, I would see the girl walking past the window of my room to remind me of her early threat. When they released me from their care, I found I had been staying at the Stephenson Rehabilitation Hospital in East Danby, which was just across the river from my home in Glendale. I was told to visit the hospital for eye check-ups once a year."

As she leaned forward to show me, you could still see a hairline crack just to the sidewall of the eye socket of her left eye. After having another shot of whisky, I asked her if she had seen the young woman again. I also needed to know if she told anyone about what the bastard had done to her.

As she moved towards me, she kissed me on my lips before moving away. She had no choice but to say no. How could the girl be so brave? I do not know if I could have gone through such a thing and survived. Somebody needed to know so this evil man could be stopped.

Yes, he was a sir, but he was not safe from prosecution. All it would take is one brave soul to show information, and his criminal activities would be in the open for all to see. Kate informed me she had thought about it but had not told the authorities because of the continuous threats of violence she had received from the young woman. "I also wanted to put it to the back of my mind and get on with my life. I needed to keep the job I loved doing, helping people to achieve their full potential."

For the rest of the evening, we lay on the bed and cuddled each other before falling asleep in the wee small hours. When she fell asleep, I left the room to record my journal, which would talk about the rape my partner had to endure. When complete, I returned to the bedroom, stripped and slipped between the sheets to cuddle my sleeping lover. When I woke from my slumber, my girlfriend was not next to me. Which worried me somewhat after the terrifying experience she had no choice but to deal with.

As I searched the flat, I found her standing on the balcony with a strong cup of hot coffee in her hands. Just the relief to see her safe was all I needed. She kissed me on the forehead before telling me there was plenty of coffee left in the pot. Leaving her to take a shower, I was happy she had done nothing stupid.

While I showered, all I could think about was how I would have handled it if it had been me. I knew my strengths; I also knew my weaknesses, which made me realise I was not as strong-minded as Kate was. There would have been a need to tell someone, but who could I tell without it getting back to my other half? Once the shower had done its job, I wrapped myself in one of the large, fluffy towels my girlfriend had brought with her when she had moved in, placing a smaller towel on my head.

I walked out of the bathroom before making my way downstairs to the kitchen to have a cup of coffee. I just hoped it was still hot once I had my refreshing brew in hand. I joined Kate on the balcony, listening to the morning song of the various birds which lived in the trees next to our house.

I asked her if she would allow me to talk to my friend Alfred about the man's evil attack on her.

She looked at me in disbelief at what I was asking. "Maggie, do me a favour and tell nobody; I just want to forget it."

I told her I would tell no one, but something so disgusting happened to my girlfriend; I just could not let the man get away with it, as if he thought he could treat a woman as a second-class citizen like they did in the past. I needed to get some advice from Alfred, and I would discuss it with him in confidence.

He was the type of man you could trust to keep something like this quiet. Leaving her once again, I went to get dressed for work. Once I was ready, I returned to the balcony to kiss her. I told her I would see her later and would pick up something for dinner on my way home. She returned my kiss before telling me she would see me later. As I left the house, I walked towards the garage to see if my car's service had been done. When I arrived, I could see George, the mechanic, washing my car. As he noticed me walking towards him, he just smiled before telling me. "It's all in the price, my dear."

I paid the bill, and he passed me my keys. Once, I was back behind the wheel of the car. I could tell he had done a fantastic job. No more could I hear the squeaking sound that had irritated me whenever I had driven the car in the past. Fifteen minutes later, I was driving into the underground car park of the House of Calamari again. As I parked up, I could see Alfred's pink Volkswagen Beetle in its usual parking spot. I could also see Lorcan's black Porsche with the gnome sticker in the back window. When I got out of the vehicle, I could see an unfamiliar yellow sports car to the left of me. I could also see a very expensive-looking Bentley parked to the right of the sports car.

Walking towards the lift, I took the elevator to the reception area.

On exiting the lift, I could see an attractive woman walking back and forth between the entrance's thick glass double doors.

Nobody could mistake her loud-southern sounding voice as she spoke to the person on the other end of the phone. Next to Alfred stood the tall, fat-looking man who I suspected was the owner of the expensive Bentley. Even before he looked at me, I could tell this was the bastard who had raped my girlfriend. I didn't want to engage in any form of conversation with the brute, but it was too late. Lorcan pointed at me to introduce me to the man. He walked over to plant a kiss on my cheek, but I moved away from him as soon as I could. It seemed he was there to see the progress of the renovations as a leading member of the tariff-setting panel.

When he spoke with me, his posh-sounding voice showed he had attended either Eton, Harrow, or Rugby. The home for the posh louts of society who, for some unknown reason, think they are the more intelligent members of humanity. The problem was this was where the male members of parliament come from. "I hear you passed your security protocols test with top marks, my dear."

I just didn't want to be in his presence after what he had done to Kate. He went over the top when he enquired how she was doing.

I had to bite my lip and return with, "She's fine." A statement that made me feel sick. This made me wonder how he knew I was her girlfriend. When Lorcan asked Sir John to take a tour with him, I was so glad when he agreed to leave me alone with Alfred. I moved forward towards him to make sure nobody could hear what I was going to say to my friend. Leaning in, I said, "I need to speak to you in private as soon as possible."

He seemed a little confused by my statement but nodded his response. I left him to make my way to my office to begin my day. Although the machine was not ready to use yet, I still had a lot of files to sort. Just after I had taken my seat in my new office, the young beauty with the posh-sounding voice walked through my door. She didn't even look at me while looking around the room. The woman left soon after, but I could hear her voice talking with her boss. "Have you not noticed something?"

His voice was just as loud as hers. "What are you on about, my dear?"

Her response sent shivers down my spine. "This is where I killed him."

The evil man's reply was just like him. "Oh, do you mean Mr Davies Senior?"

Hearing this, I had no choice but to get up from my chair so I could move a little closer to the door.

"Yes, it was quite fun."

"Just don't let the son hear you."

"I think it was next door when I hit him with the wine bottle."

Moving near the door so I could hear more of the chilling conversation, I pulled my mobile from my pocket, hoping to record the evil pair.

"I laid the room out just like you told me to."

"Well, this is why I pay you so much."

"The final touch was when I slit both his wrists."

"Did you leave the handwritten note?"

"I followed your instructions to the letter."

As the man walked out into the corridor, I had no choice but to move away so he would not see me; I didn't want to get caught recording them.

"I hired the crappiest of actors I could find to portray the police officer. Who came to investigate the suicide?"

"What did you do with the body?"

"It's buried in my back garden. The police will never find it."

"I think the son is coming back with the water you asked him to fetch for you."

"Just one more thing. Who's the black-haired beauty next door?"

"You'll never believe it in a month of Sundays."

"What's so amusing."

"The woman is the girlfriend of the woman I beat up."

"I'm sorry, you have fun with a lot of women behind your wife's back."

"Do you remember the redhead woman who wouldn't complete the job I asked her to do?"

"The one outside the file room?"

"Which one?" Lorna spoke

"The one who was standing near the filing room. She refused to do what I asked just like the girl with the black hair."

"So, what did you do with her to make her comply?"?

Sir John replies, "I dragged her into an alcove and fucked her up the arse she screamed quietly loudly but once I'd finished the woman did my filing for me. The funny thing about that incident is the woman in question is now my wife."

Lorna speaking again, "I thought I recognised her from somewhere"

I could not believe what I was hearing. I just hoped my mobile was recording it so I could play it back to Alfred or my boss Lorcan. As the couple made their way to the second floor, I needed to find some reason to follow them. I realised I could not have my mobile in my hand, as the evil pair would know I was trying to record their conversation. Making my way down the back stairwell towards the Library of Souls, I used my security pass on the door. If they saw me, I could just say I was looking for a file on my first visit to the dusty room. I needed to cover my mouth because of the serious build-up of dust coming from the old files. However, I was quite surprised when I no longer had to do it. I picked up a few files with names dating back to the early fifties, and there was not one piece of dust on it. I had noticed no one cleaning the files.

Admitting to myself that I had more pressing things on my mind, I made my way to the front of the library. I could see my boss, Lorcan, talking with the rapist and his evil bodyguard. I needed somewhere to hide just in case they came into the library.

Moving towards the back of the shelves, I found a small alcove while wondering if this would be a suitable hiding place. Only seconds went by when the voices became louder. This is when I realised my boss had brought them into the room. I was in a mild panic about how I could stay hidden while trying to listen to any conversation. I knew my mobile would be of no use at all, and my memory was not that great. I only knew it because I was crap at crossword puzzles. I thought about my journal recorder, which I had around my neck. Would it help me record a conversation? Using it daily to talk into to record my journal entries, I just hoped it would record a conversation as well.

As Lorcan opened the door, he invited the pair into the room to show them the now dust-free room.

He explained how a new filtering system simply sucked away any excess dust coming from the stored files, and it only took one press of the switch. The new filter would kick in, and after ten minutes each day, the machine would simply eradicate years of dust. If they were not impressed, I was just imagining having one of these machines in our household. No more vacuuming would be needed.

As I hid in the small alcove, I was lucky I could hear the brute talking with the attractive woman with deep black hair and blue eyes. If someone could see us together, they may mistake us for cousins, for I also had black hair and bright blue eyes. The difference, though, was clear to see the evil girl had a larger pair of breasts.

I thought my own were pert and perky, but you could see her boobs were at least twice the size of my own. Suddenly, Sir John asks Lorcan to show him some other part of the building. I thought I was now safe to move from the small alcove until I realised the evil girl had still been in the room looking through the various shelves. What was it she was looking for? I didn't know; I also didn't care. My only thought was to not get caught. As she moved from shelf to shelf, it became obvious she was looking for a file, but why? I realised I was still holding a file close to my chest. From what I could see from the front cover, it simply said a young girl's name on it. Followed by the date the fourteenth day of June nineteen fifty-seven.

I could not open the file to examine it more because I didn't want the woman to hear me. All I could hear coming from her lips were the words "damn" and "blast it." I could see her picking her mobile out of her pocket. Watching her dial a number, she waited for the connection. Once it did, I could hear her talking to the overweight man I knew was Sir John. "It's not here."

This time, I could not hear his reply, so all I could hear was her side of the conversation. "I've looked and made quite a mess, but it's not here." I could not hear his reply, but it made her quite angry. "I'm not a bloody maid. Why should I clear them up?"

I heard her curse and swore down the phone at the man before she disconnected the call. The attractive woman made her way to the front of the library to pick up the files she had dropped on the floor, cursing as she did.

It was clear the woman had been instructed to find one file, but there were thousands on the extensive shelves. Once she had done her job, she left the room to join her colleague. Turning my journal record off, I realised it had been pointless trying to record a one-sided conversation. At the least, I had the mobile I could let Alfred hear.

Now that she had left the room, I looked at the file in my hands. The name on the front cover said the file was about a young woman named Susan Farmer. As I scoured the pages, there was nothing to show why the evil pair wanted it. I remembered the back page. Turning to it, there was no blue square; it was simply a zip folder attached to the back cover. It was a generous size file that looked like a square. You could see it was one of those old dos-type files.

The machine using those types of files went out in the late nineties when the Pentium computers came in. I had no choice but to replace the disc in its holder and take it and the file back to my new office. When the evil pair were gone, I could ask Alfred or my boss about the file and its hidden contents. Leaving the room the same way I had entered was the cleverest thing to do, just in case the evil pair were still on the second floor, standing next to the front entrance of the library.

As I arrived back at my office, I glanced over the balcony to see if I could spot the man and woman. All I could see was Lorcan standing next to my good friend, Alfred. Earlier, I had placed the mystery file on my desk before leaving. Now, making my way to the lower floor, I wanted to ask if the couple had left the building.

When Lorcan confirmed they had left, he asked me why I wanted to know. I made up an excuse, saying I had just missed them. After our brief conversation, my boss returned to his office, leaving Alfred and me alone. This signalled that Alfred would follow me back to my office so we could talk privately. Although he looked surprised by my hand signals, he soon joined me. Once inside, I asked him to close the door.

As he sat on the couch across from my desk, I had no choice but to ask if he trusted me. Though Alfred didn't understand why I was asking, he nodded. I then pulled out my mobile phone to play a recording for him. I pressed play and heard only my voice narrating my daily activities. I rewound the tape to try again, but still, all I could hear was my own voice. This disturbed me. Why couldn't I hear the conversation between the mysterious pair?

Frustrated, I fast-forwarded the tape, but there was still nothing except my voice. Alfred asked me what was wrong, and I had no choice but to explain. I told him how I had overheard our recent visitors discussing the apparent suicide of Frank Davies. I revealed that the woman had admitted to murdering him and that I had used my phone to record their conversation.

Alfred stood up and asked where I had been standing when I tried to record the conversation. I got to my feet and walked towards the doorway, turning slightly to my left before stopping.

When Alfred nodded as though he understood the issue, I still didn't. Why had my phone failed to pick up their voices?

Alfred then asked me to follow him out of my office. He led me to the security office, where he examined the control panel of the security system. Pressing a button on the console, he asked me to play the tape again. This time, I could hear both my voice and the pair's conversation in full. I was baffled as to why it hadn't played the first time.

Alfred explained that this building was under Home Office control, and after recent terror attacks, a special security system had been installed. The system could record any conversation, but if the mute button in the security office was pressed, it wouldn't play back external conversations until unmuted. With the mute button now off, I could hear everything. While I understood the concept, it raised another question.

Back in my office, I asked Alfred how I could hear both sides of a conversation despite not being present for all of it. Confused by my question, he watched as I removed my journal recorder from around my neck and asked him to rewind it by about half an hour. Though unsure why, Alfred complied and pressed play.

At the agreed time slot, we heard the recent conversation between the man and woman. This time, however, we could hear both sides. The portly man, Sir John, was discussing an incident from the late fifties with his companion. He mentioned looking for some files, and she admitted to searching for them but couldn't find them. She explained how she had made a mess, tossing file after file to the floor. Sir John yelled at her to clean up and return the files to the shelves. She swore at him, reminding him she wasn't a maid. He ordered her to join him, saying the files must be elsewhere.

When the woman asked why the files were so important, Sir John replied cryptically, "For me to know and you to find out." She swore again, reminding him how dangerous she was. He soon cowered down and apologised, which revealed how scary the woman was.

Suddenly, the journal reverted to my voice, asking my girlfriend if she would allow me to tell someone about the rape. Alfred heard the word "rape," and his expression darkened with rage. It was the first time I had seen him so visibly angry. I pleaded with him to keep what I shared a secret, explaining that I didn't want to ruin my relationship with my girlfriend while I sought justice for her after the brutal assault. For the next thirty minutes, I told him everything she had confided in me.

From the look on Alfred's face, I could tell he was determined to help. He was ready to ensure the evil man responsible would be brought to justice.

Having told him what had happened, I also explained that I was unsure of the date when the rape had occurred. He assured me he would investigate and get back to me with any information he could find. Almost forgetting about the file I had in my possession, I stood up to retrieve it from my desk. I showed him the file name before handing over the DOS-based floppy disk, which I had taken from the back of the file.

As he examined the old file, he suggested we head to the storage room full of outdated computers to see if we could get one of the machines to work before they were slated for destruction the following week. For the next twenty minutes, we moved between machine after machine, trying to find one that would power on. Frustratingly, not a single one worked.

While we were struggling, Lorcan appeared, curious about what we were doing. I showed him the old 8-inch floppy disk. He chuckled and remarked, "You'll never get one of those to work," before leaving us to our efforts.

Suddenly, Alfred found a machine that flickered to life, albeit briefly. Encouraged, I jokingly told him to slap it, hoping it might work. To our amazement, when he did, the power stayed on, and the monitor flickered before stabilising. I inserted the disk into the machine and waited for it to load.

One, two, three—the screen flicked on and off, displaying a simple "Please wait" message. Then, the preliminary report screen appeared, followed by brief information about the woman on the disk. It turned out Susan Farmer had been Mr Davies Senior's first case. Back then, he conducted interviews with just paper and pen, drafting reports before recommending criminal tariffs.

Tragically, while Davies was still drafting his recommendation, someone else decided the young woman should be executed. By the time he returned to the jail to present his report, he discovered that Susan Farmer's sentence had already been carried out. Later, he learned it was Sir John Stephenson who had rushed through her execution. I was eager to understand why the girl's execution had been expedited without awaiting Davies' recommendation. But then, the machine began to smoke.

Alfred quickly ejected the disk, but in the process, it tore in half. "Damn it," I muttered. Now, we might never uncover the significance of the disk—an artefact tied not only to Susan Farmer's execution but also to the mysterious death of Mr Davies. Alfred and I exchanged glances, both grappling with unanswered questions. I wondered if the damaged disk could still be salvaged.

While Alfred went to find a screwdriver, I bent down to inspect the machine. I spotted what looked like the remains of the disk, but the acrid smell of burning was unmistakable. When Alfred returned, we turned off the machine to avoid electrical shocks and carefully unscrewed the top. Beneath the lid, we found the remains of the diskette. Though badly burnt, Alfred managed to extract it.

The middle of the diskette had been destroyed, obliterating crucial information about Susan Farmer. Using a bit of tape, Alfred pieced the disk back together. However, given the extensive damage, we needed a second machine to test if the disk might still work. Just then, Lorcan rejoined us, carrying a duplicate machine. Excitement surged through me—I could have kissed him for bringing it.

Lorcan explained that the equipment had once belonged to his father. Though it hadn't worked for years, Lorcan had repaired the wiring and the reel-based loading system. Surveying the disk's condition, he shook his head. "There's no way this will work as it is," he said. "What a shame. Once again, that evil man might get away because the evidence is gone."

But then Lorcan clarified: "You don't understand what I'm saying." We looked at him, puzzled. Lorcan explained that his father's machine was not just a player but also a recorder. He retrieved a second file from the box he'd brought with him and asked Alfred for the diskette. Alfred handed it over, and Lorcan inserted it into side A of the device. He then prepared a second disk he had in his possession.

Lorcan added the new diskette to side B of the machine and pressed the copy button. The device whirred with loud noises, accompanied by flashing lights, before coming to an abrupt stop. Lorcan ejected the disk from side B and carefully removed the damaged disk from side A. He then placed the copied disk into slot A and powered on the monitor. The machine flickered to life, and the monitor illuminated.

Despite the damage to the original disk, the copied version revealed critical details we hadn't seen before. These newly uncovered pieces of information were pivotal: they showed that Ms. Susan Farmer should have received a significantly lighter sentence. The evidence proved that Sir John had tampered with vital records, altering her age from sixteen to twenty-three. This change ensured she would be tried as an adult, leading to a death sentence rather than the manslaughter charge she would have received as a minor. As a sixteen-year-old, her sentence would have been five years for each of her three victims, served consecutively.

This evidence was what Sir John had desperately sought to destroy. Fortunately, it had been preserved on an outdated computer system, out of his reach.

Looking across at Alfred, I debated whether to tell Lorcan what I had overheard earlier. When Alfred gave me an encouraging nod, I asked Lorcan to sit down before playing a recording I had saved on my mobile phone. As he listened to the brief conversation, his face reflected growing disgust. Once the recording ended, I played a second recording, which I had documented in my journal.

When the final words faded, I glanced at Lorcan and saw tears streaming down his face. It was clear he deeply loved and missed his father despite the years that had passed. Handing him a tissue, I watched as he wiped his eyes and explained his sorrow. He believed that too much time had passed to prosecute Sir John for his crimes.

I turned to Alfred for clarification. He agreed with Lorcan but elaborated further: Sir John hadn't only orchestrated the wrongful execution of Susan Farmer. He had also hired someone to murder Lorcan's father and had raped my girlfriend. Alfred suspected Sir John believed he was untouchable due to statutes of limitations on certain crimes. However, that raised a question—if Sir John knew the law so well, why was he so intent on finding the Susan Farmer case file? Her case was far beyond the legal timescale for prosecution. What could have been so critical in that file?

As Alfred pondered, he promised to check the statute books. He had a suspicion about murder statutes. Lorcan interjected, speculating that the limitation period for murder might have been twelve years. Alfred then turned to the computer, asking Alexa for clarification, but her response was conflicting. Turning to Wikipedia, Lorcan finally found a conclusive answer: there was no statute of limitations on murder.

This revelation explained Sir John's desperation to retrieve the Susan Farmer case file. For the first time, we saw a path to justice. Yet, I still needed to confirm the statute of limitations on rape to see if Sir John could be prosecuted for his crime against my girlfriend. When Alfred asked the computer, it confirmed that there were no limitations on crimes beyond the magistrate level, including rape.

The realisation hit me hard. Sir John could be prosecuted for the heinous crime against my girlfriend. But now, I faced a delicate challenge—discussing this with her without causing unnecessary pain. If she knew he could finally be arrested, I believed she might forgive me for involving my colleagues in such a personal matter.

Looking at Alfred, I considered his offer to talk to her on my behalf. Ultimately, I declined. Lorcan then suggested an alternative: he could write an article for a magazine, framing it as though it had been written years ago. Intrigued but unsure, I asked for clarification. Lorcan explained he could craft an article about the statutes of limitations on rape and murder, embedding the key information subtly.

Alfred chimed in, explaining further: "All you'd have to do is leave the magazine open to the relevant page. If Kate saw it herself, she wouldn't feel betrayed by you sharing her story."

Journal Entry Six

After my revealing conversation with Alfred and Lorcan which I found to be quite constructive.

I gave my boss permission to make a statute of limitations story into a dated magazine article.

Which I could leave in an area of the house for her to read.

I, therefore, would not have to inform her about my conversation.

Which revealed she had been raped and abused by Sir John earlier in her career.

By doing this Alfred told me it would be Kate telling you about the article.

Releasing you of any guilt.

This way you could keep your growing relationship with your partner intact.

One hour later the article was soon ready for me to take home with me.

All I had to do is follow Lorcan and Alfred's advice to the letter.

As soon as I arrived home, I could see Kate give our love nest a spring clean so pulled the article from my bag.

Leaving it in plain sight whilst taking a refreshing shower.

Once I was dressed in some relaxing attire.

I could see Kate had found the magazine and was sitting drinking a cup of her favourite tea.

While reading what I assumed was the article adapted by Lorcan.

As I entered the room, she looked up from the magazine to ask me if I had read the article about statute law.

Looking surprised by her comment while attempting to hide the real reason I had wanted her to read the magazine.

I just said I had used the magazines to wrap up delicate items when I was packing to leave my mums.

I did not want to go into too much detail when discussing the use of the magazine.

So, I did not give the game away.

Once I had made myself a cup of the tea, she had prepared I asked her was the article any good.

Kate smiled at me before stating she felt the magazine article was quite revealing.

It could also help her prosecute the man who had attacked her.

If I wanted to go down that route but the attack had been several years ago now.

Would it be helpful to her recovery by going back over such a bad time in her life?

She then asked me for my view on the matter.

Having discovered the portly man in question was not a nice man at all.

I had also found out this was not the first time he had committed a criminal act and got away with it.

As she looked at me for my answer.

All I could do is think about what to say without giving the game away.

I needed to find a way of keeping the information I had discovered out of the conversation.

While being constructive with my reply.

As I sipped at my I tea to wait out my response.

I looked into her eyes before stating although the evil man's attack had been in your past.

I also can understand why raking it back up and bringing it back to life by taking the man to court.

I felt she should discuss it with someone who knows about these things.

She put her cup down on the tray with a smile.

When she asked me, who could she discuss such a terrible incident with without it getting out?

Hoping she would let me off the hook I suggested talking with my colleague Alfred.

He was a man of the world, and he knew how to keep a secret.

When she agreed she needed some advice about the matter?

I lied to her by saying I would leave the decision in her hands.

Once you have spoken with Alfred, we can return to discussing it.

She seemed quite happy with that.

Leaving the conversation open until she had talked with my colleague, she asked me what I had bought for tea.

I could not believe it all my effort to hide away my discussions with Alfred and Lorcan made me forget to pick up something for our tea.

When I confessed, I had forgotten to pick something up she smiled at me before suggesting we ordered in.

Wow, what a lovely idea I had no choice but to say while attempting once more to hide the truth about my afternoon discussions.

The relief was written all over my face as we spent a lovely evening together before retiring to bed.

As soon as we entered the room, I began to kiss her passionately indicating my need for sex.

As we stripped naked, we began to touch each other as we kissed.

Slowly but firmly, we embraced each other.

As I took the lead with my kisses as I moved up and down her body.

I kissed at her breasts before taking each nipple in turn into my mouth to suck on with just a little force.

Returning to kissing down her sexy body to just above her clit.

I moved back up towards her breasts again.

This time I used my teeth on her nipples biting them in quick succession.

All I could hear was her shallow groans and moan beginning to reach new heights of pleasure.

My desire to help this woman reach her first orgasmic release was my goal.

Moving down the body yet again I took her moist clit between my teeth applying a little pressure.

Slowly building the pressure of my bite till she could take no more.

Soon Kate's moaning became quite loud which met she was nearing her climax.

Biting down a little more adding a slight bit of pressure and hey presto she came in an instant.

As I began to insert my fingers one by one, I moved them in and out.

Flicking my tongue against her clit while I did so make her collapse into yet another orgasmic release.

When I released her so she could enjoy my body as I with her we pleasured each other.

For the first time since our relationship had begun.

There was no need to use the large dildo.

When she had so many other toys to help us, both reach new and exciting heights of pleasure and desire.

Minutes turned into hours before we fell once again into a deep sleep together.

When I awoke the next morning, I could see Kate was not next to me.

Dragging myself out of my bed to go and find the love of my life.

I found her in the kitchen leaning over the sink.

I asked what was wrong, but it was not long before I found out the problem.

The takeaway meal had made her feel sick.

She apologized several times but kept on heaving up plenty of carrot coloured sickness.

It always surprises me this happens even if you have not even eaten any carrots.

Leaving her to go take a shower I hoped she would be feeling a little better soon.

Once I had washed away the smell of sex from my body, I washed my hair using my favourite shampoo.

When I had rinsed the suds away, I used plenty of conditioner on my long hair.

Rubbing it to make it shine once my hair was dry.

As soon as I had finished in the shower, I stepped out onto the bathroom floor.

Grabbed my bathrobe I put it on before wrapping my hair in one of the small towels from the rail.

When I felt ready to return to the kitchen.

I found Kate still being sick, so I asked her did she need me to telephone the doctors for her.

She shook her head before heaving up again.

Seeing the takeaway menu on the side.

I put it in the bin as we would not be using their service anymore.

If they made my girlfriend feel this sick.

Leaving her once more so I could get dressed.

I could tell she would not be assessing anyone security card for at least the next few days.

Once I was dressed, I picked up the toys we had used last night to give them a wash in the bathroom sink.

Once they were washed, I returned to place them back in the drawer till they were needed again.

After cleaning my teeth, I use my favourite mouthwash to wash my mouth so my teeth would sparkle.

While looking through the supplies I had bought when at the shopping centre I found some anti-sickness pills.

Taking these to the kitchen I passed them to my girlfriend who at the time was wiping her mouth for the umpteenth time.

She took two in the hope they would work and stop her from being so ill.

Kissing her on her forehead I left her so I could go to work.

I wanted to tell the boys how Lorcan's magazine article had done its job.

Arriving at the garage there was nobody there which I found quite unusual.

Alfred was always at work before me.

So where was he?

When I parked my car in the usual spot.

I saw Alfred's car parked up I tried the lock, but it was firmly locked.

Making my way through the underground parking bay.

I found Lorcan's car, but the left passenger side door was open.

Popping my head inside the vehicle you could see it had been searched but for what?

As the mystery continued, I felt a little uneasiness creeping into my mind about what was going on here.

I needed to understand this and solve this issue developing before my eyes.

Leaving the car park, I made my way up the stairs to the reception area.

It was not the silence greeting me it was a bloodstained carpet that sent me into a panic.

I picked up the reception desk telephone to press the intercom button.

To see if my work colleagues would answer the call.

Nothing the silent response to my call was quite scary.

I needed to understand what had gone on here.

Where was Alfred, where was Lorcan and why were there bloodstains on the carpet?

I did not want to telephone the police just yet because I did not want to feel foolish if there were a simple explanation for all this.

As I made my way around the reception area, I looked at my watch to check the time.

It read nine-fifteen which was my usual time of coming into work.

So where were the builders completing the renovations of the house?

Where the hell was my boss and my friend Alfred.

They were nowhere to be found.

Walking around the large building with complete silence as my companion.

All I wanted was an explanation. Something which would solve the mystery.

Tomas One

Moving around the ground floor.

Which by now would have been filled by several builders.

Alongside Architects and not forgetting my boss Lorcan sitting in his office scouring the internet for gnome bargains.

I thought back to when I saw my colleagues last.

Which seemed to be the night before while we are discussing that bastard Sir John's crimes.

I was about to leave the ground floor when I thought about the bloodstained carpet.

Making my way there I stopped just above it.

From the staining, it looked like it had begun to dry into the carpet.

Which meant it had been done several hours before.

Bending down to touch it I found it to be bone dry.

This would also alter the time by several hours.

My problem was I was no Sherlock Holmes I was just a woman with a mystery to solve.

Just one clue would help me on my way.

Sadly, there was nothing to help me here.

I needed Alfred to talk with so we could solve the mystery together, but he was nowhere to be found.

Having no choice but head to the second floor in the hunt for clues.

One hit me in the face knocking me for six.

Touching my face, I felt several droplets of blood.

Which seemed to be coming from the top of the third-floor balcony.

Just the hope of solving this problem made me want to go on.

As I made my way up the stairwell.

I could see droplets of blood still dripping down onto the stairs.

I just hoped the blood was not coming from one of my colleagues.

On reaching the third floor I was wiping away the blood droplets from my face.

So had not noticed Lorcan laying near the stairwell with a gash on the side of his head.

I only discovered him when I fell over him.

The look of horror was plain to see written all over my face.

Yes, I had wanted to find my colleagues. Yes, I had wanted to solve the mystery but not this.

I just hoped he was not dead.

When I began to hear a slight moan coming from Lorcan.

I realised he was alive.

Bending down so I could try speaking to him his eyes were rolling in their sockets.

Which meant a possible concussion I needed to telephone the ambulance.

Leaving my bloody soaked colleague, I had no choice but to return to the second floor's security office.

Which happened to be the nearest outside phone line.

Walking through the door I headed for the console to use the telephone.

When I picked up the phone there was a flashing blue light staring back at me.

As I pressed the button the video monitor came alive.

It seemed a time-dated video had been recorded.

Looking for the manual I found it in the drawer just under the desk.

I had to press the stop button labelled yellow.

Wait a minute then press the red button followed by the orange button on the console.

Nothing happened. Looking back to the manual for advice.

I could see I had missed the most important instruction which was to press the play button.

What a fool I felt when the light in the room went dark and the video came to life.

As the recording began you could see Alfred with Lorcan in my office. Which was where I had left them the previous evening.

The video flicked to the entrance of the House which was the closest one to the reception desk.

This would be where Alfred would sit to greet any guests.

Most of the visitors were panel members from other Houses across the district.

When Chairperson Troy Castle called a meeting, the building would get quite full.

Looking closely, you could see a woman stood near the entrance.

Which gave me the feeling of Déjà vu. Why would I have such a feeling?

Thinking back the only time I had seen someone standing near the entrance was the bitch who had accompanied Sir John.

Tomas One

She was shouting at someone down the phone.

I wondered if the machine would rewind the video if I pressed the blue button for a few seconds.

Looking at the manual I realised I should have been pressing the orange button.

To rewind the video, I would press it to hold for five seconds and let go before repressing the play button.

When I did it the video had stopped just where I needed it to.

The woman was stood yet again close to the entrance.

This time she was not holding a mobile phone.

She had what looked like a walkie talkie in her hand.

Returning to the manual yet again I scanned the pages in the hope of finding the zoom-in button.

This machine was quite simple to use if you had a manual at hand.

I had to press the red button three times in quick succession before pressing the blue button once.

I then needed to press the play button again.

This would bring up a targeting system where you could use the control to move in or move out of the frame at your leisure.

Realising I was taken too long with the video.

I used the telephone to ring through to the ambulance service.

Within seconds I was connected to a woman operator who put me straight through to the ambulance service.

I informed them what I had discovered.

After asking some questions about my bosses' condition they told me an ambulance was on the way.

Returning to the CCTV station I sat down to continue watching the video. In the hope, it would explain who had attacked my boss.

If I was lucky, it may also tell me where Alfred was.

Watching the entrance of the House from what was being shown on the video.

With the young woman walking back and forward yet again as she had done with the mobile phone.

As I watched the video for any clues to Alfred whereabouts there was nothing to indicate what the girl was doing there.

Rewinding and fast-forwarding the video in the hope I had missed something was hopeless.

I need to answer several key questions.

The first was where was Alfred?

Tomas One

The second what was the woman doing outside the House walking back and forward with what looked like a walkie talkie.

I also needed to know who had made the timestamped video.

Leaving the room to get a strong drink to help me think I wish I had the master's logic.

Whenever he had a problem, he played his violin while smoking weird substances.

Until he had the answer the problem here was, I did not smoke or took weird drugs.

I also needed to check on my boss in the hope his condition was not deteriorating to a dangerous level.

Although I had taken a first aid course, I could not call myself an expert far from it.

Checking him once again I hoped the ambulance would arrive soon.

Returning to my office to collect the strong liquor to help me relax.

As I sat in my office chair drinking from my whisky glass all I could do is think about the issues in mind.

Where was Sherlock Holmes when you need him?

Finishing my drink, I returned to the security booth to watch the video once again.

What was it I was not seeing?

Back forward till my head was full of images that had no substance.

All I kept seeing was the timestamp flicking while watching the same woman walking back then forward.

What was the point of this useless video which made no sense?

Taking a second break to relax the pressure building up inside my head.

I telephoned Kate to see how she was feeling.

When she told me, she was feeling a lot better.

I asked her if she could travel here to help me solve what seemed like an unsolvable puzzle.

Having no choice but to tell her about the attack on my boss she seemed quite shocked.

Leaving my office and making my way down the stairwell I could see the two ambulance men waiting at the entrance to House of Calamari.

Wondering why they did not enter the building through see-through doors.

I discovered why the builders, and the architects had not shown up for work.

Firstly, the door was locked with a key broken in the main lock.

I shouted through the glass panel for the ambulance men to wait there for a minute.

Hoping they had understood I made my way through down the stairs to the garage entrance below.

When I walked through the dimly little garage to the stairwell, which would lead me to the front of the building.

I was happy the two men had followed my instructions and waited for me to join them seeing the big sign stuck against the wall.

Which read gas leak do not enter this revealed so much but still so little all I could think about was who was behind this.

The only person I could think about was that bastard Sir John but what did he want and why did they attack my boss Lorcan.

Escorting the men through the garage so they could come with me to the second floor.

So, they could assist my boss and get him to the hospital.

Twenty minutes went by before the ambulance operatives left with my boss in a stretcher.

They asked me if I wanted to come with them, but I had to say no because my girlfriend was on the way to the House.

As they were leaving Kate turned up to assist me in locating my missing friend and work colleague.

The first thing we needed to solve was this time-stamped video of Lorcan's attack.

Even though I had not got that far yet.

All I had seen was a single woman walking back and forward past the camera with a walkie talkie in her hand.

Somehow, we needed to understand the video to solve the mystery.

Escorting my girlfriend to my office she seemed quite shocked at the size of the room I had been given to work in.

Pouring us both a strong drink to settle our nerves I had to tell her what I had seen which was very little.

Beginning at the start when I arrived, I went through my day so far from memory.

So, she could understand my problem.

Once we had finished our drinks, we travelled to the CCTV room so I can show her the video.

After she watched the video a few times she told me where I was going wrong.

She asked me to rewind the tape and play it again, but this time stop watching the woman stepping back and forward near the entrance.

She told me to look at the time stamp.

Once I did, I could see several minutes of footage were missing from the tape inserted in the machine.

Wow, I knew my lover was beautiful, she was also great in bed, but I did not know she had such a keen eye.

I had sat and watched the bloody video several times without success.

She on the other hand watches it just a couple of times and sees where I had been going wrong.

Now I knew what to look for I checked the video once again noting down the time errors.

Whoever had videoed the time recorded tape must also have a sharp eye or was a lot more intelligent than I was.

For every second of the video, three seconds were missing.

This was the reason why I had seen the woman stuttering near the entrance to the House holding the walkie talkie.

I soon realised the machine we were sitting near must have a video correction system installed.

All l needed was to find the hidden footage before sorting the tape into the missing sections which would be quite time-consuming.

Picking up the manual to read the section on video editing.

I could see there was a skip video section installed within the device.

Why would they need something like that and what would it be used for?

I asked Kate to see if she could use her keen eye on the manual to see why this would be needed at the House.

Once again, she came out with an answer which made me want to rip her clothes from her body and make love to there and then.

Sadly, this would not be the appropriate thing to do when we were trying to find Alfred.

Showing me the instructions on how to restore the condensed video material using the built-in suppression software.

I found I needed to press the red button three times.

One-touch of the blue plus two presses of the orange and a new purple button began to flash.

Pressing the button named restoration gave us an uncompressed copy of the video to watch.

When we viewed the material this time.

It showed Alfred and Lorcan sitting in my office.

Skipping to the front entrance of House like it had done before.

Although now with the added footage it showed the woman talking with another woman.

The machine had even recorded the conversation.

When the red button flashed Kate pressed it and the machine zoomed-in catching the voices of both women.

"Are you there yet?"

"Yes, but the bloody place is huge."

"She said it would be easy to find."

"Yes, well did she take a look before sending us here."

"No of course not the portly man provided her with the details.

Showing her where you would find the back entrance to the property which led to the second-floor garage."

"Look I've been here for nearly an hour, and it is getting bloody cold out here."

"Stop moaning you're getting well paid for this."

"Yes, that may be but it's bloody cold and I can't find the back door."

"Do, you want me to come down there and do your job for you."

"Oh, I think I've found it."

"It's about time."

"Damn it, I think it's locked."

"She said the gate would be open."

"Well, it's not I've tried it three times now."

"Give it a bit of muscle."

"Oh, yes I've done it."

"Did you bring the stuff?"

"What stuff?"

"I told you this morning I had left the items we needed for the job in the boot of the car."

"When I don't remember you telling me that."

"Oh, yes I forgot you go deaf when you are licking my pussy."

"I do not go deaf; I just like to concentrate that's all."

"You better go and get it then."

"Orders bloody orders why the hell do we have to do this."

"Shut up you are making such a racket the occupants of the property may hear you."

"Did I tell you it's bloody cold out here?"

"You've got your jacket. You've got your gloves so what the hell is wrong."

"I forgot my gloves, I left them on the couch."

"Well, that was a bit silly wasn't it."

"Who was the person who packed a kettle when going camping in North Wood."

"Shut up."

"No! Come on confess your sins to me."

"Why are you dragging up old news."

"Lorna, confess your sins and I mean right now."

"Bloody hell okay I thought the campsite had electric points so we could have a brew."

"Come on tell the truth."

"No! it's embarrassing."

"What more do you want me to say."

"You also brought a toaster to use in a tent."

"Damn it, just get on with your job."

"Your, no fun when you get grumpy."

"Look, Amanda, this job should be one of those in and out jobs."

"Yes, but nobody said it would be this cold."

As we listened to the conversation, we did not know what to say to each other.

So, we continued watching the video in the hope we could discover why Lorcan had been attacked.

Also, we both hoped the video would reveal where Alfred was.

"Right, I'm at the back door where is the security console."

"Amanda darling, when we went through the plan together there would no issues."

"I'm sorry at the time you were talking to me you kept leaning over and all I could concentrate on were your breasts."

"Please keep your mind on the job we have an important task to carry out for the boss."

"Spoilsport."

"Amanda, have you found the console yet?"

"Yes, now where did I put the card we were to use."

"You better not tell me you've left it at home with your gloves."

"Lorna, ease up I was only pretending to lighten the mood."

"Please concentrate on your job. If we take too long the staff would have gone home for the evening."

"Now you know what you need to do?'

"Do you need me to go over the plan one more time?'

"I'm not that stupid once we're in the building find and locate the people in there.'

When Kate stopped the tape, I had to ask her why?

Standing up she left the room walking onto the walkway.

Following her, she said while I was concentrating on the video the phone had rung.

I had to admit I had not heard a thing.

It was the hospital.

They needed to speak to Lorcan's wife.

Just hearing that made me think about my boss.

I hoped he had not died from the gaping wound on his head.

When Kate gave the hospital, Colleen's contact details she had asked how he was.

They gave the usual response "Are you Immediate Family?"

I needed Alfred and I needed him now.

When my partner put the phone down, she looked at me.

I could see from her eyes the prognosis was not good.

Asking my girlfriend to make her way down to the reception desk.

Where she would find my colleagues address book, which would have his wife's mobile in.

I asked her to bring it back to me.

She asked me where I would be.

I had no choice but to tell her I would be in my office having a stiff drink to calm my nerves.

When she returned with the address book, I was already drinking my second shot of strong whisky.

Taking the bottle from me she picked up her glass to fill it before joining me on the couch.

For now, the video would have to wait.

Lorcan's health was more of a concern to me at this moment in time.

Although Kate did not know Colleen, I asked her to ring her for me.

When she did as instructed the mobile was engaged.

Asking her to wait a minute before trying again.

While we waited, we held hands to comfort each other.

I needed to know about my boss's condition.

I also hoped he was not dead.

When my girlfriend had finished her glass, I poured what was left of the whisky into her glass.

Returning to my office desk I pulled a second bottle from the drawer.

This was given to me by my boss to celebrate my promotion only the other day.

Now the man could be dead.

When Kate tried the mobile again this time, the call connected.

Passing it to me I spoke with Lorcan's wife.

She informed me the hospital had told her he had a deep laceration on his forehead.

They had no choice but to operate to stitch up the wound after removing several shards of what seemed to be pot like substance.

I asked her if it were gnome shards which made her laugh.

She informed me the operation did not go well.

They had no choice but to put him in a self-induced coma.

To stop the swelling on the right side of his brain.

I did not want to tell her the truth about the attack because we did not know who or why he had been attacked.

All we did know was we had the rest of the video to watch for more clues.

Asking her to keep us informed I hung up the phone.

Kate hugged me as though she understood.

I needed one at that precise moment in time alongside another strong drink.

Taking our glasses and the bottle with us we returned to the security office to watch more of the video.

In the hope, we would find my colleague Alfred alive.

Taking our seats once more we did not want to watch the timecoded video, but it was now a necessity.

As Kate pressed the button on the console the player returned to the conversation between the two women.

One of these must have been the woman.

I had met when Sir John had visited the House on the pretence of assessing the restoration of the now crumbling building.

Due to the years of neglect and underfunding.

From the conversation, it was clear they were in a relationship.

Although there was nothing like Kate and mine.

Which was growing into a loving relationship.

What was also clear from what we had heard so far, the two women worked off each other.

When we had last listened in.

One of the women were near the main entrance.

She must have been the person who had left the gas leak board on the wall adjacent to the reception area entrance of the House of Calamari.

The woman must have also broken a key in the lock.

The other entering the building from the second-floor garage exit.

This area was always locked by a security lock attached to the garage entrance.

What was not clear was if the first woman had completed her first task before going to join her partner at the garage entrance to the property.

Asking Kate to stop the machine.

I felt we had solved our first couple of clues.

Pouring a drink for us both I told her the first woman was a woman named Lorna.

Although that was all I knew about her at this point apart from the fact she was clearly off her rocker.

The second was that the evil pair were working for Sir John.

I could not prove it, but he must have been the person who supplied the security card for them to enter the premises.

As the only people who had such cards were senior panel members.

Recalling my upcoming meeting with Troy Castle.

I knew he would be very interested in this information.

After I had visited the restroom.

I returned to my chair to have another shot of whisky.

I had been quite lucky with Alcohol consumption.

I could drink and drink some more without getting that drunk.

On the other hand, it was soon clear that Kate could not take much more.

I told her to go and take a lie down on the office couch and I would return to watching the video.

For more clues to the location of my colleague.

The tape began from where my girlfriend had stopped before.

Which showed the evil women walking around the second-floor garage.

"We'll have you used the card on the panel yet?"

"Give me a second I was trying to keep my hands warm."

"You and the cold weather. It should teach you not to forget to bring your gloves."

"Get off my case will you."

"Well, what are we waiting for."

"Bloody hell Lorna, give me a second my hands feel the cold more than you do."

"Time is getting on my love."

"Fuck, you."

"Well, that's not going to happen, is it?"

"What the hell are you going on about now?"

"Get, the bloody door open and I mean now."

"What did I say early."

"You said quite a lot."

"Damn it okay the bloody doors open."

"It's about time we could have been in and out but all you do is complain."

"Well, I feel the cold much more than you."

"Let's get what we were here for, and we can go home, and I can warm you up in bed."

"Deal," "Now that's more like it."

"Will you be quiet."

"I was just saying it's lovely and warm in here."

"Listen, up I can hear someone."

"What, did you say?"

"I said I could hear somebody."

"Wow, this place is huge." "You never said it was this big."

"Amanda, will you shut up." "Look there's one of the men now."

"What's that he's got in his hands?"

"It looks like a garden gnome."

"Who the hell would want to play with a gnome in a place like this."

"Our boss said the owner of the building collected them."

"Oh, right, that's silly."

"Everyone to their own I suppose."

"So that's him then."

"Yes, his name is Lorcan."

"Hang on a minute."

"What, the problem now."

"All I was saying was didn't you kill the man's father?"

"Yes, that was one of my first jobs and what a job it turned out to be."

"So, that's my job then."

"What?"

"I was saying your job is the more important one."

"Oh, yes I see what you mean."

"I think we need to separate them to make it easier."

"You're not feeling nervous, are you?"

"No! whenever have I felt nervous."

"You felt nervous on our first date."

"Darling that was not nerves."

"You could have kidded me."

"I just wanted to rip your kit off that's all."

"You've never told me that before."

"Yes, I have many a time."

"What did he say just then?"

"Who?"

"My target. The one with the gnome in his hands."

"He's telling someone just out of view about his new gnome."

"I wonder if that's my target."

"It's a pity we can't live in such a huge space as this."

"Amanda, what are you on about now."

"I was just saying the building is so huge when the boss takes over, we could have one of these rooms as our bedroom."

"Are you off your rocker? Why would I want to live here?"

"Well, from what I've seen it looks quite nice."

"Will you concentrate on the task at hand."

"Yes, I suppose your right work first then I want to tour all the nooks and crannies this place has to offer."

"Amanda, darling I'm not moving to this Mausoleum."

"It's a pity our bedroom is so cramped at the moment."

"Okay, let's stop this right now."

"What, are you saying?"

"Bloody hell you don't half pick your moments to have such conversation when we're here to do a job."

"I know it's just."

"It's just what exactly."

"All I was saying was our bedroom is a little small."

"Why is that?"

"I don't know."

"Amanda Bloody Parker our Bedroom is so cramped because of all your clothes."

"You can never have enough clothes."

"Let's just get on with the job we're here to do then we can talk about your clothes."

"Now, you're getting grumpy."

"I'm not well I'm a little hungry that's all."

"How could you say that when I cooked you that lovely meal before we left this evening."

"Excuse me you can't cook to save your life."

"Well, you've never complained before."

"Burnt offerings is what you serve me if it wasn't for that fine arse of yours, I would have left you years ago."

"You're a damn liar."

"What now."

"You love my cooking."

"No, I love your arse so I eat your food so I can play with your beautiful butt."

"I'm going home."

"Don't be stupid, we've got a job to do."

"Well, apologise or that's it."

"Will, you concentrate on the job at hand."

"No! Not until you say sorry."

"Sorry for what."

"My cooking."

"Okay, it's fine will you do your bloody job now?"

"That's not an apology."

"Let's comprise I'll let you pour chocolate ice cream on my breasts and allow you to take your time licking it off."

"Lorna Castle I hate you."

"No, you don't, and you bloody well know it."

"Right, let's get this over with."

"Now, you want to work."

"Well, I don't want that sauce to cool down."

"What are you on about now?"

"The chocolate sauce."

"Bloody hell will you get your mind off sex and concentrate."

"Right, your always right."

"Do you want to start an argument or carry on with the job?"

"Let's just talk about this later."

"There's the man now."

"Which man."

"Your target."

"Oh, I see him now."

"Their separating the fat one is going down the stairs."

"Will you stop giving me a running dialogue."

"Okay, I get excited sometimes."

"Yes, you do."

"Now, whose minds on sex."

"Okay, let's both concentrate and get this job over with."

"I'll follow him downstairs you hit the other one."

"With what?"

"Find, something close by."

"Oh, yes."

"What are you going on about now."

"I'm improvising."

"Wow, that a big word for you, my darling."

"Shit."

"What happened?"

"I hit him with the gnome at full force."

"So, what's the problem."

"Blood sprays on my jacket."

"Is he out cold?"

"Yes, the blood thing shattered as it hit him on the head."

"So, what the problem."

"This was an expensive jacket."

"You, and your bloody clothes."

"I got this in Paris it's a one-off."

"Just do your job and I'll buy you another one."

"What have I just said?"

"Oh, well I'll buy you two jackets if you just concentrate on your job."

"I've done my part. Now it's up to you to grab the other one."

"Can, we play with him then?"

"No! We need him to get to the files the boss wants."

"I don't think she pays enough."

"When Sir John hires us he's very generous with the cash."

"She pays quite well."

"No! How can I keep up with fashion trends on what she pays?"

"Let's just talk about this later we've got work to do."

Having no choice but to press the pause button once again.

So, I could go spend a penny.

On my return, I thought I would go and see if Kate were awake.

So, I could update her on what I have heard so far.

Arriving at my office I found her sound asleep so left her there.

Leaving the room to return to the security station I poured myself a strong whisky before resuming the video once again.

Hoping it would not be too long now having found out it was this girl named Amanda who had attacked Lorcan.

I felt for the man while awaiting news of his condition from his wife Colleen.

From the video, Alfred had gone down the stairs with the two women following him.

I did not want to hear they had beaten him up as well just to get their hands on a few files.

Watching the evil pair following my friend was not something I ever want to see again.

The woman named Lorna had grabbed hold of her surprised victim.

While the one named Amanda had hit him square in the jaw knocking square off his feet.

It seemed he had not heard them following him because he was wearing headphones listening to his favourite show tunes.

When the tape suddenly ended, I hoped this was not the end of the video.

Rewinding the tape before playing again several times but there was nothing.

Damn it where the hell is my friend.

Almost a minute went by before I began to hear conversation yet again but there was no picture.

What had they done to Alfred more important where were they?

Having no choice but to just listen to the two women threaten what seemed to be my work colleague was quite upsetting.

Stopping the tape so I could find something to wipe away my tears.

I was joined by my girlfriend who must have heard me crying at the developing story.

As she took me by my hands, she sat me down on the couch to cuddle me.

Which it seems was something I needed due to watching the heart-breaking video.

Almost fifteen minutes went by while we just sat there together.

As we kissed, I knew I had found the woman of my dreams.

Telling her what I had learned she told me to go and take a rest and she would listen to the conversation.

Feeling she was right a rest was something I needed.

So, I kissed her before leaving her to go take a rest on the couch.

As I kicked my trainers off, I got myself comfy and in no time at all, I must have drifted off.

Journal Entry Seven

Waking up in a cold sweat, I must have had a nightmare about those two women torturing Alfred. Hearing me scream, my girlfriend rushed into my office to check on me. I apologised to her for disturbing her, and she hugged me, which I felt was just what I needed after such a scare. I just hoped she could tell me if she had learned more about my friends' condition and location.

As we made our way back to the security station, she explained that she had waited for me to wake up so we could listen to the voices on the recording together. Although I was slightly disappointed, I understood why she had waited. When we were both ready, Kate pressed the button. I just wished the video would come on.

The evil pair knew they were standing in an area without cameras, having thought about their early conversations. It made me wonder if they were intelligent or just plain psycho. Suddenly, without warning, I saw what looked like a hand before it went blank again. Then it happened again. Even though it was quite blurred, we could just about see the two women, and it was then I noticed Alfred. They had him tied to a chair. One woman was shouting at him, while the other slapped him if he didn't tell them what they wanted to hear. Then the camera went off once again.

I tried to adjust the camera, hoping that it wasn't on our side causing the blur. When the camera came back on, we could now see the two women clearly. I wouldn't say I liked Alfred's look— you could see he was full of bruises. I must have pressed the wrong button on the console, as there was no sound this time. Asking Kate to press a few buttons allowed the picture to stabilise, but it continued to go on and off. Finally, we found the correct combination, and we could now hear the sound. This time, we could see a clear picture.

"Look, we haven't got all day. Give us what we need, and you can go about your daily business."

"I told you I can't gain access to the folder until I've had my security clearance upgraded by Mr. Castle."

"Should I hit him again?"

"Give me a minute to think about it."

"Oh, sorry, I didn't hear you."

"Now look what you've done. You hit him too hard."

"I said I was sorry."

"Go fetch some water so we can wake him up."

"Since when was I classed as your slave?"

"Do you want me to open my legs this evening or not?"

"Enough said. I'll be back shortly."

"Right, I'm back. Should I pour it over him like they do in the movies?"

"I don't know. Just make sure you wake the fool up so we can grab those files Gabrielle wants."

"Did I tell you I didn't like her?"

"Yes, many times. You only dislike her because she's beautiful."

"No! I dislike her because she doesn't pay enough."

"You mean she doesn't pay you enough. She has always paid me well enough."

"I don't like her also because she nearly killed you."

"Okay, I'm sorry, but she apologised later."

"The bitch should have compensated you loads. All she does is pass a few jobs to you she needs taking care of."

"Now, you know that's not true. You're just jealous."

"Jealous of that? I don't think so."

"Gabrielle has a stressful job. So, she likes to relax once her shift has finished."

"Yeah, yeah, let me finish that one—she likes to take occasional drugs."

"Wow, you don't like her, do you?"

"You do not understand, Lorna. I love you, and she nearly took you away from me."

"It was lucky, then, that you were there to help me."

"Yes, there she was, stoned out of her face while you were nearly dying."

"Amanda, darling, calm down. You'll give yourself a heart attack."

"There you go again, trying to make a joke out of it."

"Who am I with?"

"What do you mean?"

"You know what I mean."

"You are with me."

"Yes, I'm with you because I love you, not her."

"So, let's get on with the job, and tonight, I'll show you who I love."

When Kate stopped the tape, I was a little taken aback. She asked me if I recognised the location where they were holding our friend Alfred. I asked her to play the tape again so I could try to pinpoint the location. The House of Calamari had so many areas, some of which I had yet to explore. Watching the two women abuse our colleague was not pleasant, but sadly, it was the only way we could find him. I told her if I recognised the area, I would signal her by tapping her on the knee.

"Are you going to stop wasting our time, Mr. Banks?" one of the women said on the tape.

"I cannot tell you what I do not know. I cannot access the files without my card being upgraded," Alfred replied.

"Should I stab him a little with my knife?"

"Did you hear? My girlfriend wants to play with her sharp knife."

"Please, stop this. You're at least a day early," Alfred pleaded.

"Please, Lorna, let me stab him."

"What do you mean?"

"Your father was going to upgrade our security cards when we visited him tomorrow."

"Shit, darling, I think the bastard recognises you."

"You've got to let me stab him now."

"Crap! Why would that bitch send us here for information when he hasn't got it?"

"That is why I hate her. Do you think she wants us to get caught?"

"What day is it?"

"It's the nineteenth. Why?"

"Bloody hell, it's us. We've got the date wrong."

"Do you mean I can't stab him with my shiny new blade?"

"Put it away, Amanda. All I can do is apologise to you," Lorna said, turning to Alfred. "My issues are with my father. Having you recognise me has caused a problem that needs to be rectified. There's also a second problem I must deal with. A friend of a friend of Sir John Stephenson hired me. They promised I could resolve the delicate issue regarding those files my father insisted on locking under extra security. Our boss this evening wants those files, which you've kindly informed us are inaccessible tonight because we arrived a day too early. This, I admit, was my error."

She paused, her tone calculating. "I need to think about how to continue with this challenging issue. My friend and I must withdraw for a while to consider what we can do to complete this evening in a way that will satisfy us all."

When I hadn't tapped my girlfriend on the knee, she inquired if I knew the location where they were keeping him prisoner. I had no choice but to tell her I had only seen part of the annexe. I mentioned the second-floor garage as a possible location. Leaving the console, we descended the stairwell toward the garage to see if it matched the area from the CCTV recording.

As we opened the door, we were met with pitch darkness. Glancing at my watch, I realised it was late. I hadn't considered that we'd both slept for a while—Kate because of alcohol consumption and I because of nervous stress. It was useless; we were failing our friend. All we had to go on was a time-stamped recording showing those evil women discussing what to do with

Alfred. All I could hope for was that he wasn't dead. Time was slipping away, and we still didn't know where my colleague was.

I thought about informing the police to aid us, but then I remembered hearing Sir John's confession. He'd hired someone to pretend to be a detective when Lorcan's father died under mysterious circumstances. This meant we had no choice but to go back to the tape again. Only by watching the tape could we discover where my friend and colleague were being held. I took another large drink to steady my nerves before pressing the console button one more time, knowing that every second was one second too late for Alfred.

Watching the tape, it was clear my colleague was in serious pain and anguish. When the two women reappeared in front of Alfred, one was carrying what looked like a large bag, its contents obscured.

"Right, Mr. Banks. My girlfriend and I have come up with a solution to our immediate problem of you recognising me," Lorna began. "When we left early, we returned to our dogging van to talk about this. You understand the term 'dogging,' don't you?"

Alfred remained silent, prompting her to sigh in annoyance. "I see. I gave you a little time to answer me. Sadly, you remained silent, which I felt was quite rude."

"Amanda, darling, I give you permission to hit him."

"Yes, I love to hit people," Amanda replied gleefully.

"Dogging is something couples do if they've been together for several years like we have. It's a way of spicing up a poor sex life," Lorna explained.

"Our sex life is grand, so why are you saying this?" Amanda interjected.

"Amanda, we talked about this back in the van."

"No, you talked. I licked your pussy."

"You were listening to me, though."

"How many times do I need to tell you I like to concentrate when licking fanny?"

Lorna sighed again. "I'm sorry, Mr. Banks. This is quite embarrassing when you have a girlfriend who doesn't listen to instructions."

"That's not fair. You told me to go down on you. While you were thinking about the problem we faced this evening, I listened, and I did as instructed," Amanda protested.

"Right, let's just agree to disagree."

"You're not telling the man the truth," Amanda snapped.

"Okay, what the hell is your problem?" Lorna asked.

"You said our sex life was stale and boring. If that's the case, then why is it I can get you to cum within five minutes?"

"Can we discuss this later once we've dealt with the issue?"

"No! I want to discuss it right now," Amanda retorted.

"Bloody hell, Amanda, we spent twenty minutes discussing this."

"Yes, and I said I was busy."

"You do my box in sometimes. That's why we go dogging—to spice up our sex life."

"You never said our sex life was boring before."

"It isn't. I love you, but sometimes I want a little spice in our lives."

"Okay, let's just get on with it. I don't want to miss my program."

"What program?"

"The Prada walkway is on the fashion channel."

"When?"

"Tonight, at ten o'clock."

"What do I do when you're watching that?"

"Now, whose memory is terrible?"

"When it's on, you are fucking me from behind with our favourite dildo."

"Oh, I see, and you watch this regularly?"

"Not. If we're dogging, I record the program to watch on our return."

"Well, let's get this over so we can go home."

"Now, Mr Banks, while my girlfriend was busy in the van, I devised the perfect plan to stop you from communicating with my father. Now, you have seen me this evening."

"Amanda, darling, open the bag and pass me the hammer and the two long nails I have in there."

"Woah, I like it!"

"I cannot crucify you, but I can do one better. I can use these nails on the palms of your hands to attach you to the wooden chair. First, the right palm; hold him down, Amanda. Perfectly struck now, the left one. There you go again. What a bloody excellent shot."

"Should I clean up the blood?"

"No, let him suffer."

"He looks as though he's passed out."

"Which is good, I suppose, because the next part is going to sting. Put your protective gloves on, my love, and pass me a set. Now, hand me the protective eye shield," Lorna instructed.

"Please be careful with the spray bottle. It contains sulfuric acid."

"Wow, how lovely," Amanda replied sarcastically.

"Stand back so the spray doesn't catch you," Lorna continued. First, she sprayed one hand to the left and then one to the right. "Good, it's working a treat."

"He's moving. Should I hold him down?" Amanda asked.

"No, just step back now. The final spray—one to eye one, then one to eye two."

"Wow, it's bubbling. It must hurt him," Amanda observed.

"As soon as he wakes up, he'll want to touch his eyes."

"Oh, you're so wicked, Lorna. He'll never get to speak to your father now," Amanda said with glee.

As Kate pressed the button on the tape, I believe we both felt sick. I just hoped they had not blinded our friend. I wished we knew where he was because he would need specialist care for the extensive wounds on his hands—not to mention his face. I took another large swig of whiskey before refilling both our glasses.

When my girlfriend pressed play again, I saw what looked like the stairwell to the annexe. Stopping the machine, we both headed toward the third-floor annexe. Upon entering the room, a foul smell made us both gasp for air. As we reached what appeared to be a doorway, Kate opened the door to let in fresh air for our tightening lungs.

Descending the stairwell to the rooftop, I finally saw our colleague. The smell of rotting skin was overwhelming. It was fortunate, in a way, that he was unconscious. I used my mobile to call the ambulance service for the second time that day.

Realising we had no choice, I also contacted someone I trusted in the police force. Within thirty minutes, Alfred had been freed from the chair and was on his way to the hospital for life-saving treatment.

We returned to my office to escape the sight of the horrific scene we had just witnessed. Once inside, I poured myself another stiff drink to calm my shattered nerves. Kate went to fetch the whiskey from the security office floor, and when she returned, we both took a strong drink before preparing to talk to the young, attractive, blonde-haired WPC who had arrived.

The officer, WPC 2936 Sarah Dunn, began by asking us about Lorcan's earlier attack. I explained that we only knew about the attack and its timing because of the date-stamped recording. She requested a copy of the tape, but I informed her that the facility was a government-run site, meaning we needed explicit permission from the Home Office to release it.

"Why are you being obstructive to my investigation?" she asked, frustrated.

I had no choice but to explain that I wasn't trying to hinder her investigation but could not release anything without proper authorisation. I asked Kate to explain the rules of non-disclosure while I stepped onto the veranda to make a call.

It took several attempts to reach someone in the Justice Department due to the late hour. When a man finally answered, he transferred me to the correct office. After waiting on hold, accompanied by grating opera music, a helpful woman picked up and expedited the process. With her assistance, I secured permission to share the tape with the WPC.

Returning to my office, I found the atmosphere had relaxed as Kate explained the situation to the officer. I offered to burn her a copy of the tape and asked if she wanted to view it. She declined, admitting she had just joined the Langley force after being transferred from Hanley headquarters. This was her first investigation since her transfer, and she confided that her previous station had ostracised her because of her appearance.

This made Kate and I reflect on Sir John's attitude toward women, but I chose not to dwell on the past. Instead, I warned her about the tape's graphic content, including violence and the actions of two very disturbed women. Kate advised her not to watch it alone.

Once the copy was ready, we escorted her to her car in the underground garage. As soon as she left, all I wanted was to collapse into my girlfriend's arms. We decided we had a decision to make stay at the House of Calamari or make the fifteen-minute journey home they decide this by stating although the couch option would be a comfortable option but they both preferred their own bed so went home.

Journal Entry Eight

I do not recommend being woken from a perfect slumber by the woman you love trying to shove a phone into your ear. Opening my tired eyes, I saw a naked Kate telling me there was someone on the phone. Wondering why she looked wet, I realised the phone must have rung while she was showering.

"Hello, Maggie, is that you?"

Having no choice but to say yes, I sat up at once when I discovered it was Lorcan's wife, Colleen, on the phone.

"He's gone, Maggie."

"Excuse me?"

"The injury to his head was just too much for him. Lorcan's dead."

"I was by his bed when all the machines started beeping. Several nurses came rushing into the room with what they said was a crash trolley. They tried everything, but his injuries were too severe. They announced his death at 6:25 am. I'm sorry for telephoning you this early, but you are the only person I could think of."

"Can my girlfriend Kate and I condone your loss?"

"He was only fifty-six. I must go. I need to contact the family to arrange the funeral."

As soon as I put the phone down, I stripped off my clothes to join my girlfriend in the shower. I needed her more now than ever. On entering the shower, I cupped her large, firm breasts with both hands while kissing her neck. Just the touch of this beautiful woman made me feel quite horny. Having sex, they say, is a great release for being stressed.

I had to admit the stress we had both been through was bad. I could not believe Lorcan was dead. As I turned her around so I could kiss her passionately, I needed to embrace her warmth. Her kind-heartedness was what I wanted. Planting slow kisses down from her breasts to her navel and back up again turned us both on.

When I dipped down again, I kissed around her clitoris while I entered her moist fanny with two fingers. Soon, my fingers were moving in and out as I flicked at her clit. The moans and groans from Kate showed me she loved the attention. After a nightmare twenty-four hours, I felt we both needed to take some pressure out of our lives. As I pushed my fingers in and out at speed, she soon came.

Once she had reached her orgasm, we swapped over so she could help me do the same as the warm shower washed over our bodies. Twenty or so minutes later, we left the shower to continue our lovemaking on the bed. When we began to fuck each other by rubbing our clits together, it was not long before we both came in unison.

Pulling at the drawer entrance, I grabbed our favourite toy to do its business. Just the feeling of pleasure the large dildo would give you when doing its job. First, it was me fucking Kate, and then it was her doing me until we found our orgasmic pleasure centre. As we both continued to pleasure each other—pussy, anus—the thrill of the moment took us to heaven several times that morning.

We needed to release the pent-up stress and anger we had no choice but to see the night before. When we were spent, we had no choice but to return to the shower to wash away the serious number of orgasmic juices we had allowed to escape while making love.

Once we had finished and were back in the bedroom getting dressed, I realised I had not told Kate about the devastating news Colleen had shared earlier. When I told her, she broke down in tears. She had known the man a lot longer than I did. Passing her a few tissues so she could wipe her eyes, I hugged her for a minute or so.

When the phone rang, I moved across to my side of the bed to pick up the receiver.

"Miss O'Neil."

"Yes, who is this, please?"

"It's about time we spoke."

"I don't recognise the voice. Who is this?"

"My name is Troy Castle; I believe you met my estranged daughter."

"Yes, have you heard the news?"

"Colleen telephoned me this morning with the shocking news. Lorcan was a nice man."

"Your daughter's girlfriend killed him."

"I spoke with the hospital this morning about Alfred. He's in intensive care; they are doing everything they can for him."

"Your daughter is plain evil."

"All I can do is apologise to both of you. I see from my diary we were meant to meet under different circumstances today. Instead of you coming to me in Glendale, why don't we meet at the House in about an hour?"

"Kate and I wanted to attend the hospital but were advised against it at this time by Troy Castle."

"They wouldn't tell you anything."

"Why not?"

"I've had him put under armed guard so nobody apart from me and close family can speak to him. Your daughter used a hammer on both his palms and sprayed sulfuric acid on them. She sprayed it in both eyes just because he recognised her."

"My daughter and I have not spoken in over twelve years. She blames me for her mother's suicide."

"So, you want to meet up this morning under the circumstances? We could postpone the meeting until I can get over the stressful episode we had no choice but to witness yesterday."

"This morning would be a perfect time to meet up. For one, you will need to upgrade your security pass so you can see the hidden files my daughter wanted to access. Secondly, I want to talk about Lorna. I feel you need to hear the truth behind the many lies the girl has told over the years. Also, now that Lorcan has gone, his wife Colleen and I have spoken about the future of the House. Although Colleen is grieving for the loss of her husband, she wants a speedy handover so she can leave the area."

"What are you saying? I do not understand."

"This is why we should meet up this morning before the news leaks out about the devastating incident which happened at the House last night."

"Kate and I will be there, Mr. Castle."

"Thank you for understanding, and I'll see you there in about an hour."

As soon as I had put the phone down, I returned to the side of my loving girlfriend to ask her what she thought about the conversation.

Although she had only heard my side of it, she had heard Mr. Castle's name mentioned. I told her what he had said about our dear friend Alfred and how the hospital was doing all they could for him at this time. I then moved on to tell her about the meeting arranged for an hour at the House.

She shook her head from side to side, asking if it was too early to talk about such things after both my colleagues had been attacked in such devastating ways. I agreed but reminded her that we also needed time to mourn our friend's passing. I suggested moving the meeting forward and asking for some time off to grieve. We didn't know what the future held for us, but we wanted to be together.

Although the meeting was set for an hour, we put on our coats and made our way to the car for the short journey to the House, aiming to get it out of the way. Upon arrival, we found Mr Castle standing outside the second-floor reception entrance, talking to a locksmith who was working on the jammed lock—damaged by one of the perpetrators. When I looked at Mr. Castle, he noticed our early arrival and asked if we wanted to speak with Colleen. I immediately agreed so that we could offer her our deepest condolences.

As we walked toward the car, Colleen stepped out of Troy's vehicle. She was dressed in black, wearing a short, see-through veil over her eyes. I hugged her, and then Kate did the same. Once Troy gave us the nod, we entered the House together. It was clear that Colleen, like us, wanted this meeting over as soon as possible. We escorted her to what had been Lorcan's office, a room that now felt cold and lifeless.

The memories of Lorcan overwhelmed me—his laughter while buying a simple gnome or the mischievous satisfaction of outbidding Stan on a rare find. Tears filled my eyes again. Kate, too, was in tears, which confirmed that this meeting might have been too soon. Troy took Lorcan's seat while I wiped my eyes and left to fetch chairs with Kate's help. Upon our return, Mr. Castle handed us an itinerary for the meeting:

A: House of Calamari (change of ownership)

B: Lorcan's wishes

C: Lorcan's funeral

D: Lorna Castle

E: Restoration of the House

F: Upgrading security

G: A worrying concern (shares in the Houses)

I hoped the list wouldn't be as extensive as it seemed. Mr. Castle explained that Colleen was there only to address the first few points: the change of ownership, Lorcan's wishes, and the arrangements for his funeral. Her family was coming down for the service, after which she planned to sell her house and return to her childhood home in Danby.

Before starting, I requested an additional agenda item: time to mourn our loss. To my relief, Mr. Castle agreed. Kate then asked for an update on Mr Banks' condition, but Troy could only repeat what he'd told me earlier that morning.

Noticing Colleen's unease with the delay, Mr. Castle began with the first item: the change of ownership. His secretary, Mrs. Coulsum Wish, had prepared a legal document requiring Colleen's signature and two witnesses. It became clear that Kate and I were the witnesses. After signing the document, Kate noticed the figure—fifteen million—offered by Mr Castle for the House, which was well above its value due to years of neglect. She smiled at Colleen before signing. Once completed, Troy handed Colleen a cheque from a brown envelope.

The meeting moved on to Lorcan's wishes, written years earlier after his father's premature death. He had wanted Alfred to take over the House's operations. The mere mention of Alfred's name brought tears to my eyes. Kate comforted me as I struggled with the loss.

Next, Colleen informed us that Lorcan's funeral would be held the following Wednesday at the Glendale synagogue at 2 p.m. With her part of the meeting concluded, she stood, shook Troy's hand, and kissed Kate and me on the cheek before leaving the room.

Once Colleen departed, Mr. Castle hesitated before continuing with the agenda, unsure whether to discuss his daughter Lorna. He eventually explained her troubled history. Lorna had been a difficult child with severe mental health episodes, for which she had been sectioned multiple times. Troy recounted how these issues dated back to his earlier life, when his wife, Meg, had suffered health problems after giving birth to their fourth child, Sarah. The third daughter's name was Mary. Unknown to Troy, Meg had been having an affair with a man named Dr. Shane "Shagger" MacDougal, who pretended to be her psychiatrist. When the truth emerged, Troy was devastated to learn the child was not his biological child. Despite loving Sarah, he ended his marriage and split his family in two.

Joanna sided with him Lorna sided with her mother Mary was too young to make a decision, so the fourth child from the illicit affair with Sir John who often used the name Shagger to hide his illicit affairs was discovered, and Sarah wasn't Troy's daughter the child was put up for adoption.

Having been cut her off from any form of financial restitution due to her betrayal, she had no choice but to go back to Sir John for help. He took the girl and put her up for adoption under his wife's instruction in exchange for a financial package to keep their affair from becoming public. For years, she tried to find her daughter while becoming even more depressed. The problem was the girl's identity had been changed to protect her for future adoption.

I had to stop him here because Kate and I both needed to ask about a young woman Alfred had told us about. Her name was Lillie Cole. Was this the girl his late wife had with Sir John? He informed us that even he could not find out due to the strict laws on adoption. I asked him to investigate, suggesting there must be a backdoor access route he could use. Troy said he would ask a friend of a friend if there was some way to discover the truth.

Continuing his story, he told us about his wife, whose depression had worsened to the point she turned to drinking. At the time of her death, she was living with Lorna, who was on heavy drugs to combat her serious mental health issues. "Therefore, she hates me," he said, "claiming I left my wife with no choice but to take her own life. Sadly, I admit I was a bitter man back then who refused to help her in any way. Since that time, my daughter has done everything to get back at me. I never thought she would go this far. This morning, I placed a warrant on both their heads. If spotted, they need to be detained."

I asked him not to go soft on her and suggested a shoot-to-kill order for both women. Kate reminded me we were in England, not America. Moving on with the itinerary, we discussed the restoration of the House. We all agreed it should continue. Troy said he would double the budget for repairs so they could be completed within a few months. While he was here, I asked him about Sir John, his role with the panel, and how it worked, given their history.

Troy stood, turned to the first cupboard on the left, and pulled out some fine Italian brandy he had bought for a friend. He poured us all a large glass before returning to his seat. He explained that Sir John, now an ex-MP, had many friends in many places, owning several businesses, even a hospital. They had never fully agreed on the operations of the panel. Sir John's views on criminal restoration conflicted with Troy's responsibilities as Chairperson of the Tariff Setting Panel.

Kate decided to be open with him about their past. She relayed her tale of how Sir John had raped her and mentioned that Mr Castle's daughter was working for him. The anger was evident on Troy's face as Kate wiped her tears with a tissue. Troy asked why she had not pursued prosecution. Kate explained that Lorna, Sir John's daughter, had threatened her with extreme violence. This was one reason she hadn't had him arrested.

The main reason, she continued, was that Sir John had connections with several barristers, some of whom she had met and others who were under the radar. Not all barristers were competent or ethical. She mentioned one barrister, known for taking money to look the other way—Cecil "the Hitman" Higgins. His reputation came from his clientele of gangsters. She also described the grim process that often humiliates victims by digging up their past relationships. If it came out that she was a lesbian, the case would likely be closed.

Moving on, Troy asked for our security cards. We handed them over, and he opened his briefcase. Taking each card in turn, he pressed mine, a blue card, onto a pad before pressing a button. Moments later, he returned it to me, now black with a slight hint of red, indicating Level A grade security. He repeated the process with Kate's card.

Once finished, Troy mentioned he would arrange for my girlfriend to be transferred to the House, which pleased us both. He also informed us of our promotions: we would gain seats at panel meetings and secure voting rights. As he prepared to leave, he noted that, with Alfred incapacitated, the House would need a caretaker boss. Since Kate had been with the panel longer, she would take that role. I would step into Alfred's shoes as the receptionist—a significant promotion without which the House could not run.

Walking him to the now-fixed front door, he informed us that he would contact the HR department at the Home Office to make our promotions official. Though we were already earning decent salaries, the promotions would nearly double our wages.

Journal Entry Nine

It has been six weeks since I lost my boss, Lorcan Davies. There is so much to catch up on. His funeral went off without a hitch, even though Stan, my boss's chief rival, brought some unexpected guests along. These included Betty Harris and her boyfriend Clive, who lived in Clacton, as well as their son George, who had a habit of spitting whenever he talked. Colleen was surprised when this group contributed to the funeral costs by purchasing the complete collection of my boss's gnomes.

Moving on, the house re-modelling is underway. Troy has sent Kate to the States to build connections for the justice department. We talk on Messenger every night. Meanwhile, I've had some good news about Alfred, though he will remain in the hospital for the foreseeable future. The doctors are pleased with his effort to help himself use the spray designed to alleviate the hitching in his hands—an issue stemming from the injuries inflicted when the evil woman nailed his hands to the bench and sprayed acid on his palms. The damage left him with severe problems at the wound sites. He has now managed to reduce his scratching to every three hours.

The doctors are particularly concerned about his facial injuries. Since his palms are too damaged to apply the cooling cream, he will always need assistance to spray his eyes with the cooling mist every two hours. Builders, who have been incredibly supportive, are working to demolish the old annexe, with its cold, damp, and empty rooms, to construct a lovely new home for Alfred. This new space will include a rooftop garden and an area for his guide dog, Bonnie.

Alfred is officially blind in his right eye but retains limited vision in his left. The acid damage has caused the skin around the injury to resemble rotting flesh, reminiscent of monsters from old Universal Horror films. Bonnie, an intelligent Labrador whom Alfred personally chose, has been trained to meet his needs as best as possible. Alongside the spray, Alfred must take several painkillers, which Bonnie helps him manage. She signals when it's time for his medication.

During the day, a carer helps Alfred with his spray and medications. Once they clock off at ten each evening, Bonnie takes over. Due to the pain in his hands and his visual impairment, Alfred's medication is administered in six equal-sized liquid doses. Bonnie barks to signal the order of the medication, ensuring he takes it correctly. Some of the medication is extraordinarily strong, requiring precise intervals of fifteen minutes between doses.

Once the new home is ready, Alfred will return. He tells me via messenger that he is adapting well to the changes in his life and describes Bonnie as a godsend. Without her, he wouldn't be able to leave the hospital. For now, hospital staff are available around the clock, working with the doctors to refine ways to support Alfred and Bonnie through the night. With the need to spray his hands every three hours and his face every two, they are exploring additional medications to eliminate the need for frequent spraying altogether.

The bond between Alfred and Bonnie is remarkable and continues to strengthen. The more the dog learns, the closer Alfred comes to returning home. I deeply respect his tenacity, spirit, and adaptability during this challenging period of change. It saddens me that such a tragedy has befallen a man I admire.

Meanwhile, it is with regret that the evil woman and her girlfriend remain at large. Despite an extensive search, they have yet to be found. With my one true love away in Sugarland Texas, working to advance the justice panel's connections. Our first-panel meeting is scheduled for this Saturday afternoon, with Kate joining us via Skype to provide an update on her progress. It makes me wonder if Sir John will recognise her, considering the attack he committed against her all those years ago.

Journal Entry Ten

Well, my first-panel meeting has just finished. I didn't know they went on so long. The itinerary included several items, including Kate and my introduction to the rest of the Houses. I met so many interesting and diverse sets of characters. I cannot wait till my lovely girlfriend returns from the States next Tuesday. The look on Sir John's face when she spoke was priceless, which showed he remembered her. I do not think he liked it when we both outvoted him.

He wanted to make changes since Lorcan's sad departure, but Troy Castle had the final say on the vote. The look of dismay when Troy turned down the bastard's proposal was unforgettable. I do not think Sir John had been told that Troy now owned the house. When Kate returns, I will have a lot to tell her at a twice-monthly panel meeting about how the system works.

Once the meeting had concluded, Mr. Castle took me by my hand and led me into his office. As soon as we were there, he laughed aloud, which is something I must admit I had not seen coming from the man recently. "Oh, girl, the look on the man's face when you voted him down." Pouring us a large brandy, he asked me to take a seat. "As this was your first-panel session, you won't understand how it works yet."

However, Kate was not on screen for more than fifteen minutes while discussing her successful connections to the Justice Department. Her casting vote in all six votes held went against anything Sir John wanted. "Let me tell you, girl, you could have cut the atmosphere with a knife, as there are so many appeal house representatives and secretaries. The more panel sessions you and Kate attend, the more you will discover.

Sir John's influence spread across at least nine of the Houses present today. This means he can, if he wants, swing a vote in his favour. If you do the math, there are sixteen-member houses. Each member gets to cast a vote. With Sir John's control, he could get most articles through a vote with at least a nine-seven split. Well, this was until today. Now, you and your partner have a vote. The same ratio no longer helps him control how the panel votes. The vote is now on an equal footing for the first time in a long while. He probably did the math, too.

When Alfred returns, Sir John can be outvoted. This would be something he would not like. The man has a lot of money and pays well for information—anything he can get against a panel member who would vote with us so he can get them to change their vote in his favour."

Yes, the man has power and money, but all the power in the world would bring just as many enemies as friends. If you do not live for something, you will die for nothing. It was a saying I had heard once but needed help remembering the author. It was a terrific way to sum up the challenging road that lay ahead.

Journal Entry Eleven

Although the last two entries have been quite short, I feel this one will be at least double because of the amount of news I have to put in my journal.

Kate's back from her visit to Texas. All she could do was talk about this chatty American. Eira Jepson would be my Stateside counterpart. The American Appeal Houses are at least ten times the size of ours. They take their rehabilitation a lot more seriously than we do, maybe because they have a lot more states to sort out. The Stetson-wearing cowboys all walk around with guns attached to their belts. When she was shown around a typical house, there were at the very least seven floors per house, plus a physiatrist bay. The amazing thing there at any time was that they had three floors with six rooms, using the same equipment we were about to use. I felt it would be great to have him discuss rehabilitation houses with Troy. I understand their budget is much higher than ours because of the prisoners who pass through their doors each year.

On our first night home, I had missed her so much. All I wanted was to make love all night, but that didn't happen. She suffered from severe jet lag, and she also had the painters in. So, sex was off the menu for the near future. When she finished, I came on so we would have to wait for the right time to have fun.

Now for an update on our friend and colleague, Alfred. We have been given the green light so he can return home to the house once his flat has been finished in what was the old annexe. I am meeting with Troy to discuss his progress in finding out if Lillie Cole is the daughter of his late wife. He also said he has had a few leads in the hunt for his daughter and her murderous girlfriend.

Because of the events of the last few weeks, I will also get an update on completing the house's renovations. However, they were returned when we had to add the alterations to the annexe on the list. I also have a lot to discuss with Kate now, she is my new boss, to talk about the hidden messages in the files those bitches tried to get their hands on. Troy said he would also attend the meeting because of the sensitive nature of what the files held. Now we are working together we need to separate are working life from our home life. Because of our busy lives, we miss each other at night. When I come home, she will be asleep or vice versa.

I miss the sex so much. This and our move to the new house in Hanley will go ahead as soon as we have found the time to sign the contracts with the estate agency. We seemed not to have time to spend even a few minutes together since our promotions. Alfred never complained. He just got on with his job, which I had not realised was so complicated. He had so much to deal with in such a fleeting time.

Tuesday came and went, followed by Wednesday. I had no choice but to put the brakes on. I needed sex. I needed my girlfriend to spend more than five minutes with me. On Thursday evening, I had to arrange a meeting with my girlfriend, which felt strange, to say the least. I made us a lovely steak dinner with asparagus leaves and new potatoes. I bought several bottles of red wine to drink with our meal. Once the meal was served, we ate together while taking the time to talk about anything other than work.

After finishing the meal, I put the dishes in the dishwasher while Kate gave us both a relaxing bath. Twenty minutes later, we were top and tailing each other in the hot steaming bath, taking turns to wash each other all over. Once we had finished, our bodies looked like red hot prunes, our skin had tightened so much because of our time in the bath. Once we retired to the bedroom to dry each other, Kate pulled out a blindfold; it was quite a surprise. All I could hear was her taking something from our wardrobe. As she re-joined me on the bed, she kissed me down my neck. This was something I had missed. Just the gentle kisses at the base of my neckline were a major turn-on. When she handed me a toy, it felt quite bulky, with several ridges. Just the size of it surprised me. When she allowed me to remove my blindfold, I saw what seemed like a large white bag full of new toys for us to play with.

Returning to feeling the ridged toy, it was at least twice the size of our regular strap-on dildo. Although this didn't attach a strap, it had two different endings. Kate informed me her American friend had taken her to a sex supermarket—something I had never seen—where she had bought several toys. As she opened the bag, there must have been at least twelve different-sized dildos, several bottles of spray with different flavours to spray on clits, and what looked like a ridged cushion. This, she said, was the cushion of dreams.

When she ask me to take hold of it? It was quite heavy, but the remote control had several buttons. What shocked me more was the price I felt she deliberately left on the device: three thousand eight hundred dollars. I was shocked she had spent so much on her credit card. She asked me to sit on it, showing me why it was worth every penny. As she turned the device on, she asked me to stay still. When the ridged pillow moved, I felt a powerful surge just around the edges of my fanny. The more it moved up and down, the wetter I became. In no time at all, I was screaming with pure pleasure, making Kate laugh. I had felt nothing like it before. When she told me I had only tried the second of the five buttons on the device, I knew we would have a lot of fun with such a machine.

This was something I had missed—spending quality time with the woman I loved with all my heart. Toy after toy, spray after spray, we tried them out, giving them all a rating out of ten. It made us both realise we had missed each other.

Now she had Lorcan's job. She found it involved a lot of travel and a lot of learning about how different countries treated their prisoners in terms of rehabilitation. As we took a breather to eat some ice cream, we discussed our move and the thought of buying modern furniture. When she pulled out her diary, I was a bit disappointed that it was only to find a date we could get together to sign the contracts. It made me quite happy. Yes, we both had busy careers. We both needed to earn the pennies to afford our alternative lifestyle together. We had to promise each other that we would spend quality time together.

When we returned to the bedroom to make love again, I wanted to see how Kate did on the vibrating cushion. As I played about with the many settings, I would laugh at her reaction when I moved the buttons up and down. Several hours went by in a blink of an eye. We certainly made up for all the sex sessions we had missed because of work. The number of orgasms we had was amazing. It was not until the wee hours that we fell asleep in each other's arms as we used to when we first got together. Although we had not been together that long, we knew we wanted to spend the rest of our lives together, which meant marriage. As Kate slept, I looked at page after page about women marrying other women. The proposals and the rules differed from when a woman married a man. I wish I had Alfred here to talk to about it. I knew he was only a phone call away, but I quickly removed my search history so my girlfriend would not see my recent searches on gay marriage.

The next morning was soon upon us. Yes, we had had a brilliant night together. The only problem was moving. Kate's head was between my legs, which was where she had been just after the fast-paced dawn was approaching. I also had to admit the bedroom stunk of raw sexual energy. Moving her head slowly so I could get up from the bed, I needed a shower to wash away our sins from our several trips to heaven and back again. I tried not to disturb her, but I did with a bang when I fell over one of the large dildos, banging my knee on the bedframe. When Kate roused herself too quickly from her slumber, she looked at me with one eye open, the other still firmly closed, with sleep crystals in the corner of her left eye. I apologised, but she was gone as she collapsed back into the sleep her body needed.

Picking up several toys from the floor, including the one I had stubbed my toe on, I made my way to the bathroom to take a refreshing wake-up shower. Placing the cum-soaked toys in the sink, I pulled back the shower curtain and stepped in. Turning the tap on, I allowed the hot water to cascade down my body, as I needed to feel awake once more. After twenty minutes, I turned the shower off and stepped out onto the mat. I sang to myself as I dried my body with one of Kate's fluffy towels again.

As I returned to the bedroom, all I could hear was grunting from my girlfriend beneath the quilt. Picking up what was left of the spray bottles and the rest of the toys from the floor, I left my lover to get some sleep, knowing we both had a busy day full of meetings ahead. I returned to the bathroom and chucked the empty spray containers in the bathroom bin before washing the various dildos and other sex toys we had played with the previous evening. The only one I could not wash under the sink because of its size was the expensive vibrating cushion my girlfriend had brought back with her from Texas.

Once I had finished giving the cushion a good wipe over, I took it back to the bedroom. After briefly returning to the bathroom to retrieve the other toys, I returned to the bedroom in the hope that Kate would be ready to get up. After putting the toys back in their respective resting places, I put my hand under the covers to grab a leg. As I pulled it, all I could hear was a slight moan. Pulling it again, I heard the word "spoilt sport." On my third and final pull, she squealed. She was getting up now please leave me alone. Leaving her to wake up, I walked from the bedroom to the kitchen to put the coffee on. I knew she would want it after her shower.

Calling out her name, I heard nothing. Returning to the bedroom, I found the quilt lying in a crumpled heap on the floor. Putting my coffee down on the coffee stand, I stripped the bed. The wet stains on the sheets showed we both had a great night. I placed the quilt cover, damp sheet, and pillowcases in the wash basket. I drank a little more of my hot coffee before looking for clean bedding to put back on the bed. Stepping back into the hallway, I could hear my lover trying her best to strangle the cat as she sang what was a familiar pop song.

Part Three

Journal Entry Twelve

A few short hours later, I was sorting out the itinerary for the forthcoming meeting between Kate, Mr. Castle, and me, which should cover several topics.

The meeting could take several hours because we must discuss several items:

A: Hidden Files/Need for Information

B: Lillie Cole/Who Is She

C: Sir John Stephenson/Future Panel Meetings

D: Alfred/Bonnie

E: Future Business of the House

F: Priory Lane Inspection

G: Funding Proposals

H: Anything Else

I also understood this would be the first time I would meet Mrs. Wish, Troy's private secretary. She had worked for him for several years.

As soon as I filed the paperwork, I prepared the bottles of fresh water and the stronger drinks if necessary, for after the meeting. Leaving the printer behind, I walked across the hallway before knocking on my girlfriend's office. I waited out of respect for her position of command until she allowed me to come in.

On entering the room, she was on the phone with Mrs. Wish. It seemed Mr. Castle would not be long before we could start our meeting. While we waited, we had the opportunity to discuss allowing ourselves a time slot so we could sign the new property paperwork at the estate agents in Hanley.

Looking at my watch, I knew we needed the meeting to start on time if we were going to make that trip. I also wanted to take another private trip, but if I had time, that could wait until we were finished for the day. I knew I would need to make an excuse for why I needed to see my friend George at the garage.

When I decided I wanted to look for a decent engagement ring, I made up my mind to propose to Kate. Shortly afterward, we saw Mrs. Wish and Mr. Castle enter the House. We left Kate's office and headed to the new boardroom next to her office so we could begin our meeting on time.

As I sat in the new, comfortable leather chair, it showed the budget had been spent well. Shuffling the papers, I felt a little nervous because this would be my first meeting as the Receptionist, bringing a small tear to my left eye. When Kate noticed, she passed me a few tissues to compose myself. Using a small silver bell I began the meeting this made it sound quite official, as though we were introducing ourselves to the world. We recorded all the meetings so everything would be open and professional while I ran the House.

However, this section was more for Troy to discuss the hidden files and why they were needed. I opened the floor to allow him to discuss the first section of our meeting. Just as he was about to speak, he allowed Mrs. Wish to hand Kate and me a file that looked quite old. It made me wonder if it had come from the Library of Souls before the new dust prevention system was installed.

Once she handed us both a copy of the file, she asked us to wear protective gloves. Mrs. Wish told us the paper had an acid-based touch within its pages, which could burn us if held for too long. After we put on the gloves, Troy told us Frank Davies had compiled the pages when he was on the panel. This was well before there was ever a tariff-setting panel.

Inside its pages, it discussed his hopes for the adoption of the panel. He had arranged several meetings with officials from the justice department of the Home Office. We saw the same report about his suspicions that someone was altering his work as we turned the page.

Troy asked us to pay close attention to the two reports about a young woman named Susan Farmer. The files date back to June of nineteen fifty-seven. You can see two different versions of the same report from the file, which showed that the original had been tampered with in not one but three separate places.

First, according to the first report, the girl's age was sixteen; according to the adapted file, she was twenty-three. Secondly, her crime was poisoning her uncle with the help of her older sister. The older man had won on the pools, and they thought he had a sizable amount of money. The girl took her own sister's life alongside the woman's fiancée to gain the total amount of seven hundred and fifty thousand pounds, which turned out to be an error because of a mistake with the pools' computer regenerating old winning slips.

When the error was fixed, it was because too many people had the same number of X's on the form. The prize amount was reduced from the sizable seven hundred and fifty thousand top prize to a small five-pound win. This entire file had been changed to suggest the girl had killed a doctor alias a certain overweight man had used in the past.

Because the girl was tried as an adult, the recommendations were altered, so she received a death sentence instead of a much lighter sentence due to her age. We needed to know why he felt he had to interfere with Mr. Davies's case file. Troy said it might have been the simple idea of interpreting the rehabilitation act, having had many arguments over the act with Sir John, who felt that once a person had crossed the line, they should be punished—not given some "piss-arsed" sentence in hopes they could rejoin society once rehabilitated. Guilty was guilty, plain and simple, with no redemption for their crime.

Maybe it was his way of trying to stop the beginning of the rehabilitation law used today when dealing with the criminal mind. We all knew the man was only interested in helping himself. The problem we all had was that he had many friends in high places, who received bribes to look the other way whenever he wanted to do something.

Kate and I also needed to understand the connection between the three case files that were removed from their original locations to the dust-free room within the annexe. All three files had been moved yet again because of the renovation work and the changes to the building after Alfred's attack. Once

Mrs. Wish had removed the tampered files from in front of us, she asked us to remove our gloves.

After we handed her the gloves, she placed them in the bin. She then passed us another set of protective gloves to wear. Wondering what she was up to, I had no choice but to ask, yet the woman gave me a simple look. I understood I should wait for an explanation rather than try to jump the gun. Apologising for my eagerness, the woman nodded her acceptance.

Once she saw we were wearing our new gloves, she showed us a sample and explained why we needed them. Using a simple piece of paper, she took a spray bottle from her left jacket pocket. At that moment, she reminded me of Q from the James Bond movies, attempting to demonstrate an invention for a spy to use on his next mission.

When the paper was sprayed with just a little of the liquid, it looked like any other soaked piece of paper. I asked Kate to turn off the lights. Once my girlfriend had done so, she returned to her seat. We could all see the paper had turned a violet colour, which Mrs. Wish told us was ultraviolet. After removing her protective gloves, she picked up the paper from the table, touched it several times, and then deposited it in the bin.

She asked me to turn the lights back on, but we could see nothing on her hands. When she used an ultraviolet wand over her hands, we could see the stains the paper had made. Troy looked at me before asking if I had held the three files. Wondering why he would ask, he told Mrs. Wish to use the ultraviolet wand on my hands. They turned the same colour as hers had.

I could not understand why, since I had showered after touching the files with Alfred and Lorcan only hours before they were both attacked. Troy informed me of the added security: he had the files sprayed with ultraviolet spray. Even if you showered or bathed, the evidence would remain hidden on your hands until a second spray was used to remove it.

To demonstrate, Mrs. Wish took a second bottle from her pocket and sprayed the liquid generously over her hands. When using the wand, the evidence was now gone. Although I had protective gloves on, the wand still did its job, which I found strange. When the Asian woman allowed me to remove my gloves, she sprayed my hands with the same liquid.

Once again, she used the wand, and the ultraviolet evidence was gone. She asked me once more to put my gloves back on. Then she passed us some glasses to wear, which Kate and I thought was strange. She mentioned that these were not ordinary reflective materials; they were ultraviolet detector glasses. Then she asked Kate to retrieve the files from her office.

On her return, we could see they were soaked in ultraviolet liquid. I asked if my girlfriend had known about the spray when collecting the three files from their storage places in the annexe. When Mrs. Wish said no, I asked Kate to remove her gloves. Picking up the wand, I saw her hands were also covered with the ultraviolet spray. When Mrs. Wish used the second spray, I could see it was gone because I was wearing the reflective glasses.

Once Kate was given another pair of gloves, we all looked through the files. Troy informed us not to consider the files important when looked at separately. As he turned the three files to their relevant back pages, they each had some writing on them, but it was unintelligible when viewed one at a time. Only when they were put side by side could we read the hidden message. Kate and I knew this message got Lorcan killed and Alfred attacked, so its importance had to remain hidden.

Troy surprised us by showing us that when they were put together in the correct order, there were not one but three separate time-coded discs for John Smith, Brian Cross, and Jenny Louise Harper. When I picked up the first disc, it differed from the old 5.25 and 8-inch discs we had seen. It was more like a thick, grey-looking diskette with several ridges on it.

When Mr. Castle asked us to come with him to the new control station, which was now on the third floor, we knew there must be something important stored on the diskettes. When we arrived at the control room, we had no choice but to watch the awful time-coded recording, which revealed how Lorcan had lost his life and how our colleague had life-altering injuries inflicted on both his hands and eyes.

Mr. Castle told us not to go into that room but to walk past it to the locked room next door. As we arrived, he pulled a key chain from around his neck and used it on the door. After he invited us in, we found this new room was twice the size of the old control room next door. I was surprised to see a more complex machine in front of us.

The video screens were twice as large as those in the other room. The control deck looked as though it had far more buttons to touch or press. As he asked his secretary, Cully Wish, to pass me the new manual, he said we would get used to the new console in no time.

He asked us to sit in front of the console and turn the key on the operating deck. The difference was obvious: this machine would not work without the key inserted. Passing me the spare key, he asked me to put the first of the three ridged-looking disks into the tray. He then gave me the other two disks, which he also asked me to insert. Once I had done as he asked, he pulled a final diskette from his pocket, which surprised both Kate and me.

Mr. Castle explained this was the control diskette. He asked me for a password. Looking at Kate, I didn't know what to say, but the word *love* came to mind when I looked into her eyes. He then asked Kate for a simple code, so she gave him a combination of our birth dates. Turning to Cully Wish, he asked her to add another password. She used the name *Calamari*, which was quite an easy password. Then he entered another mix of numbers—fourteen six fifty-seven. I knew this came from the Susan Farmer case file.

Seconds later, the room went dark, and the monitors turned on. A female voice was heard. When a face appeared on the screen, it was of a young, attractive woman in her mid-twenties. "Hello there, my name is A.R.I.E.S.," she said. This stands for *Automatic Recording Interactive Enhanced Security System*. It gives added security when accessing sensitive data streams from around the globe.

When the computer asked us for our ID cards, I could see that this software was extraordinary and well worth its million-pound price tag. As a drawer opened, we put our cards in one by one. The woman on the screen read our names before verifying our identities. By accessing the sensitive material we had provided when taking our security protocol card test, once named, it gave us our cards back.

When the machine asked if we would like to see the files added to the machine, I said yes a bit too loudly before apologising to the group, feeling like a spy in a movie downloading sensitive information.

The screen went blank for a second before playing the first time-coded video hidden within the three files. We could see the recording had happened some time ago. It showed a large office-like room with a roaring fire to the right of the large leather chair in which a portly man was sitting.

I tried my best to remain silent while we viewed the film. It showed three men in the room: the first was Sir John, the second was the sniffling rat Cecil "The Hitman" Higgins—the most corrupt barrister in the country—and the third was a tall, stout-looking man in his early forties.

Sir John smoked a huge cigar while sitting in his chair. It was Mr. Higgins talking to the third man: "Right, Tony, it is agreed Mr. Stephenson will loan you one million pounds for three months. When the loan period ends, you will return the money with a further £500,000 in restitution. Do you have anything to say before signing the agreement?"

Kate observed the man, who seemed to be swaying as he tried to listen to the corrupt barrister. Never do a deal when intoxicated was a simple but effective rule. You could sign your life away without knowing it.

When the tape stopped, I felt quite concerned for the man. Looking across the room to where Mr. Castle was sitting with a remote control in his hands, I noticed he controlled the machine. He mentioned the third man was a salesperson named Tony

Harper, who had worked for Sir John for several years doing anything the man asked. The problem was, Tony was a known drunk and a gambling addict.

He had always wanted to run his own business, helping people fill in their tax records. All he needed was a sizable amount of money to get started. Having no choice but to ask his boss for the funds—because his credit rating had fallen through the floor due to his regular drinking and gambling at the dog track—Tony had turned to Sir John. At one time, the bank would have offered him a loan with a sizable interest rate, but over six months, his credit rating went from 997 to 327, which barred him from normal credit. After watching his credit line decrease, he thought he could win it all back.

I feel I should mention here that Tony used to beat his wife if she didn't give him money to lose at the track. When the woman had enough, she stood up to him and asked for a divorce. He never thought she would give up on their ten-year marriage. One of the case files was about the man's daughter, Jenny, who had witnessed the regular beatings over the years. This left the young girl with severe mental health issues and a raging temper boiling on insanity. We are not here to discuss her case this morning; I used her case to hide these video files.

Just like the other two, they also held media-related files. As Mr. Castle pressed the button on the remote once more, we returned to watching the video. When Tony was asked again if he could see any reason he could not fulfill his end of the agreement in the time allowed, he moved forward before collapsing to the floor.

The portly man stood up from his chair to look at the unconscious Tony on his office carpet. Turning to his friend Cecil, he had no choice but to ask how many drugs he had slipped into Tony's drink.

"I looked at the packet your friend supplied. It said to add two capsules to any drink, when it actually said two-quarters of a single pill to be added only."

"You haven't killed him, have you?"

"Any drug-taking in his class has trial and error."

"How will he agree to the loan terms if he's dead?"

Watching the shady barrister check the passed-out man for a pulse, he soon confirmed Tony was merely asleep.

"You'd better wake him up. I want this agreement signed this evening."

Not wanting to upset his major client, Cecil tried to wake Tony with little success because of the strength of the drug he had used. He had no choice but to tell the portly man, who had returned to sitting in his favorite chair smoking another cigar, that he had failed for the night but promised to "resurrect" Tony and try again the following evening.

This seemed to anger the man. Within a minute, he informed the barrister he would give him one more night, but he would only pay half the man's bill due to him not getting Tony to sign the paperwork. He also demanded a special set of terms and conditions be added. When Cecil found out what they were, he had no choice but to agree.

The portly man passed him the updated terms he wanted added to the contract. Once Cecil read them, he had to tell Sir John nobody would ever agree to such terms.

"I don't give a damn. Just write it up and get the idiot to sign it, or he won't get a bloody penny."

"Please, Mr. Stephenson, you can't make me do this. Tony's a friend."

"Do you want to work in this town ever again?"

"Yes, I want to work, but this contract isn't workable."

"I was told you could get anything or anyone to sign an agreement. Am I wrong?"

The man looked shocked, but he also knew he needed to work. He wanted to earn money to feed his wife and seven children and give his two mistresses a sizable allowance to keep them sweet.

When Mr. Castle stopped the tape again, Kate asked him if he knew what the small print held that made the barrister shake in his boots. When Cully handed us both an enlarged copy of the agreement, it was clear nobody would ever sign such a downright evil piece of legislation. I knew the portly man was all for himself. The suggestion that a man needed to agree to his family being killed if he didn't honor the agreement within the allotted time limit was pure evil. Yet, thinking about Tony, there was not much redeeming about him.

How such a dangerous individual could have anything to do with the panel was beyond me. Troy had wanted the man evicted from the panel for quite some time because of his irregular and immoral activities, but the man was going nowhere because of the number of illicit friends within the sixteen-household community.

Mr. Castle also felt he needed to mention that when he had discussed the issue privately with a few members, he was always told the same roundabout answer: they owed the man a favor or money, or he had something on them, and they were not going against such a powerful man. One member told me in strict confidence it was not the man they were afraid of but "the bitch he had a connection to." When he said that, Kate and I knew exactly who he was talking about. The look of stress and annoyance was felt whenever her name came up.

Returning to the illicit contract with its not-so-friendly terms and conditions, I asked if Tony ever did sign the contract.

"Let me continue with the last part of the tape," Mr. Castle said. "This will answer your question."

"Cecil, is the man awake, or do I have to reduce your payment yet again?"

"Yes, I gave him plenty of coffee with just a touch of the drug you asked me to give him."

"Will he sign?"

"I told him about the added terms, and he agreed to sign immediately."

"Excuse me?"

"I repeatedly told him about the added clause. All my friend would say was the woman had kicked him into the long grass. He also said none of this will matter because he'll get your money back to you within the month."

"One month. The cocky little shit doesn't realise I meant it. If he can get the money back to me in time, I suppose I'll have to get the girls to do something else. Right, Cecil, have the contract typed up and on my desk by Friday at the latest."

When the tape stopped, I looked at Troy with a worried expression. I asked him about the young girl, knowing I might have to interview her one day. All he would say was that she was a special case with a severe, uncontrollable rage issue whenever she thought about her father.

Seeing how much time we had spent on just the first tape, I asked for a one-hour rest break to eat and refresh ourselves before continuing. Kate agreed because she could not understand why Tony Harper would have signed the form—even if it had been for a trillion dollars. She would never sign something so evil. Troy mentioned he had a little information that could wait until after lunch. Just the look on his face showed it was not going to be good news.

Journal Entry Thirteen

After lunch, we had no choice but to return to the new control room. While sitting in the comfortable console chairs, Troy told us the news about Mr. Harper. With his gambler's optimism, Tony felt he could double or even triple the money loaned by Sir John—even though the hefty price tag of his family's life was now attached to it.

Once he had the money in his bank account, he headed straight for the greyhound track in East Danby. He had several contacts there who could supposedly give him sure-fire tips on securing the extra money he needed. What could go wrong? He had a full million pounds at his disposal. He was meeting up with his long-time gambling partner, Gina Wild, head nurse of the Priory's third floor. All Tony could see was a successful night in front of him. At first, his tips were like gold dust—everything he picked came in. As the money rolled in, he was soon up by a cool two hundred thousand in one night.

Drinking to his success was his downfall. He didn't know when to turn off the tap. After a few too many losing bets, he had loaned Gina some of his winnings so she could pay off a few known loan sharks. Near the end of the night, he won big. He let his close friend keep what was left of her share, and he headed home to celebrate with his sister-in-law, Elizabeth, or Betty for short.

He wanted her to get out of bed to celebrate with him as soon as he arrived home, throwing money at her while carrying yet another bottle of gin. Betty had only taken him in because she felt sorry for him. For some unknown reason, she could only see the good in the man—even when she had no choice but to visit her sister in the hospital after Tony had beaten the woman to a pulp.

"Men would be men. All they need is to be kept in line. If you obey the simple rules of courtship, nothing can go wrong."

We could all see where this story was heading, but we felt we would not understand the entire picture without hearing the whole story. You could see the eager look in Mr. Castle's eyes— he wanted to tell us what happened to the money, to Mr. Harper, and to the contract. Most of all, he wanted us to know how this tragic story ended.

As he continued, he explained that a few short hours later, Mr. Harper would never see the light of day again. The problem was, Tony had listened to Betty's rules when she took him in: no drinking, no swearing, and no beating his girlfriend. Because he was in such a good mood, he wanted to break all three rules in one night. Betty warned him to calm down, but he only shouted at her. When she ignored him, he saw red and swore at her, then threw an empty bottle of gin at her head.

"Come on, bitch, I want some fun. Let's fucking drink to my success."

The problem here was his mentality—he had allowed the drink to take over all reason.

"I'm going to save your sister's life, even if the bitch wants a divorce."

He pulled the contract out of his pocket when Betty asked what it meant. He also had a few banknotes he had collected from the teller at the track. When Betty saw the extra terms of the contract, she called him a fool.

"Nobody would sign such a thing; you are a fucking fool."

"Ah, you're breaking your own rules. Come on, drink with me. I'm feeling wonderful."

He grabbed her by the hair when she said no for the second time.

"Come on, I want some fun."

"Get off me, you idiot. How could you use my sister as a tool to get your hands on some money to lose at the track?"

"Fuck her. She wants a divorce."

"Tony, I'm going to bed. You can sleep this off on the couch."

"I'm not tired yet. I want to drink. Come on, bitch, let's drink to my success."

"You're bloody crazy. How could you have used my sister as leverage? If you do not pay the money back, this man may kill your wife."

"I can get the money back plus loads more before the month is out."

"You don't understand. Have you read this bloody contract?"

"No, I didn't need to. I have tuition."

"You have what?"

"I've got tuition. Gina told me so."

"No! You have not been at the track with that pisshead."

"Come on, Betty, let's have some fun. I won several races with her help."

"You promised me you would stop drinking. You promised me you would not gamble anymore. And what do I find you doing? Not only are you gambling for cash, but you're also gambling with my sister's life."

"The man would not pay up if I didn't agree to those terms and conditions. I can win the money back in a month with my tuition."

"Your *tuition*? Don't you mean *intuition*, you drunken fool?"

"Why are you saying these things to me when you know I'll have to hit you to stop you from talking like this?"

"Hit me. It'll be the last thing you do."

"No one can tell me what I can or cannot do, Betty Harper. Take this for your troubles."

Troy had seen the police record, which he pulled from his briefcase to show us. As I looked down the page, it was clear Tony was dead. The fool had beaten Betty senseless, but with her last effort, she stabbed him in the heart before collapsing to the floor.

Looking at Kate's reaction, I saw the horror on her face as she asked Troy about the woman. He explained that when the police broke into the flat, they found Tony Harper dead next to Betty's cold, battered body.

I was shocked. Not only had the man signed his wife's life away, but he had battered her sister to death and died in the process because he was blind drunk. When asked what happened to the money, the police only found half of his dog-track winnings. To this day, the million-pound contract, with its extra terms and conditions—putting a death sentence on Mr. Harper's ex-wife and her family—didn't appear.

I didn't want to know, but I needed to know the answer, which took a lot of work. The man's wife didn't even last a month. When Troy Castle informed us that once the contract failed to be paid back in full with interest, Sir John was heard saying, "All is fair in love and war. It was simply business, my dear." This showed the man was callous, but it also seemed he was above the law for some unknown reason.

Having to ask for another break because I needed to see George about something important, Kate asked me if I had a problem. I had no choice but to lie to her, even though I hated it, but it was all for a noble cause. Troy seemed a little put out when he saw how much of the meeting we still had to discuss, reminding me we had a lot more to get through.

I had to lie once more, telling him the man was off on his holidays the following day, and he was the only person I trusted to fix my car. When Kate looked at me with a puzzled expression, I knew I needed to get out of there before my lover realised I was lying. Mr. Castle asked how long I would need. I really needed all day, but I said I would only need an hour for a first look at the jewellery store. When my girlfriend wanted to come with me to sign the paperwork for the new property, I could not say yes—even though the garage was right around the corner from the jewellery store.

Needing a get-out clause, I pretended I had just received a text from the garage. The man's flight was rearranged, and he would see me on his return. Luckily, they all believed me.

As I sat down next to my girlfriend, she looked at me again with a puzzled expression. When Troy pressed the button on the remote control, the second tape began to play. Watching the tape, I saw it was a low-grade CCTV recording. Then the woman named A.R.I.E.S. came back on the viewscreen, informing us she could enhance the video, but it would take some time. When Troy asked if the third tape was the same quality, the machine answered yes.

Noting the time on his watch, he decided there was no point in watching something so low-grade. He suggested we suspend the rest of the meeting until ten o'clock the following day. That would give the machine enough time to work on the two remaining videos. Even though I didn't want to admit I was relieved by the second abrupt break, I knew Kate and I could take the opportunity to sign the contract in Hanley.

When we made our way to the underground car park, we briefly discussed our upcoming journey. I wanted to go to the high-street jeweller to look for a nice engagement ring so I could ask Kate to marry me. She mentioned she wanted to pick up a few items from the Brookfield shopping centre. So, we agreed to drive our own cars once we had signed the alternative housing forms and paid the fees. We would see each other later, back at the house.

I kissed her on the lips before leaving together to make our way to the estate agency. Twenty minutes later, we arrived in unison outside the agency. Walking in together, we spoke with a young woman named Heather, who informed us the house we were interested in was situated in a lovely area of the town. We were invited to sign on the dotted line once we had paid our deposit and agreed to pay the rest within six weeks.

After Kate and I signed the agreement, the woman smiled at us, clearly due a large commission. We didn't mind, because the house we wanted was lovely. We had so many ideas for transforming each room of the four-bedroom property. Because of the extra space, one room could be an office so we could work from home. Another could be a place where we could relax, light incense sticks, and make love on the large rugs we intended to buy. That would still leave our bedroom, and we could even make a "pleasure room dungeon" if we fancied a bit of BDSM. The possibilities were nearly endless.

As we left the agency, we kissed each other with excited glee. Kate left me there to shop while I went to the jeweller. I just hoped she would say yes. Arriving at the store, I must have walked around looking at everything with a budget in mind, but the only ring I felt Kate would love was twice my budget ceiling.

Leaving the shop, I felt quite disappointed with myself. Turning to take one last look, I saw in the reflection of the window a perfect diamond staring back at me. Checking its price, it was just over my budget.

Was my girlfriend the woman I wanted to spend the rest of my life with? Yes. Did she make me happy? Yes, again. So, was she worth the extra grand? Most definitely.

I walked back into the shop and came back out with the perfect ring for my beautiful bride-to-be in no time. Next on my shopping list was something special for tea, a large bottle of bubbly, and her favorite flowers. What could go wrong? Once I bought everything on my shopping list, I headed home to propose.

You can rehearse once, twice, or even three times, but my nerves returned with a bang. I wanted the night to be special for both of us. When I arrived at our house, Kate's car was already there. Getting the items from the back of the car, I made my way inside. Putting down everything on the table, I could smell something coming from the kitchen. Was that fresh salmon? Walking into the kitchen, I saw a pan bubbling with rich, dark green savoy cabbage, along with fresh asparagus and new potatoes on the stove. Opening the fridge, I noticed a bottle of the finest bubbly cooling.

What was going on here? Making my way out of the kitchen, I spotted the first of several rose petals on the stairs. As I slowly walked upstairs, I heard music from the bedroom—the music we always played when making love. Following the trail of rose petals into the bedroom, I saw the bed was freshly made, scattered with rose petals across the duvet cover.

As I turned around, Kate appeared behind me, covering my eyes with her hands. The woman of my dreams lifted my hair and kissed the nape of my neck, which she knew I loved. I did as she asked when she told me to turn around slowly. The moment I met her gaze, she was already down on one knee with a large diamond ring in her hands, asking me to marry her. All the nerves left me in seconds. I said yes to her proposal before helping her up, smiling with absolute joy and happiness.

As we kissed, I wanted to strip her bare and make love to her right then and there. I could not believe we had both had the same thought at the same time, which proved we were made for each other. We went downstairs to have the special meal she had spent so much effort cooking. When she noticed the flowers in the hallway alongside the food I had bought, she smiled.

I then pulled out the ring from my pocket to show her that I had also been planning to propose. We kissed each other passionately. It was only then I noticed we had both bought the exact same ring. That afternoon, Kate had purchased hers from another branch of the same jeweller in Brookfield's shopping centre.

Once she served the meal—one she had slaved over in the name of love—we took our seats at the table. I realized this was no ordinary tea with the woman I loved; this was a meal I never dreamed I would experience, given how my nerves used to get the better of me. Yet since meeting her, something changed within me. Now, three months later, we were having our engagement tea. Yes, we had plenty to talk about and much to arrange, but for one night, we shut out the world and all the problems we were forced to deal with because of our jobs. Making our way to the bedroom to make love, we knew it was more than love. It was a desire in our hearts to fulfill each other's dreams—together, forevermore.

Journal Entry Fourteen

We were both asleep the following morning when the phone shook me awake.

"Hello, I'm sorry for calling you this early. Mr. Castle wants to crack on with the itinerary. Therefore, can you meet him in the A.R.I.E.S. security station within an hour?"

I could not believe it when I looked at the clock—it was not even six a.m. As Kate moved closer to me for warmth, I had no choice but to tell her about the phone call. She looked up at me in disbelief, then turned back over to sleep. Shaking her once more, all my wife-to-be could do was shift her body away from me until she nearly fell out of bed, muttering something foul under the covers. She pulled the covers back so I could see her face.

"Does he know what bloody time it is?"

I didn't know what to say to her, but we did have an afternoon off.

"One afternoon off doesn't deserve a call this bloody early in the morning,"

she complained.

I had to agree before inviting her to join me in the shower to wash away our sins from the night before. Two hours later, we stood outside the control room—but nobody was there. Kate looked at me, annoyed at being dragged into work this early.

"Where is he? I'm knackered."

I had to consider her feelings because I didn't want to upset my girl. I just hoped it was not a dream and that I had not dragged her out of bed for nothing. Luckily, it was not. I spotted Mrs. Wish walking through the reception doorway, followed by Mr. Castle, using the newly installed lift at the back of the building. I could see Mrs. Wish's hands were covered in oil residue, so I had no choice but to ask why.

She explained they had been on their way when a fast car nearly ran them off the road. All I could wonder was if the car had been a yellow sports car. Cully said she had spent the last twenty minutes changing a tire, which was why her hands were covered in grease. Excusing herself so she could wash her hands and freshen up, she left us.

As we took our seats, Kate served everyone some strong coffee. Troy apologized for the early call, explaining he had always been a man who liked to rise with the sunrise. Just the look on my girl's face when he said that was a picture.

When Mrs. Wish returned, I inquired if the two tapes the machine had been enhancing were ready. Mr. Castle checked and said it was all set. It made me wonder what was on the second and third tapes that needed to be hidden.

When the second tape started, it looked like a CCTV camera view showing what appeared to be an entrance to a park. Although the high-tech machine had enhanced the footage, the video quality still left much to be desired, and the audio was strange. Nonetheless, we all watched to see what it showed.

The footage revealed the camera moving up and down a pathway. The clock on the tape said it was 3:37 a.m. Standing up to fetch myself and my colleagues a second cup of coffee before returning to my seat, I wondered why this footage was important to the portly man. Looking across at Mr. Castle, I could see he was keen to understand the tape's relevance to our investigation.

Just then, I saw what looked like that now-familiar yellow sports car pulling up. Two women got out of the vehicle. They entered the park and walked down the path to meet someone. I was taken aback when I saw that idiot Karl Thornton stepping out of the bushes into view. The problem was the camera was on a timer, moving up and down the pathway a few meters from the entrance into the park and then back again. Luckily, the three people had not noticed the camera, so they had no idea how long it might be recording them.

Although there was no audio to confirm what was being said, it was clear they were handing the idiot some money. I nearly fell off my seat when I saw they had a photo of my dad. As I recalled the court case, Karl had said he was paid to take out my father before changing his story.

When Mr. Castle pressed a button on the console, we heard some audio:

"Right, you know what to do?"

"How much is here?"

"There's plenty enough for you to have some fun with. You'll find the car parked in the car park of the Bearded Tavern.

The keys will be under the driver's front wheel. My friend here will have fixed the target's car so he must take a bus home. Do not fuck it up. The car is an expensive model. Do not race it; just get behind the wheel and drive it into the bus stop."

"I can do that. It's pretty easy."

"Once you've completed the job, keep your mouth shut or my friend here will have your guts for garters. Right, that's it. Do this right, and I'll double your money. Well, you can leave now."

Seeing the young lad run up the pathway and out of the park, I hoped I would get some information that would explain why my mum now had a practical stranger in her house, instead of a caring, loving man. As the camera returned to the two women, you could see they were deep in conversation about the car the young lad was given to use to take out my father.

"Why did you have to give the guy my car?"

"Don't worry about it, Amanda. I've already added the cost of a new car to our fee."

"The portly man said he would buy me a new car; that's nice of him."

"Well, the simple answer is that he's not. He doesn't know I'm charging him

for a new car."

"Oh, so he's not being nice to me."

"Darling, I charge the guy a flat fee. He moans about it, but I tell him

to pay up, and he does. It's quite simple."

"No, you've lost me. So, who is paying for my new car then?"

"You are, from the money I give you."

"So, you're buying me a car, then."

"Don't worry about it, darling. All you need to do is follow my instructions,

and everything will be just fine."

"Lorna, I'm not going down on you at this time in the morning."

"Did I ask you to?"

"No, but the way you're talking, it's as if you want sex."

"I always want sex, but I said it can wait until we get home."

"So why are we standing here still?"

"We're waiting for someone."

"Who?"

"A friend of a friend."

"If it's that Gabrielle, I'm going home."

"No, the portly man said I was to meet a mechanic to give him

some instructions."

"What instructions?"

"He's going to fix the car for us so if that idiot goes over forty miles

an hour, he'll simply crash—job done."

"So, who's going to pay this man for doing the job?"

"Darling, I need a favour."

"No, I'm not sucking the guy off."

"It's just a small favour, and you'll get well paid for your trouble."

"Why can't you do it?"

"No, that would be beneath me."

"So, tell me again why I've got to take some greasy guy's cock in my mouth?"

"Amanda, do you want a new car?"

"You bitch, that's blackmail."

"When did I say I was a good girl?"

"I hate you."

"No, you don't. Look, he's coming down the path right now."

"Lorna Castle, you're a bitch."

"Yes, I know, and you love it."

"Where are you going to be?"

"I'll wait in the car. Now get to work. It'll soon be over by the look of him."

"Wow, you were quick. I told you it wouldn't take long."

"He got it out, took one look at my tits, and he came all over my hand. Pass me a few of those fresh wipes. Men are only good for one thing—to get money out of. Otherwise, they're useless in bed, fart, burp, and complain a lot. They claim they're the stronger sex, but get them to give birth or have the symptoms, and they soon change their minds."

"I have never been into the creatures. I prefer the gentler sex. They have more drive, do not moan as much, and are always ready for a fun time."

"So, I'm on a promise then."

"Amanda, darling, you know I'd never refuse you."

As the tape was about to end, I was amazed at how this million-pound machine had not only enhanced the video quality but also brought the audio to life. I could see why Alfred had wanted such a machine. Just as Mr. Castle was about to stop the tape and move the meeting along to the third and final tape, the A.R.I.E.S. woman appeared on the screen to ask if we would like to see the new footage the CCTV camera had caught.

This surprised us all.

The first video highlighted a dodgy deal that went to trial. The second revealed the truth about my dad's accident, alongside the deal struck between those evil bitches and the idiot Karl Thornton. It showed that he had been about to tell the truth but changed his story for some reason. Now, the machine had found even more footage.

I asked for a break so I could use the facilities. On my return, I offered everyone another drink. Several cups were passed to me for refills. Once we were all seated, Troy pressed play again.

It showed the entrance to the park once more. As the camera moved up and down in its permitted angle, we spotted what looked like a heavy-set, tall man carrying something over his right shoulder. When he entered the park and made his way down the path, at first we could not see what he was carrying. As the camera zoomed in, it became clear it was an old rug.

I assumed he might be dumping rubbish in the overgrowth, but that was just wishful thinking. The reality was much more horrific. As the hand of a woman fell out of the rug, we realized this camera had caught the man dumping a girl's body. It also showed the name of the park—less than a minute from Kate's and my current love nest. I was so glad we were moving away soon.

I looked across at Mr. Castle to see if his reaction matched mine. He rewound the tape to try to get a clearer image of the man. Only then did Kate notice the machine was not playing with any inserted tape. The camera was showing live images from the device at the side entrance of Stanley Park Lower Glendale.

Troy began checking the machine for faults but soon realized it was working perfectly, which meant we now had not one, not two, but three killers on the loose. As we continued watching for more clues, the clock read 8:00 a.m.

With no choice but to watch, we could see the man was doing something with the body. Unfortunately, all we could see was the tall man's back. He was standing just to the far right of the camera's viewing angle. When he came into view again, I nearly fell off my chair.

The man removed the girl from the rug before placing her directly to the right of the camera, giving us an "eagle-eye" view of what he was doing. He seemed to pull some pieces of wood from inside the rug, constructing something. Once finished, he picked up the young girl's naked body and placed it on top of the wooden object, which looked like a crude cross.

Kate covered her mouth in shock when Cully shouted, "He's not about to crucify the girl, is he?" After repositioning the corpse several times, he banged nails into her feet, securing her lower half to the base of the cross. Then he nailed both of the corpse's palms. Finishing his grisly task, he drove one more nail directly between the dead woman's eyes.

When he was done, he picked up the cross as though it weighed nothing, stood it upright, and leaned it against the nearest tree. Then he seemed quite pleased with himself. He took a camera out of his pocket, snapped a photo, and, apparently satisfied, walked up the pathway. Only then could we hear him humming to himself, as if he was proud of his work.

He exited through the gates but stopped where the CCTV camera was located. The man must have seen the flashing light showing he was being watched. He climbed the pole and looked straight into the camera, moving his eye directly in front of the lens for some unknown reason, making his eye look enormous from our side.

"Hello, hello, anybody there?"

After that, he jumped back down to the ground. He must have spotted someone coming, so he ran in the other direction. Mr. Castle was in shock at what we had just witnessed. I felt sick watching the man do that to a young girl. How could we continue viewing the third tape now?

Because the location was only about ten minutes from our current building, I asked Mr. Castle for a brief break so I could see the site for myself. Kate looked at me as though I were asking to watch a live horror film. Cully said there was no way she wanted to stand just meters away from a dead girl's body.

As morbid as it was, I felt I had to see it for myself—one day I might have to interview this man to draft a report on him and his reasons for crucifying a young woman. When I explained my reasons, they understood but didn't want to accompany me, each giving a simple but valid excuse to stay behind. Kate turned her head away, and Cully said her religious beliefs forbade her from going. Troy said he wanted to continue with the meeting but allowed me to attend the scene during my lunch break.

Standing up to offer everyone a choice of refreshment, they all chose whisky. I poured them each a large glass, filling it to the brim, then resumed my seat to listen to the third tape. I just wondered what it would reveal.

Journal Entry Fifteen

After we had all taken time to consume a stiff drink (we definitely needed it after the "tall man" incident), we were ready to move on with the day's itinerary. Although the original meeting was supposed to last a few short hours, it had already taken two days. We still had several sections of the itinerary to complete, including the third tape—the last hidden file.

When Troy received a nod from each of us indicating we were ready, he pressed the button on the console. When it started, it looked like a scene from a film you might see at the cinema—an old-fashioned pub scene from a war movie, just before the brave soldier went to war. The pub was crowded, and wartime music played on the radio. I could see my girlfriend taking notes of everything she observed, while Cully fixed her eyes on the viewing monitor. Mr. Castle's hand hovered just above the "view" button, as though anticipating we might see something we had no choice but to witness.

Ten minutes passed, and I still could not understand why we were seeing the same scene. Nothing was happening, so why was this tape among the three hidden files? Then a man and a woman entered the pub, laughing and joking with each other. At least it was something different than just a pub playing old tunes on the radio.

When the view shifted to show the reflection of the pair in the bar's mirror, it was a welcome change. Then the viewing monitor went dark for a moment before coming back to life, showing the same scene but with no music this time. Even the bartender had changed. It seemed to be daytime now.

The man from the previous evening entered the pub, approached the bar, and flashed some identification. He asked if the pub had any CCTV. When the bartender asked why, the man showed him a picture. The bartender stepped back a little, gasping as though shocked by whatever he saw in the photo.

From the image now on-screen, we could see the man from the previous evening showing the photo to the pub's regulars. Only when one of them was handed the picture did it reveal the same laughing woman—but now she appeared battered, with a phallic object inserted where the sun doesn't shine. Once again, Cully had to ask for another drink to calm her nerves. After I refilled both her cup and mine, I continued watching.

The footage showed the pub regulars staring strangely at the police officer as he took back the photo. When the officer asked loudly if anyone had seen the woman the previous evening, some of the regulars remained silent, just staring at him, as though they remembered seeing him with the now-dead girl.

The camera went dark again for a moment, then returned a minute later. This time, we saw another pub scene—people singing along to the music, appearing to enjoy themselves. The pleasant scene was interrupted when a man and a woman entered together. They looked like a normal couple until the man turned towards the camera. We recognized him as the man from the previous evening with the deceased victim. The scene played out for several minutes before going dark once more.

When the system came back on, it was the same pub again, but during the day. The man from the previous evening returned, showing the regulars a similar photo of yet another woman he had been with the other night. The only difference was, this time he had another man with him. When they showed the photo to the men in the pub, they pointed to the first man, saying he had been with the now-deceased woman. When the other man said that the first man was the lead detective on the case, Troy had no choice but to pause the tape.

I realised the tape was about ex-detective John Smith. The footage showed he was the man with the woman, so how could he claim he was innocent? We had all seen the evidence not once but twice; what more proof would anyone need of the man's guilt?

After a group discussion on the evidence we were shown, Mr. Castle pressed the button once again. The tape now displayed interview room footage from a police station: the same man we had all seen earlier was being questioned by senior detectives.

The tape ran for fifteen minutes, showing the man repeatedly stating he was innocent. Photo after photo displayed to him showed another dead girl. Then the tape went dark once again.

We looked over his preliminary case notes, which indicated he had been guilty of taking eighteen women for a drink in a local pub—only for them to be found beaten to death the very next day, with what looked like a phallic-shaped candle sticking out of their anus.

When the machine was turned on once again, extra footage was shown from a different angle, and we watched with fascination. The video this time showed the first two scenes again.

It showed the man in the pub with the victims, but because of this new angle, we could see another man looking in through the window. When the camera zoomed in, we could see that the man reflected in the window and the man at the bar looked similar. Was this evidence to support Mr. Smith's claim of innocence or not?

Once Mr. Castle switched the tape off, we needed to discuss this new piece of evidence. It could be critical for Mr. Smith's tariff. If the man had simply been doing his duty investigating the murders of these young women, the tape we had all just seen could potentially free him from prison.

Taking a second look at the Ex-Detective Inspector's preliminary case file once again:

Preliminary Case File

45/01141984

Name:

John Smith

Age:

45

Last Known Address:

Held at Fallon Wood Correctional Facility while on remand; moved to Maiden Vale Men's Prison.

Sentence Given:

Twenty-five years to life

Appeal Date:

24 January 2000

Appeal Decision:

Denied Parole

Assessment Hearing Held:

16 March 2000

Records Passed to Host *19 April 2000*

New Case File Classification Number:

45/01141984

Records Reviewed by Host:

Parole Appeal Denied (Reason Given: No New Evidence)

Determination Report Findings:

Does not admit guilt

Final Report Decision:

Without a guilty plea, the ex-detective inspector will serve out his sentence in full.

Description:

Brown Hair, Brown Eye Colour, Height 6 ft 5 in, Shoe Size 12

Distinguishing Marks & Tattoos:

None

Preliminary Case File History:

Ex-Detective Inspector John Smith was reportedly chasing a serial killer. Several victims were discovered. Witnesses identified Mr. Smith as the killer when he was detained for questioning; he could not give a reasonable explanation as to why all witnesses pointed in his direction as the man they saw with the victim before they disappeared.

Arrested and charged with eighteen suspicious deaths.

Final Classification:

Overwhelming evidence pointed toward Mr. Smith, who would not admit his guilt. It showed the man had never been believed to be innocent of these gruesome murders. Troy said he would speak to the Justice Minister at the Home Office once we had concluded our meeting.

Since we no longer needed to view any footage, we returned to the boardroom to finish what was now becoming a lengthy meeting. I felt this would be a perfect opportunity to leave and check out the entrance to Stanley Park, which was only five minutes from Kate's and my home, and ten minutes from work.

When Mr. Castle looked at his watch, he nodded but told me not to be too long, as we still had a lot to discuss. Kissing my girlfriend before I left, I headed out to check the location where we had seen the tall man crucify a young woman's body only a few hours ago. Taking my car, I arrived in no time.

The entrance was covered in police tape, and a crowd of onlookers wanted to see what was happening. When I noticed WPC Sarah Dunn standing near the gate, I had no choice but to approach her to see if she could provide any relevant information about this awful crime. When she noticed me, she smiled before telling me she would be off duty in about half an hour. She said she would come over to see us when she was free. I asked why, and she told me:

"This isn't the first, and this won't be the last. The man in charge of the investigation is a bigot and seems to hate women. His philosophy is that women are only good for three things: cooking, cleaning, and sex. They should not be allowed out of the house. Today, females of the species impede a man from doing his duty."

Wow. What an outdated way of thinking. If I met him, I would give him a piece of my mind. I thanked her for her candor before informing her I would see her when she was available.

Even though the woman had officially been at my workplace, I was surprised she had been allowed to attend the scene if her boss thought of women as second-class citizens—the weaker sex. I headed back to the house to inform the group of my findings. I also intended to tell them about WPC Dunn's visit to discuss the latest attack by the tall man. We had all seen it on the CCTV camera earlier that morning.

I saw Kate and Cully waiting in the boardroom as I entered the building. Wondering where Troy was, my colleagues informed me he would be back shortly. He had gone over to the Justice Department to update them on our recent development regarding Mr. Smith.

I told Cully and Kate about WPC Dunn's upcoming visit to the house to discuss the tall man and what she knew about it. When Cully heard this, she seemed surprised, but then I explained how the woman's boss treated women. She said, "Let the bastard stand in front of me and tell me I am only good for three things. I would certainly give him what-for."

From what I had seen of Mrs. Wish, I believed she was a God-fearing woman, so when she swore, it shocked me to the core. Looking back at the itinerary, we still had a lot to cover. When a meeting takes two days to complete, you need to ensure everyone is on the same page. This was one reason we kept updating the preliminary reports, minus what we had already discussed.

When I took a second look at the list, it shocked me how slowly we were completing a meeting that I had initially believed would take only a few hours. This gave me a simple idea on how to proceed with such a lengthy discussion: we needed to delegate time to each subject so there would be no delays. Those headings with two subjects, for example B, C, and D, would be given more time than those with only one heading.

We decided on one hour each for the double headings and half an hour for the single subjects left to discuss. If needed, we could split it into two days once again:

B: Lillie Cole / Who Is She

C: Sir John Stephenson / Future Panel Meetings

D: Alfred / Bonnie

E: Future Business of the House

F: Priory Lane Inspection

G: Funding Proposals

H: Anything Else

With Lillie Cole being the next subject on the list, we aimed to see if there was any updated information on the young convict. Was she the overweight man's daughter or not?

With Mr. Castle still a no-show, I turned to Mrs. Wish to see if she had anything new to share about the young woman. Cully informed us that Troy had found little about her, but he did have an answer to one question we needed to resolve. When she left the room to take a phone call, I looked across at Kate to tell her I loved her. She looked back at me, making sure no one saw her blow kisses in my direction like a little schoolgirl. It made me laugh before I blew one back. She caught it with her hand and rubbed it across her breast. I could not wait until we moved. I also could not wait until she was my wife.

Journal Entry Sixteen

When our fun and games were interrupted by Cully's return, we saw Mr. Castle had just returned from his trip to the Justice Department. When they were both seated once again, Troy told us he had been to see the Justice Minister and showed him the evidence we had gathered on Mr. Smith's behalf. The man seemed surprised to see such evidence, given that the convict had already served twenty-one years of his sentence. Not once had he admitted his guilt during that time. Because of the serious nature of the crimes, this new evidence could free the man and see him sent for a retrial. He would be released on bail to await another trial, which would give him a sense of freedom.

I was pleased with that outcome and hoped for the best for the man. When I asked Mr. Castle if he had any news about Lillie Cole, he seemed quite happy to state there had been no news of any link to the portly man—although he had spoken with the social services, who were trying to locate her original paperwork. I was somewhat disappointed by the news, as I had hoped the girl would at the very least get to know who her parents were.

When Troy received a phone call, we all laughed at his "playschool" ringtone. As he stepped out of the room to take the call, he nodded several times in approval. When he finished, he returned with a clear smile on his face. He had now confirmed that the portly man was indeed Lillie's father. This meant Mr. Castle's ex-wife was her mother. He also arranged for Sir John to receive a copy of the matching document. This made him smile.

I had to ask why he felt this was good news. "My darling, Lillie will at least know who her father is. Also, that bastard will have trouble with his wife, who hates children. Although his wife was party to the deal which saw the child put up for adoption, she never wanted to know what happened to the child. Now it has been confirmed there is a connection between him and the young woman. I would love to be a fly on the wall when that secret is exposed. I have sent the evidence in a letter to his wife."

You could see his satisfaction written all over his face. This was clearly revenge for all the heartache he had suffered. He asked if I would like to be the one to tell Lillie about this development. I couldn't believe he offered me the task of informing the young woman who her father was. I asked if it would mean my first actual interview using the machine. When he confirmed it, I was happy to use the machine for real, but not thrilled about telling a girl that a murderous bastard was her father.

This was a perfect time to discuss the man and his control of the panel. We needed to ensure this man could never again control the panel's voting system. Troy mentioned that the man had taken what was once a fair voting system and twisted it so it always went in his favor. Now that Kate and I had a vote, hopefully this could not happen—but only time would tell.

I asked Mr. Castle, if he was the chairperson, why he couldn't stop these irregular, rigged voting procedures. He liked my suggestion but didn't know how to implement such an order when Sir John owned several houses and therefore loyalty in the voting. "Yes," I said, "but the chairperson must approve all procedural ballots. This means laying down the law to those houses, stating that if they cannot have a free, unbiased vote, then any future vote from those houses with a biased voting system will be discounted until they can be free of any mismanagement."

Troy laughed at my suggestion. When I asked him why, he said Sir John would never see his control diminished by such a new voting rule. "Yes, but what can he do if you force the houses under his control to play fair in love and war? If they do not comply, they can be forcibly evicted from any future panel meetings until they have cleaned up their acts. Nobody can force a house to vote with them just because the leader has done something they regret. From the next panel meeting onward, they must sort themselves out, or a vote will decide whether these biased houses can attend future panel meetings."

When Cully interrupted me, she informed us about the panel rules. No house can be forced to take a vote in anyone's favor, and if found to be biased, those houses can be evicted from the panel.

Troy looked up from his notes at Mrs. Wish. "I've looked at all the rules and procedural commandments, but I've never seen that rule."

The woman smiled. "Well, it's there now, if you care to look."

As we all did as she instructed, we saw this new rule, but the way she had introduced it made it look as though the panel—including Sir John—had already voted and agreed to it. Kate said we must wait and see at the next panel meeting.

"In the meantime, why don't you send a copy of the rules to each house? Make sure this rule is highlighted," she added. "Then, people can only say they've seen it."

I asked if he (Sir John) could be devious enough to want to control the panel. Could we not be just as devious?

When Troy asked what I meant, I turned to Cully and asked when any vote was implemented and whether all house leaders needed to sign it. She nodded but still tried to determine what I was asking for. I then asked if Sir John felt he owned the panel, why couldn't we stop those houses he felt were under his control from voting in his favor?

Even Kate didn't understand what I was getting at. So, I asked again if the panel members needed to sign off on every vote, whatever it was, after it happened. If that was the case, this new rule we had just implemented would have voting signatures attached.

When the three of them thought about my suggestion, they all said in unison that it was downright devious. Its simplicity would instantly cancel Sir John's control over the other houses.

Troy mentioned he had wanted to wipe the smile off that "bastard's" face for far too long. "Now, we can get the houses to behave regarding a vote."

I turned to Cully and asked how long it would take to make the necessary changes.

"I've already done it with a simple bit of cut and paste," she said. "They'll never know it's a forged document."

"Now we have that sorted out, we should discuss Alfred and his new pal Bonnie's new apartment. What's the progress on the build?"

Kate said she had talked to the architect, who informed her the place would be ready by the following Monday. They had completed the flat by clearing out the old rooms, and now they needed to create a garden area for Bonnie to do her business.

Although it would be nice to welcome our colleague back into the fold, we would all need to adapt to his disabilities in the workplace. Because the place is so large, I feel lifts should be installed to help him get around. I know this might slightly delay his homecoming, but it would be beneficial in the long term. We also need handrails he can use to guide himself from his apartment to every floor.

With modern technology, we could make these rails talk so that he knows where he is at any time of the day or night. Yes, it will take us some time to adapt to our friend needing his dog with him to help throughout the day, but the sooner he's back home, the better. I thanked Kate for her input regarding our friend.

"Let's move on to the next item on the itinerary, which is the future of the house," I said. "We have now been given a large enough grant to help us remove all the old clutter from the rooms. We need to use these empty spaces, which could bring extra funding to the place. Yes, this is a government-run facility, but we need future investment to prevent it from falling into disrepair again."

I opened the floor to see if anyone had ideas. At first, there was complete silence in the boardroom, until Cully suggested she move her offices into one of the now-empty rooms on the right side of the second floor. This gave Troy the incentive to suggest moving his own office to the second floor as well, possibly right next door. Renting space in the building would bring in extra money.

I looked at Kate, then at Cully, and finally at Troy. "How will you rent something if you own the building?"

He laughed and explained, "The extra funding could go toward anything Alfred needs, such as a medical bay for any necessary treatment. This wouldn't affect the house's budget, which we can leave for other adaptations."

He suggested we take a tour of the building to see what adaptations we could install to help our colleague when he returns from his extended stay in the hospital. We then adjourned the meeting so we could take that tour. I decided to begin at the top of the building so we could map out the areas most in need of adapting.

As we made our way to the top floor, we discussed which adaptations a blind person would need. Cully used her iPad to look up suggestions while also taking photos for size and suitability. Alfred was not fully blind, but he was close to it, so we needed to treat him as though he were. Using this approach would help him adapt more quickly once he returned to the house.

Journal Entry Seventeen

As we were finishing our inspection of all three floors—noting where adaptations could be placed to help our colleague navigate the building—I noticed we had a visitor.

Making our way to the reception area, we found WPC Dunn, who had come to update us on the Tall Man investigation. Since it concerned all of us, we invited her to join us in the new boardroom so she could give us her perspective on the case.

Once we were all seated, I allowed Sarah to inform us about the grisly discovery found in the park early that morning. She began by telling us that the lead detective had ordered her to keep her head above water or he would find another reason to have her suspended. I asked if this was the same idiot who treated women with contempt.

When she said yes, the man sounded just like the portly man. I thought she had been transferred to a new station in Langley.

"Yes," she explained, "but because of the latest incident here in Lower Glendale, the bastard brought his entire team over from the Hanley district to use our base in Langley, which is just over the water from Lower Glendale."

Troy interrupted to ask for the man's name. Once Officer Dunn provided it, he allowed her to continue. She said that ever since she had been a recruit, this man had picked on her from day one. In the three years she had been on the beat, she had been suspended for at least half that time.

Mr. Castle asked if there was any reason for this. What could she think of that she might have done wrong? Sarah told us her uniform was always pressed and tidy, her long hair was pinned neatly beneath her cap, and she was never late for a shift. There was nothing to warrant such attention.

Looking at Troy, I could see he and Cully were taking notes about the man. "Now," Sarah continued, "this morning was my first shift after yet another suspension. I recall the boys having a meeting about the Tall Man. When I butted in to ask a question, I was treated like an alien. My sergeant was ordered to escort me out because that room was 'for the boys.' I felt so ashamed to be an officer of the law.

"I looked at the man I had treated as a friend as he grabbed me by the arm and forcibly removed me from the room. I was shocked when Sergeant Fox told me I was being suspended yet again. I asked him, 'What the fuck? What have I done now?' He said he was following orders from Detective Northman.

"I couldn't understand why I was being suspended and physically forced from a room just because I was a woman. I had no choice but to shout at him for being weak and not standing up to that senior detective. How can I respect anything you say from now on when you suspend me for being a female police officer? All he could say in his defense was that he owed the man, so he had to do as he was told."

Troy had heard enough. He stopped Officer Dunn to ask one question. "Why did you join the force?"

Sarah looked at him and said, "To catch criminals—not to sit behind a desk filing paperwork or stand near a park gate to stop people entering a crime scene until the senior detective has decided he's seen enough. That's what I've been forced to do for the other eighteen months I've been on duty. Now, tell me what you want to know about the Tall Man."

"Everything you know, in your own words," Troy clarified.

"Yesterday's crime wasn't the first. It was the twenty-first such crime. Each body is placed in a different location. I've been suspended so many times that I made it my personal goal to track and trace the location of each body drop."

Sarah pulled out a large map and placed it on the table. "All the body-drop locations are here. From this, it nearly forms a sign of the cross. I believe it would be a complete cross if—sadly—six more women lose their lives."

As we all examined the map, it was clear a pattern was emerging. Troy asked what the lead detective was doing about the large number of bodies cropping up across the map.

"I don't think he's looked at the track-and-trace aspect of the investigation. Every time I tried to make a simple observation, I was put on suspension."

We couldn't believe what we were hearing. How could a man overlook such obvious evidence?

"I can tell you one thing," Sarah said. "He isn't looking at the map. He's more interested in keeping his head just above water. Whenever I was allowed near the station, I was told to leave the investigating to the men—only they can solve such a crime."

Troy looked unhappy but stayed calm as she spoke. "I even talked to Sergeant Fox about the investigation. He told me to stop bothering the 'menfolk'—that they knew what they were doing."

Mr. Castle asked her to come with him to see the Justice Minister about this man and his so-called "glory boys' team of buffoons."

"We need to stop this man in his tracks," he said. "We can't allow him to complete his sign of the cross. I'll make sure someone listens to you, my dear—don't worry."

Once Sarah picked up her map, Mr. Castle said he had no choice but to adjourn the meeting. If he could get someone to listen—just once—to a woman who had more evidence than this so-called detective, then maybe the blatant sexism could be dealt with.

"Because a woman's place was in the home? Not in my book," he said. "Women are just as vital as men. I've never heard of someone being suspended just for being female. That man needs a full dressing-down before the Tall Man claims another victim right under his nose."

I had never seen a man look so angry, but it was the truth. A serial killer might move across towns and cities simply because of a bigoted idiot and his wild notions of what women are good for. I hoped Troy could find someone who would listen.

Now that the meeting was adjourned, we only had three more items left on the itinerary. My upcoming visit to the Priory needed to be arranged once we had finished our meeting.

Turning to Cully, I asked if we needed Troy here to discuss this trip.

"No, my dear. I can arrange with Ms. Wild to show you around this coming Monday," she said.

We were just about to move on to discussing some funding proposals when suddenly the overweight man turned up, looking red-faced and angry.

"Where's that man?" he demanded.

I had no choice but to ask who he was referring to.

"That bastard, Troy Castle! Tell him he won't get away with this recent rule change."

Cully stood up to face the portly man and spoke her mind. "What rule? No new rules have been invented or made up. So, explain yourself or get out."

"Do you know who I am?" he growled.

"Everyone knows who you are, Sir John. You're a bigoted idiot if you think you can barge into a meeting to call out the chairperson over a rule you signed over a year ago."

"I signed nothing like this!" he shouted.

The angry man threw the rule book down on the table, pointing to the very rule we had all added.

"Well, as you can see, this rule was signed by all the houses, and from what I've seen, you were the first to sign," Cully said.

"No, I would never sign a rule discounting a House vote if they're found to be biased," he snapped.

"Sir John, would you like me to read the meeting minutes from last spring, when we had this meeting?"

"No," he grumbled. "Just tell him I want this rule voted out at the next meeting."

"Nobody can change a rule unless all houses agree."

"No, where is that in the rule book?"

"Page fifteen, rule ten, if you care to take a look."

"It's bloody not right. It's unfair, and I want it removed from the statute books immediately."

"I cannot see the rules as being unfair. What surprises me is that you wanted the rule added."

"No, I would never have said that about a rule."

"Do you want me once again to read the meeting minutes back to you, Sir John?"

"No."

"Well, you can leave. I will note your intrusion into our meeting, and I feel Mr. Castle will demand an apology."

The man didn't look happy as he stormed out of the building. As soon as he was gone, we congratulated Cully on her strength and for being an excellent actress. She laughed before saying,

"I am so glad he didn't want me to read the minutes back because there was no speech by Sir John. I was just glad his memory's not as great as that bellowing voice he has."

As we moved the meeting along to my upcoming inspection of the Priory, Kate asked if she could come too, since she wanted to see the infamous third floor for herself. She asked Cully if she could arrange this for the middle of next week. She nodded and put it in her diary before telling us both that we would need to speak with Gina Wild so she could take time out of her busy day to show us around the place.

Just out of curiosity, I asked Cully if she knew how many patients were currently on the third floor. Mrs. Wish replied that she needed an up-to-date figure. When I asked about Lillie Cole, I wondered if she would be there when we visited. Cully said she didn't know but suggested that if I asked Troy, he could find out Miss Cole's current location.

Just then, Mr. Castle walked through the door of the boardroom with a wide smile on his face. When I asked why he was grinning so broadly, he said it was because he and our young friend, WPC Dunn, had gone to see the Justice Minister about the Tall Man and ex-detective John Smith.

When she showed the minister her map, he was shocked at the quality of her work. I explained to the minister about the bigoted detective in charge of the investigation, who continually suspends the young officer whenever she wants to suggest they look at her notes regarding the Sign of the Cross killer. When the minister took the time to look at the map, he could see that the young woman had simply been doing what the lead detective should have done in the first place. The Justice Minister sat there, looking quite uncomfortable; he realised something needed to change if they were ever going to catch this killer.

As we sat there, he picked up his phone.

"Can you connect me with Detective Inspector Jack Northman?"

Seconds went by until he could speak with the man.

"Jack, it's me, Roy, at the Justice Ministry."

"Sir, what can I do for you?"

"I just wanted to catch up with you to see how far along you are in trying to catch this killer they call the Tall Man."

"I'm sorry, we're having problems tracking this man's movements. He's been busy dumping several girls around the city."

"I was asking because I have a young lady here alongside Mr. Castle. The young woman tells me that every time she suggests something to you, you suspend her. That can't be true, can it, Jack?"

"Women, what do they know? They're only good for three things. Every time this young lady feels she can undermine my boys by making these wild suggestions, I have no choice but to act because it's not good for team morale."

"Jack, the woman has some leads, which she has kindly shared with Mr. Castle and me. So tell me, if this woman is 'only good for three things,' as you put it, how come she's done more than you in the last eighteen months?"

"No, my boys have done a lot of work on the case, but we're not ready to make an arrest yet."

"So, why haven't you paid attention to what this woman's been offering you and your boys? From what I've seen, she has some very good leads. Do I need to make a change at the top and give her the power to take over this investigation?"

"No, just give me some time to review the evidence my boys and I have collected."

"I feel you are misguided in your views of women. Officer Dunn has done more work than your team, and this cannot continue."

"Look, sir, a woman would impede my boys from concentrating on their work."

"Jack, I'm sending this woman over so she can show you how to do your job."

"Sir, I cannot work with a woman undermining me in the office. She'll get in our way."

"Jack, do I have to suspend you?"

"No, sir, I'll take your suggestions on board."

"So you'll allow me to send WPC Dunn so she can help you this afternoon?"

"Sir, I can't work with a woman. It will cloud my mind. The problem is that Miss Dunn is quite attractive, and my boys might not concentrate."

"Jack, you will do as you're told, or I'll suspend you. Do you understand?"

"Yes, sir, but can I suggest sending the young officer over so that one of my boys can take her evidence? That way, we can see if her ideas pan out."

"Now you're telling me you want to steal her work and use her suggestions yourself?"

"No, that is not the case. I can do my job. I caught the notorious killer, John Smith."

"Let's agree to disagree on that subject because fresh evidence has come to light suggesting the man could be freed."

"No, you cannot do that. He was my finest collar."

"From the evidence shown at the trial, it was an open-and-shut case because the CCTV footage showed you what you wanted to see. This recent evidence Mr. Castle has shared indicates the man may, in fact, be quite innocent. What do you say to that?"

"I was John Smith's deputy. There were just too many people saying he was guilty."

"So, I bet you saw a perfect case to get an early promotion."

"No, sir, I would never have thought that. I just believed the man was guilty, that's all."

"I have one more thing to say before I let you go. From now on, you will treat Miss Dunn with the utmost respect, or you'll be out on your ear if I find evidence to the contrary. Do we understand each other?"

"Yes, sir."

Wow, I bet he didn't like that ultimatum. Would the man allow her to show them what she had?

"The man is an idiot with outdated theories on how to treat a woman. I think eighteen months is far too long for any criminal to be on the run. I believe this insane man might have been caught months ago if he had allowed Officer Dunn to help with the investigation. If you recall Brian Cross, I discovered he was still on the loose. There needs to be a serious rethink at the Langley station. I suggested the girl be promoted to sergeant so she can pursue a detective's badge. The minister agreed with me. When I left the young lady with the minister, he discussed moving her back to the Hanley branch so she can begin her detective training once she's helped that buffoon, Northman, catch this killer. Now promoted to sergeant for her good work, he felt the Tall Man could be caught with her forward thinking rather than that man's archaic views on women, hopefully in the not-too-distant future."

Moving on with our meeting, I told Mr. Castle how Cully had arranged for Kate and me to visit the Priory for our tour the following week. He said it would be quite an interesting excursion. Once again, we needed to shift the meeting so we could discuss future funding proposals and ensure the house was always up to date.

I opened the floor for suggestions. Kate was the first to propose that we contact our friends from Texas. They might use one or two of our empty rooms to work from if they were ever in our neck of the woods. I asked her to arrange that and update us on future developments at the next meeting.

The last part of our long-drawn-out meeting was to see if there was anything else to discuss before closing. Cully informed Troy about Sir John's interruption and explained how she had sent him off with a flea in his ear. She also recounted how we had fooled him with that simple cut-and-paste method we had discussed earlier. Mr. Castle seemed quite pleased, leaving me free to close the meeting.

Journal Entry Eighteen

I must apologize for not writing sooner; I have been incredibly busy since our long-drawn-out meeting, which covered so many topics. Kate and I are in the middle of packing to move into our new home at the end of the week. Because of the size of this new place, we've even discussed installing a dungeon so we can indulge in some BDSM—a harness in the ceiling and a wall covered in various toys and whips to try out on each other whenever we feel like adding a little extra fun.

We are set to visit the Priory tomorrow to see the other side of the machine I use regularly. I cannot wait to see the third floor and learn something about each resident. Troy has arranged for me to interview Lillie the next time she's brought to the Priory. Mr. Castle explained she would need a few days of treatment before I can speak with her using the machine. Currently, because of her manic episodes, she remains a prisoner at the notorious Parkinson Hall. Kate mentioned she would love to see that place and find out why it has such a poor reputation— perhaps we'll discover what it's really like to live there every day.

It even gave me an idea for a sex game in which we could indulge our fantasies: one evil guard, one naughty prisoner. Just the thought gave me quite a thrill. That thought led me to take Kate to the bedroom for a fun night.

The next day, when the alarm jolted me from sleep, I felt wonderfully relaxed after our night of experimentation. It's surprising what you can do with a bit of imagination. Pulling off the covers that hid my sex-kitten girlfriend, I slapped her arse to get her to move so we could shower together. Once we had washed away our night of pleasure, we went back to the bedroom to dress.

I realized we hadn't been in this property very long, but the new place we bought in Hanley will definitely be our forever home. Now that we know about the Tall Man, we're more than happy to move.

Over our morning coffee, we discussed Sarah's search for the evil man. The next time we see her, we plan to wish her good luck in capturing him. It still shocks me that he's killed twenty-one women already. I'd love to discover his motive—maybe one day I could interview this monster by having him sent to the Priory.

Kate reminded me he must be caught first before he can be sent anywhere, and I already have my work cut out interviewing Lillie Cole. A hint of sadness passed through me when I realised I would have to tell her the truth about her father. After we finished breakfast, we returned to the bedroom to finalize our dressing.

Most of our clothes were already packed, so we left just enough outfits on the rail for each of us. Once we were ready, we headed out to make the short journey to work for another day of filing on my part, while Kate had several funding calls to make.

Journal Entry Nineteen

As we arrived at work, we went to the underground car park. As usual, Kate parked her car on the left, and I parked mine on the right. I got out and saw Alfred's pink Volkswagen Beetle, which made me sad, knowing he could never drive his beloved car again after the ferocious attack by those two bitches who were now on the run.

Looking across the car park, I spotted a large removal truck, which could only mean that Cully or her boss was moving their belongings from the Glendale offices to the House of Calamari. We made our way to the lift, which would take us to reception, and soon discovered it was indeed both of them moving in. If Alfred had been here, he would have ensured the removal crew didn't make a mess.

I kissed Kate before we separated—she headed off to her office, while I made my way to mine. As I looked over the banister rail, I could see Cully instructing two of the removal staff, who were carrying a filing cabinet, to be careful with the walls since they'd only been painted the other week. That office was the second to be completed after my own.

Turning to my desk, I noticed my fiancée had left me several files to look over, each a potential candidate for an interview using our new machine. Yes, I needed to keep busy, but the sheer number of files was too much to tackle all at once. So I took the first half and placed them on my to-do cabinet. After making myself a cappuccino, I set to work, looking for those cases that stood out as especially unusual. The first dozen I read didn't pique my interest at all.

When I left my desk to walk over to the veranda, I could see Troy and Cully still deciding where they wanted to place everything. Then my newly installed phone rang, so I returned to my desk to answer it. It was Sarah, asking if she could come and see me—and if Kate knew how we could help her with her investigation. It was nice to hear her voice.

I needed to know if she had been transferred back to the Hanley station. Her honest reply was no. She explained that things had been non-stop since the Justice Minister promoted her. Jack Northman had been forcibly retired, a new man was now in charge, and even the desk sergeant who had sided with that idiot Northman was fired. The atmosphere changed overnight, and her new boss encouraged her to pursue her detective badge. She studied like crazy at night, hoping to move from the traffic division to the murder squad, which was where she wanted to be.

Any suggestions she had regarding the case, her new boss accepted without question. He made several changes, ensuring everyone had firing-squad training, ever since the Justice Minister ordered a shoot-to-kill policy on the Tall Man. Speaking of him, three more bodies had been discovered in different areas of the city. I asked about her cross theory—how many more bodies would it take to complete a perfect cross? She said there were three left to go, which led her to believe there was a religious aspect to these crimes. The complication now was the latest victims had been men, not women, which changed everything they thought they knew about the killer.

Returning to her request, I asked how Kate and I could help. Sarah wanted to discuss our roles within the House so she could complete her exam testing. She also needed help visiting the

Priory and the notorious Parkinson Hall women's prison. I told her I could get her on the visiting roster at the Priory the next day since Kate and I were already going there. Unfortunately, she'd have to check with the Justice Minister again if she needed access to the prison. She sighed but readily agreed to join us on our trip to the Priory.

I gave her our address and told her to be there by eight in the morning so we could leave together. After I hung up, I headed down the back stairwell to see if Cully and Troy were done settling in. When I reached Mrs. Wish's office, I saw her and Mr. Castle sitting together, each with what smelled like a strong brandy.

They noticed me, and Troy asked if I wanted a drink to celebrate their official move into the House. I smiled at them both but explained that I needed to see Kate first about the following day.

"Tomorrow? What about tomorrow?" Troy asked.

I reminded him about our Priory visit scheduled for the next day.

"Oh, about that, my dear. I'm sorry. I've got to suspend the visit because of the minister's new shoot-to-kill policy. We must go through gun training school, which I've arranged with the ministry."

I accepted the stiff drink he offered, feeling I needed it after learning we'd be handling firearms. When Kate joined us, we all sat drinking Mr. Castle's strong brandy until the bottle was empty. Then, I left to return to my office.

I had no choice but to call Sarah to explain that our trip to the Priory was off until further notice. She thanked me for letting her know and said she'd see me at the gun range the next morning. Even though I'd just had three strong brandies, I felt unsure about this gun training.

Going back to Cully's office, I asked why there was such urgency for this action. Troy looked a bit merry, and although he spoke with a slight slur, I attributed it to the drink. He said that no one—neither women nor men—was safe from this monster. The ministry felt a blanket order across all houses and police forces was needed. Gun training for all of us would begin the next day.

Part Four

Journal Entry Twenty Part One

Our training at the Hanley gun range had barely begun when we first caught wind of the case of the Tall Man.

Detective Constable Sarah Dunn—new on our team, but already a force to be reckoned with—had been chasing down leads in the hunt for this elusive serial killer.

But the thing was the Tall Man wasn't a simple mystery.

We had one, just one blurry CCTV image from Stanley Park in Lower Glendale, and that was it.

No eyewitnesses. No other clues. Just that single frame of a shadowy figure, his face hidden. That solitary photograph was the only tangible evidence we possessed, while it confirmed his existence, it left us with more questions than answers.

But the most disconcerting aspect of the case wasn't the faceless figure lurking in the shadows—it was his choice of victims.

The Tall Man had been targeting college students, but disturbingly, among the dead were men. Three victims, to be precise.

This curious deviation from the expected pattern of his targets introduced a new layer of complexity to an already confounding investigation. What connected them? What was the motive behind such chilling selections? And could we uncover any patterns before more lives were tragically taken?

It was a significant departure from what you'd expect in these kinds of cases, and it immediately complicated the investigation.

The thing that made this case so unnerving was that the murders didn't happen where the bodies were found.

The victims were brought from other locations—dumped in various parts of the city like discarded objects.

Whoever the Tall Man was, he knew how to cover his tracks.

And as the bodies piled up, our leads seemed to slip further away, leaving us with nothing solid to go on.

As the weeks dragged on, the pressure to solve this case intensified. The Minister for Justice was breathing down our necks, demanding results.

It wasn't long before we were handed extra resources: more officers, more training, more equipment.

The department went through a massive shake-up, with personnel being reassigned to different roles.

It felt like we were being prepared for something big, but the more resources we had, the more we seemed to be spinning our wheels.

The department's old house—once a storage lot—was now buzzing with police vans and patrol cars.

The Minister even suggested leasing out the garage and storage rooms to help fund the upkeep of the property.

It was a decent idea, but it didn't take away the fact that the case was still going nowhere.

Then came the news that John Smith—who had been locked up for crimes he may not have committed—was being released on bail.

The news stirred up a lot of anxiety, and the media jumped on it.

But while the town was gripped by this development, we were just not buying it. No, the Tall Man was still out there, lurking in the shadows, and we had to stay focused.

Kate and I spent more time at the gun range. The city felt like it was teeming with danger, and we weren't about to be caught unprepared.

The uncertainty of John Smith's release kept us on edge, but we knew it was a distraction.

The real threat was the Tall Man, and he was still waiting.

The so-called "Sign of the Cross" map, which had plagued our every thought, was tantalizingly close to completion—just one more victim was needed.

Yet, we were still no closer to finding Brian Cross, the escaped prisoner, whose whereabouts continued to elude us.

We had learned that the Tall Man was clever, moving his victims to different locations before dumping their bodies, making the investigation even more complex.

Time was running short, and the urgency only increased as we realised that locating the killer was key to keeping John Smith out of jail.

Alfred, too, was still recovering—weeks of hospital treatment ahead of him. I wished he were with us on the ground, not holed up in that quiet residential wing at the hospital in East Danby.

At least he had his dog, Bonnie, keeping him company as he struggled to manage the pain from the attack that had nearly ended his life.

Meanwhile, Sarah was working tirelessly, spending most evenings studying for her Detective Two badges under the Minister's watchful eye.The Minister had high hopes for her, believing she was the key to unraveling the entire mystery.Her quick thinking and ability to perform under pressure had proven invaluable to the team.

Through long nights, she sifted through records of past criminal activity in the area, spanning over thirty years.

And then, just two days after the announcement of John Smith's upcoming release from prison, we were hit with a new horror: A young female student was discovered, brutally beaten, and subjected to an unspeakable act.

The press, ever quick to sensationalise, dubbed the killer the "Black Candlestick Killer," a title that stuck. They scrambled to make sense of the spree, digging into the history of his gruesome killings, but we knew we were only beginning to understand the true scope of this nightmare.

"Uncovering the Truth: The Triplet Revelation"

The media, with their insatiable hunger for a story, made sure their customers—everyone—was well-acquainted with the history of the man's killing spree.

John Smith had been anxiously anticipating his release, but the press had other plans. Sensationalised headlines flooded the newspapers, portraying him as guilty even before the trial had begun.

Yet, deep down, we knew the truth: John Smith was innocent of the crimes he had been accused of.

In an effort to shield him, we asked for the news to be released early—three days ahead of the planned schedule—to try and prevent the tidal wave of press frenzy from overwhelming him.

We hoped that the killer, emboldened by the recent attention, would return to his twisted ways.

The murder of the young woman marked the first time since John's imprisonment that a victim had been claimed.

And, as expected, people all too eager to cast blame were quick to point fingers at him. But this time, they would have to come to terms with the uncomfortable truth—John Smith was innocent.

After twenty-one long years spent behind bars for crimes he didn't commit, the realisation was bitter. The man had suffered far too long for sins he had never committed.

The problem we faced was both simple and complex: Why would anyone want to frame John Smith for these grisly murders?

To find the answer, we needed to sift through all the witness statements, each one pointing to him as the double of the killer.

But there was something more behind it—something we needed to uncover.

Sarah, ever diligent, balanced her studies and job while tirelessly tracking down the Tall Man's whereabouts.

Meanwhile, Kate, assigned as our research assistant, had been diving into the case files with relentless determination.

It didn't take long before the brilliant woman, who would soon become my wife, cracked the case wide open.

A regular at the Grange Pub—a gentleman who had frequented the establishment for over thirty years—became a focal point.

According to the landlord, this man had been giving misleading statements to the police, a fact that had surfaced as we combed through witness testimonies.

This same man had been traveling across the district, providing conflicting accounts to multiple police forces.

What was even more troubling was that, in some cases, the same victim's name appeared two or even three times across different statements.

In her relentless pursuit of the truth, Kate uncovered something startling—an updated photo of the elderly man standing between two boys who looked strikingly similar.

The photo was taken outside the old orphanage in East Danby, just across the river from our new house in Hanley. This seemingly innocuous picture would turn out to be a key piece of the puzzle.

The orphanage had been demolished in the late nineties and replaced by the Stephenson Rehabilitation Hospital.

It was at this very hospital that Kate had once been an unwilling patient, the aftermath of her trauma caused by the infamous Portly Man.

Was it some miraculous coincidence, or perhaps an accident, that made the striking similarities between Sir John Stephenson and John Smith so undeniable?

Kate brought the two photos across to Cully's office, where we examined them side by side. I showed her the first photo, and she instantly identified the boy as Sir John.

When I showed her the second boy in the photo, she identified him the same way. But when I pointed out the overweight man in the image, she was startled to realise that both photos actually featured John Smith, not Sir John.

Kate, still visibly confused by the uncanny resemblance, stepped over to one of the filing cabinets.

She retrieved a large bundle of photographs from a box in Troy's private collection and invited Kate to sift through them for any other images that might show the two boys.

Kate, with her sharp eye, identified seven photos out of thirty-two that stood out. And then, with her trademark brilliance, she pointed out something strange in two of the images that seemed to hold the key to the puzzle.

Realising she needed a closer look, Kate returned to her office to grab a magnifying glass. When she returned, she studied the images with greater precision.

It didn't take long before she noticed something extraordinary—there was a third boy, positioned to the right of the first photo.

In the second photo, the same boy appeared on the left side of the frame. Piecing the photos together, it became clear: there weren't two twins—there was a set of triplets.

The need to speak with the Portly man to show the man pictures from the past in the hope he could prevent more deaths by revealing all he knew was now a must. The tension in the dimly lit room was palpable as the portly man shifted uneasily in his chair, beads of sweat glistening on his forehead. The air conditioning was either absent or ineffective, adding a layer of discomfort to an already oppressive atmosphere. His hand trembled slightly as he dabbed at his face with a handkerchief, his demeanor betraying a deep unease.

"What is going on here? Why have I been summoned to see these images?" he demanded, his voice tinged with a mix of irritation and apprehension.

Kate, seated across from him, smirked subtly, her eyes gleaming with a rare triumph. She seemed to relish the reversal of power, watching him squirm under her unwavering gaze. The photograph she held in her hand was the catalyst for the unfolding drama—a seemingly innocent snapshot of three boys standing in the sun, their youthful faces masking the dark shadows of a shared past.

"This," Kate began, holding up the image for all to see, "is the key to everything. The three Johns. Or should I say, the three Waynes?"

The portly man's face darkened. "What the bloody hell are you showing me these for? I'm busy and cannot waste valuable time looking at old photos of children."

Kate leaned forward, her tone sharp. "Come on, John. You're not fooling anyone here with your pompous, self-driven air of imaginary importance. You're a man with a secret. Now tell us, or get out, because there's a killer on the loose."

The man bristled, his defiance faltering under the weight of Kate's accusation. He reached for the edge of the table to steady himself, his hand gripping it with a force that betrayed his inner turmoil. As the beads of sweat collected on his brow, his eyes flickered to the photograph. A flash of recognition, quickly suppressed, passed across his face.

"Is that you, Mr. Wayne?" a voice interjected, breaking the silence. The question came from Mr. Smith, who sat opposite the man. His gaze was steady, a mixture of curiosity and disdain etched into his features.

The portly man's lips parted, and a weary sigh escaped. "Yes, Mr. Wayne, it is I, the other Mr. Wayne."

Recognition dawned between the two men, but it brought no joy. Instead, a shared dread seemed to seep into the room. The photograph was more than a relic of a carefree afternoon; it was a reminder of a long-buried history that had warped and destroyed lives.

Kate's voice sliced through the tension. "What happened that day? What turned a friend into a killer and a boy with aspirations into a bastard like you?"

Mr. Smith's expression softened as he glanced at the photograph, his gaze lingering on the boy he once was. He cleared his throat and began to speak, his voice thick with emotion.

"That day was... unforgettable. A rare sunny afternoon in an otherwise miserable summer. The smell of sweet tobacco hung in the air—not the smoking kind, but the chewing variety. And him. That man. The one who ruined everything."

He paused, his hands gripping the arms of his chair as he struggled to continue. "He told Eric his disfigurement was a sign from God, a mark of his worthlessness. But Eric wasn't the only one. We all suffered under his twisted reign. The cane, the freezing showers, the humiliations. He called it God's tears, cleansing us of our evil. It was his excuse to torment us."

The room was silent except for the faint hum of the lights overhead. Mr. Smith's words painted a vivid, harrowing picture.

"Shower nights were the worst. Twelve boys, chosen at random—or so he said. Not only that he would have Eric sit on his knee. While we were ordered to do Shakespeare's Plays, If the performance were bad, he would cane us before we had to do it again. When I must recall those nights of pure pain and misery. Yes, many had to endure cold showers while trying to perform the plays he wanted us to perform for him.

If there were no good sex scenes in the play, he would add them. On a good night, I would only have to suck off three boys before he let us stop. he'd beat us. Eric... Eric had it the worst. He was the director, forced to punish us when we failed. And when we didn't meet his standards, he'd make the boy suffer."

Kate's eyes narrowed, her jaw tight. "Go on."

On a dreadful night, and there were too many of those. I would have to sodomise at least six boys before I got to rest up. Whenever someone could not perform their duty, he would have to beat them with the man's waggle stick.

This stick was a very thin piece of wood with very sharp and rough edges to the ridges of the piece as it went down. There were seven sharp pieces on the declining slopes of the stick. The evil bastard would make the young lad hit you with it clean in your balls. One, maybe two hits would be fine. Anymore, there would be blood dripping down onto the shower floor. The man would say these were God's way of telling us that we had not performed his play correctly."

Mr. Smith's voice trembled as he continued. "Ughh, If the performances were bad, he'd add... scenes. Awful, unspeakable acts. I don't know how many times I prayed for it to stop. But he had us under his control. He used pain, shame, and fear to break us. And Eric... Eric bore the brunt of it. He'd walk through shards of glass, beaten and bloodied, while we watched, powerless to help."

He further stated "He would clap his hand with intense excitement if we did a decent job. While shouting out some words in Italian, which began with Bravo, Bravo Bravissimo. When we were all allowed to kneel at the man's feet. The poor lad had to endure alot. I cannot say if I am right, but this may have been programming like brainwashing."

Tears glistened in his eyes as he turned to the portly man. "You remember, don't you? You remember what he did to us? To Eric?"

The portly man's face was ashen. He nodded slowly, his voice barely above a whisper. "I remember."

Kate's voice was like a hammer hitting a nail. "Then tell us. Where are Eric and that man now? We need to know. For justice. For redemption."

But the portly man's lips pressed into a thin line. "I can't," he muttered. "Not out of loyalty to that monster, but to Eric. He's my brother. I... I can't betray him."

A heavy silence fell over the room. Kate's glare could have pierced steel, but even she couldn't force the words from him. Mr. Smith, however, seemed determined to break the stalemate. He stood, his voice steady and resolute.

"Enough secrets. It's time to end this. Eric deserves peace, and so do the rest of us."

As he spoke, the weight of years seemed to lift from his shoulders. The photograph—a snapshot of a long-lost summer—was more than just an image. It was the key to unraveling a history of pain, betrayal, and ultimately, redemption.

Journal Entry Twenty: Part Two

Being yanked out of bed at an ungodly hour is never recommended, but we now had mandatory gun training ordered by the justice minister, coupled with regular early morning meetings. The upside? Extra pay to compensate for this grueling new regime.

At our first early morning meeting, we were introduced to Staff Sergeant Tracy Howard, who was tasked with training us in the use of a newly designed Heckler and Koch machine gun. Additionally, we had to master an advanced stun gun—slightly too heavy for my liking, as I managed to break two nails handling the damn thing. The two-hour training session was followed by an introduction to the teams we'd be working with.

Kate was assigned a team of eight highly trained officers from S019, while I was given my own team of eight. Meanwhile, Detective Constable Sarah Dunn, newly fast-tracked, was assigned a special research team dedicated to the Library of Souls Archive. Their mission: dig up anything to aid in our hunt for the three killers—Brian Cross, the Tall Man, and the Black Candlestick Killer, now identified as Eric Stephenson, brother of Sir John Stephenson.

We were also instructed to keep any progress confidential, except for discussions with Cully Wish, Troy Castle, and our colleague Alfred, the tariff-setting panel chairperson. Any other disclosures required express permission from the justice minister.

Luckily, we had the powerful A.R.I.E.S. system to assist Sarah's team in processing and uploading data. Regular panel-based boardroom meetings were to update the sixteen-panel members, but morning meetings remained strictly off-limits for disclosure.

When I dared to ask how long this early morning routine would last, the justice minister's scowl answered louder than words. As much as Kate and I value our beauty sleep, I never want to see that look again.

Once the first training session and meeting concluded, we returned home utterly drained, opting for much-needed rest instead of our usual afternoon fun. That day, sleep was the only thing on our minds.

Journal Entry Twenty-One

Two Weeks Later

Two weeks of early mornings and relentless training later, Kate and I finally adjusted to the routine. Unfortunately, Detective Constable Sarah Dunn's research team had no significant updates from the Library of Souls.

At least one part of our lives was back on track—our sex life. Our healthy experimentation and occasional BDSM fun in our newly built cellar dungeon added some excitement to our otherwise monotonous days.

But excitement came unexpectedly one evening while I was tied to the rack with a vibrating dildo teasing me mercilessly. Kate was also indulging, using another throbbing toy on me when the phone rang loudly. Helpless and restrained, I could only hope Kate would answer it.

By the time she returned, the answering machine had taken over, but duty called. She freed me from my restraints, and I rushed to the shower to clean up after multiple, overwhelming orgasms. As I descended the stairs, refreshed, Kate informed me of new evidence in our hunt for the killers.

Once Kate cleaned and sanitized the dungeon, we quickly prepared to meet Sarah and her team at the House of Calamari.

There, an enthusiastic Sarah briefed us on her latest discovery. While combing through archived files in the Library of Souls, her team uncovered evidence linking the killers to secret tunnels. These tunnels, built beneath church altars during the witch trials, had been used by corrupt church officials to accuse wealthy landowners of witchcraft and seize their estates.

The revelation confirmed Sarah's theory of a religious connection to the killers. It explained how they evaded authorities for so long. Everyone congratulated Sarah and her team, while the justice minister pressed her for details on the evidence's origin. Sarah explained that the files had been in the Library of Souls all along, hidden in plain sight.

Journal Entry Twenty-Two

Part One: A, B, C Twist

With this new lead, our team shifted focus to mapping out the tunnel network beneath Glendale. The challenge? Glendale isn't a quaint town but a sprawling city. Planning safe routes and strategies became imperative, especially as we faced not one but three dangerous serial killers.

Each killer posed unique challenges. The Tall Man, for instance, was a giant of a man—built like a fortress and terrifyingly strong. Capturing someone of his stature required meticulous planning.

Then there was Brian Cross, who had evaded capture for years. His escape and prolonged freedom raised questions about our system's vulnerabilities.

Finally, the Black Candlestick Killer, Eric Stephenson, tied the case to a disturbing familial connection with Sir John Stephenson. The justice minister demanded swift action but understood the necessity of a solid plan.

Troy Castle, Cully Wish, and Detective Constable Sarah Dunn's team were assigned to brief the panel members on our findings and objectives. Their goal: align everyone under the minister's directive and ensure our operations moved forward without interference.

The hunt was officially underway, and with Sarah's discovery of the tunnels, we finally had the breakthrough we needed to corner the killers.

Part One: The A, B, C Plan

The research team split into three groups to tackle their objectives efficiently. Their goal was clear, and their plan was methodical:

- **A:** Research the religious angle to locate the address of Harold Cross Senior.
- **B:** Locate the whereabouts of the sadistic priest who abused the boys at the orphanage. The orphanage, demolished to make way for a hospital owned by Sir John Stephenson, had been the site of unimaginable horrors.
- **C:** Map out the underground tunnels discovered beneath the altar of every church in Glendale.

Once these three tasks were completed, the team would reconvene to finalise their end goal.

Sarah suggested that part of the research team return to the records department to focus on Part A within the Library of Souls. Meanwhile, Troy Castle, Cully Wish, and Alfred would tackle Part B, meeting Sir John and John Smith to gather testimonies and uncover leads on the sadistic priest and Eric Stephenson. The rest of Sarah's team would work on solving Part C.

Research Station A: Locating Harold Cross

With a clear target in mind, the team delved into their research. They quickly discovered that Harold Cross Senior had passed away twenty-one years ago. His only surviving family was his son, Brian Cross, who lived at 51 Parkview Terrace, Higher Glendale — conveniently close to a church.

The team uncovered startling details about Brian's son. He had undergone a medical procedure as a child due to a congenital condition; he was born with both male and female genitalia. The operation, only partially successful, left remnants of female anatomy intact. With this revelation and the address in hand, Part A of the research was completed.

Part Two: Unveiling the Truth

Troy Castle and his secretary, Cully Wish, worked alongside Alfred George Banks and his dog, Bonnie, to tackle Part B. Their task was to interview Sir John and John Smith about their experiences at the orphanage. Both men had grown up there, enduring the twisted rule of Father Peters, a priest infamous for his sadistic treatment of the boys.

Sir John Stephenson's Testimony

Q: How long were you at the orphanage?

A: About three years, with my younger brother Eric, before I was adopted.

Q: Did Eric join you in your new home?

A: No, we were separated, and I never saw him again.

Q: Who were the "Three Waynes"?

A: It was what Eric, our cousin John Smith, and I called ourselves. We idolized the action hero John Wayne.

Q: Can you describe the location of the orphanage?

A: It was in East Danby, near the Mallon Stone River.

Q: What do you know about the tunnels beneath the churches?

A: There were three interconnected tunnels linking the churches and the orphanage.

Q: Did you hate your brother?

A: No, but his port wine-stained face made him a target for Father Peters' cruelty.

At the end of his testimony, Sir John attempted to access the A.R.I.E.S. machine with a full can of soda, prompting suspicion. Bonnie's timely intervention prevented any damage, but Sir John's intentions remain unclear. He was arrested pending further investigation.

John Smith's Testimony

John Smith's responses added little new information, apart from confirming that the tunnels were remnants from the 1600s, created during the witch trials. He provided several notebooks that helped map the tunnels but offered no new leads on Father Peters or Eric Stephenson.

With this, Part B of the research was reluctantly closed.

Part Three: Mapping the Tunnels

The research team turned their attention to Part C. They confirmed that the tunnels connected churches across Glendale, a network built centuries ago. The team decided to focus on East Danby, where three churches were directly linked by the tunnels. The plan was to map the tunnels using the A.R.I.E.S. machine, then deploy search teams to locate and apprehend the perpetrators.

The Three Targets

- The Tall Man
- The Black Candlestick Killer
- Brian Cross, aka the Sign of the Cross Killer

The team's immediate goal was to secure the area and begin mapping the tunnels. They also sought to capture Father Peters, whose abuse left a legacy of pain and suffering. With Sir John now imprisoned and stripped of his position, the team had to rely on other resources to track the killers.

Despite setbacks, the team remained resolute. The discoveries they made shed light on the horrors of Glendale's past, fueling their determination to bring the perpetrators to justice. The underground tunnels, steeped in dark history, would soon become the stage for a new chapter in their mission to rid Glendale of its monsters.

Journal Entry Twenty-Three: Part One

The Search of Church One: Team One

Team Leader: Maggie O'Neil

Today was the first time in two weeks that I got to spend some time with Kate, my soon-to-be wife. Sadly, it wasn't for intimacy, but a simple chat and a tender kiss. My team stood nearby, readying the equipment we would need for the first of three searches scheduled for the day. When the team signaled their readiness, I gave Kate another kiss and a hug, whispering my love to her before my team and I moved out. Kate stayed behind outside the church, monitoring radio chatter from all three teams and staying in contact with the criminal justice minister.

Meanwhile, back at the House of Calamari, Alfred, his assistant Coulsum Wish, and Bonnie, his loyal Labrador, monitored the Aries Machine. The machine was tasked with mapping the underground tunnels beneath the three churches in East Danby.

As my team entered the quiet church, we prepared to descend into the tunnels beneath the altar. One by one, eight officers and I made our way down, bringing our equipment along. Once inside, I signaled the first minister and the other two teams, notifying them that we were beginning our search.

Stan Fellows, the leader of the armed task force, handed out echo signaling patches to the leads in the team. These patches were to be placed on the tunnel walls and activated so the Aries Machine could map the area. The atmosphere in the tunnels was eerie. Though they were over three centuries old, the structures were remarkably solid, with smooth, white walls. It was disconcerting to stand in such an ancient and secretive space.

The team split into two groups of four, each heading in opposite directions to map the area. Twenty minutes later, Stan's team reported hitting a dead end. Allan Bishop's group signaled that they had met up with Team Two from Church Two. With the first section mapped, we prepared to return to base to await updates from the other teams.

Just as we stepped out of the tunnels, static interference disrupted the radios. A blood-curdling scream cut through the static on Kate's radio, sending a jolt of fear through me. I immediately contacted Sarah Dunn's team. She decided to continue her search but sent half her team to retrace their steps, hoping to meet up with Kate's group.

The static persisted, and my anxiety grew. Then came the confirmation from Sarah: there had been a serious incident in the tunnels. We needed an ambulance immediately.

The first minister, alerted by the escalating chatter, ordered me to stay put until he and a heavily armed backup team arrived. While waiting, I sat on one of the equipment boxes, straining to hear any movement. A sudden noise echoed through the tunnel. Moments later, a blood-soaked officer came stumbling toward me, his eyes wild with panic. He fired his weapon blindly behind him until his magazine was empty.

"What happened? What's going on?" I shouted, but the officer collapsed, mumbling, "Too big... he's huge... Oh, my God, help me."

Fear gripped me as I thought of Kate. Was she safe? Was she alive? I radioed for assistance, and soon the minister arrived with twelve heavily armed officers, two paramedics, and a doctor. The injured officer was examined; his right arm was broken, his face bruised, and he was in deep shock. He was rushed to the hospital for treatment.

Shortly after, Sarah's team emerged from the tunnels. Their expressions were grave. "Team Two... they're gone," Sarah said quietly.

I froze. "What do you mean, gone? Where's Kate?" My voice wavered, dread taking hold.

Sarah's gaze dropped to the ground, and my heart shattered.

Journal Entry Twenty-Three Part Two

The Search for Research Team B

As the remaining members of the search team gathered near the entrance of tunnel one, I felt a wave of anxiety, especially with Sarah standing beside me and the first justice minister by my side. We were all wearing headphones, listening intently to the radio chatter from Kate's team.

They had just planted sonar devices on the tunnel walls near entrance two when the conversation began normally. However, things took a turn when a small room was discovered nearby. The team entered, but it turned out to be empty. Just as they were about to leave, a second room was found. It was within this room that one of our many questions was answered.

The playback of the radio recording revealed Kate's voice, speaking into her radio while scanning the room. She reported the discovery of a large, black-covered leather two-seater couch. Unfortunately, her next words would be far more unsettling: the decomposing body of Father Peters, the sadistic priest we had been searching for, was found in the room. To our horror, Kate reported that his head had been removed and was placed on the coffee table directly in front of his body.

Then, a team member found the light switch, and a gasp echoed through the room. There, sticking right through the top of the bloody corpse, was a large stick. As Kate examined the body more closely, she recognized it as Father Peters' Waggle

Stick, the instrument he had used to torture the orphaned boys while forcing them to perform Shakespearean plays.

Upon further inspection, it was revealed that one of the priest's hands still clutched a remote control. When Kate picked it up, the video player on the center wall flickered to life. The video revealed a haunting scene: several boys were desperately trying to act out a play while Father Peters shouted at them with a booming voice, sometimes commanding, "No, no, no," or laughing and shouting, "Yes, yes, yes."

The next sounds from the tape came from across the room. One of the team had found another body. It was the missing serial killer, Eric Stephenson. As Kate approached the body, she noted that he had hanged himself, but the placard hanging from his shoulders bore a strange message: "I'm sorry, Mr. Wayne." Kate interpreted it as an apology to John Smith, who had served a twenty-one-year prison sentence for crimes he hadn't committed.

As the team exited the room, an unsettling noise was heard near the entrance to the first room. Static crackled over the radio, followed by screams. "Shit, he's here. Oh my god, he's bloody huge. We're going to need more men." Then, all fell silent.

We removed our headphones and understood immediately: something terrible had happened in the tunnel just below the entrance to the second church tunnel. Sarah then approached me, confirming what we feared. When she arrived with her team, they discovered the remains of several men from Kate's group. The scene was horrific and undeniably gruesome. Police officers lay scattered across the boxes they had brought with them, some with limbs torn off and thrown about the room. Eight heavily armored officers had stood no chance against the Tall Man.

The first minister, visibly shaken but maintaining control, immediately ordered us to return to the House to discuss a plan of action. I, however, was consumed by the thought of having to leave the tunnel without knowing where Kate was. That was something I never wanted to endure again.

Journal Entry Twenty-Three Part Three

We need to find Kate.

As we all gathered in the center of the House of Calamari, there was a slight sense of panic in the open space in front of the reception desk. When the First Minister spoke, for some unknown reason, his words seemed to give the men a bit of hope, as if there was light at the end of it all.

He began by asking everyone to bow their heads in prayer for the men who had lost their lives when the Tall Man appeared out of nowhere. After a one-minute prayer for the fallen, he spoke about being prepared and mentioned that more training would be needed to face such a monster, one that had wiped out eight good men in less than a few minutes.

One man suggested carrying grenade launchers, but the idea was quickly dismissed, as we didn't want to destroy the tunnels. The minister then asked for volunteers to go back into the tunnels with the ambulance crew to collect the bodies of the fallen men. Understandably, no one volunteered, and the minister had no choice but to select the taller men in the group. Fifteen men were chosen to escort the ambulance crew and protect them while they did their duty.

After they left the room, those who remained were informed that anyone entering the tunnels from now on must have written a letter to their families and prepared a will in case of another tragedy. The minister opened the floor for suggestions on how to tackle this evil monster and locate my fiancée Kate, who was still unaccounted for.

Troy Castle was the first to speak, suggesting that we upgrade the Aries machine mapping system to make it easier to track the monster and his victims. He also mentioned that the mapping of the tunnels was still ongoing, but this could wait until the machine upgrade had been completed.

As I sat there, listening to all of this, my thoughts were consumed with wondering where Kate was and hoping she was still alive. Just then, Alfred entered the room with his dog Bonnie. He had some news about a trace of where the Tall Man had gone. He informed us that when the First Minister had added the sonar beacons to the tunnel walls, it hadn't just recorded images but also several blimp responses. When the minister asked him to explain, Alfred told us that he could track the killer's last movements using these blimp responses.

Finally, there was some good news that lifted the spirits of the group. It was decided that Sarah Dunn, Coulsum Wish, Troy Castle, and Alfred would immediately begin tracing these blimp responses. The rest of us were ordered by the minister to write letters to our families and prepare our wills. He also added that anyone killed in the line of duty would receive a payout of up to a quarter of a million pounds, in addition to their remaining pension, for their families.

As I thought about Kate again, my mind returned to my dad, who that reckless boy, Karl Thornton, had nearly killed, leaving him a shell of the man he once was. My mother had become a virtual widow, with what remained of my dad being a man who merely existed day by day with little to no memory of the past.

The First Minister then approached me, gave me a hug, and reassured me that Kate would be found. He walked away to meet with the team members responsible for tracing the blimp responses, as he wanted more information on how they worked.

It was fortunate that the design team had included a sonar beacon system when they created the Aries machine. As Alfred sat down next to Coulsum Wish, the woman explained how the blimp responses worked and their effectiveness in tracing the Tall Man's last movements. Alfred then spoke to the machine, asking it to track the blimp responses. Suddenly, the machine mapped out a trace using dots and dashes, much like Morse code. Within minutes, the machine produced a map that the team could follow to track the monster.

As the minister reviewed the trace, he saw a clear location to follow underground through the tunnels. Sarah then suggested adding a street map and overlaying it with the simple track-and-trace map, which would allow two teams to operate: one above ground and one below. We later found that not long after the first tunnel turning left, we reached a dead-end. However, when the Aries machine produced the new maps, we saw a blockage in the tunnels from years ago. This blockage had closed off an area, but there was still access further left at the abandoned church near the Brookfield Tunnel.

The machine then displayed an alternative map, showing both the street and tunnel views. This new map revealed that the teams would need to travel above ground for about two miles before splitting up, as the blocked tunnel had been reopened. The Brookfield tunnel could still be accessed, and a team could enter it and track the Tall Man's whereabouts. Most importantly, it also showed the potential location of Kate and the person who had taken her.

When the minister heard the good news, he still insisted that we have more training at the gun range and wear an upgraded version of the body armor, which would take a few days to arrive. Teams were drawn in lots and divided into two heavily armored groups: one for above-ground missions and the other for venturing down into the tunnels when needed.

I didn't want to go home during my off-duty time, as I missed Kate terribly. So, I stayed with Sarah Dunn and her girlfriend, Patricia, a traffic warden in Glendale. The two women had met at the police social club, and I had met Kate around the same time. While Sarah prepared some food, I talked to Pat. The woman was about five feet three with a medium-sized waist, short legs, and a large bust. Because of her walking around the city, she had to change her shoes regularly, as they were one of the five allowed expenses. She wore a pair for six to eight weeks before needing to replace them.

As Sarah served the meal, I could see she noticed me trying to hold back my tears. I was heartbroken over Kate, unsure of what would happen next, especially after the massacre in the tunnel. As we ate in silence, I could tell Sarah shared my worry for Kate's safety.

Once the plates were cleared, Sarah offered me tea or coffee, but Pat spoke up, offering me something stronger to calm my nerves. As the evening came to a close, we all prepared for an early start at the gun range. It was then I learned that all staff at the Tariff Setting Panel were also required to take gun training, in addition to the police officers who carried firearms.

As I laid down on the couch, I couldn't sleep. My thoughts were consumed by Kate, and I hoped she was safe. I must have fallen asleep in the early hours, only to be woken by Sarah, who asked if I wanted to use the shower before the hot water ran out. I thanked her for letting me crash at her place, as I didn't want to be alone.

After a quick shower, I dressed and waited for Sarah and Pat to get ready so we could head to the gun range together. Patricia, who had to leave for her job at the city police station, offered to drive us. After a brief hug between Sarah and Pat, Sarah and I headed into the range together.

Journal Entry Twenty-Four Part One

Train, Train, and Train Some More

When Sarah and I arrived at the gun range that morning, we were both surprised by how crowded it was. The sheer number of people there made it impossible for us to start right away, leaving us to sit on the benches for nearly four hours, waiting for a free booth. It was agonising, especially with the weight of Kate's absence pressing on me. Sarah tried her best to keep my mind off it, but the worry was relentless.

Eventually, I asked Sarah if there might be a way to secure a private area for our team so we could train without such long waits. She agreed it was a good idea and called the minister, who supported the suggestion and promised to arrange it. From that day forward, training priority would be given to those directly involved in the mission.

When our turn finally came, Sarah went first. Unsurprisingly, she scored a perfect twenty out of twenty. When it was my turn, however, my performance was dismal—I only managed to hit four out of twenty targets. On my second attempt, I improved slightly but was still far from meeting the standard required for the team going into the tunnels.

Sarah, ever supportive, pulled me aside. She told me I wasn't focusing properly and reminded me to look down the barrel and concentrate. She gently urged me to stop thinking about Kate for the moment, even though she knew how much I was struggling. Taking her advice to heart, I tried again. Sarah even stood behind me, guiding me on when to shoot and where to aim. While I initially thought this approach was futile, it helped me improve my score to nine out of twenty.

Unfortunately, time on the range was limited due to the increased demand following the tunnel massacre. The owner gave me one final attempt, during which I barely managed to scrape a passing score of eleven. While it was technically a pass, it was clear that it wasn't good enough for the underground team.

Frustration and despair overwhelmed me as I realised how far I was from being ready. Sarah handed me her handkerchief as tears threatened to spill. All I could think about was Kate— where she might be and whether she was safe. The idea of her being held captive by that monster was unbearable.

As we left the range, we found Patricia waiting outside, smoking a cigarette. It was clear I wasn't the only one worried about a loved one. I hugged Pat and reassured her she had nothing to fear, especially with Sarah's perfect score. They laughed it off, but the tension was palpable.

Back at the House of Calamari, Sarah lingered to say goodbye to Patricia, while I waited near the entrance. We bumped into Coulsum Wish, who was taking Bonnie out for her morning walk while Alfred received his treatment. His condition required regular applications of medication every three hours— a brave man enduring so much.

Despite all this, I couldn't shake my feelings of failure. Kate's absence weighed heavily on me, and I knew my poor performance was letting the team down. When Troy Castle heard about my scores, he demanded I return to the range and practice until I was ready. He wanted me to lead the underground team, but at that moment, I was far from capable.

I asked Sarah to come back with me for support, and she agreed. With Patricia back at work, we hailed a cab to the range. By then, the minister had arranged for a private training area, away from the public distractions.

When we arrived, the owner's wife escorted us to the new section. Sarah went first, as usual, scoring a flawless twenty out of twenty. It was my turn next. Without the crowd to distract me, I managed to score fifteen out of twenty on my first attempt—a significant improvement. On my second go, I scored another fifteen. Encouraged by the quiet atmosphere, I pushed myself to do better. After three more attempts, I finally achieved a score of eighteen, leaving me in awe of my progress.

The owner's wife calculated my average at seventeen, which was a massive improvement. Sarah was visibly impressed, and for the first time that day, I felt a glimmer of pride. After two full hours of training, we returned to the House of Calamari to report my progress to Troy and the minister.

Though my average was respectable, the final decision was that Sarah would lead the underground team, while I would head the overground team. While I was initially disappointed, I understood their reasoning. The day ended with a mix of emotions, but I felt a renewed sense of purpose. The fight to bring Kate back wasn't over.

Journal Entry Twenty-Four Part Two

Are We Ready?

With our own private training area now set up at the gun range, both teams have been training relentlessly. While my shooting improved significantly without the distraction of the public, I know it's still not up to par for the demands of the mission. I'm not ashamed, though—this operation requires the best, and I recognize that I'm not yet at Sarah's level.

Sarah, on the other hand, is exceptional. Not only does she consistently achieve perfect scores at the range, but her skills as a researcher are also invaluable. I hope Jack Northman regrets the way he mistreated her when she worked under him. Thankfully, she's now part of a team that truly values her intelligence and expertise.

The mission ahead is dangerous, but we're hopeful it will be successful.

Step One:

Teams One and Two will begin their search at East Danby, near one of the tunnel entrances. The teams will make their way to The Brookfields, an abandoned church, where they'll split up. Sarah's team will enter the unblocked tunnel system, while my team will continue navigating the backstreets.

If we locate an address for the Tall Man's base, the teams will regroup to surround the property. One team will enter from the top, the other from the bottom, and both will converge in the middle.

Both teams are equipped with the upgraded stun pistols and Heckler and Koch machine guns, capable of firing up to one hundred rounds per second. With the shoot-to-kill policy still in effect, team leaders will decide the best course of action based on the situation:

- Attempt a surprise attack using the stun pistols.
- If that fails, execute the shoot-to-kill order.
- Map out the tunnels for future operations.
- Return to base with either Kate's safe recovery or confirmation of her fate.

Meanwhile, the first minister and Mr. Castle have enlisted American engineers to upgrade the Aries machine's search pattern software to its highest capacity. According to meteorologists, D-Day will begin at dusk on the next full moon—tomorrow.

A press release has already been issued, urging the public to stay indoors until the madman is captured. In the meantime, team members have been encouraged to spend a little time with their families before the mission begins.

Journal Entry Twenty-Five Part One

D-Day

The police force gathered in the large hallway of the House of Calamari, awaiting final orders. The first minister and support staff stood by as a priest blessed the teams, praying for their safe return.

The latest update confirmed that the Aries machine's mapping system upgrade was nearly complete. With this news, both teams conducted final checks on their weapons and protective suits to ensure they were ready for any attack.

Once the signal was given, both teams departed for East Danby, the starting point of the search. Each team comprised twelve heavily armed officers, led by Sarah and me.

When we arrived at the designated area, Sarah and I conducted radio checks to ensure communication with the base staff was functioning properly. Once confirmed, we received the final instructions to aid the sonar beacon back at the House of Calamari.

To enhance the Aries machine's capabilities, sonar blimp monitors were to be dropped every ten meters along the search route—both in the tunnels and above ground. The initial five miles of the search would focus on the area surrounding Brookfield, believed to be the Tall Man's hideout.

At Brookfield, the teams would split up. My team would continue above ground, while Sarah's team descended into the tunnels. As they moved through the tunnels, they would deploy sonar blimps at regular intervals, allowing the Aries machine to map the area in real-time. Any changes in the terrain would be immediately relayed to both teams.

At our first checkpoint near the tunnel entrance, the first sonar blimp was deployed. With everything in place, I'm ending this transmission and going radio silent to allow Sarah's team to report their movements along the tunnels.

My team and the support staff will monitor and listen in. The hunt for the Tall Man begins now.

Journal Entry Twenty-Five Part Two

Before heading down the westward tunnel, Sarah thanked her team for their dedication that morning. She reminded everyone to check their equipment and inspect their armor for any vulnerabilities. Once Paul Scott Jackson, leader of Police Team A, gave her the nod, they began their journey.

Sarah kept her radio on, maintaining communication with the base as she led her team. "Welcome, everyone, to this podcast. As we proceed, I must stress vigilance. These tunnels are wider than the ones I've explored before. Interestingly, the walls here are light green instead of white, and the lighting is sufficient, so we don't need our torches for now."

She continued, "These tunnels were upgraded at some point, but during my research in the Library of Souls, I found no records of them. It wasn't until our team at the house uncovered an old police file from the early twentieth century that we learned of their existence. Dropping the first sonar blimp now. The Aries machine should pick it up instantly."

Mrs. Wish's voice came through the radio. "Sarah, the machine just registered the sonar blimp. You can continue, and in a few minutes, the map on your device will refresh."

"Thanks, Cully," Sarah replied. "Team, we're moving forward. Oh, hold on, there's a fork in the tunnel. Cully, do we split up and drop sonar blimps in both directions or stay on one path?"

After a brief pause, Cully responded, "Sarah, the first minister and Troy Castle suggest posting two officers at the second tunnel's entrance to wait for further instructions."

"Understood. We'll take a short rest here," Sarah confirmed.

Ten minutes later, Cully's voice returned. "Sarah, Sir John Stephenson has confirmed the second tunnel is a dead end, used as a tool drop during the hospital's foundation upgrades. Maggie's team has now reached the hospital, so you can proceed along the first tunnel."

The first minister expressed gratitude to Sir John for the information. Sarah's team resumed their journey, noting the cold and flickering lights in the tunnel.

"Cully," Sarah asked, "Can Sir John provide more details about this tunnel?"

Sir John's voice came through. "Sarah, I apologize for my past actions. Prison has taught me many lessons. The land above your location was farmland in the eighteenth and nineteenth centuries. When I purchased it, I ignored the tunnel maps provided. If my solicitor, Raymond Anthony Castle, retrieves those maps, he can bring them to the house for upload."

The first minister interjected. "Sir John, if you assist us, I'll reduce the remainder of your sentence and allow you to personally deliver the maps."

"Thank you, but I feel I must serve my time. However, I'll ensure my solicitor delivers the maps immediately," Sir John replied.

The team at the house prepared to receive the maps. When the solicitor arrived twenty minutes later, the maps were handed over to Alfred, who worked alongside the American technician to upload them into the Aries machine. Ten minutes later, Sarah's monitor refreshed with the updated map.

"Cully, Maggie, do you see the updates?" Sarah asked.

"Yes, I see them," Maggie confirmed. "We'll continue above ground."

Sarah's team moved westward through the tunnel, dropping another sonar blimp. Sir John advised, "Ignore the side tunnel near your current location; it leads to an unused hospital outbuilding."

Shortly after, Cully informed Sarah, "There's interference in Maggie's radio. She'll need to switch it off and on again."

"We'll move slightly left to avoid the interference," Sarah suggested, and the issue was resolved.

With Sir John now equipped with a monitor, he provided additional insights. "Years ago, when I walked my dog in this area, I dismissed the tunnel's significance, focusing instead on building the hospital. The nearby outbuildings and houses complicated the original plans, so the car park was relocated."

The first minister, Roy, added, "As a former councillor for this area, I'm aware that most of the buildings were purchased, except for one owned by the church.

Journal Entry Twenty-Five Part Three

Let's Update the Maps

As we awaited the existing maps of the tunnels that Sir John had inherited from the previous landowners, the team grew restless. Sir John, who hadn't understood the maps' significance at the time, had tossed them aside in his office. His focus had been on building the hospital as quickly and cheaply as possible to maximize his profits from the government's funding. Though the hospital had been constructed over twenty-five years ago, progress for both teams was stalled until the maps could be uploaded to the base's mainframe.

Twenty minutes later, a portly, slightly balding man in a posh suit arrived at the house carrying the maps. Mrs. Wish greeted him and escorted him to the support team, who eagerly awaited the materials he had once deemed worthless. To the search team, however, these maps could prove invaluable. The maps were handed to Alfred, who, with assistance from an American technician upgrading the Aries machine's sonar capabilities, uploaded them to the system. Ten minutes later, Cully announced: "Sarah, darling, the maps are now uploaded. Your monitor should refresh shortly, displaying the updated information."

"Yes, Cully, I see the updates now. Maggie, are you there?" Sarah asked.

"Yes, I'm here," Maggie replied.

"Do you see the updated maps?"

"Yes, I have them. My team will continue above ground toward the next sonar blimp drop."

"Thank you, Maggie. My team will proceed west through the tunnels. As we pack up and move, we've discovered another tunnel opening here. Please advise."

"Sarah," came Sir John's voice over the radio, "at your current location, you'll find the back entrance to the hospital's outbuildings. It leads nowhere important, so you may disregard it."

"Thank you, Sir John. Moving further into the tunnels now, we've dropped another sonar blimp. Cully, has the machine received the information?"

"Yes, Sarah," Cully replied. "The machine has updated, revealing another tunnel opening. Sir John, can you see the screen?"

"Unfortunately, no," Sir John answered. "I have radio access but no monitor. Could one be provided? I might offer better guidance."

"Troy Castle here," another voice chimed in. "We'll dispatch a monitor immediately. Your assistance is much appreciated, Sir John."

"Anything I can do to help," Sir John replied solemnly, "I will. Consider it penance for past misjudgments."

"Sarah," Cully interrupted, "could you ask Maggie to reset her radio? We're experiencing interference."

"Yes, Cully," Sarah responded. "Maggie, please switch your radio off and back on. Does that improve communication?"

"Oh, yes," Cully confirmed. "That's much better."

Moments later, Sir John received his monitor. "This technology is remarkable," he marveled. "Looking at the maps now, I see that I ignored an area during construction. The hospital's car park was originally planned for that site, but we moved it due to the presence of several outbuildings and homes nearby. I regret not mapping it further."

"Sir John," another voice cut in, "this is Roy, your First Minister. Before my current position, I served as a councilor, and that area was my responsibility. There are indeed several outbuildings there. Most were acquired through compulsory purchase, except one house, which remains church-owned."

"Cully, darling," Sarah interjected, "I told you there was a religious connection. Can we retrieve the address of the church-owned house?"

"Alfred is on it," Cully replied. "We have the address now: fifty-seven Jurby Avenue. Stand by for further instructions."

Journal Entry Twenty-Six Part One

The House at the End of the Tunnel

The support team deliberated their next steps. A single house linked to the church had been identified, and it needed to be searched. The critical questions were whether the house was still occupied and, if so, by whom. Most importantly, could this be the home of the elusive killer known as the Tall Man?

"Maggie, darling, it's Cully. We at the house need an update. What can you see from your position?"

"Understood," Maggie replied. "I've sent Paul Scott Jackson with two team members to scout the houses. Please hold for their report."

Moments later, Maggie continued, "Paul's team has returned. There are six houses to the left and three to the right of the property. All are abandoned, boarded up, and empty—except for the house in the center. It stands out with black metal railings enclosing a courtyard.

"We entered the courtyard and found a large property with three floors. There's a staircase attached to the side leading down to a garage, which is open. Inside, the garage is filled with wooden crates labeled 'Book Depository.' Each crate is marked with an address: 14 Shannon Street, East Danby town center. If needed, we could dispatch a team to investigate this location later. Please advise on our next steps."

"Sarah, darling," Cully interjected, "why don't you and your team join Maggie's in the garage? It seems crucial."

"We've reached the end of the tunnel and can see the property. Team One is ahead of us, and we'll rendezvous with them now."

"Cully, darling," Sarah reported, "we've joined Team One in the garage. The structure is extensive, with three side rooms. Maggie's team is searching them as we speak. Meanwhile, my team is investigating sounds coming from above us. The noise seems to be a record player or tape machine. Is there a detailed map of this property available?"

"Alfred is working with the Aries machine to retrieve information. It should update on your PDA soon."

"Thank you. The monitor has just updated," Sarah confirmed. "Maggie's team found a storage room with more crates identical to the ones here. In another room, they discovered a corpse of a young woman on what appears to be a mortician's slab. It seems this is where the Tall Man kills his victims before disposing of them.

"They also found a map with several X's marked on it— likely body dump sites. Another disturbing find is a skeleton with an axe embedded in its skull. Identification near the remains reads 'Brian Cross,' the escaped serial killer who disappeared years ago."

"Sarah," Roy, the First Minister, responded, "if this is true, the only thing left is to capture the Tall Man. We're close to resolving this."

"Yes, sir. We're installing cameras in the garage now. Once set, we'll observe the area above us through small ceiling openings. If the church records reveal the killer's identity, we'll know exactly who we're dealing with."

"Sarah, darling," Cully said, "Alfred's back from treatment and ready to assist. He's accessing the church records now."

Alfred added, "The records show the property was owned by Harold Cross Sr. and passed to his son, Brian Cross, and Brian's wife, Betty. With Brian's remains identified, we can confirm his death."

Sarah nodded. "Yes, Maggie found Brian's skeleton in a cupboard. The young woman's body was likely his latest victim, waiting for disposal. The map on the wall matches earlier dump sites, except for one difference: the next marked location is Howarth Street Park.

"Should both teams stay here, or should one move to the park to intercept the killer?"

"Stay put," Roy advised. "If the body is still in the house, the killer must return to retrieve it. Prepare for an ambush."

"Understood," Sarah replied. "Maggie, have your team hide behind or inside the crates near the entrance. My team will conceal ourselves in the room with the young woman's body. When the killer comes down, we'll apprehend him."

"Sarah," Paul asked nervously, "are we shooting on sight, or should we attempt to stun him?"

"That depends," Sarah replied. "If you can, stun him. But if he poses a threat, you have permission to act decisively."

Roy's voice came over the radio, firm and clear. "Be cautious. We can't afford another team loss. If stunning doesn't work, take him down."

Journal Entry Twenty-Six Part Two

Music Sweet Music

Both teams positioned themselves in the large, open garage-like structure, hiding behind or inside the many crates and boxes. The tension was palpable as Maggie broke the silence.

"Sarah, can you hear the music coming from upstairs?"

"Yes," Sarah replied. "It sounds like soft show tunes from the early sixties. My mum had records with the same tunes. She'd play them while cleaning when I was at school. Sometimes, she'd fall asleep on the sofa with the record still spinning."

"I need to move," a voice interjected. "I think I've got a cramp in my leg."

"Who's speaking?" Sarah asked.

"It's Luke Conway," he replied.

"Are you with Paul's team?"

"No, I'm with John's team. Maggie is leading us."

"What seems to be the problem, Luke?" Maggie inquired.

"I'm cramped in this box. There's hardly any space, and my right leg is killing me."

"Try moving to one of the larger boxes in the corner," Maggie suggested. "Look for the ones labeled 'Book Depository.'"

"I see them. I'll move now."

As Luke shifted to a new hiding spot, Sarah spoke again. "Maggie, the music is getting louder. Are the cameras ready?"

"They're unboxed but not installed yet," Maggie replied.

"Who's handling that?" Sarah asked.

"It's John here. Frank and I can install them, but we'll need to be careful not to make noise and alert the man upstairs."

"No problem," John assured her. "I can set up a camera in less than five minutes."

"Luke, did you bring the ladders?" Maggie asked.

"Uh... we might have a problem," Luke admitted.

"What kind of problem?" Maggie pressed.

"Someone forgot the ladders back at base."

"Damn it!" Maggie exclaimed. "I told Allan to fetch them. Allan, was that your responsibility?"

"With all this new equipment to manage, I only have two hands," Allan replied. "I'll head back to base and grab them."

"Be quick about it," Maggie ordered. "We need those ladders for the cameras."

Cully's voice crackled over the radio. "Sarah, darling, one of the logistics team will deliver the ladders to the house entrance. Your team member can meet them there."

"Cully," Sarah replied, "our man has already left the garage and is out of radio range."

"No worries," Cully assured her. "I'll use the Aries machine to contact him. I've programmed your radio signals into it. It shows Allan Bates heading for the ladders. I'll inform him to meet James Ayrey, who's bringing upgraded soundboards and cameras. Once the new equipment is installed, you'll hear everything happening above you."

"Thanks, Cully," Sarah said. "We'll wait for them to arrive."

Ten minutes later, Maggie spotted movement. "I see them coming."

The logistics team arrived, and James Ayrey introduced himself. "All right, who's Sarah and Maggie? Let's get these PDA monitors upgraded first. This new soundboard is state-of-the-art. You'll hear the difference immediately."

James worked quickly, replacing the boards. "Maggie, your monitor is ready. Plug in your headphones and let me know what you hear."

Maggie did as instructed and gasped. "I can hear the music more clearly now—and voices. They're coming from upstairs."

Sarah leaned in. "Once the cameras are installed, we'll confirm if the voices belong to the perpetrator."

James continued upgrading the equipment. "While I work, Maggie, why don't you move to the right and Sarah to the left? Describe what you hear so we can gather intel."

Cully chimed in. "Maggie, can you give us a running commentary for Base Camp?"

With her headphones on, Maggie moved across the garage. Suddenly, she froze. "Oh no. I think I hear..."

"What is it, darling?" Cully prompted.

"It sounds like someone using a toilet and humming a tune—poorly. It's the Three Little Pigs, but off-key."

"What tune is it?"

"Three Little Pigs," Maggie confirmed. "Bloody hell... the bastard."

"What's wrong?" Sarah asked, joining Maggie's position.

"It's Kate. He's singing to her in a childish voice."

Sarah listened intently. "I hear it now. He's moving into another room. I can also hear sobbing—Kate's sobbing. They're directly above us."

"We need those cameras installed now," Maggie urged.

James reassured them. "We've set up three cameras, but they're facing the wrong direction. Give me ten minutes to reposition them toward your location."

"Be as quick as you can," Sarah urged. "We don't know how much time Kate has left."

Cully spoke again. "Maggie, while James works, continue describing what you hear. It's important for the record."

"I... I can't," Maggie said, her voice trembling. "Hearing Kate—it's too much. She's my one true love."

Cully's tone softened. "We understand, Maggie. Step outside and take a moment to collect yourself."

"Thank you," Maggie whispered.

"Sarah," Cully continued, "you'll need to take over. I've set the Aries machine to record everything you say in case it's needed later. Please describe what's happening."

Journal Entry Twenty-Six Part Three

Listening to a Three-Way Conversation

With the cameras now installed, every team member could hear and see the activity in the rooms above the large church house. Paul's team positioned themselves on the left side of the garage, while John's team occupied the right. Meanwhile, Sarah and Maggie took positions near the staircase entrance for better proximity to the source of the sounds. Once the upgraded PDA monitors were functional, the logistics officer finished his work and left, heading back to base.

"Cully," Sarah began, "I'm ready to provide a running commentary on what both teams are seeing and hearing above us. From the camera feed, it looks like the occupant upstairs has just left the bathroom and is heading down the hallway, humming what sounds like a children's tune."

"Understood," Cully replied.

"Cully, can you upload the preliminary report for Brian Cross again? I think there's critical information about his son and daughter we might need."

"Give the system a moment," Cully responded.

"Maggie's back now and standing beside me," Sarah added.

Cully's voice returned shortly. "The report indicates Brian Cross had two children, Harold and an unnamed daughter. There's limited information about the daughter. Regarding Harold, a medical note mentions he was born a hermaphrodite. Brian and his wife, Betty, insisted on a medical procedure early in Harold's life to make him male. However, the surgery wasn't successful, leaving Harold with severe mental health challenges.

"School records mention Harold exhibited uncontrollable behavior, severe depression, and anxiety. The last record shows the sister began taking control of him, and whenever this happened, another child would get hurt. Harold was eventually removed from school and home-schooled. No further information is available about the sister, not even her name or whereabouts."

"Thank you for the update, Cully," Sarah said.

Maggie, now calmer, chimed in, "Thanks for your support earlier. I feel better now."

"All of us back at base are hoping for Kate's safe return," Cully reassured her.

"Thank you," Maggie said, handing the commentary back to Sarah.

Sarah resumed, "From the camera views, we see a large hallway upstairs with several closed doors. Maggie and I can hear voices coming from one of the rooms."

"Cully," Sarah continued, "now that we know Brian Cross is dead, what do we know about his wife, Betty?"

"Alfred and I will check her records," Cully responded.

As they moved closer for a better view, Cully updated them. "According to the Aries machine, Betty Cross filed for divorce from Brian several years ago and left the property. We don't have further details or any updated medical records for her."

"Thanks, Cully," Sarah replied. "From this new position, we can see Kate. She's restrained at the foot of a large pine bed. Apart from some bruises on her face, she doesn't appear to have sustained serious harm.

"We can also see Harold Cross, though his back is to us, and there are two women in the room speaking with him. Unfortunately, we can't identify them. Kate seems to be signaling us with her fingers. She points to the man with one finger, then raises three fingers and wiggles them. She's trying to say something, but it's unclear what she means. It's frustrating not to have a clearer view to interpret her signals."

Cully responded apologetically. "I'm sorry, Sarah, but the logistics officer hasn't returned to adjust the cameras for a better angle. Troy Castle has also left the room. I believe he's gone to track the man. We'll update you if he finds anything."

"Understood," Sarah said.

"Alfred has stepped out again for medical treatment," Cully added. "At the moment, it's just me here at base."

Journal Entry Twenty-Six Part Four

What is Kate Trying to Tell Us?

"Thanks for the update, Cully. Let me continue with what's happening here. I'll keep the camera focused on Kate while I relay the conversation in the room. Watch her closely; maybe you'll be able to figure out what she's trying to tell us.

"Here's what I'm hearing from the room. The voices seem to belong to Harold, his sister—still unnamed—and possibly their mother, Betty Cross. Harold is complaining to his mother, accusing his sister of forcing him to kill young women. I'm panning the camera to stay on Kate, hoping her signals will reveal what she's trying to say.

"Whenever Harold speaks about his sister, Kate points directly at him with one finger. When the two women speak, she raises three fingers and wiggles them toward the camera. She also shakes her head as if saying 'no.' I can tell she's desperately trying to communicate something, but I can't figure out exactly what."

"Cully, can you interpret what Kate might be trying to tell us?" Sarah asked.

"Sarah, could Maggie provide any insight?" Cully replied.

"I'm sorry," Maggie admitted, "I have no idea. It's definitely something important, but I can't decipher it."

"Right," Sarah said, "whenever Harold speaks about his sister, Kate points at him. When the women speak, she raises three fingers and wiggles them. I'll point the camera directly at Harold when the women are speaking. Hopefully, this is the clue Kate's giving us."

"Sarah," Cully suggested, "can Maggie position a second camera slightly to the right of Harold to give us a better view?"

A sudden noise interrupted them.

"What was that?" Sarah asked sharply.

"Sorry, it's my leg," Luke replied. "I've still got that cramp in my left leg."

"Luke, was that you?"

"I'm sorry, but I couldn't stay still anymore," Luke said, shifting uncomfortably.

"Can you two be quiet?" Sarah snapped. "You're making too much noise!"

"I already said I'm sorry," Luke muttered. "But the cramp is unbearable."

The conversation was cut short by Sarah's alarmed voice. "Damn it, I think you've alerted him! Harold's off the bed and heading for the door."

"Hide!" someone whispered urgently.

"Oh my God," Sarah whispered, her voice trembling. "Look at the camera pointed at Harold. Now that he's moved, you can see under the bed. There are skeletal remains there. Could it be his mother?"

"No," Maggie said, shaking her head. "That's impossible. I distinctly heard two women speaking to him earlier."

"Cully, can you play back the recording for us?" Sarah requested.

"Give me a moment. Alfred's back now, and he'll handle it. I need to step away for a moment," Cully said.

Alfred's voice replaced Cully's. "Hello, everyone. I'm back. It's clear tensions are rising here. Luke, you're clearly struggling. I suggest you return to the house to avoid jeopardizing the team."

"I'm sorry," Luke replied, visibly ashamed. "I know I've compromised things. Please forgive me. I'll head back now and hope you all stay safe."

"Luke," Alfred added, "I don't want to reprimand you, but you must understand the danger here. The man upstairs is a known serial killer responsible for the deaths of over twenty-one women and several officers. Please be careful."

As Luke left, Alfred continued, "Sarah, Maggie, listen carefully. The Aries machine has recorded the conversation in the room. Before I play it back, I need the entire team to withdraw from the garage and return to the house. This recording may confirm or refute whether there are truly three people in the room."

The team quietly packed their gear and exited the garage. They moved together this time, abandoning the earlier two-team approach. Back at the house, it was decided that two fresh teams would take over operations, heading across town to await further instructions.

Journal Entry Twenty-Seven Part One

A Conversational Interpretation

"Now that everyone's back at the house, we need to analyze the conversation from earlier and determine if it's the voice of one man using ventriloquism or genuinely a man and two women. To do this, we'll try two approaches.

"First, one of us will read the conversation as though it's one man mimicking three voices. Then, we'll reenact it with one person voicing Harold and others taking the roles of the two women. Afterward, we'll overlay the recording into the Aries Machine for analysis. Only then can we confirm whether it's one man or three people.

"Paul Scott Jackson, what are you doing eating ice cream in here?"

"Sorry, Cully. I was hungry after standing in those cramped boxes, hiding from that serial killer."

"Wait, that's not mine, is it?"

"I, uh… I went to the loo, and on the way back, your apartment door was open. I got curious and peeked inside. Then I saw the fridge and thought I'd just have a look. That's when I spotted Ben & Jerry's Cookie Dough ice cream—my favorite. I couldn't resist."

"Paul, I'll forgive you this time because we've all been under a lot of stress. But just so you know, I don't even like Cookie Dough ice cream—Bonnie does."

"Oh… uh, sorry, Bonnie."

Suddenly, someone exclaimed, "What's that smell?"

"Not me!" Luke protested. "Don't blame me. I've already got enough grief with my leg cramps."

"Maggie, darling?"

"Oh, please, don't look at me. Women don't fart; we perfume."

"No one's blaming you," Cully interjected. "It's Bonnie. She needs a trip to the garden after gorging herself this morning on chews, bones, and three tubs of Cookie Dough ice cream."

All eyes turned to Paul.

"Fine," he groaned. "I'll take her out to make up for stealing her ice cream."

"Thanks, Paul."

Once Paul had left the room with Bonnie, someone suggested, "Can we open a window? It smells terrible in here."

"All right," Cully said, "let's focus. Who's going to portray Harold, Betty Cross, and Sarah for this reenactment?"

"I'll do Harold," someone volunteered. "I'll try a Scottish accent to make it realistic."

Harold: "Mother, she's doing it again."

Betty: "She's doing what, Harold?"

Harold: "She's picking on me like she always does."

Betty: "Sarah, stop picking on your brother. You know how sensitive he is."

Betty: "All right, Harold. I've told her off for you. Now, are you going to introduce me to your friend?"

Harold: "She's not my friend! Sarah brought her here."

Sarah: "That's not true, Harold. She was with those men in the tunnel."

Betty: "Harold, are you and your sister keeping secrets from me?"

Harold: "No, Mother! It's Sarah! When we were coming back through the tunnels, we ran into those men with guns. You always said we couldn't show anyone where we live, or they'd take us away from our lovely home."

Betty: "I believe you, Harold, but Sarah, is he telling the truth?"

Harold: "It's not fair! Why does she always get to be in control? I'm old enough to bring young women back here so you and Sarah can have your fun with them!"

Betty: "Harold Cross, stop sulking! Or I'll tell your father about this."

Sarah: "Mummy, I think you've forgotten something."

Betty: "What now, Sarah?"

Sarah: "It's about Daddy."

Betty: "What about him?"

Sarah: "He's downstairs… in the cupboard… with an axe in his head."

Betty: "What? You didn't hurt your father, did you, Harold?"

Harold: "No, Mummy."

Betty: "Sarah, did you?"

Sarah: "No, Mummy."

Betty: "If neither of you hurt him, then who did?"

Sarah: "Take a guess."

Betty: "Was it this girl?"

Sarah: "No, Mummy. It was you."

Betty: "Me? Stop this nonsense! I would never hurt your father."

Sarah: "You don't remember, do you? You hit him with the axe because he kept bringing women here to play with, and you got jealous."

Betty: "No, that can't be true. Why don't I remember any of this?"

Sarah: "Maybe because you're dead."

Betty: "Stop it, Sarah! That's not true!"

Harold: "She's right, Mother. You took all those pills and went to sleep. You've been dead for a long time."

End of Conversation.

Journal Entry Twenty-Seven Part Two

Time to Confront Harold Cross

After analyzing the conversation both ways, the Aries Machine confirmed that Brian and Betty Cross had been dead for some time. However, it couldn't conclusively determine if the voice was from one man or a brother-and-sister duo continuing their father's dark legacy.

The First Minister, along with Troy Castle—the current owner of the House of Calamari—arrived for an update. The two teams that had replaced the initial teams during the analysis reported back with crucial information: Harold Cross and his captive, Kate, were still inside the house but had gone eerily quiet. The whereabouts of Sarah Cross remained unknown.

Following the updates, the First Minister and Troy Castle decided not to delay further. It was time to capture Harold Cross, and, if she existed, his sister Sarah, while rescuing Kate from the house and the tunnels below.

The plan was to strike at first light, giving the teams one last evening with their families.

Day of the Attack

The morning of the operation was marked by heavy rain lashing down on Glendale, but by 8:00 a.m., the skies cleared, and the sun shone brightly. At the boardroom table, First

Minister Roy, Troy Castle, Alfred, his dog Bonnie, and Cully Wish waited for the teams to return to the house.

By then, the house was bustling with activity as police officers joined Maggie O'Neil and Sarah Dunn to prepare for the mission. The First Minister's brother, Franklin Davenport Roy, and his wife, Jane, held a brief church service for the team. After the service, the First Minister ensured all weapons were thoroughly checked, leaving no room for error.

The Plan

8:15 a.m.: Teams One and Two would leave the house and head to the Brookfield Viaduct entrance to the tunnels.

8:30 a.m.: Teams Three and Four would move toward the property.

Each team was equipped with W23 stun grenades for emergencies and V.N.A. smoke grenades to force the Tall Man, Harold Cross, out of his position on the top floor. The plan was for Teams One and Two to enter from the garage upward, while Teams Three and Four would create a diversion with smoke grenades on the second floor. The hope was to force Sarah Cross, if she existed, to reveal herself.

A shoot-to-kill policy was in place for Harold Cross. If he resisted or posed any threat, the teams were authorized to act. The ultimate goal was to rescue Kate alive.

The Operation

At 8:15 a.m., the First Minister pressed the action alarm, signaling Teams One and Two to set out. Fifteen minutes later, the signal was given for Teams Three and Four, which included Maggie O'Neil and Sarah Dunn, to move in.

By 8:38 a.m., Teams One and Two reached their positions. Smoke grenades were launched into the property's windows but were met with an unsettling silence.

At 8:50 a.m., Teams Three and Four arrived, launching additional grenades into the second-floor windows. Again, there was no response.

Ten minutes later, more smoke grenades were deployed—five to the top floor and three to the middle floor. This time, there was movement inside the property, though not the escape they had anticipated.

The First Minister ordered another round of smoke grenades. Suddenly, the Tall Man appeared at the garage stairwell, using Kate as a human shield.

The Confrontation

Maggie and Sarah spotted him and rushed into the garage to save Kate. They fired stun grenades as the Tall Man charged at them with Kate still in his grip.

Maggie locked eyes with Kate and saw the sheer terror in her gaze. In a split second, the rest of the team arrived, firing more grenades at the Tall Man.

But the monster, in an act of pure brutality, used his immense strength to decapitate Kate before anyone could intervene.

Maggie and Sarah screamed in anguish as they launched their final grenades, bringing the Tall Man down. He collapsed on top of what remained of Kate's body.

When the attack ended, Maggie stood in the wreckage, overcome with despair. Kate, her girlfriend and teammate, was gone. Tears streamed down her face as she cried out in grief.

"What will I do without her?"

The mission had ended, but at a devastating cost.

Journal Entry Twenty-Eight

Part One: Reflections After the Jurby Avenue Attack

It's been several months since the attack on the house at Jurby Avenue, the place where my fiancée lost her life at the hands of that madman known as the Tall Man. As I revisit the case notes and write this entry, the weight of everything that unfolded that day still hangs heavy on my heart.

After the fire brigade cleared the property we assaulted in our desperate attempt to save Kate, the entire building was thoroughly examined. On the top floor, the true extent of the horror was revealed. That was where Kate had been held, tied to the bedframe of the monster while he slept soundly, undisturbed by the suffering he inflicted.

The investigation brought to light a grim reality. There was no sister. The man's mother, Betty, had been dead for years, her skeletal remains still lying in her bed. Beside her were two items: a remote control and a confessional note. The note detailed how she had killed her husband, Brian Cross, the man infamously known as the *Sign of the Cross Killer* for his brutal murders of young women.

The floor below bore the brunt of the damage from the grenades we deployed, desperate to force the Tall Man out and save Kate. The plan, tragically, didn't succeed. Her life was taken in the most horrifying way imaginable—first by decapitation and then by her body being crushed beneath the killer's own lifeless corpse.

The grenades neutralized the Tall Man, but they also robbed me of the love of my life.

I recently completed my final round of therapy, though I'm not sure if it's enough to help me move forward. Sarah Dunn, one of my colleagues, has since transferred back to Langley. She blames herself for throwing the grenade that provoked the killer's final, brutal act against Kate. In an attempt to ease her guilt, I told her I believed it was me who threw it, though the truth is lost in the chaos of that moment.

I lost more than just Kate that day. I lost our home as well, unable to keep up with the mortgage after her death. For now, I'm living in Sarah's old flat, sending her as much rent as I can manage to keep a roof over my head.

I have a meeting with Alfred next Monday, hoping he has work for me at the House of Calamari. I'll take anything to keep my mind occupied. Troy Castle has also reminded me of my pending visit to Priory Lane Psychiatric Hospital for the Criminally Insane.

Keeping busy is the only way I can stop myself from drowning in memories of Kate.

Tonight, I'll attend a benefit at the police officers' club in Higher Glendale. It's a memorial for the families of those killed in the tunnels by that monstrous man.

Tomas One

This entry ends here for now. The story will continue in
Book Two: Jenny's Revenge.

The End for Now